Blood of
the Red Rose

P J Gray

Clink
Street

London | New York

Published by Clink Street Publishing 2018

Copyright © 2018

First edition.

ISBN:
978-1-912562-72-5 - paperback

About the Author

Philippa began writing when she was a child, illustrating her own handwritten books for the enjoyment of her friends, and had her first short story published when she was ten. She started her first novel after her eldest daughter was born, 27 years ago, writing when the baby was napping in the afternoon. Many rewrites and crises of confidence later it has evolved into Blood of the Red Rose and its 'coming soon' sequel Tears of the White Rose. Philippa has two daughters, four grandchildren and lives in Cyprus with Paul, her husband of twenty-two years, their two dogs and four cats.

For my husband Paul who always believed in me.

Characters

Edmund Beaufort	Duke of Somerset
John (Jack) Beaufort	Younger brother of the Duke Somerset
Marguerite of Anjou	Queen of England – wife of Henry VI
Edward of England	Prince of Wales – son of Henry VI
Richard Neville	Earl of Warwick – also known as 'Kingmaker'
Anne Beauchamp	Countess of Warwick
Katherine Neville	Illegitimate daughter of the Earl of Warwick
Isabel Neville	Elder Daughter of the Earl of Warwick
Anne Neville	Younger daughter of the Earl of Warwick
Edward of York	King Edward IV of England
Richard Plantagenet	Duke of Gloucester – brother of Edward IV
George Plantagenet	Duke of Clarence – brother of Edward IV
John Neville	Duke of Northumberland – Earl of Warwick's brother
George Neville	Archbishop of York – Earl of Warwick's brother
Veronique de Roet	Katherine Neville's (Warwick's daughter) mother
Jasper Tudor	Earl of Pembroke – King Henry VI's half brother
John Courtenay	Earl of Devon
Stephen Thevenot	A Knight of Yorkshire

House of Beaufort

The Principal Members of the Neville Family.

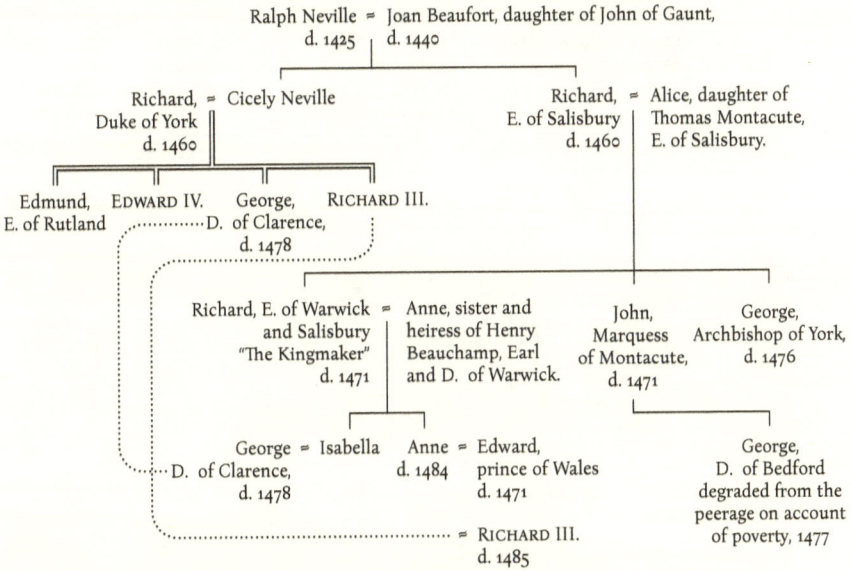

Ralph Neville = Joan Beaufort, daughter of John of Gaunt,
d. 1425   d. 1440

Richard, = Cicely Neville
Duke of York
d. 1460

Richard, = Alice, daughter of
E. of Salisbury   Thomas Montacute,
d. 1460   E. of Salisbury.

Edmund,   EDWARD IV.   George,   RICHARD III.
E. of Rutland ·············D. of Clarence,
d. 1478

Richard, E. of Warwick = Anne, sister and   John,   George,
and Salisbury   heiress of Henry   Marquess   Archbishop of York,
"The Kingmaker"   Beauchamp, Earl   of Montacute,   d. 1476
d. 1471   and D. of Warwick.   d. 1471

George = Isabella   Anne = Edward,   George,
····D. of Clarence,   d. 1484   prince of Wales   D. of Bedford
d. 1478   d. 1471   degraded from the
peerage on account
= RICHARD III.   of poverty, 1477
d. 1485

House of York

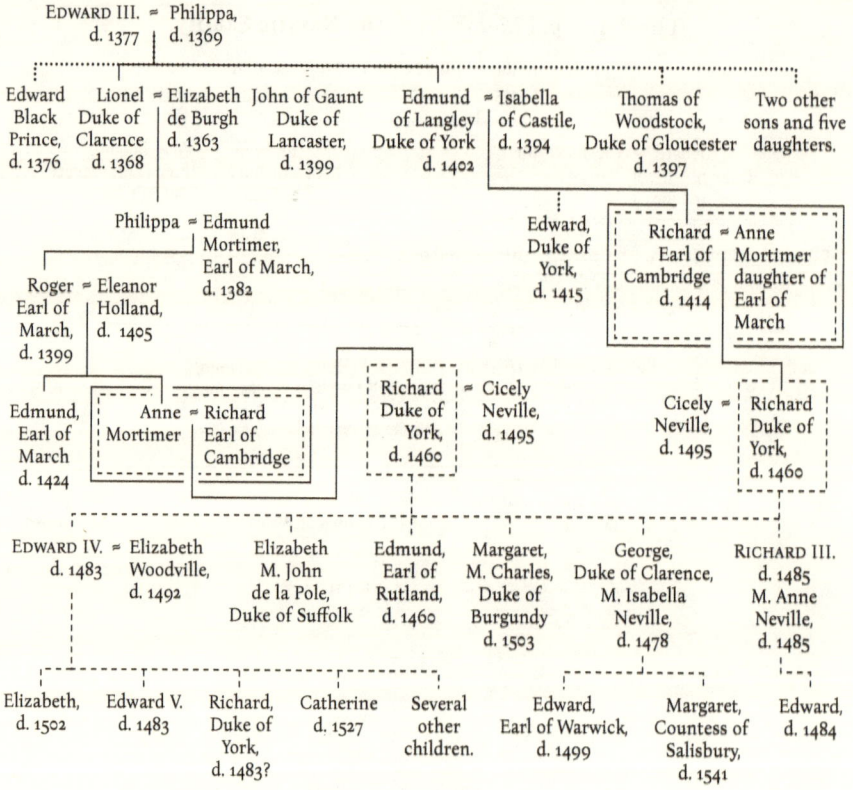

EDWARD III. = Philippa,
d. 1377 | d. 1369

Edward Black Prince, d. 1376

Lionel Duke of Clarence d. 1368 = Elizabeth de Burgh d. 1363

John of Gaunt Duke of Lancaster, d. 1399

Edmund of Langley Duke of York d. 1402 = Isabella of Castile, d. 1394

Thomas of Woodstock, Duke of Gloucester d. 1397

Two other sons and five daughters.

Philippa = Edmund Mortimer, Earl of March, d. 1382

Edward, Duke of York, d. 1415

Richard Earl of Cambridge d. 1414 = Anne Mortimer daughter of Earl of March

Roger Earl of March, d. 1399 = Eleanor Holland, d. 1405

Edmund, Earl of March d. 1424

Anne Mortimer = Richard Earl of Cambridge

Richard Duke of York, d. 1460 = Cicely Neville, d. 1495

Cicely Neville, d. 1495 = Richard Duke of York, d. 1460

EDWARD IV. = Elizabeth d. 1483 Woodville, d. 1492

Elizabeth M. John de la Pole, Duke of Suffolk

Edmund, Earl of Rutland, d. 1460

Margaret, M. Charles, Duke of Burgundy d. 1503

George, Duke of Clarence, M. Isabella Neville, d. 1478

RICHARD III. d. 1485 M. Anne Neville, d. 1485

Elizabeth, d. 1502

Edward V. d. 1483

Richard, Duke of York, d. 1483?

Catherine d. 1527

Several other children.

Edward, Earl of Warwick, d. 1499

Margaret, Countess of Salisbury, d. 1541

Edward, d. 1484

House of Lancaster and Beaufort Family

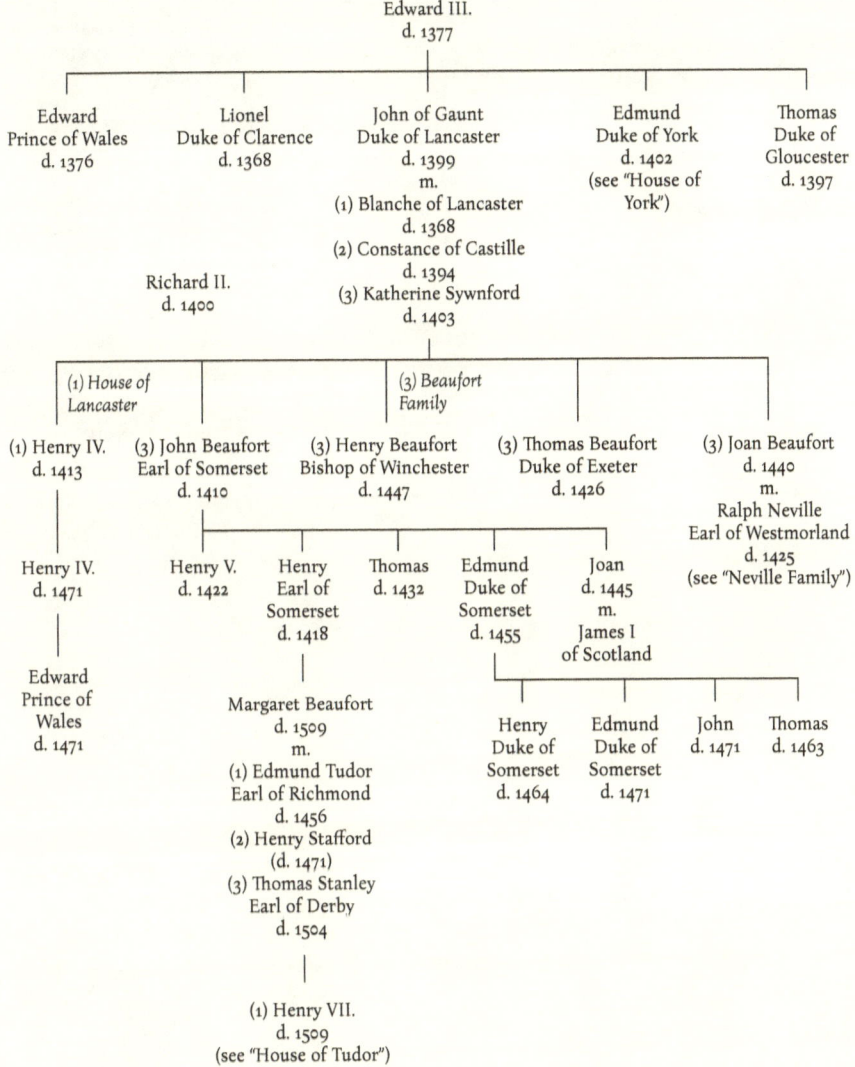

Prologue

Ludlow 1460

The woman's scream echoed in the street even though it was alive with noise, sending shivers up his spine and prickling into the back of his neck. Pushing it to the far reaches of his consciousness, Edmund Beaufort looked down at the sobbing child and, exasperated, scooped him up by the back of his tunic and dumped him unceremoniously on the horse's neck in front of him, with a curt, "Stop snivelling, child. You are not hurt." He looked down then at the woman, dishevelled, her bright hair escaping from the decorum of her headdress, and the other boy feigning bravery.

"Madame, why are you still here?" he asked, his normally husky voice cracked with the strain of shouting, his distinctive honey-gold eyes meeting her clear grey ones.

"I did not think the armies of King Henry made war on women and children, my Lord." She lifted her chin defiantly. He bit back an oath and spat on the ground, more to enjoy seeing her flinch than because he needed to. She was a beauty, there was no doubt of that but, damnation, she was so prim and pious.

"They do not, Madame. My brother must have overlooked that he had such prestigious guests." He raised a mocking eyebrow. "Otherwise I am sure he would not have missed the opportunity to call on the great Duchess of York."

He smiled sardonically, suddenly looking very young for all that he was twenty-one. "If you would accompany me, Madame, my men will take you to the priory. I am sure that my brother and the Queen will call on you as soon as they can." The scream rang out again with

1

blood curdling resonance and then stopped abruptly. The boy on his pommel burst into loud wails once more.

"Richard, hush." His mother admonished.

"Is this a boy or a girl, Madame?" Beaufort tugged the child's head back by the hair and looked into his face. The boy stopped wailing and stared at him, wet midnight blue eyes meeting hard gold ones. The woman flushed and glared at him.

"He is a seven-year-old child..."

"I am a boy," the child said.

"Then behave like one."

"I am afraid." The little boy's bottom lip trembled and something akin to empathy stirred in Beaufort's heart.

"That's stupid," the older boy said contemptuously. Beaufort glanced at him, taking his measure and laughed unkindly.

"Don't listen to your brother, lad, for it is he who is stupid," he said to the boy on his pommel. "It's wise to be afraid, it is just not wise to show it. You lift your chin, put your shoulders back and look the fear in the eye." The little boy stared at him with his solemn dark eyes and then nodded carefully.

"Yes, my Lord," he said and straightened his back, wiping a small hand across his tearstained face. There was a loud crash and the sound of clashing weapons; he flinched but kept his back straight. Edmund Beaufort almost smiled until the woman said loudly.

"For the love of God, my Lord, get my sons out of here. They should not..."

Anything else she had to say was drowned out by the sound of hooves galloping around the corner and the metal ring of armour in the saddle.

"Beau!" a tall man astride a big black destrier called out, raising a hand and bringing the armed men behind him to a stop. The woman riding at his side smiled, her huge luminous black eyes shining as she came to a showy stop, her gossamer veil barely hiding her lustrous black hair, her fitted riding clothes showing off her tiny frame to full effect.

"Ah, you are still here, Madame?" she asked, her smile widening. "Enjoying the show?" She turned away without waiting for an answer, her glance taking in the scene. "My Lord Beaufort," she acknowledged, sharp eyes on the boy on the front of Edmund's horse and the pretty picture of the proud, pale-haired woman before him. "I hope you are not getting sentimental on me." He flushed, his skin staining to the roots of his hair, his youth obvious once more.

"No, Madame." He met her eyes and the flush darkened further.

"Good." Her voice was a caress. "I care not for sentimentality. I have high hopes for you, my Lord, and I would hate you to spoil everything by being sentimental." She turned to the man at her side. "Somerset, get the Duchess of York and her brats to the priory, I think they have had enough fun today." She turned back and smiled again at the young man. "While your brother escorts her sainted Grace to the priory, I think you can escort me to Ludlow Castle, my Lord Beaufort. Let's see what we can find of interest there."

"Yes, your Grace." He handed the boy to his brother and turned his mount so that it was alongside hers, looking down at her, wearing his admiration like a badge. "It would be an honour, your Grace.

Calais 1460

The child with her nervous, twisting little hands was the first thing Richard Neville saw as he stood in the doorway of the tower room. Feeling a surge of surprised tenderness, he hesitated on the threshold until a movement to his left drew his attention. The eyes he met were warm and brown, curved at their corners by a soft smile of recognition; a smile that had once melted his heart, in a face that he used to hold so dear. He showed nothing of his shock, whilst inside he recoiled, and if she was surprised at his lack of reaction, she did not show it, sinking before him in a low curtsey, eyes first cast down and then lifted, still glowing, to rest on his face.

"Well well!" he said softly.

She kept her eyes on his face as if taking in the detail and reacquainting herself with more than seven years of wear and tear, of weathering and wars. A nerve twitched in his cheek as he took warm fingers in his icy ones, automatically brushing lips against knuckle. Her skin was feather soft and smelled of rose petals, and his stomach lurched as dormant memories raised their heads. He let go of her hand, afraid he may betray himself by trembling, yet wanting to gaze at her and take in her heady honeyed beauty once more.

"As you can see, Madame, your presence here is unexpected to say the least." His voice at least was his own and he managed a bitterly ironic smile. The woman swallowed, dropping her gaze.

"I am sorry, my Lord. I should have sent word but I was afraid that you would not receive me."

His stomach flipped again at the remembered cadence of her speech and he cursed the memory of which he had always been so proud wondering why, after all these years and so many women, he still remembered Veronique de Roet so clearly. Every inch of her was familiar to him, from the depth of her creamy-white forehead to the silk-soft curve of her breasts and the tiny little mole that nestled between them. She lifted her thickly lashed lids and looked directly at him, brown eyes soft and beseeching. His mouth twitched at one corner in an attempt at a smile and he shook his head.

"So instead you just descend upon me like an avenging angel." He arched well-defined eyebrows coolly, and the teasing words did not quite hide the real anger that lay behind them. He watched her poise retreat a little, and felt some grim satisfaction as he saw that she was uncertain what to do. He could see that she had not expected his hurt to be still raw, not after more than seven years. "Well here I am, Madame, so what brings you here?"

"I…" Veronique faltered, her eyes moving unconsciously to the child still seated. "I came to bring you a gift."

His gaze followed hers to the forlorn little figure, still staring at the stone floor. A cold ache of realisation settled in the pit of his stomach and reflected in the deep emerald of his eyes. He moved the three paces that separated them and caught her shoulders,

"Mine?" His voice was hoarse. She nodded again.

He turned and crouched before the little girl. She did not move yet he sensed the instinctive fear within her.

"Bonjour, ma petite. Hello, little one," he said in the same soft tones he used for his own small daughters, "Comment t'appelle tu? What is your name?" She gave him no response either by word or deed but maintained her gaze in her lap, her knuckles whitening as she gripped her hands more tightly together.

"Katrine!" Her mother's voice was sharp with irritation, an obviously all too familiar sound to the child, yet one which made him start with surprise that her tone could be so harsh. The little head jerked back and he was struck first by the incredible whiteness of her skin, almost chalk like in its pallor except for the blue veins that tracked their path across her temples, and then by her eyes.

He felt the gut wrenching jolt of shock for the second time in minutes and as his stomach lurched he was forced to put out a hand to steady himself. Taking a deep breath, he caught her chin in his hand, turning her face up to study it more closely. She stiffened slightly and her pupils dilated. His mother's eyes! Cool hazel, flecked with bright green. Jesu', his mother's face!

"Christ!" he muttered without thinking. Something flickered in her face; a flash of fear gone almost before it came and a rush of tenderness besieged his heart once more, stronger this time because he knew. Poor babe looked like she had never seen the light of the sun, unnourished by the warming winds and freezing snows. "It's alright, sweetheart," he murmured, "I will not hurt you." She seemed to relax, her eyes becoming round and wondrous, losing their eerie knowing look and his mother retreated into their depths.

He supposed it was not entirely unexpected that the one woman he had loved should have borne his child but it was sad that when a man was as willing as he to acknowledge all his children, he had so few.

"Why did you not tell me?" He did not turn as he spoke, not sure if he could bear to meet her gaze. She had been the one real love of his life, the only one who had made him suffer the agony of emotions he had never known he possessed. And she had been the one to let him down; not just once in leaving him like she did, but twice in keeping silent about this child.

There was no answer, the room quiet behind him. He made to rise, thinking that she wanted him to confront her, but the child caught his sleeve, looking expressionlessly into his face.

"My mother has gone, my Lord," she said flatly in French, her voice betraying nothing. He looked behind him and true enough there was no sign of her presence except for the child and the faint scent of roses in the air. He ran to the door where he could hear her footsteps pattering lightly on the stone steps.

"Veronique!"

If he ran he could catch her, but he knew that would be of no use. It was what she had meant to do from the start.

"Veronique!"

When he turned back to the child he saw that she had not moved, but the wet track of tears glistened on her white skin. He sighed softly and reaching down swung the girl up into his strong arms.

"Mama may have gone, sweetheart," he murmured against the top of her bright, burnished head, "But papa is here now."

Chapter One

Northamptonshire May 1464

Edmund Beaufort rolled onto his back, sweat slick on his sides as his chest still heaved with the exertion of his release. Automatically he reached for the girl and drew her to him, her head on his chest, his hand stroking her hair as he fought the desire to put distance between them. He never understood a woman's need for talk and affection after coupling, that sort of intimacy eluded him. He was a man who took his pleasure and then moved on. He ran his free hand through his dark hair and over his damp face, rubbing his eyes vigorously to get the sweat out of them, and then shifted the pillow behind him, propping him up better. The girl stretched and smiled, like a sleek, well-fed cat, and nipped his skin with her sharp little teeth.

"You are restless already," she said, as he flinched from her bite. "I can feel it. You can't wait to leave."

"It's nothing personal, Izzy." He dropped a kiss on the top of her head and slid out from under the covers, taking her words as a cue to extricate himself. "You know that." The girl sighed and sat up, a swirl of dark hair encircling her voluptuous shoulders.

"I suppose you will be gone for months again?"

"I don't know." He glanced over at her as he fastened the cord of his braies and then dragged on his chausses. "Depends what happens." The girl pouted, full red lips sulky.

"I don't know why I let you do this to me!" she said, sullenly. He grinned, his hard face lightened suddenly by the smile.

"Because you love me and I give you what you want, sweetheart." He gave her an arrogant wink.

"Huh. A quick tumble and then off you go again." Tears filled her eyes, more self-pity than real sadness but he softened all the same.

"Ah, Izzy!" He sat down on the bed and caught her hand, his bright gold eyes appraising her warmly. "I cannot help the way I have to live. You know that I see you as often as I can."

"Aye, me and a dozen others." She grimaced sourly and he grinned.

"But you are the one I always come home to, darling." He did not refute it but kissed her palm and then the tips of her fingers.

"Oh Beau!" She used the familiar family nickname, pushing him away in exasperation. "I'm not a child to be bought off with sweetmeats. I did think that you might do me the courtesy of at least staying the night. I am not a whore you know; I don't do this for anyone but you."

"Do I treat you like a whore?" He stood up abruptly and went back to dressing, pulling his linen shirt over his head, tousling his hair appealingly. "I look after you as best I can Izzy, you know that."

"Aye, but I'd rather see you than you just look after me." She flung back the covers and went around the screen to the garderobe.

"Saints preserve me from demanding women," He muttered under his breath, irritated that she, who was usually the most easy-going of his women, should suddenly take on so. It was not like he could help his lifestyle, moving as he had to from one safe place to another, dodging those loyal to Edward of York who hunted both him and his brother, hoping to curry favour with the new King by delivering the most valuable of deposed King Henry's supporters.

"I can hear you," she called sharply from behind the screen, and he laughed.

"I can hear you," He mimicked back unkindly and laughed harder as she flung a gutter insult at him. Suddenly there was a loud rapping on the door and a young voice called out.

"My Lord, my Lord. An urgent message, my Lord!"

"Come," he called, his heart in his mouth. This was what he had been waiting for; a message from his brother telling him when and where to meet. The door opened and his squire came in with a dishevelled travel stained messenger in tow. His gut contracted at the sight of the man's face. "Well?" he snapped.

"My Lord." The man knelt and handed him a piece of parchment. "I have scoured the north for you, only by chance finding that you were here." He read the words on the letter, his face turning to stone. He felt rather than saw Izzy come and stand next to him, discreetly robed, her perfume filling his nostrils, as instinctively she placed her hand on his arm.

"Tell me," he said hoarsely to the kneeling man, unshed tears fringing his lashes.

"It was a skirmish in Hexham, my Lord. My Lord Somerset had ordered a foraging party to hunt for supplies as meat was getting low. Warwick and Montague took us by surprise; we did not even know they were in the area. They took your brother and Warwick had him tried and executed at Hexham more than three days ago on York's instruction. I have been looking for you ever since."

"Jesu." Izzy moved closer to him as if trying to instill comfort by the very nearness of her body. He shook her off and moved away from the group, the tears threatening to spill.

"How could he be so stupid?" He thumped his fist into the wall, not feeling the bruising impact or the blood running down his knuckles. Izzy signaled for the men to leave, shutting the door behind them.

***

"Beau," she said softly as soon as the door closed. He turned, leaning back on the wall, his face a mask, his eyes hard and glittering like a hawk's.

"Don't," he said thickly.

"I am so sorry, love."

"I said don't!" His voice, always husky, was now cracked and hoarse. He slid down the wall until he sat on the floor, and laid his head on his knees; harsh, silent sobs wracking his body, tearing at her heart. She didn't try to comfort him, she knew that he would turn on her, hating as he did to be caught in any show of emotion, preferring all to believe that he was as hard underneath as the face he showed to the world. Instead she went over to the small table by the hearth and poured him a cup of rich red wine. She waited for a moment until his shoulders stopped heaving and then knelt beside him.

"Here," she said quietly. He took the cup, drained it and then flung it into the wall, where it shattered, scattering pieces across the room. She flinched at the sound but said nothing, merely went and filled another one and brought it back. This time he drank more slowly, one arm still round his knees, his tearstained face averted from her.

"It's over," he said, his voice breaking, "It is all over." He leaned his head back against the wall and closed his eyes, more tears squeezing underneath his lids and tracking down his high cheekbones. She sat cross legged on the floor next to him, her elbows on her knees, her chin resting on her hands. They had known each other since he was fifteen and she was thirteen and they had been lovers on and off for more than seven years yet still she knew nothing about what went on inside his head. But what she did know was that this was probably the biggest, bitterest blow he had suffered in his life. He and his brother, the Duke of Somerset, had planned so meticulously what they were going to do and how they were going to rid England of the usurper, Edward of York, and win the throne back for their captured King Henry, and now Hal was gone and Beau's grief was not just for his lost brother but for his lost Lancastrian cause.

"What will you do?"

"I will have to leave the country."

"Could you not go to Edward of York...?"

"Go to York?" He stared at her incredulously. "Prostrate myself before that whore's son?"

"He forgave Hal..."

"Aye and then executed him!" He spat the words at her furiously. "Anyway, I don't want his forgiveness.!" His voice broke again and tears spilled once more as he snapped his lids shut against them. "It is King Harry's forgiveness I should be asking," He whispered.

"Ah Beau, you are too hard on yourself." She shook her head but he ignored her.

"I can't stay here," was all he said. Izzy sighed and then smiled sadly.

"No." She reached out and touched his hand tentatively and he didn't shake her off. "Stay the night though Beau. It's foolish to go now."

"Yes, you're probably right." He opened his eyes and looked at her. "You're a good friend, Izzy," he said softly. She smiled, getting to her feet and taking the cup once more from his hand, taking it over to the table and refilling it, and drinking from it herself before she brought it back to him.

"Poor Hal," she said, looking down at him. "I suppose that makes you Duke of Somerset now?"

"For what it's worth." He snorted through his nose, pushing the grief for his brother to the back of his mind to be dealt with later. "I doubt that I'll be receiving investiture soon!"

"No." She held out her hand to him; he took it and pulled himself to his feet, wiping his free hand across his face.

"I will miss you, Izzy." He reached for her and pulled her to him in a wordless hug.

"Where will you go?" She pulled back and looked up at him sadly, realising that this was probably the end for them. He touched her face with long fingers.

"I shall go to France." His eyes took on a golden tenderness that she had never seen in them before.

"France?"

"Yes." His face softened and suddenly he looked very young for his twenty-five years, young and very appealing. "I will go to France, to serve my Queen."

Middleham, Yorkshire
Christmas 1464

Anne Beauchamp, Countess of Warwick, sat on the dais, the edge of one delicate forefinger crammed into her mouth, neat white teeth gnawing absently upon it, her round blue eyes fixed on the slender figure of the girl who she saw as the cause of her problem: a child brought into her household on the careless, thoughtless whim of the husband she had loved since she was betrothed as a child of eight. Thirty years of unquestioning devotion she had given him, according him the honour and respect she felt he deserved, aware as she was that he was a man of so many talents, which outweighed so many faults. Even if she had not been able to express her love in the way he craved, she had been sure that he was aware of her feelings, had been certain that he knew just how much of herself she had given to him. She had never been a demonstrative woman, raised in a household lacking in overt expressions of affection, her own father, late Earl of Warwick and

11

bequeather of the title, often absent fighting in France and overseeing the household of the young King Henry. She had never been able to respond to her husband's caress as he would have liked, had not been able to give him the passion that he needed, and although she knew that she was physically to his taste, their relationship in bed had not been successful. But all the same she had thought that he cared for her, that he respected her enough, loved her enough, even, to be discreet about his infidelities, and for her part she had never complained about his unfaithfulness. And he had been discreet; that was until he had fallen in love with that little French whore. She shuddered at the memory. One of the Queen's ladies and only fifteen, Veronique de Roet had been one of the most beautiful girls Anne had ever seen; sweet, innocent liquid-honey, a woman put on earth for the pleasure of men or, in this case, for the pleasure of Richard Neville. Anne had not realised at first that he was in love with her, had thought it was another passing fancy of lust, until he began to parade her for all to see to the detriment of his wife's dignity. Anne had left court then, retired home to lick her wounds and wait for him to come to her. And so he had, some six months later when the girl had gone from court back to France, a defiant loser in the game of love, making it clear that he only returned because it was his duty and because he needed to get an heir to the Warwick fortune, and from then on all he offered her was gratitude for the riches she had brought him, and polite, almost impersonal concern for her welfare. After the birth of Isabel and then Anne too, he had never shared her initial disappointment in their sex, always sure that a boy would follow. But so far the boy had not come and after six miscarriages in four years she seemed to have finally stopped conceiving. Even so, she had never truly believed that he could be so unfeeling that he would bring that woman's child into her home.

Anger still welled inside her as she remembered Richard Neville arriving at their city home after Edward of York's great victory at Towton, where Edward had defeated Harry of Lancaster and they had ridden victorious into London. Warwick had declared him King of England, much to the Londoners' delight; and not caring that she had worried herself sick at the rumours of his death at St Albans, he had breezed in like a whirlwind, sweeping the children off their feet in great hugs of exuberance, full of stories about his infernal cousin how he, Warwick, had made a king and talking interminably about their prowess on the field of battle. He had not given a thought about her worry, not a thought, thinking only of the power he was to gain, the power he so craved. She had withheld her resentment, slipping into the background, curbing her desire to shout at him, knowing that she could speak to him when they were alone, her love for her daughters overcoming her desire to hurt him. Then as they had sat alone in the solar, the servants retired for the night, his squire and her Lady preparing their bedchamber, he had blithely announced that his bastard child was coming to live with them in their household, in her home, with her children, without a 'by your leave' or any semblance of discussion. All the memories of her humiliation came flooding back and she had been unable to curb her tongue, lashing him with all his past wrongs until, infuriated that he just stood and laughed at her she had mustered all her strength and swung at him. But he was far quicker than she and he had caught her arm and thrown her over his shoulder, carrying her into their bedchamber and throwing her onto the bed. He had then sat down beside her and proceeded to tell her all the details of his affair, how much he had loved the girl and how he would never have come back to her bed had it not been for the need to conceive a male heir. Then he had slowly undressed her and made love to her with an impersonal tenderness and emotional detachment that had broken her heart. Afterwards she had lain there silent and dazed, the love she had borne him for so long, turning to ice. She knew now that she was nothing more to him than the mother of his legitimate offspring, a failure in her attempts to give him the longed-for son, the benefactress who had brought him his wealth and status. She remembered fondly the child he had been when they had wed; full of ambition even then, goaded on by his father, over-proud of his ancestors. She had been a good catch for the son of the Earl of Salisbury, even if he was descended from John of Ghent, her inheritance making him England's premier Earl, and yet it had been she who had thought herself so lucky to wed this handsome boy, she who had been overawed by him. There had been nothing humble about him, nothing that made her think he would ever be aught but arrogant, and still she had loved him with the childish devotion of an eight-year-old, which blossomed into adult love and respect. That was, until now. They were of an age, she and

Richard, both thirty-four, yet somehow his age seemed to matter little and hers to be an ever increasing spectre on the horizon. She knew that her looks would soon begin to fade, and as she approached those years that childbearing became impossible instead of improbable, there would be nothing to keep him at her side. How unfair it was that women were only useful to their husbands for such a short span of their married life, and a man could produce until death. How sad it was that a woman should suffer so and a man should take all the pleasure. Only she knew how the miscarriages had affected her, how hard it was to begin yet another pregnancy so bound to end the same way; yet it was her duty to do so and duty was a diet she had been raised upon. She touched her stomach lightly, still taut and flat after two daughters and one full term still born boy, a stomach she was proud of and yet seemed no longer able to bear fruit. Every one of her last six pregnancies had ended after three months, and every one of them a male child, and every time she had seen the weary disgusted light in her husband's eyes, seen how he thought of her and her inability to breed. She knew that he could never credit that he was at fault, even though he had not one male child to his name, and few enough children from his many affairs, but then it was not in his character to admit any failure of any sort. The fault could only lie with her, and if that be the case there seemed little point in coming home, save to see his children once in a while.

Anne shook herself out of her thoughts, her eyes re-focusing on the group playing with the puppy in the corner of the busy torchlit hall, softening at the sight of lovely golden Isabel and dark dainty Anne. It was almost time for the younger children to be in bed but she delayed summoning their nurse, happy to indulge them for a little longer in their play. She loved her daughters with a passion few would understand, tried to instil in them the values she had grown up with, but their father was critical of her protectiveness, insisting that they should see something of the harsh realities of life, should see for themselves how difficult it could be in the world outside. He was hard on them at times, unafraid to inflict tough punishment for what he saw as weakness, hating Anne's vulnerability and her seeming constant need for protection, irritated by Isabel's vanity and scalding temper. The only one who seemed to meet his approval was the wretched bastard with her quick tongue and the devil in her. He laughed at her antics in the stables, how she competed with the squires on her pony, willing to jump where the poor pony would not. Often Anne had complained to him that he indulged her at the expense of his true children, but he would merely give her one of his sardonic smiles and tell her not to fret, their inheritance would be little affected by a child who would inherit nothing. And suddenly, the boy Gloucester, who she had earmarked for her own little Anne, had taken a fancy to her and seemed to include her in all his activities. She knew she was silly to worry about something like that, after all Dickon of Gloucester would hardly be allowed to wed a bastard, but she knew Anne already cared for Dickon, and she had been but eight when she had fallen in love with her own Richard. It was not unfeasible that 'the child', Katherine would form an attachment to Gloucester and him to her. She studied the girl carefully, watching her pretty little cat-like face as she and Dickon talked animatedly over the little dog. There was no sign of much in the hazel eyes, save a desire to put her own point of view across, hands flying in gallic fashion as she gabbled in her silly accented English. Anne was irritated that her youngest daughter seemed so much taken with her half-sister; it had been the blight of her life when she had noticed the attachment the two girls had formed for each other and no matter how hard she tried there was naught she could do to alter it.

'Jesu" she thought irritably, 'how could Dickon take so quickly to this girl who behaved like a boy, and who had even mastered the quintain much to both Richard and Dickon's delight. Anne had to admit that she had the makings of real beauty, although her colouring was all wrong; the alabaster skin laced with blue veins, her russet hair which seemed to have a life of its own, tumbling from her head in a cascade of wild, unmanageable curls which had to be wetted and scraped back to get them into anything like a decent braid; but she was going to be lovely all the same. Huge eyes lay along sharp cheekbones and a full expressive mouth announced the beauty to come. She snorted out loud, startling herself and Joan Scrope, Lady of Masham and her oldest friend, who sat beside her.

"Is aught wrong, Nan?" the older woman asked. Anne shook her head with a rueful smile.

"Nothing more than usual." Their eyes met in a quick flash of understanding.

"She is a strange child, that girl of his." Joan rarely minced her words, but Anne valued her for that, preferring her company to many others who would not have dared to raise the subject.

"Mmmmmm." Anne did not trust herself to comment and seeing her friend's obvious distress, Joan changed the subject.

"Have you heard from the Earl?"

"Yes, he's spending New Year with the King, so I know not when he will be home. He sent gifts for us all and the children." The last was said a trifle defensively.

"Well when you are so close to the King as he is, duty does always come before family, does it not?"

"I suppose, though it would be easier if Richard did not enjoy his duty so much. It means everything to him to be close confidant to the King." Anne shook her head. "I fear we come a sorry second."

"Well they do say that the King is but a figurehead and my Lord Warwick is the real ruler." Joan grinned impishly and Anne smiled.

"Or at least Richard says that," she countered with a laugh, glad that Joan had shaken her from her melancholy.

"And the boy of Gloucester, how has he been?"

"Oh, he has settled admirably considering the way his life has been turned upside down, what with his father's death and suddenly having a King for a brother. I was a little worried as he was so quiet at first but Richard said that he is always so." She bit her lip and forebore to add that he was not so shy with 'the bastard' suddenly.

"A real feather in his cap bringing the boy into his household; a responsibility not every man would relish, the King's brother as his ward. But I would suspect the Earl is up to the task." The older woman laughed again. "It is a true mark of the King's respect for him."

Anne said nothing. She had no love for her husband's cousin, now King of England; in fact, had never liked him and could not see what Richard saw in him, hating his easy ways and immoral reputation, knowing that such a man would be nothing but a poor influence on her husband. But it was not just this hat brewed against him, it was a feeling of mistrust, an instinct that there was more beneath the surface of his fun-loving nature than met the eye, and that her husband would have to tread very carefully if he was to retain his hold on the reins of governance. Not that she would ever have aired such an opinion, for she was but a woman, not expected to voice her thoughts on such matters that were best left to men, but she had them all the same and many a time her instinct had been right whilst Warwick's political acumen had failed him.

Warwick would have to tread carefully with this nineteen-year-old boy, so confident in his own military prowess and with good reason to be. Not many could show the skill and leadership he had shown on the battlefield and win the crown, even from so hapless a King as Henry VI. His father, the late Duke of York, had not been able to accomplish that feat in ten years yet Edward had done it in less than ten months. Her husband would of course say that was because Duke Richard had not used the silky skills of Richard Neville to make him a king, but Anne was sure it was Edward's own magnetism and charisma that had won his crown, not her husband's.

"They say that the morals of the court have come way down the castle walls since Edward became king," continued Joan disapprovingly, though Anne thought she would probably be the first to forgive a man such as Edward of York should she meet him face-to-face. "It is said that he has a different woman each night, and nothing must ever come between him and his pleasure."

"Then that is where he and Richard differ, for power comes between him and his pleasure, not the other way about." Anne grimaced in distaste. "Though I have often wondered who the pleasure is for; it is for certes not my idea of it."

Joan laughed in obvious agreement with her friend; the pleasure was all for the man, there was nothing in it for a woman.

"These wantons do it for what they can reap, not for pleasure; that I'll wager. There can be small pleasure in being a man's mistress unless it's for the gifts a generous lord might give!"

"No gift can be big enough to pay for the risk of becoming with child!"

"Perhaps not to you or I, Nan, but to these whores it's just a price to pay." Joan glanced across the room to where Warwick's daughter was playing with little Anne and Dickon. "After all, if a man acknowledges his bastards, then it's a goodly income."

Anne followed her gaze and smiled bitterly.

"And if he takes the child into his home, it is the wife who pays the forfeit for his whoring. The whore can continue without the encumbrance of the child." She turned back and met the eyes of her longstanding friend with calm surety. "I don't think I can ever forgive him that, Joan. Not for bringing that girl into my home. Even after three years I cannot forgive, and each time I see that girl it reminds me of how I suffered when he left me for her whore of a mother. He humiliated me and now I am forced to care for the child. Jesu' he would try the patience of a saint!"

Joan patted her arm reassuringly but Anne knew that Joan thought she was luckier than most wives, and that if the price to pay for a husband who kept his hands to himself was to bring up his bastard then Joan would have happily taken it, not that she had ever said so in as many words but their friendship was such that she didn't need to.

"What is done, is done, sweeting," Joan said softly, "and brooding on it will not make it vanish. It's time to make the best of it."

Anne looked back at the child and sighed softly.

"Perhaps you are right, Joan, perhaps it is time; though what 'the best of it' is, I am not so sure."

Middleham
January 1465

It was the baying of the hounds that first alerted Kate that the Earl was home, followed by a great clattering of horses' hooves on the cobbles of the bailey and the sound of shouting voices floating up toward the hall. In the chamber where she was having lessons with the other household children, the occupants jerked up their heads and looked quickly across at each other. Their tutor moved across to the high window and looked out, then, turning back to his pupils, smiled and nodded.

"My Lord Earl is here," he said in his soft voice and all the children held their breath in anticipation. As with any child, for Kate, the lessons were sometimes a bind to be endured under sufferance and avoided whenever possible, though in later years Katherine Neville would thank her father's farsightedness, as a man of progressive thinking who saw fit to educate his daughters in the arts of reading, writing, Latin, French and basic mathematics. She knew that the Countess was inclined to think it a waste to educate girls in such a fashion for it gave them ideas above their standing in the real world, though perhaps, Kate thought, that was because she was envious of their learning and probably wished her own father had not been so keen to merely educate her as a lady, with only French, reading and needlework.

"I think that as this is a special occasion you may leave your books and go to greet the Earl." The tutor was kinder than some they had endured, and a man with an eye for who his pupils were. As of one movement they all jumped up and rushed from the chamber, Dickon and the other boys leading the way down the winding staircase, taking the steps two at a time, whilst Kate and her sisters followed at a more sedate pace.

The hall thronged with men; a buzz of voices reaching her long before she could see, coupled with the barking of excited dogs and the clatter of metal on wood as swords were unbuckled. Kate took in the scene around her, following her sisters, always slightly behind them, afraid to push herself forward. The Countess was already by Warwick's side, greeting cup in hand, her expression politely welcoming as though he were no more than a stranger warming himself at their hearth. She saw the admiring glances of some of the men as the Countess moved among them, and the irony struck her even at such a tender age. How odd that men should so envy her father something that seemed to bring him so little joy.

Dickon was the first to greet the Earl, a rare smile about his lips as Warwick ruffled his hair, and laughing as Dickon murmured something in his quiet tones. It was not so long since they had parted, for Dickon had arrived home from Durham but a week before, having spent almost a week with Edward, celebrating the new year. He had been quiet when he had returned and Kate had guessed that he would have liked to have stayed.

"Have you no greeting for me Katherine?" The familiar, low voice broke into her musings, startling her so that she jumped and then flushed. She realised, to her dismay, that half the men in the hall were watching her.

19

"Forgive me, my Lord. I..." She stopped and shrugged, and he smiled holding out his hand to her.

"You were too busy watching everyone else to care about your poor weary papa, eh?" He teased her lightly and she flushed deeper.

"No! I was just waiting." She took his hands and dutifully reached up to kiss his cheek, stunned afresh as she contemplated that this wonderfully beautiful man was her father. His colouring was striking, the emerald eyes and chestnut hair, but his face was too finely boned to be classed as handsome, his nose too long and his mouth too wide, but women especially seemed to like him for eyes followed him wherever he went. All three girls looked on him as a kind of romantic hero who had fought with the handsome Prince for a kingdom and won. It mattered not that he had lost some of his battles like the second one at St Albans that had caused the Countess such worry and that perhaps Edward was the real conquering prince; to them he was the invincible Knight he told them he was, the man behind the throne who guided the handsome young King and ruled the land. It was an ideal that he had subscribed to well, making sure that all those close to him realised that Edward relied on his judgment, that he needed Richard Neville close to his side.

"Are you well, child?" He broke once more into her thoughts and she realised that she stared at him. Quickly she dropped her gaze.

"Yes, thank you, papa." He let go of her hands, his expression bemused. She knew that he would have liked her to hug him but somehow, she couldn't. She was not like Anne and Isabel who loved open shows of affection, like a hug in Isabel's case or Anne being nestled on his lap. She knew that sometimes he was hurt by her lack of affection and she wished she could reassure him that she loved him more than anyone else in the world, but she could never say the words when it came to it and was left tongue tied and embarrassed.

"And have you been good and done as you were bid, whilst I have been absent?" He flashed a quick look at his wife as he spoke, but the child merely smiled and nodded, seeming not to see his glance.

"Of course, papa."

"Good." There was nothing more to be said, yet distance seemed to hang between them and once more she longed to cross it and throw her arms around his neck but instead stood politely with her hands demurely folded. He turned back to the rest of his family, smiling benevolently, the jolly father just returned from campaign. "I expect you all wish to see what I have brought you, eh?" he asked indulgently, and Anne squealed with delight.

"Ooh yes, papa!" As her father began to produce gifts for all, Kate hovered uncertainly, still feeling like an intruder on a family gathering. She wondered unexpectedly if her mother ever thought of her and supposed that she did not for there had been no letters in the four years since they parted. It was the first time in a long time that she had let herself think of her mother, for even after all this time it was too painful to recall the years before she had come to her father at Calais; hard years of her mother's uncertain temper, constant reminders that she had been the ruin of her mother's life and that the beautiful Veronique had never married because of her; none wanted a woman who had a bastard, for bastards were the fruit of sin and no man wanted a wife who had such an open reminder of her sin. Yet it had been the sudden possibility of her mother's marriage that had forced her to bring her child to Calais, when she had become the heiress to her father's lands and there had suddenly been suitors for her hand. So she had rid herself of her child in the best way she knew how. Kate had not wanted to leave her mother, for all her moods, for she loved her. And though she had come to love her father, even his presence could not always make up for the loss of her mother.

"Katherine?" Warwick's voice was soft as he held out a slender cloth-wrapped cylinder. She looked up at him and saw that his green eyes were filled with tenderness as he met her gaze, just the two of them left as the other children had wandered off with their gifts.

"What is it, papa?"

"Open it and see." She reached out and took the cloth, noting its weight as she unwound the wrapping.

"Oh!" she breathed, staring down at the jewel-handled knife in her hand, etched on the blade with her father's insignia of the Bear and Ragged Staff. "Oh papa, thank you!" That her father could know how much she had envied Dickon the knife that Warwick had given him for his name-day seemed extraordinary, unaware as she was how obvious it had been to Richard Neville at the time and suddenly she flung herself into his arms, both surprising and delighting him as she kissed his cheek before burying her face in his neck and hugging him tight. "Oh thank you, Papa, thank you," she said again. Warwick laughed and hugged her back, his smile radiant.

"If I had known it was this easy to win your affection I would have brought you a knife years ago," he said teasingly as he set her on her feet and kissed her forehead, one arm still round her narrow shoulders. "Lord knows you are hard to reach sometimes!"

"I'm sorry, papa," she said in a small voice.

"For what, sweetheart?"

Kate shrugged, her eyes suddenly bright with unshed tears.

"I never seem to be what anyone wants me to be," she said quietly.

"Who says?" Warwick stopped and turned her to face him. "Who says you are not?"

"Maman used to, ma mère says I am a hoyden not a lady and I know I do not always please you." Her bottom lip trembled. "I don't mean to be disobedient, papa."

"Katherine, listen to me." He took her face in both his hands and looked into her eyes. "You do please me, more than you can ever imagine and I really don't care what your mother or your stepmother might have said. I am very proud of your reading and writing and your hard work in the schoolroom and I am proud of the way you sit a horse and the skill with which you ride it and if you want to learn sword play with my squires and Dickon then do it. I want you to be happy here at Middleham, Katherine and to feel that this is your home but up to now I have never been certain if you are?" He ran his thumb along her cheekbone, wiping away a spilled tear. "Are you happy?"

"Yes, papa," she nodded vigorously.

"You are sure?" He smiled, his almond eyes crinkling at the corner and furrows appearing round his wide mouth.

"Yes, papa." And suddenly she realised she meant it. This was her family now, there was no going back to those days in France. She owed this family her love and loyalty, owed it to the father who loved her, the little sister who had become her friend, and even to the countess whose coldness she understood. None would ever call her fickle like her mother; none would say that she had no idea of family ties. "I am very happy."

Anjou, France
February 1465

Marguerite of Anjou, former Queen of England, stood at the bottom of the stone steps leading into the hall and watched Edmund Beaufort sitting on the dais, chewing the inside of his lip and staring broodingly out over the busy hall as his young brother chattered in his ear. She swallowed and took a deep breath, swept as always by a sense of loss at the sight of him, and now, after yesterday, by a surge of embarrassment. The sense of loss came from years gone by and a love that was now just a memory, a man who was dead and gone; the embarrassment from what had happened last night and the sick cold feeling in the pit of her stomach at what she had done. She made as if to move across the hall and then stopped, putting her hand on the wall to support herself. Somehow she had to face him and pretend that nothing had happened; somehow she had to get past his beauty and become his Queen again, his liege Lady. That she could have humiliated herself so in front of him was mortification enough, but now she would have to face his arrogance and superiority, his looking down at her and enjoying knowing that she wanted him from the supremely lofty position of having denied her. Anger roiled in her gut and she felt physically sick at his rejection, and a picture of his face as he recoiled from her flashed through her head, the expression of horror in those extraordinary eyes imprinted on her mind forever. Until that point he had looked so much like his father that she had been completely beguiled by him and his adoration, beguiled by his dark harsh beauty and his tender hawk eyes. She had thought that he wanted her, had not realised that it was a courtly idealization, and starved of love she had opened herself towards him like a flower moving toward the sun, but she had misread the situation and now the damage created between them was irreversible. She knew that at thirty-four she was still a very beautiful woman and even though Edmund Beaufort was nine years her junior, she could rival anyone of his own age, yet he did not want her, somehow did not think of her as a woman he could fancy, idealizing her instead as his Queen. She thought of the day more than three months ago, when he had arrived at her little court, a truly magnificent, angry young man, broken by his brother's death and the

23

loss of their cause, trailed by his unhappy young brother who had suffered the consequences of what had obviously been dark days. He had knelt at her feet, a taller, leaner version of his father, the man she had loved so much and who had dominated Henry and ruled with her for nearly ten years, and he had swept her back to a time gone by; a time where she reigned supreme as the beauty of the court, loved by this man's father who she had loved wholeheartedly in return because he was sharply clever and because he had that supreme masculine arrogance that his middle son had inherited in full measure. It was funny how different the three Beaufort boys were: pretty Hal had been a soldier in his own mind but could never translate it onto the battlefield, his father's favourite but never talented enough to fulfill his ambitions; and young Jack, a blurred version of both his brothers, an open, honest and good-looking face but not striking like either Hal or Edmund (she preferred to think of him as Edmund but his family called him Beau)

According to the old Duke, both he and his son looked like his grandsire, John of Ghent, who in turn had looked like *his* father Edward III, dark haired, with an aquiline beauty that turned heads and hearts alike. All the boys had inherited the looks and spirit of these fine warriors in some measure but it was Edmund Beaufort, the younger, who had it all. He had always promised real battlefield potential, real soldiering skills and his father had been proud of the man he thought he would become. But now that King Henry, her husband, was captured and a prisoner of Edward of York, and most of his Lancastrian allies had made their peace with Edward or disappeared into the Welsh marches, Somerset was here without chance of much fighting, chafing at his inactivity, callously seducing her women and then leaving them without a backward glance. Even seeing all that and knowing the type of man he was, she had still thrown herself at him, thinking that he used her women as a substitute for her. How stupid she had been to think that it was her he wanted and how humiliated had she felt when he had gently disengaged himself and stepped away from her, bowing deeply and backing out of the room, wishing her goodnight as he always had done and pretending that she had not just tried to seduce him. But she had seen the glimpse of shock and then horror in his eyes as he had slipped out of her embrace, and now it made her insides shrivel with pure embarrassment as she contemplated what had happened.

Steeling herself, she moved away from the wall and began to walk across the hall, inclining her head as men bowed and women curtseyed, not looking at the dais but knowing that he must have seen her, was probably watching her. She did not look at him until she had mounted the steps and he was on his feet, an uncertain smile on his face, his eyes wary as he drew her chair back and bowed deferentially. She favoured him with a dazzling smile and he relaxed visibly, pushing her chair in for her and waiting for her to signal that he could sit. Once he was seated she leaned in towards him and said softly,

"Do not even begin to think that I have forgotten how you insulted me last night, my Lord Somerset." She felt him stiffen and smiled to herself maliciously. "To attempt to seduce your Queen could be construed at the very least as insolence and at the most as treason and should not go unpunished." She did not look at him, but heard him draw a sharp breath and felt his glittering, gold eyes burning into the side of her face.

"Madame?" His always husky voice was almost a whisper in his shock.

"I am not flattered, my Lord, that one such as you should think he is a fit mate for a Queen." She turned then and met his gaze coolly, daring him to challenge her, her voice still low. "You are not half the man your father was." He searched her face, still disbelieving what he was hearing. She could almost see the turmoil in his mind as he struggled with how to deal with this unjustified attack, and then she saw the light die in his gaze as he realised he had no choice but to go along with her game.

"Forgive me Madame," he said tonelessly

"I am not sure if I can, my Lord. I think it might be a good idea if you left my court for a while." She turned back to look out over the hall, but when she glanced at him from under her lashes she saw that his face wore a wary expression and his eyes were hard.

"Yes, Madame."

"I hear that the Count of Charolais is looking for good soldiers. I thought you may be able to go to Burgundy and hone your skills serving with him." She turned back and smiled at him with cool politeness, a smile that he did not return, merely looking at her with an expression that made her want to reach out to him and touch his cheek. She knew she was being grossly unfair and that made her more intent on achieving her goal, so she met his expression levelly and finally he nodded.

"Yes, Madame," he said quietly.

"Your brother Jack may stay if he wishes or he may go with you, whichever you choose. Edward will miss you, of course" She glanced at her son but he was watching some jugglers and laughing. "But he will be glad to see you when you return, and you will have more skill in tutoring him by then. I will not expect you back for at least a twelve-month, my Lord."

"Yes, Madame."

"Good. So we understand each other then, my Lord Somerset?" She arched a defined brow and after a moment he nodded.

"We understand each other perfectly, your Grace." He inclined his head, his expression like granite, and she felt another sense of loss sweep the pit of her stomach. She had lost the father and now she was to lose the son, and the loss of them both was entirely her own fault.

Chapter Two

Middleham, December 1467

Stephen Thevenot pulled his cloak about him and cursed loudly, the sudden outburst startling both his chestnut stallion and his young squire.

"Goddamn this cold," he groused petulantly, "and this sodding rain. I swear if it were not the Earl of Warwick I were visiting I'd be turning back to the warmth of my own hearth." His young companion grimaced at his master, flashing a large gap where his front teeth should have been.

"It's not so bad, my Lord. We've been out in worse and, anyway, think of the fine hospitality we shall receive, not to mention the gracious ladies!" Stephen rolled his eyes at the boy's one-track thoughts.

"Have a care, Harry!" he cautioned. "You don't want to be losing any more teeth. Jesu', it's bad enough that they fall out without having them knocked down your throat."

Harry laughed, obviously proud of his hell-raising, unable to see anything wrong in brawling over a wench; it was part of growing up after all.

Stephen sighed. 'The joys of youth,' he thought caustically; what a shame they seemed to have passed him by. His mind shifted once again to the reason for his summons to the great Earl's Christmas festival. A possible marriage, the letter had said, between Stephen and the Earl's natural daughter, an honour not to be spurned even if the lass was a bastard. One could not afford to care which side of the marriage contract she had been born when she carried such a good dowry and a chance of allying himself with the Earl's noble family.

He allowed himself a small smile of satisfaction at being on the receiving end of such an opportunity, wondering briefly what it was he had done to bring him to the Earl's attention, though if the rumours he had heard were true, my Lord Warwick was devoting himself much to family matters these days. The King and the Earl had had yet another difference of opinion, but they always managed to resolve them so he saw no reason to think that this time would be any different. A sudden gust of wind and driving rain took his breath away, whipping off his hood and hammering into his face.

"Christ Jesus!" he spat angrily as soon as he was able to speak. The chestnut shied skittishly and it was all credit to his superior horsemanship that he managed to stay in the saddle. He shook his head to clear his vision from the onslaught. "Damn this fucking rain!" He fought to bring the stallion under control, and turned back to his squire, his face stark and pale against the dark fur of his cloak, his thick brown hair plastered to his forehead. "Are you alright, lad?" The boy's voice came from some way behind him, almost carried away by the wind.

"Aye, my Lord. Just keeping out of the way of that brute of yours. He's too flighty to be out in this if you ask me."

"Well, no one asked you," returned Stephen drily. "And how will he ever learn to behave if he's not ridden." There was no reply and he smiled grimly. None of the servants thought much of his passion for breeding and schooling fine horses, thinking it not a decent pastime for a noble knight; they felt it lowered his social standing, and there was no greater class-conscious folk than servants. He cared little for their opinion, indulging his passion shamelessly, and had made quite a name for himself as a man with a well-stocked stable worth passing an eye over. That was why he rode the young chestnut, for he was by far the best looking stallion he had bred so far and it would do his reputation no harm to be seen riding him. "Jesus Wept, how much farther is it? It will be dark soon and then where will...?" Another icy blast smashed into his face corking his words in his throat as easily as stopping up a keg and he swore viciously against it. Then as if from nowhere the great keep of Middleham castle loomed ahead of them, almost black against the stormy skyline.

"Christ," he whispered, awed by the sheer magnificence. "Sweet Jesus Christ." He turned in the saddle and met the round eyes of his companion. "It makes my little place look humble, doesn't it lad?" And too full of wonder to lie, the youth nodded dumbly.

Stepping into the inner bailey was like entering another world. So, sheltered was it by the high curtain wall which surrounded it that the wind seemed to pass by with hardly so much as a whistle, leaving only the rain to fall at a much gentler pace, less uncomfortable than the heavy lash he had endured on the long journey. Swinging out of the saddle, he threw the reins to Harry with instructions on what to do with the young horse, and then made his way to the great entrance. As if by a sorcerer's wand, a young man appeared before him, an easy grin of rakish charm across his face.

"Sir Stephen Thevenot?" he inquired with a quirk of dark eyebrows. Masking his surprise, Stephen nodded and the lad inclined his head. "My Lord Earl is expecting you." He clicked his fingers to a young page who scurried up the stairs whilst they followed at a more leisurely pace. He pushed his way through a throng of people in the great hall, Stephen blinking his eyes against the sudden pall of smoke which seemed to hang in the air. He was led to another doorway and ushered through, finding himself in the great chamber where the air was much cleaner and there were far fewer people. He felt suddenly at a loss, realising with an embarrassed start that he had no idea what the Earl looked like, much less in which part of the chamber he may be in. He hesitated, a fraction nonplussed what to do.

"Thank you, Rob." A quietly authoritative voice spoke somewhere to his left and the youth at his side bowed before retiring to the hall. Turning he found himself being regarded appraisingly by a pair of the greenest eyes he had ever seen, set in a striking, finely boned face. Gems glittered at the man's throat and fingers and his forest-green tunic was set with tiny rubies, leaving Stephen in no doubt of who he was. "Sir Stephen. I bid you welcome to Middleham. I hope your journey was not too arduous in this dreadful weather." He came forward, clasping Stephen's hand in a firm handshake.

"Thank you, my Lord." Stephen sketched a suitable bow and then grinned ruefully, aware suddenly of his very disheveled appearance compared to the Earl's supreme elegance.

"I fear that strong wind and rain is not conducive to visiting. I must look as though I were dragged here through a bush, not to mention a few puddles!" He cursed himself for the uneven cadence of his voice indicating his nervousness to all. The Earl was only a man after all, not a God, and it was hardly likely that he was about to conjure the King from nowhere. He was relieved to see Warwick smile with disarming familiarity, designed, with success, to put him at his ease.

"I'd wager a hot bath would revive you, lad, and a change of clothes eh?" He clapped Stephen on the shoulder. "I'll have you shown to your chamber and a bath will be prepared for you. Then you can join us for supper." It was not a suggestion but an easy command.

"Of course, my Lord." Stephen smiled again, "Anything as long as I am spared facing that abominable storm again." Warwick's grin broadened.

"I see I have you in the right frame for a bargain," he said very quietly, a subtle reference to his reason for inviting the young Knight to his home. Stephen smiled tightly.

"Perhaps you could have done even better had you sent for me in a blizzard." Their eyes met for a fraction and the Earl also began to laugh, and Stephen felt that perhaps this would not be quite the formal occasion that he had anticipated.

Once immersed in the blessed warmth of his bath, his skin scrubbed until it tingled, he felt better. He was a rare breed of man who hated to be filthy, bathing, much to his household's amusement, as often as weekly, and insisting on his tunics being well perfumed with jasmine and musk before they were packed away. There was little he hated more than stinking of putrid stale sweat, whether it was his own or his horse's.

Reluctantly he stood up in the water, drying himself vigorously with the rough towel provided before climbing out completely and moving closer to the blaze which flared comfortingly in the hearth. He looked at his reflection in the glass which stood in one corner of the chamber, an expensive accessory which very few could afford in the vast quantities as seemed to be here in the castle. He wondered for the first time if he might hold any appeal for a young lass. He knew scarcely a marriage that was founded on love, in fact most were content to resign themselves to mutual tolerance, or if they were fortunate, affection. That was how it had been in his first marriage; wed at fourteen to a girl his own age, they had spent ten tolerable years together before she had died after her sixth, or was it seventh, abortive pregnancy, her blood poisoned so that she had passed away in raving fever. He had mourned her sincerely enough for she had been as good a wife as any man could hope to have, except for her inability to provide an heir, and he had felt a curiously empty sense of loss without her, but he was not fool enough to harbour romantic notions of a second wedding. Not at his age. At twenty- six he guessed he was in the prime of his manhood, yet he felt jaded, with his youth far behind him. Physically, he thought, grimacing, he was in good shape. His skin was smooth, his torso reasonably muscular, and if his conquests were roads to follow he was personable enough to look at, but inside he felt fatigued, unable to muster the joy to indulge himself with enthusiasm in anything frivolous. He sighed wearily and reached for his clothes, wondering what could have happened to young Harry, resigned but not irritated by the boy's wayward spirit. He felt fleetingly envious of such freedom and then snorted a mirthless laugh at his morbidity. 'Come on Thevenot,' he thought ruefully, adjusting his rich rust tunic over his shirt, 'it is time to impress your host with your eagerness to follow the Bear and Ragged Staff wherever it chooses to lead you.'

On his way from the tower lodging he decided to quickly look in on the chestnut and make sure that Harry had settled him properly. He was awed by the massive stable complex in the outer court of the huge Castle, combined as it was by various businesses thriving on the Earl's considerable trade. There were farriers and slaughterhouses, feed buildings, great stone blocks housing the harnesses of their only mode of transport, not to mention the living quarters of all those folks who worked amongst the animals. He gazed jealously about him, conscious suddenly that the rain had stopped and the sky become a little brighter. It must be nigh three in the afternoon, he thought, almost time to dine, so he had better be quick.

He found the stallion knee-deep in soft straw, munching his way quite happily through a large quantity of what looked like fine quality hay. His coat was dry and shone with his squire's exertions and he looked contented after his soaking. Stephen smiled and shook his head wonderingly. He may be a young hellion but none could fault the lad on his diligence, for he undertook tasks normally considered to be beneath a squire's duties with unmatched cheerfulness and never once in the years they had been together had Stephen heard the boy complain.

"Jesu', Rob, if she catches me I will be in such trouble." Stephen swung round at the quiet voice which seemed so close.

"Well it was you who wanted me to do this, not I." More whispers but deeper this time. Intrigued, Stephen moved across the stable and peered over the half door into the next one. He was not sure what he expected to see, but he was surprised to find two lads indulging in gentle swordplay. One was the squire who had escorted him to the Earl; the tall, broad youth with the rakishly lopsided grin. The other, with his back to him, was a good head shorter, skinny in stature and sounded much younger. The older lad seemed to be tutoring the other who had difficulty holding the sword upright.

"Now, parry, parry, thrust. Come on! You need to put yourself behind it. Parry, parry.... oh Jesu'" Exasperation made the bigger youth shout and the other muttered 'shhh' crossly. They began another exchange and Stephen started to lose interest, thinking he must get to his host in the hall, when suddenly the point of the older boy's sword tweaked the younger's cap off his head, revealing a thick waist-length braid of the richest russet that Stephen had ever seen. Christ, he thought with shock, it was a lass!

"Damn you, you...you...whoreson," she hissed, flashing the heavy steel dangerously close to her opponent's face. Laughing the youth parried the blow with ease, dodging neatly aside. The girl spat another particularly unladylike invective, which had Stephen biting his lip to avoid laughing aloud, and swung again with her lethal blade. Unfortunately, her opponent caught his foot, unbalancing and falling heavily into the straw behind him, and regardless now of discovery, she whooped like a banshee, placing her right foot on his chest and the point of her sword at his throat.

"Now beg, Rob Percy," she crowed delightedly, "Beg for your life." Stephen grinned broadly and decided it was time he retired.

***

At supper, the food was as plentiful as it was unsurpassable, and the wine a rich full-bodied red from the finest vineyards of Bordeaux, yet Stephen felt himself unable to do it full justice, so overtaken was he by the excitement of his surroundings. Almost ignored were the great platters of hare and rabbit, the huge trays of almond capon and rich stuffed chicken, and the urns of broth and pottage. Appetizing smells of herbs and spice assaulted his nostrils, but caused little activity in his stomach as he watched the laughing crowds of revelers, jesting as they tucked into fine fare. The first course had been preceded by a fanfare and two pages walking ceremoniously across the hushed hall bearing a massive and ornately carved sugared subtlety, crafted in the exact replica of Middleham castle. Marchpane soldiers in Warwick livery stood on the battlements and on the keep flew a sugared standard bearing the insignia of the Bear and Ragged Staff. It was now set on the dais close to the Earl for all to admire, and Stephen wondered, 'if that was the noble work of art for the eve of the Christmas festival then what would be in store from them tomorrow.'

He spent much of the evening watching the antics of his companions as they enjoyed themselves, a pastime which he frequently enjoyed at large gatherings. He found his attention continually drawn to the dais where his host sat with his very attractive lady, holding court like a king in his own domain. He supposed that was what the great Earl was here in Yorkshire, for his name was revered as no other had ever been. To the folk of the county, he was their Lord, and it was his approval they sought, not that of the King. If it happened to coincide that Warwick and his King were in agreement then all well and good, if not then it was the Earl they would follow wherever he chose to lead. Also on the dais was the Earl's daughter, the Lady Isabel, one of the fairest creatures he had seen in a long while, if you ignored the petulant droop to her mouth and the restless discontent deep in her blue eyes. Beautiful to look at but difficult to please, he guessed. She was at present bestowing her attention on one of her numerous Neville cousins like one granting the ultimate favour as the lad tried vainly to make her laugh. Her father watched her with evident pride, murmuring something in his wife's ear. The countess smiled somewhat frostily and Stephen guessed that the Earl and his wife were not the happiest of couples. He had been disappointed to note that neither of the Earl's younger daughters were on the dais, and he wondered why, for it was unlikely that they would have been left out of such an important celebration, not at the respective ages of eight and thirteen anyway. He was surprised by his overriding eagerness to see the prize

Warwick was dangling before him, though he managed to convince himself that it was merely natural curiosity that sparked his interest. It was not as if he was willing to wed her, whatever she was like, for all his eagerness to ally himself with Warwick, and he would never take a woman who was defective in any way, be it mind or body.

He had caught sight earlier in the evening of the lad who had been coaching the lass in swordplay, and his humour was rekindled by a hint of scratch at the boy's throat. She was definitely a hellion that girl, he thought grimly, and then found himself scanning the chamber to see if he could see her, looking out for the distinctive russet of her hair.

The noise level in the hall had taken on almost unbearable proportions as the conversation became louder and more increasingly intoned with raucous and bawdy laughter. Thick, eye stinging smoke palled in the air, though all seemed oblivious to it save he, and the atmosphere became hot and oppressive. He was beginning to think of ways of making an escape into the cool night air when he caught a movement to his left, just the smallest flash of blue and a swirl of red, but his attention was riveted immediately, for there was no mistaking the colour. He swung slightly in his seat in an attempt to catch a glimpse of the girl, but could see nothing except a crowd of laughing youths. He slipped out of his seat with a mumbled apology to his neighbour and the excuse that he must get to the privy, and sidled his way around the wall in the direction of the throng. Perhaps it was the blatant disregard for convention that he had witnessed in the stables, or the obvious enjoyment with which she had beaten her companion that had stirred him, or perhaps even the merest chance of a challenge offered by her outrageous behaviour, but whatever it was, it was the first time in a long while he had felt his interest sparked enough to push him forward.

He was almost out of the door before he actually saw her, leaning back against the stone wall, holding court, the youths of the household clustered round her, laughing and teasing but listening to what she was telling them. She could be little more than fourteen but she was already beautiful, a thick and luxurious braid hanging down her back, escaping curls framing a pale, finely-boned face which was hollowed out into shadows under high cheekbones. Her eyes were huge, and though he could not see their colour, they reminded him somewhat of a cat's in the way they lay slanted above her cheekbones. The crimson slash of her mouth was at once sensuous and innocent, and he swallowed, taking a deep breath, forcing his nerves to steady, only half aware of his surroundings. Perhaps she sensed the intensity of his gaze, or maybe it was mere coincidence, but she raised her eyes to his, smiling suddenly, changing the whole aspect of her face to impish mischief, destroying his struggle for control. He dropped his gaze, like a callow boy, and turned away, bumping against someone in his embarrassment.

"I see you have spotted our little hellion," murmured a familiar, quiet voice close to his ear. Stephen jerked his head up and met the green eyes of his host, self-conscious colour creeping up his neck and into his face. He nodded with a weak grin, knowing it was too obvious for him to deny, having been caught out so blatantly. "Don't you think she has the makings of a beauty?"

"Yes, my Lord."

"She takes after her mother in that respect, though she is not much like her at first glance." He raised his hand in authoritative gesture and the girl moved away from her companions, dropping her gaze demurely. Warwick slipped a familiar arm about her shoulders and smiled. "This is Stephen Thevenot, sweetheart. He would like very much to meet you." The girl looked up and gave him a friendly smile, holding out her hand for him to kiss. He took it between stiff fingers, bringing knuckle to lips, then was jerked out of his fragile composure by the Earl's next words. "This is Katherine, my daughter." Unable to stop himself he swung round and stared at the Earl before he laughed, a sudden sharp sound. His wily host had obviously been watching him all evening to see if he would see the girl, knowing how lovely she was and obviously prepared to rely on her charms to ensnare him. He suspected though that the Earl did not realise just how successful his little ploy had been. Feeling chagrined and ridiculous, Stephen looked down at the girl who was still regarding him with a direct, curious stare, and gave her a very stiff smile. She smiled back shyly.

"I concede defeat, my Lord," he said coolly, not taking his eyes from her face. "You need but name your terms."

"I'm sure you will find them most favourable."

"I'm sure I will, my Lord. for a man who is apparently such easy prey."

Suddenly he snorted a mirthless laugh and Warwick stared at him for a moment, then his mouth quirked and he grinned wolfishly.

"Aye, lad, but the bait was the best I had to offer." The two men shared a look and the young girl at her father's side stared at them both as if they had quite lost their senses.

***

"It is a fine evening for stargazing." The voice behind her was soft and well-modulated. She started, whirling round, expelling a sharply indrawn breath in a puff of icy smoke.

"Jesu', my Lord, you did make me jump!" Shock made her sound sharp and Stephen Thevenot raised a cool eyebrow.

"Forgive me, I did not mean to startle you." He stepped forward and came to stand before her, his smile not quite reaching his eyes and she felt her anger subside to be replaced by a sudden prickling at her neck and a sense of apprehension.

"I'm sorry but I don't much like surprises, my Lord."

"I will remember that." He smiled, his outer calm unruffled by her rudeness. "Would you like me to leave?" But he made no attempt to go. Recalling the talk her father had had with her that morning about being courteous and ensuring that her future husband had no complaints about her behavior, she grudgingly shook her head.

"No, my Lord. I am happy for you to stay."

She turned back to look out over the battlements and felt him move to her side and do the same.

"How could I refuse such a gracious invitation," he said drily. She bit back a sharp response but instead deflected his attention with a gesture, attracting his attention to where the moon lit up the hills. "Do you not think this place beautiful, my Lord?" He followed her gesture, screwing up his eyes as if trying to see what she saw.

"The barrenness you mean?" He pitched his voice at the same soft level of hers. She nodded, still staring out across the vast, dark moors, her eyes seeing nothing but the memories of childhood.

"When I first came here I thought it was the loneliest place anyone could live, so far away from what had been my home especially as I had been raised to believe that the English were barbarians and when

36

I arrived here I began to think it was true. But this place has a way of making you love it, and it was not long before I realised that I had grown to love it very much." She turned her head slightly and glanced into his face, encouraged to go on by the interest she saw there. "I am afraid, my Lord. I feel as if part of my life is ending, although for a new beginning, but it's hard to leave it behind so suddenly." It was a long spontaneous speech and suddenly she felt a bit foolish. Stephen didn't respond for a moment, merely leaning forward and looking down at the bailey below them.

"When I was fourteen," he said finally, keeping his eyes ahead of him, "I was wed to a lass my own age and was told that I was a man, ready to make my own way in life. It was the most frightening experience of my life, and hers I would imagine. But we muddled through those early times and had a good life until she passed away." He turned to look at her. "As I am sure we will too."

"Did you love your wife, my Lord?" She felt him start, obviously taken aback, but his voice was edged with wry humour when he spoke.

"Do you wish for romance or honesty, sweetheart?"

She flushed, realising that she must sound very young to him and that she was prying into a part of his life that was his own, and one he might not wish to reveal.

"Forgive me, my Lord, I do not have the right..."

"Actually, you probably do, and in truthful answer to your question, no I did not love my wife."

"Did that not make it difficult, my Lord, being married?"

"No. We had friendship and cared enough for each other to be able to live in amity and I mourned her when she died. But I did not truly love her."

Part of Kate was relieved by this statement for she had no wish to compete with a dead woman; it was well known that the dead were perfect in the eyes of their loved ones. But part was saddened that sometimes it was necessary for the sake of making a good marriage to sometimes settle for second best, as her father had done. They were silent for a while, their intimacy shattered by her awkward questioning, neither quite knowing what to say to bridge the gulf between them.

Slowly he turned to her, reaching to touch her cheek with the back of his hand, seemingly reassured when she did not shy away from his caress.

"It is up to us to make this union an amicable one," he said quietly, his dark eyes on hers. "If you are prepared to be guided by me then there is no reason for us not to be successful."

"It is a wife's duty to be guided by her husband." Kate dropped her gaze demurely, parroting her father's words to the letter. If Stephen was surprised he did not show it, he merely smiled and nodded approvingly.

"Then I can see that we will be the best of friends," he said softly and reaching into the pocket of his tunic he took out a leather pouch, removing a small object from it. "I would like you to have this." He took her left hand in his and slipped a ring on the middle finger. She stared at it, spellbound, taking in the intricately wrought gold and the flawless ruby set within its midst. "This is my betrothal gift to you. I wanted to give it to you privately rather than in the prying company we shall be forced to endure on New Year's Day." He kissed her palm, his lips cool against her skin.

"It is beautiful, my Lord, and it fits like it was made for me. Thank you!" She smiled up at him and then gazed back at the ruby ring and felt a surge of pleasure at her first real piece of jewelry.

"I will try to be a good wife to you, my Lord," she murmured haltingly, uncertain how to express these new feelings which rose within her. "I promise I will try very hard." He still had not released her hand but he reached out with his free hand and cupped her chin gently, holding her gaze for what seemed like an age, and then finally he smiled.

"Come. It is cold out here," he said, dropping her chin but keeping hold of her hand. "Let us go back to the hall."

Obediently Kate followed him with her hand in his, the ring heavy on her finger and the knowledge that his smile had never once reached his eyes.

Bruges, Burgundy
July 1468

"Lucy." Edmund Beaufort's voice was a fierce whisper. "Psst, Lucy." The girl swung round in the dimly lit doorway, dark eyes startled, and then her lovely, heart-shaped face broke into a huge smile.

"My Lord!" she breathed, hurling herself into his arms and covering his face with kisses, her long dark braid of hair swinging behind her.

"Alright, alright!" He held her off laughing.

"What are you doing here?" She kissed his lips ardently.

"I've come to see you." He grinned, making her heart swoop.

"But I thought you had to go back to Angers last week?"

"I got half way there and then I had to turn back." He nuzzled her neck. "I missed you too much."

"You are such a liar. You didn't even go did you?" Stepping back, she shook her head, and he spread his hands and shrugged disarmingly.

"No." He had the good grace to look abashed.

"You bastard!" She put her hands on her hips and glared at him and he laughed silently. "You just said that so you didn't have to see me."

"Come on Lucy, don't be harsh." He grabbed her hand and kissed her palm softly, his beautiful eyes glowing in the dim light of the oil lamp at the door

"You're locked out again aren't you?"

"Yes." He nodded, his expression still contrite. "They barred the door at cure-feu and I can't get in without waking the landlord. I have been out here for an age hoping that you would come to put the rubbish out!" She softened unwillingly, her heart betraying her, giving her voice a rough edge as she spoke.

"Well you can't sleep in my chamber; Tom's home tonight and all the rooms are taken, what with the Duke of Burgundy's wedding and all, we are full up to the gills. You'll have to sleep in the bar." He grimaced expressively at her words, not wishing to think particularly about his patron's marriage to his enemy's sister. It felt like the ultimate betrayal that Charles of Burgundy was marrying Edward of York's sister in two days' time, especially when he had always patronised the House of Lancaster.

"As long I don't have to sleep in the privy, I don't care." He reached for her and pulled her into him, his hand in the small of her back, pressing her against him, his mouth covering hers in a hot, probing kiss, memory of their passionate encounters rekindling his interest and pushing away his unwelcome thoughts.

"Who is it, Luce?" A man's voice drifted through the open door and the girl jumped, dragging her lips away from his.

"It's the Duke of Somerset, Tom. He's locked out again." She pushed him away with obvious reluctance and gestured him through the door and into the sparse public room of the tavern.

"My Lord!" The big man behind the bar held out a meaty hand, his broad face split into a huge grin. "Long time no see!" Beau grinned and shook it strongly, happy to dispense with formality for the sake of the girl, who stood tensely beautiful at his side.

"Tom," he said

"Have a drink, my Lord?"

"I might have had too much already. I have been across town, entertaining." He winked at the barman who laughed.

"I'll take that as a yes then." Tom smiled and then jerked his head at the voluptuous, dark haired girl. "You go on up, Luce; I'll be up in a while."

"Alright." She nodded dejectedly and then curtseyed to Beau. "Goodnight, my Lord."

"Goodnight, Lucy." Both men watched her leave the room appreciatively and then Tom reached for two cups and a flagon and poured some wine. Beau dropped some coins onto the counter and the big man grunted his thanks.

"You do not need to, my Lord," he said quietly, but Beau smiled.

"I would have no one say I do not pay my way, Tom."

"Are you staying for the wedding, my Lord?"

"Yes." Beau gave a short laugh. "My brother and I are guests."

"They say she is a beauty." The man made a curvy woman shape with his hands and grinned lasciviously. "And nearly six feet tall!"

"Yes she is, I can vouch for both." Beau laughed. "Though not my type. I don't like blondes and I prefer to bend down to kiss my women rather than meet them at eye level."

"Duke Charles will have to stand on a bench I think." Tom grinned again and Beau nodded.

"I think he may have met his match with this one. If she is like her brother Edward of York in more than just looks, then she will be used to getting her own way and not afraid to use any of her charms to get it."

"Is the Duke looking forward to his wedding?"

"Yes I think he is." Beau grimaced wryly. "Much more than I am."

"Why's that, my Lord?"

"Makes my life a touch difficult, Tom." Beau leaned his chin on his hand morosely. "I guess it is back to Anjou for me."

"Why's that, my Lord?" the big man asked again.

"Well I cannot see Margaret of York being a friend to me, considering that my loyalties do not lie with her brother, and even if she was it would be very awkward to stay. I think my Queen would have something to say about it." He smiled bitterly.

"I've heard she can be a fiery one, that Marguerite of Anjou?"

"Yes, so have I." Beau deadpanned and the other man laughed.

"Why do you do it, my Lord?" Tom asked with real interest.

"Why do I do what?"

"Why do you stay in exile like this, flitting between courts, eking out a living as a soldier when you could be in England being the Duke of Somerset?"

"I am the Duke of Somerset!" Beau drew his brows together in a mock frown.

"Not in England where you should be."

"True." Beau shook his head suddenly. "And the answer is fuck-knows. I get little thanks from either side."

"Then why do it?"

"Because I pledged fealty to my Queen and I pledged to serve Duke Charles in times of war. The lot of the nobleman, I'm afraid, is to serve a liege Lord or Lady."

"I used to envy the nobility their riches but I don't envy you your ties of loyalty. At least I am my own man and not pulled from pillar to post by my ties of fealty, and loyalty and all that goes with it." Tom spat into the rushes crudely. Beau yawned and rubbed his face tiredly and then drained his cup.

"That had best be my last Tom, or I shall get maudlin and start blubbing all my woes to you and you will never get upstairs to that lovely wife of yours." He smiled at the other man who grinned appreciatively.

"I'll get you a pallet and some blankets, my Lord, and you can sleep by the fire." He moved out from the bar and across the room towards the door. "I can wake one of the girls for you if you want?" Beau shook his head.

"No it's alright thanks, Tom. I think I have had too much wine for that." He smiled suddenly. "My life is not so bad you know; at least it is never dull."

Bruges, Burgundy
July 1468

"You have to admit, Beau, that these Yorks are a handsome family!" Jack Beaufort murmured in his brother's ear. Edmund Beaufort flicked a glance at him and snorted.

"You think?"

"I do, yes. That girl is lovely, so was her mother and look at her brothers Clarence and York; hardly gargoyles are they?" Jack grinned and Beau laughed.

"Not my type," he said dryly.

"What, Clarence and York?" Jack deliberately misunderstood him.

"Any of them." Beau glanced back at the woman on the arm of her new husband, his patron Charles of Burgundy and had to admit they made a handsome, if slightly incongruous, couple. Him dark, her fair; him broad and average height and her willowy and almost as tall as Beau; but while he could see that she was pretty he could not see anything in her that would draw him to her. He didn't like blondes much even though they were the fashion of the day; he found them too cool and ice-like to appeal to his palette. He liked exotic and exciting women and, although he would never class himself as a romantic, since he was a boy, when his mother had told him the story of Katherine Swynford and his ancestor John of Ghent, he had had more than a hankering for redheads. "When I was first at court, when our father was still alive, Cecily Neville, our Duke Charles' mother in law, was considered one of the most beautiful women there, but she always seemed like the Queen of Ice to me and so damned virtuous it set my teeth on edge. I can't say I ever envied Richard of York his bed-sport!" Beau pulled an expressive face and Jack laughed softly.

"Trust you to bring it back to that. Do you ever think of aught else?"

"I think about many things. But if we are talking about women then that is what it comes down to."

"You're such a romantic!" Jack shook his head in mock horror. "You are beyond redemption."

"Funny, that's what my confessor keeps telling me." Their eyes met and they smiled strikingly similar smiles, sharing a common joke. But there was a restlessness and emptiness inside him that would not go away. He knew that much had changed in the last four years since he and Jack had traveled to France to be part of Marguerite's exiled household. He had come as a young man still full of ideals and hope, had fastened his loyalty and devotion to Marguerite and she had sucked him dry, taking all from him and giving nothing in return. She had taken advantage of his loyalty; had ruled his life, allowing him no freedom or comfort, expecting his devoted loyalty while she gave him nothing but poverty in return. When money ran out or things became too difficult they came back to Burgundy and Charles' army or his court and then, pockets filled and guilt building, they would return to Marguerite and her ingratitude. He had become tutor to her son, had taught him the arts of soldiery and chivalry and Edward had made an apt pupil; a boy to be proud of and he looked on him as his own son. But Marguerite would not allow him a life; he had to take his pleasures where he found them and more than once he had found himself on the end of her icy jealous wrath for philandering with her ladies. The boy who had once worn his heart on his sleeve was now a man who kept his thoughts behind a closed mask, a hard and cynical coiled spring; a man who stored up his emotions to the point of eruption, who did not show anything except the courtly devotion expected of him to his Lady and her son, and who took physical pleasure in the arms of whores and village girls. His elder brother Hal had once warned him that Marguerite was a jealous and capricious mistress who had used their father's love mercilessly to achieve her ambitions and to protect her son, but he had not listened and had willingly given over his loyalty, and now she held it in a vice that she would never release, leaving him an emotional husk. He knew that Jack loved and admired him, but he also knew that sometimes his brother wished that they could just go home.

"This will be fun." Jack's voice interrupted his thoughts. He looked up and saw that Charles was bringing his new wife towards them to present them to her. Both men dropped to one knee as he approached them, their heads bowed.

"My dear," Charles said in his warm, clear voice, "these are my good friends Edmund Beaufort, Duke of Somerset and his brother John Beaufort." He gestured to them to rise and Beau bowed first over Margaret of York's hand, meeting cold blue eyes with hard gold ones.

"Madame," he said softly, grazing her knuckle, lips compressed against laughter as her hand twitched in his, knowing she was fighting the impulse to snatch it back.

"The Duke of Somerset?" She arched well plucked and defined brows sardonically, her voice cool and malicious. "I had heard that was a vacant title."

"Did you Madame?" he said, blandly, his mouth lifting at the corner. She turned to Jack.

"I'm glad to see you have not taken any titles you have no right to, my Lord." Jack flushed but managed a small smile.

"No Madame," he said quietly. "I have taken nothing, as yet, from Edward of York." Charles looked from his wife to the two men and then back to his wife.

"These men are at my court on my invitation, Madame. I hope that is not going to cause you a problem?" His brown eyes were cool as they regarded Margaret's fair young face, his meaning clear even though the words were conciliatory. A flush spread up her neck and delicately infused her cheeks.

"Of course not, my Lord." She looked at him through long gold lashes. "I am well aware of your kinship with the House of Lancaster; I just hope that you will in time feel as close a kinship with the house of York." Charles smiled at her and then nodded at the two men as they moved on.

"I just hope that you will in time feel as close a kinship with the house of York," Beau parodied unkindly, not quite under his breath.

"Beau!" Jack admonished softly. "Don't!" The older man regarded his brother levelly for a moment and then sighed.

"Ah fuck, I'm sorry!" he said crudely. "It's just I hate them and everything they are and stand for."

"I know Beau, but you knew he was marrying her and you knew you would have to meet her."

"True, but I still find it hard, especially as she looks so much like her pious prig of a mother." They turned away and began walking across the hall, their stride in perfect tune. "I think I might go back to Angers for a while." Beau rubbed his hand over his day old stubble in a tired gesture.

"Are you sure you want to do that?" Jack looked surprised for Beau had left the sparse court of Marguerite in a high temper when she had berated him publicly for his lack of effort on securing money for her from her nephew Louis, even though he, himself, gave her at least two thirds of the pension that Charles of Burgundy gave him.

"She will have got over it by now." His brother's eyes shadowed and his mouth turned down at the corners as he remembered Marguerite's white-faced fury and her scathing lashing tongue.

"I don't know how you put up with it."

"Because there is nothing else is there?" Beau kicked at an imaginary stone with the pointed toe of his boot, his shoulders hunching. "There is Anjou and there is Burgundy. I don't want to be here so I have to go to Anjou and when I don't want to be in Anjou I have to come here; there is nowhere else to go and anyway I want to see my boy." Once outside the hall they walked for a while in companionable silence, heading without need for words, for their favourite inn by the river.

"By the way, I heard all is still not well with Warwick and York, even after the charade of Warwick taking our new Duchess to her ship to sail for Burgundy." Jack shoved open the low door and held it open for his brother to duck under. Tom, the landlord, greeted them with a smile and poured a jug of ale for them before they even asked. Beau dropped onto a bench at an empty table and Jack sat opposite.

"Thank you my friend." Beau smiled at Tom as he brought the jug to the table and gave him some coins "Aye, I had heard that too." Beau carried on the conversation as if they had not been interrupted. "I cannot see how the two of them can keep the peace. It seems to me it has gone too far. I had heard that even Warwick's brother Montague is wavering in his loyalty, especially now that York has taken away his Dukedom of Northumberland and given it back to the Percy's."

"York is trying to buy Henry Percy, for all the good it will do seeing as Percy is only interested in Percy. But then I can understand the strategy, after all the Nevilles have far too much power in the north. Warwick is well thought of up there." Jack raised his eyebrows sardonically.

"It's a mistake to allow a man like Warwick a power base like the north. He has always been one for getting his own way and York will reap what he sows up there." Beau shook his head in disgust, morosely tracing the pattern of the wood on the table with his forefinger.

"I wonder why he cannot see that?"

"Because he trusts too readily and cannot believe that any would go against him. I am not sure if it is naivety or arrogance but it is a character flaw for a king."

"It will be interesting to see how it all ends. It would be good to see York get his comeuppance." Jack smiled wistfully.

"Well it affects us little. Even if they fall out completely and declare war on each other it will help us not at all. We cannot exploit it as we have no funds, no men and no way of raising either." Beau sighed heavily, a cloud of depression descending over the table He tried to think of something else to say but could not, instead staring into the bottom of his cup as if he might find inspiration in its depths.

"What say you?" Jack said suddenly, "that we buy ourselves a couple of girls, get some wine and get totally and uproariously drunk and let nature take its course?"

"Nature taking its course would be a limp dick, a sour gut and a bad head!" Beau laughed shortly, but good humour sparked up in his hard face "I have a better idea," he said. "Why don't we buy a couple of whores, plunder their treasure until we can do no more and then get totally and uproariously drunk?" His brother grinned.

"Well if you put it like that," Jack said softly, "why don't we?"

London
September 1468

"Richard! Richard!" Richard of Gloucester looked up to see Kate running towards him down the wharf as he disembarked from the barge which had just brought him up the Thames from Westminster, hair flying behind her, almost tripping over her skirts in her desire to reach him. "Richard, I can hardly believe it is you!" she flung herself into his arms, completely disregarding decorum and almost knocking him off his feet. He laughed and pulled her to him in a breathless embrace, and then, still grinning, held her off at arm's length, looking at her appraisingly.

"Well, well cousin, you have changed." He looked her up and down appreciatively and she grinned.

"And you, Richard, why I would swear you have even grown." The tone was slightly mocking, but what she said was true for their eyes were no longer level. Still slight of frame with hair so black that it shone faintly blue, he was much less pale than she remembered and his eyes were much lighter, like twilight sky. He slipped a friendly arm about her shoulders and they turned up the passageway back toward the house, chatting easily.

"So how is life treating you?" He winked at her, a man of the world at sixteen. "And how is your husband?"

"Oh he's all right I suppose." She pulled an expressive face.

"Is there aught wrong?"

"No. Only that I'm not sure what he expects of me. I am too young for all the responsibilities of a husband and household just yet," she laughed, looking up at him from beneath long dark gold lashes

"Many girls of fifteen are fully wedded-and-bedded wives Kate," he said, thinking that this truly lovely girl should be one of them and faintly envious of the Yorkshire squire who was to get her. If anyone was ripe to be bedded it was her.

"I know but papa thinks I am too young and am not mature enough. I think he prefers me to be where he can keep an eye on me."

"Or he is too soft to let you go." Richard smiled, knowing how much Warwick doted on this daughter. "Still getting into scrapes then?" She laughed.

"My Lady stepmother still scolds me every day for my behaviour. If she had seen me running down the quay to meet you just now she would have locked me in my room for a week I'm sure!" He joined her laughter.

"Some things never change," he said softly, and she leaned against him momentarily.

"No, some things have not changed, but some have and I don't know whether papa will welcome your visit here today."

"I had thought on that," he muttered, kicking at a stone on the path. "But I had to try, Kate. I could not just pretend..." She understood his feeling for this, The Herber, her father's house in London, had been his home as much as hers not so many months ago, and now because he had chosen his brother the King over her father, it was possible that he would not be a welcome visitor.

They had been in London for some weeks and, at first, it had seemed like the reconciliation between King Edward the fourth and her father was complete. The King was still surrounded by his wife's Woodville kin, but he had seemed eager to welcome his dear cousin Warwick back into the fold as if nothing had come between them. However, it soon became apparent that her father would not be given the same kind of power, for the King had decided that no one should ever have the hold over him that Warwick had done in the early years and so his role in government would be superficial. Admittedly he had been given an honoured part in the proxy wedding of Edward's sister, and also in the task of escorting her on the back of his destrier out of the city but that was not likely to satisfy him for long. He did not just want to appear to be powerful, he wanted to *be* powerful. Her father felt that the King had betrayed him; firstly, when he married Elizabeth Woodville and secondly when he had ridiculed his wish for an alliance with France. That he might have offended his King with his enjoyment of his title of 'Kingmaker' bestowed upon him by the commons did not cross his mind. But this was something that had obviously rankled with Edward for some time, and although he had done his best to ignore it, it had finally blown up into sour resentment and an almighty row and now there was little chance that their friendship would survive on its previous footing.

Kate stopped walking and pulled her arm from its place in the crook of Richard's elbow.

"I know where there is one who will welcome you heartily," she murmured. He stopped walking and looked down at her.

"She did forgive me then?"

"She would forgive you anything and you know it." His shoulders relaxed and he grinned.

"Will she see me?"

"Why think you I risked my Lady stepmother's displeasure and came to greet you like a common fishwife. It was not for my benefit I assure you."

"Ah and I thought you loved me." He laughed but there was something in his look which made her blush. He looked away self-consciously. "Actually, I thought it was to warn me of my reception... and because you were pleased I was coming." For a second his dark eyes searched her face and then he smiled. Kate snorted but did not respond to his teasing.

"There is none here except Anne and I. Papa is at Westminster, the Countess and Isabel have gone calling and Francis was sent to the Fitzhugh's to spend some time with his wife." She gave a passable imitation of Warwick when she spoke the last words and wagged her finger sternly as Warwick did when making a point. "But if the Countess returns before you are gone, your reception could border on the icy. She likes me better than you at the moment as she has borne the brunt of papa's displeasure since your 'desertion'."

"And he still harbours a grudge against me?"

"I fear so Richard. He feels you played him false after all the years of living under his roof. He thought that with your's and George's support he could have been reconciled with the King much more quickly." There was no judgment in her voice and Richard sighed.

"But Ned is my brother Kate..."

"I know." Impulsively she hugged him, and slipping his arms around her he held her close in an embrace that was as strangely tense as it was comforting.

"Ned is my brother," he repeated, softly this time. Kate pulled back from him and looked up into his face, her hands still resting on his shoulders.

"But papa was never one to appreciate loyalty to any cause but his. Nor does he take kindly to ingratitude and that is how he views your actions. Surely you can understand something of what he feels?"

"No, Kate, I cannot understand and I wish I had never been forced into this position. If I blame anyone for where I am now, I would have to blame your father." He smiled suddenly, wonderingly. "You hold no illusions about your father, do you?"

The question was unexpected and she flushed guiltily, pulling away from him and turning towards the house, conscious she was almost being disloyal.

"I am just honest," she said stiffly. "But that does not mean that I do not love and honour my father. I would follow him to wherever he chooses to lead me, not because I always agree with him but because I do owe him so much."

"And Anne, what does she feel?"

"You know how she feels, Richard, she is torn in two and she ever will be unless this is resolved."

49

He gave the briefest of satisfied smiles and for an instant Kate glimpsed another Richard, ice cold in the depths of his dark blue eyes and then it was gone. He took her hand and squeezed it.

"Come," he said with a quick easy grin, "let's go inside, I have a fancy to see my other little Neville cousin."

The reunion was a happy one, for Anne was delighted to see him and though Kate felt that it would not be proper to leave them completely alone together, she retired to a window seat in the corner and tried her best not to eavesdrop their conversation.

Anne reacted to Richard with an appealing mixture of the old adoration and a new self-consciousness which had come with the impending onslaught of womanhood. No longer could it be called a childish devotion, for it was an adult emotion with a new intensity which embarrassed her. As for Richard, he had long passed through the stage where he had no time for girls and he reveled in her attention. He complimented her on her gown and told her how pretty she had become, pulling a strand of her shining dark hair which lay loose about her shoulders, remarking on its softness, laughing as she flushed the colour of rose petals and stammered shy responses. Kate suspected that Richard had recently experienced some success with the opposite sex and that this was the reason for his new, confident manner. He was a man now and it sat well with him. He may be slight of build but he was strong and his features were arranged pleasantly with those startling twilight eyes and neat bone structure. When he laughed, he radiated a shining warmth and his voice was now quite deep and well modulated, no longer the scratchy fluctuation of youth. He was at that moment relating a story which had been well circulated, telling the latest tale of one of Edward's many blatant infidelities and of how Elizabeth had been unfortunate enough to walk in on him when he was in a delicate embrace. Seeing his wife had caused Edward no embarrassment, nor stopped him in his act of making love; he had merely smiled and told her that he would come to her chambers shortly. So, the humiliated Elizabeth had been forced to withdraw gracefully to avoid total ridicule. Kate could not help but feel sorry for her and wondered who should have been so unkind as to let her enter her husband's chamber when they knew that he was with his latest conquest. She also knew that Richard disagreed with Edward's lifestyle, yet there was no disguising the satisfaction in his voice as he told the story. She found it difficult to believe how a woman reputed to be so beautiful was so capable of alienating all around her, not only the women, which may be understandable, but also the men. There had to be many flaws in her character for men, normally so susceptible to feminine beauty to be unable to forgive her. Or perhaps they were afraid of the position she held in Edward's affections, in case it undermined their own influence. She wondered if Edward would brook interference from a woman, Queen though she may be.

"Is Elizabeth Woodville very beautiful, Dickon?" Anne asked suddenly. He stopped smiling.

"Yes, she's very beautiful."

"And does she love Ned?" Unconsciously she used the King's familiar name.

"Yes, she does. Though I think she does not love many of his friends or kin." His voice was even, giving nothing away, but his eyes were cold. "She does love her brothers and sisters though."

"You cannot fault her for loving her family."

"No, I cannot." He laughed suddenly, not entirely with mirth. "But there are a lot of them."

Kate turned away from their conversation, looking out of the window onto the river which ran so close to the house. The warm May sunshine gave a murky sheen to the Thames, making it gleam like gemstones as the traffic of varied vessels moved up and down. Looking down she saw that a barge bearing the unmistakable insignia of the Bear and Ragged Staff had pulled into the jetty. The occupants were already walking toward the manor house. It was her father and with him was the tall, slim and beautiful figure of Richard's brother George, his bright-blonde head glinting in the sun, his mouth turned down in a petulant line.

"Papa and George are here," She cried, jumping up from the window seat. Richard crossed swiftly to the window just in time to see George disappearing down the passage which led to the inner bailey. He looked at her warily and she shrugged; there was nowhere for him to go. Instinctively Anne moved closer to his side, either to protect him or be protected from her father's wrath, Kate was not sure. He put his hand out and rested it lightly on her shoulder, and Kate felt a pang of envy for their empathy. Then the chamber door swung open and Clarence entered followed by Warwick. They stopped in the doorway, the Earl with a delicate eyebrow raised at the sight of his cousin and his daughter standing so closely together. The atmosphere in the chamber tensed almost visibly. But the Earl's voice when he spoke was quite amiable.

"Well, Richard, have you come to renew your acquaintance with my family?" The only sign of displeasure was the use of Richard's full name "I see you have found a welcome in my home?" Anne flushed scarlet but Richard inclined his head, a smile illuminating his face but, she noticed, not quite reaching his midnight eyes.

"Having grown up in your household, my Lord, I have learned to expect nothing less than a welcome when I come here."

"Even now?"

"Aye, my Lord. Pettiness is not the nature of Warwick and having presumed upon your natural benevolence all my life I saw no reason to stop now."

Warwick stared at him for a fraction and then gave a sudden burst of laughter.

"Sweet Blood of Christ, Dickon," he swore, "you have style, I have to give you that. Is this what you have learned at that damned corruption they call court?"

Richard smiled again.

"Perhaps some of the folk I am forced to mix with have left their mark of sophistication on me," he grinned, "though not by my choosing of course." It was a subtle illusion to his brother's wife's kin and one which was designed to get him into Warwick's good graces.

"Of course." Warwick warmed visibly.

"My little brother has become quite a ladies man, cousin," George joined the conversation, smiling maliciously. "Why, only the other day I heard tell..."

"Shut up, George!" Richard cut him off quickly, flushing as Anne stiffened under his touch and moved away. Warwick laughed again, catching Kate's glance and rolling his eyes.

"Well I see you two do see eye to eye as always," he said, smiling at them while Richard scowled and George smirked. "Well, now that you are here Dickon you may as well sup with us, unless you have more pressing engagements elsewhere?" The invitation was accepted gracefully and the Earl clapped him on the back while turning the conversation to merrier matters.

Kate was relieved that when the Countess and Isabel arrived home, the Countess took her cue from her husband and made Richard feel welcome, his defection into Edward's camp quite ignored. The conversation had dropped easily into familiarity of long the acquaintance and there was much talk of the Queen and her kin at the table, although Richard avoided taking part in the discussions, only giving non-committal answers to the questions that were posed to him. It was obvious that he did not trust that his word would not get back to his brother.

As usual Clarence's voice was loudest in protest against the King, pretending to Isabel, who was not the least taken in by his protestations, that he came to see her in open defiance of his brother's wishes. In his strange paranoid nature, he truly believed what he said and really considered himself to be badly treated by Edward. It was hard for Kate to see how he could believe that for he appeared to lack for nothing, and everything that George wanted, Edward gave him. Kate wondered if that was because Edward found him difficult to love and so, in guilt, gave him honours. She would not be surprised for to her George was impossible to even like, let alone love, and what Isabel saw in him she could not even begin to imagine. What a tangled web this was, George and Isabel, Richard and Anne destined for each other and yet unlikely to be together. How would they reconcile themselves to that? She suddenly had the feeling as she watched them all together that this was like the last supper and that Judas Iscariot had already done his worst.

Anjou, France
October 1468

Edmund Beaufort led the black stallion from the stable block, keeping tight grip on its head as it danced showily across the yard, its steps high, the feathers around its hooves blowing in the draught its feet created. Edward of Lancaster, once feted Prince of Wales and now exiled pauper, stared at the horse and then at the woman next to him, his face breaking into a huge dazzling smile.

"For me, maman?" he whispered. Marguerite of Anjou looked across at the man holding the horse and then back at her son, Edward.

"Yes, for you, my love. But you must thank my Lord Somerset for him, not me. It is he who has paupered himself to get you this prize." There was an edge to her voice which was lost on the boy but not on the man. He met her gaze levelly.

"It is important for the boy to have a decent horse and to learn the art of mastering a destrier, Madame," he said quietly.

"For what exactly, my Lord?" She arched her defined brows over her beautiful black eyes.

"For his self-respect as a man if nothing else, Madame."

"He is fourteen, Somerset!"

"Aye, Madame, and I was at court at fourteen with my father, learning the art of cavalry at his side, as I am sure that you remember. I had my own sword and my own destrier at that age." Edward looked from one to the other, quite used to the tense relationship between the two people he loved most in the world.

"Maman," he said in a soft conciliatory voice. "I am not a child. Somerset is right, I cannot ride palfreys all my life." He kissed her cheek and smiled, his young face lighting up. "Please, maman." She looked at him for a long moment and then nodded almost imperceptibly. He gave her a lightening hug and then turned to the horse. Meeting her eyes over the boy's head, Beau gave her a half smile of gratitude but she was already turning away and walking back toward the hall. He turned back to the boy and boosted him into the saddle.

"Right, my Prince," he said, flashing the boy a determined grin. "Let's see what you and this animal can do." He gestured to the waiting groom to bring him his own stallion and vaulted aboard. "To the training ring." He swung his mount around and cantered behind the big black beast, a huge well of pride in his chest as he saw how well the boy handled the animal. This boy was the one thing that kept him loyal to the Lancaster cause. His idealistic love for Marguerite was long buried, iced over by her deception and then by her bitterness. By the time, he had come back from Burgundy, a year after joining Charles' army, she had turned into the hard-embittered woman that she was today, her beauty curdled by the sourness of her temper, and her attitude towards him one of ambivalence. She had drained everything from him, playing on his guilt at rejecting her and screwing every ounce of emotion out of him, and squeezing all his funds out of him He had given her all he had, barely leaving himself enough to keep himself and Jack in food and clothes, and still she wanted more from him. It was as if she would take everything from him because he had denied her himself and he had given and given and given until he had nothing left to give her and now all that was left was his devotion to her son, this boy who he had taken under his wing and who he loved as if he was his own. This boy who was going to be a great man, in spite of his mother and hopefully because he, Edmund Beaufort, had helped to instill the right values in him.

His time serving Charles of Charolais had taught him much about the art of soldiering and shown him that he was a good commander and an able battle strategist. He had served Charles on and off for three years, coming back to Anjou regularly to see Edward and then always going back before things became too difficult. That was until Charles had gained his duchy of Burgundy and married Edward of York's sister, and then somehow it had seemed impolite to continue to impose on Charles' hospitality, although Charles still paid him quite a nice pension for the services he had rendered him over the last years. So back to Anjou he had come, while he decided what else he could do, and with him he had brought this stallion for Edward, the sort of present a father gave his son because that was how he looked on the boy.

"How long are you going to stay this time, Somerset?" The boy's newly broken voice cut into his thoughts.

"I don't know, Edward." He flashed a brief smile at the boy. "I will not be going back to Burgundy to serve Charles, not now he is wed to York's sister."

"No I suppose not." The boy glanced across at him. "You could stay here though."

"I can't stay for too long, lad, Jack and I need to earn our living."

"Doing what?"

"Selling ourselves as soldiers, I suppose." Beau looked thoughtful

"Mercenaries, you mean?"

"I'd like to think I was a bit more honourable than that!" Beau laughed. "I would say that I pledged myself to Charles when he needed me and I would like to think I would do the same for another lord. But as they are paying me for my services then I guess it would be fair to call me a mercenary, yes!" He laughed again and Edward was puzzled.

"Why is that funny?" he asked shyly.

"For the very reason that it is not. Here I am, born of the blood Royal and a premier Duke of England, living in France and selling myself as a soldier to the highest bidder!" He snorted and then took pity on the boy. "Ah, lad, I am just being contrary." He smiled at him, his eyes warm and tender. "I am just teasing. I plan to stay as long as I can before your mother gets sick of me and sends me on my way." Edward laughed at that.

"Ma mère gets sick of everyone except me," he said ruefully. "But at least when you are here she does not coddle me so much. I really thought that she would not let me ride this stallion but, because you bought him for me and begged her, she did." He looked up at the older man. "It is good when you are here, my Lord, for I feel at least there is something for me to learn and at least ma mère lets me out of her sight."

"She has no one else, lad." Beau glanced sympathetically across at his young companion. "Your father is imprisoned and she has only you. She must sometimes feel that you are the only reason for her to be thankful for her life."

"I suppose." The boy was thoughtful for a moment. "But it is hard sometimes to have to live up to that."

"I know." He smiled at the boy again. "But, when things get tough, just think of it from her point of view. You are not only precious to her but you are the Prince of Wales, King in waiting, and she just wants to protect you so that when the time comes you are ready for your destiny."

"But will the time ever come?" Edward sounded skeptical.

"It will come, lad, and when we least expect it." Beau spoke with a conviction he did not entirely feel, not because he did not believe their chance would come one day but because he was not sure how they would finance it when it did. Charles of Burgundy had allied himself with York and King Louis was a friend of Warwick so chances of large sums of money from either of those sources looked unlikely.

"Well I hope when it does come I get a chance to fight." Edward swung his sword arm and flexed his fingers. Beau smiled.

"Being in the thick of battle is not for the fainthearted, lad," he said, appraising the boy with his extraordinary eyes. "It is fast, noisy, confusing and exhausting and sometimes it is hard to distinguish friend from foe. Many a man has been killed by mistake by a comrade, I can tell you; so don't be too quick to want to jump into the centre of it!" The boy's face dropped into sulky lines and Beau softened. "You will be a great battle commander, Edward, if you continue to learn as quickly as you are now. You have a good mind for strategy and as long as you give your opponent the right amount of respect you will always have the chance to defeat him."

"And Edward of York deserves respect?"

"He does as a battle commander, lad, and as a fighter. There are few like him and he is a great warrior King, an inspiration to his men who has been known to fight on foot at their side. Not necessarily something I would advocate but he is a lesson in drive and inspiration." Beau grinned. "He is also an arrogant show-off who has been lucky not to get himself killed; but I believe he thinks of himself as invincible, and perhaps because of that he has been unstoppable so far."

"And you, my Lord, what about you?" The boy looked at him eagerly.

"Me?" Beau raised his eyebrows and then shook his head slightly. "I think I am an able commander and a good strategist, but I have lacked the chance to truly command an army; I came closest when I had command of the vanguard for Duke Charles of Burgundy." He smiled at the boy. "Perhaps we will have to learn together what it means to command."

"I heard my uncle Jasper Tudor tell ma mère that you are a good soldier." Edward flashed him a grin and Beau laughed.

"Did he now?" He felt an extraordinary sense of pleasure that the dour Earl of Pembroke would think so highly of him. "Well that's good to know."

"That's the first time I have ever seen you blush, Beau." Edward burst out laughing and the older man grinned a little sheepishly.

"I guess we all like praise, lad, especially when it comes from someone we respect."

"I always thought uncle Jasper was a bit of a bore." Edward was obviously surprised that his mentor liked the older man so much. Beau shook his head vigorously.

"No, lad. He is a fine man and a good soldier. He might be a bit dark and dry sometimes but I would much rather have him fighting on my side than against me. He has a force of spirit inherited from his Welsh side and is as crafty as a cat when it comes to battle tactics."

"Really?" The boy looked skeptical.

"There are no cleverer fighters than the Welsh, lad, and your uncle Jasper certainly has a goodly amount of Welsh blood in him!"

"As did my grandmother Catherine!" the boy quipped, and they both looked at each other and burst out laughing.

"Don't ever let your father hear you speak like that of his mother." Beau remembered to admonish when their mirth had died down. "He doted on her as he dotes on her Welsh offspring. It broke his heart to take them away from her and if he had been older he would not have let it happen, would probably have let her live out her life in obscurity, so just tread carefully. And around Jasper as well. He is very proud of his Welsh blood, and will brook no mockery of his father. Owen Tudor may have been a mere groom but a queen saw fit to mate with him and marry him and for Jasper that is good enough. After all he is descended from the Royal House of France, no less." He smiled to soften the rebuke. "You wouldn't like it if people said things about your mother."

"They already do when they think I cannot hear them." The words were out of Edward's mouth before he could stop them. Beau's expression darkened.

"And what do they say?" he asked quietly. The boy flushed and looked away.

"That my mother and your father..." He trailed off, staring at the ground beneath his stallion's feet. "That we are brothers and that is what started the war with York. They did not want a Beaufort bastard on the throne."

"Look at me, Edward." The older man's tone was gentle. The boy looked up, his skin still stained red. "It is not true."

"How do you know?" Edward asked in a small voice.

"Because firstly, your mother is virtuous and she would never do anything like that." He was pleased at the certainty in his voice. "And secondly, my father loved my mother and although he cared very much about your mother and father, it was my mother to whom he was most attached and finally, do you look anything like me?" He grinned and spread his hands. "Do you remember Hal?" he asked "Well my mother, my father, Hal, Jack and I, we all have eyes in varying degrees of brown and black hair; but you, well you have blue black eyes just like your Mama but you have the same brown hair and expressions as your father so how anyone could say you are a Beaufort...?" He shook his head and the boy grinned back.

"You're right," he said, his grin broadening, "I could not be a Beaufort, after all I am only average in both height and looks, not 'beau' like you!" He laughed, delighted with his pun. Beau laughed with him, indulging him in the distraction from such a dangerous subject.

"I have heard the ladies call you 'Le jolie garçon' or 'le jolie prince'," he teased.

"Pretty oy!" Edward pulled a face. "You get handsome and I get pretty. Great!" He glanced at Beau slyly. "Mind you, I am 'boy' and you of course are not."

"Are you saying I am old?" Beau rose to the clumsy challenge, the game familiar. "I will show you who's old, my boy; last one to the river does an hour at the quintain!" They looked at each other for a moment and then the boy whooped noisily and spurred the big black stallion forward, Beau, laughing, followed in his wake.

Chapter Three:

Middleham, February 1469

The warmth of the hall was a welcome relief from the cold February wind, and Stephen was thankful to be able to unfasten his travel cloak, albeit with numb fingers, and allow the heat from the hearth to seep into his bones. The thick white carpet of snow beyond the castle walls had begun to drift, and more than once he had found his strong stallion floundering chest high against a wet wall, unable to find a grip with his flailing hooves. It had taken all his skill as a horseman to stop the chestnut from panicking and he now found that he was tired, almost to the point of exhaustion, and after only three hours in the saddle.

He waited slightly impatiently by the grate, leaning against the iron guard rails, as close as he dared so that he could benefit from the blaze of the fire. He had come in answer to an urgent message from his father-in-law, received late the night before, requesting his presence at the castle at the earliest convenient moment. The messenger had been able to tell him nothing, except to allay his fears that his wife was ill or had had an accident. So he had set off as early as he dared on the cold winter morn, waiting only for dawn to break before he, his squire and the messenger, young Robin Percy, set off for Middleham. It had taken three hours to cover a distance which usually took no more than one and they had all been chilled to the very marrow of their bones by the time they arrived. He thrust his blue tinged fingers almost into the flames before him, wondering where the Earl might be to keep him waiting so long.

"Thevenot!" hailed the now very familiar voice, a hand catching his shoulder and breaking into his irritated musings. He swung round, looking up to meet Warwick's disconcertingly green eyes.

"My Lord," he acknowledged stiffly, finding that his voice was hoarse from shouting against the wind and that his lips were still numb and wooden.

"Christ Jesus, lad, you look half frozen. Come on, let's get you some food and something warm to drink." Warwick took his arm and guided him towards the solar, clicking his fingers to a page and indicating he wanted food and wine brought in. "By the look of you I'd say 'twas not the best of journeys." Stephen snorted mirthlessly.

"'tis cold enough to freeze the vitals out there, my Lord, as my stallion did discover each time he stepped into a drift." His voice was as dry and humorless as his laugh, but the Earl grinned all the same.

"Be thankful, lad, that it was the horse that did have such a distasteful experience." He steered Stephen through the door and into the smaller, warmer chamber. There were two men arguing furiously in one corner, one of whom he knew and the other he did not, though he could tell at a glance that he was a Neville. "Thevenot, you do know my cousin, the Duke of Clarence.?" Stephen nodded and bowed courteously, hiding his dislike under a passable smile. Clarence inclined his head sullenly, not very interested in his cousin's husband. "And this is my brother," continued the Earl, "his Grace the Archbishop of York. George, this is Stephen Thevenot, husband to my Katherine." The Archbishop favoured Stephen with an infectious grin.

"So you are the lucky man, eh?" he said with a quick ribald chuckle "A beautiful girl, if ever I saw one." Stephen was slightly taken aback by such freely expressed, worldly talk from a priest of the church; it may be common practice for a priest to lay with women, but it was usually done under a cloak of piety. He returned the smile somewhat stiffly.

"Aye, my Lord, and I do know it. I go home in some frustration each time my Lord Earl does summon me here." All the men laughed and Warwick clapped him on the back amiably.

"And let me add, brother, he needs little encouragement to bring him here. I know not whether he answers my requests or his own callings when he comes." They laughed again and Stephen flushed, slightly embarrassed. George Neville came easily to his rescue.

"I think it is the lure of virginity that does attract him, Rich, for you must admit, when a man nears the age of thirty they are few and far between, unless you seek the bed of a girl as young as your Kate." Warwick grinned.

"So speaks a man of the cloth," he teased benevolently, and the Archbishop gave a disarming shrug accompanied by a rueful smile. Irritated at being excluded from the conversation so far, Clarence waved an impatient hand and muttered with a petulant twitch of his mouth,

"'It is all very well discussing the obvious charms of my sweet cousin, but has any yet elected to inform Thevenot why he has been called here today?"

"Give the man a chance to eat, lad," murmured Warwick quietly, "and then we will down to business." Clarence subsided back into his window seat, growling something Stephen could not hear, drumming his fingers restlessly against the stone sill. He was glad that Warwick seemed able to handle the youth for he guessed he would be overbearing if left to his own devices.

At that moment, a page came in carrying a tray of hot spiced wine and some food. Stephen's stomach leaped suddenly, galvanised by the stirring smells, a gnawingly ravenous ache in its pit. He helped himself to a hot pastie and some wine, easing back onto the settle to eat and listen to what was to be said.

"I cannot say that I am entirely sure what you do intend Rich," began the Archbishop conversationally.

"Christ on the cross, cousin, do you have no grasp of words?" Clarence glared at George Neville. "It is quite simple; we intend to stir up a rising." Stephen almost spat his pasty, crumbs scattering from his mouth as he spluttered and choked, jerking his smarting eyes up to stare at the beautiful young man, all hunger forgotten. He thought for a moment that he had not heard correctly, but one look at the Archbishop's stunned face showed that there was nothing wrong with his hearing.

"Yes, George is right." Warwick's silky tones cut smoothly through the atmosphere, ignoring the two men's reaction. "It's quite simple, brother. Conyers will raise the standard of discontent, calling himself Robin of Redesdale, a good name for the common folk to follow seeing as they love a Robin, wherever he may come from. We will not be overtly involved as we will be in Canterbury and none will know that we are behind it. I just want to drag Ned out of his damned complacency and show him that he cannot slight the Nevilles, not when we have the power of the north behind us."

"But if he does not know you are behind it then how will he deduce that you have such power?" The Archbishop's usually deep, well-modulated voice was almost unpleasantly shrill with surprise.

"Because he will have to recall me to put down the rising. Northerners will not follow him, they will wait to see what I do so I need to be in favour and following Ned willingly or the rising will escalate." Warwick gave a smug grin, but George Neville looked unconvinced.

"But he never banished you in the first place, you chose to absent yourself."

"True enough, dear brother, but he will have to ask me back on my terms, or he will have to fight for control of the north. Quite simple would you not say? I will not be mocked and insulted by his damned pox-ridden kin. How he can bear to surround himself with such scum I know not, but I intend to rid the court of them if it's the last thing I do."

"And so it may be," muttered George Neville drily.

"Ballocks!" The Earl was moved enough to retaliate with a gutter oath.

"What does our brother John say to this...this plot?"

"He was not told of it. His loyalty to Ned and even his dislike of that itch's kin would not make him sanction such a scheme." Clarence's voice held reluctant admiration for his noble cousin.

"Then it will fail." The Archbishop's voice held a note of finality. Clarence spat a particularly unpleasant invective in his face.

"Shit! I see you have not the liver for this kind of adventure, my Lord!"

"No, cousin, but neither do I turn my coat so often nor so swiftly as some." It was a quiet and effective thrust at Clarence's fickle and dubious loyalties. Only a few short months before he had ridden by his brother's side to the Archbishop's palace and taken away the Seal of Office, stripping George Neville of his office of Lord Chancellor, and yet now he was swearing himself to be a staunch supporter of his cousin. The only person Clarence supported unwaveringly was Clarence, a trait which did not attract much sympathy with the very familial Archbishop whose fealty to his eldest brother could never be questioned.

"I hope you do not aim to insult me, cousin, for I do not take kindly to slurs."

"If the cap fits then wear it, George!"

"Stop bickering, for Christ's sake." The Earl's voice cut through their venom. "It is serious business we discuss here."

The Archbishop snorted with sudden dry mirthlessness.

"Serious business, Rich? By our lady! It is more than that, it is treason. If you are discovered, Ned could condemn you to a traitor's death and be fully justified!" He stood and moved closer to Warwick, looking long into his face. "Is that how you want to die, brother?" he said softly, "To hang by the neck, have your guts pulled out and all your limbs ripped from your body; all done whilst you're still live. Is that what you want?" Warwick stepped back a pace, his face blanching slightly beneath his weather-beaten tan and the fear in his brother's eyes.

"For Christ's sake, George, it will not come to that. Do you think that there will be anything that links us to these risings? How stupid do you think I am?"

"It is not that I think you are stupid, although this undertaking is foolhardy to say the very least, it is the risk that you take, man; the risk not only of your life but leaving nan and the girls with nothing if you are linked to treason."

"Ned would not make war on my family."

"No, he would not, but he would take everything they have. A king, no matter how merciful and conciliatory, can never have enough land or enough wealth. You do need to be very sure that this scheme will work before you set off down this route."

"My Lord Warwick?" Stephen's voice broke into their heated discussion. "Perhaps if you could outline your plan in more detail then it may be easier for a simple man like to me to understand. At this moment, I am struggling to see the link between the action you intend to take and getting back into the King's favour." Thankful for a reason to turn away from the Archbishop, Warwick smiled at his son in law.

"It is relatively simple, lad," he said. "If I hold the country then Ned will have no choice but to keep me in favour. The more unrest there is then the more he needs me to ensure peace. He will need to treat with me and if he doesn't then he will regret it."

"So if he doesn't bring you back to favour then you will declare against him?" Stephen met his father-in-law's gaze levelly. Warwick nodded almost imperceptibly.

"Yes, I will declare against him."

"How do we know that we can trust him?" Clarence's jabbed a finger towards Stephen. "Just because he is wed to our Kate does not mean that he is on our side." Stephen stiffened and stared at Clarence with open dislike, but it was Warwick who spoke quietly.

"Stephen is loyal to me and to me only, is that not right, Stephen?"

"Yes, my Lord."

"Unto death?"

"Unto death, my Lord." Stephen bowed his head in assent.

"And gentlemen, therein lies my superiority, for I have worked hard to gain the loyalty of my Lords in the north; a task I was set by my cousin, but I believe I have succeeded beyond even what he could have envisaged. He should have realised that I would settle for nothing less than an equal share of power; he should have realised that the Nevilles would not tolerate their standing being eroded by low-born Woodvilles. And now I am going to make sure that he takes note of my discontent and acts in my favour, or he will suffer the consequences." He looked slowly around the room, meeting the eyes of each man in turn and then he smiled his brilliant, engaging smile. "I made the King and I can unmake him. I hope he realises that before it is too late."

***

"You wanted to see me, papa?" Kate came into the solar and shut the door behind her softly.

"Ah, Katherine." Richard Neville was seated in the window embrasure, his back to the intricate leaded glass. He looked uncomfortable for a moment and then gestured to the cushioned seat beside him. "Sit down, sweetheart." Kate grimaced inwardly at the seriousness of his expression and wracked her brain to think of what she might have done wrong.

"Have I done something to displease you, papa?" she asked softly. Her father shook his head and smiled.

"No Katherine. I am not displeased at all." He took her hand, warming her cold fingers in his. She braced herself, aware that whatever was coming may not be to her liking. "You are fifteen, almost a woman grown. It is a fact, and many girls are wedded and bedded by your age and Thevenot has more than proven his worth by showing himself loyal so I have decided it is time that we let him bed you." He leaned back in the window seat, his face shadowed by the stone frame so she could not read his expression but she guessed that he was once again feeling uncomfortable. This was normally a conversation that would have been undertaken by her mother but she knew he would not trust it to the Countess as he would not be certain that she would be kind and she had little liking for the act a married couple must do in bed. She was not sure how she felt about it herself, especially with her husband who was almost a stranger to her. Somehow their conversation was always awkward and never achieved the level of intimacy that either of them would have liked. He was handsome and tried very hard to be engaging but he was cold and self-contained and every encounter left her feeling dissatisfied. She was so taken up with her thoughts that she forgot about her father and when she did not speak he leaned forward and looked searchingly into her face. "You do know your duty, don't you?" he asked awkwardly.

"Of course, papa." Kate nodded hastily. "Ma mère explained to me before my betrothal." Warwick looked irritated for a moment and then took a deep breath.

"I have taken the liberty of having your things moved from Anne's chamber into the large chamber in round tower and I have told Thevenot that he may join you there this night." He smiled and Kate smiled back dutifully, hiding her apprehension and hoping he could not hear her thudding heart.

"Will I have to leave Middleham, papa?" she asked quietly. "Will I have to go and live in his manor?" Warwick shook his head and relief flooded through her. She could not bear the thought of leaving her family so suddenly.

"No, sweetheart." He reached out and touched her cheek. "Not yet. He will stay here with us for now."

"And when Stephen is away I can still stay in my new chamber in the round tower?"

"Of course." He looked surprised that she should ask. "It would make no sense to keep moving your things. But I am sure your sister will not mind if occasionally you want to share her room again."

"And there will be no fuss over our bedding this evening?" She almost shuddered at the thought of everyone smirking and dancing her to bed.

"We will have a quiet supper this evening in the solar, just family, and there will be no fuss or ribaldry, I promise." Warwick's expression softened and he cupped her chin. "I know how little you like to be the centre of attention."

"Thank you, papa." Her response was fervent for she could think of nothing worse than crude jokes at her expense as everyone laughed outside her bed curtains. Warwick did not let go of her chin but looked deep into her eyes, his own reflecting deep green in the light.

"Do not let my wife taint this night for you," he said very softly. "There is pleasure to be had in the marriage bed. Follow your husband's lead and all will be well." He laid his lips against her forehead briefly and then let go. "Now off with you child, I have work to do."

***

She lay staring up at the canopy over the bed, the cresset snuffed out so that she could see nothing in the darkness, but she could feel the warmth of her husband laid beside her, his back towards her and his face toward the hangings. She did not know if he slept but she hoped so.

It had all started so well. He had led her from the solar to the round tower, stopping once in the shadow of the stairwell to kiss her and she had responded as best she could, following his lead as her father had told her. Once in their chamber he had helped her undress until she was in her chemise and then asked for her help with the laces on his tunic and shirt. She had found it almost enjoyable as she helped him out of his clothes until he stood in just his braies, his excitement obvious. Once under the covers he had removed his braies and helped her out of her chemise before pulling her to him and kissing her, his hands exploring her body eagerly, his breathing ragged. She had followed his movement, stroking him as he stroked her, her hands running down his back and over his buttocks, her stomach swooping as he whimpered at the touch of her fingertips on his spine. She had felt a warmth spreading through the pit of her stomach which she could not identify and a feeling of excitement like something wonderful was going to happen. And when his fingers had slipped into her secret place between her thighs she had masked her initial shock and given a small whimper of pleasure, tentatively reaching

68

out to touch his erection, her fingers stroking the shaft from top to bottom. She had been unprepared for the violence of his reaction at her touch when he had growled, hissing a sharp breath down his nose and pushing her roughly onto her back, the tip of his penis slipping inside her and nosing against the barrier of her maidenhead. She felt him thrust as if he would break it and then, somehow, it had all gone wrong as he groaned, shuddered and then cried out in anguish, warm sticky wetness seeping onto the sheet below her. She had lain very still, not sure what to do or say as he rolled away from her and buried his face in his pillow. After a few minutes she had reached out to touch his shoulder but he had shaken her off, sitting up only to snuff out the cresset, before laying rigidly with his back to her.

"You unmanned me," he had whispered through clenched teeth. "Your whore's tricks unmanned me."

"I am sorry." She heard the tears in her own voice, not knowing what she was apologising for but responding to his anguish. "I am so sorry."

"Who taught you those tricks?" His jaw was rigid.

"What tricks, my Lord?" She was crying now at the injustice of his anger.

"Who showed you how to touch a man?"

"No one." She reached out to him again but he slapped her hand away. "I just wanted to please you."

"Well you did not please me!" His voice was low and menacing. "You displeased me."

"I am sorry, my Lord." She bit back a sob and ran the back of her hand over her eyes, afraid of the threat in his voice but determined not to show it.

"You will not speak of this to anyone."

"Of course not, my Lord." She was horrified that he had thought she would. "I would never..."

"See that you do not." He cut her off and threw himself away from her, his back rigid and the conversation ended.

And so now she lay confused and afraid in the dark with a naked stranger, a man she barely knew, who happened to be her husband and who happened to be very angry with her, all because she had tried to please him in bed.

Anjou, France
August 1469

The room was cold even though it was still August, a draught flickering the torches on the wall. It was just another thing that Edmund Beaufort hated about the palace at Bar in Anjou; it was old, cold and draughty even in the summer months, and keeping warm seemed to be an ever losing battle. He leaned back against the mantle, the flames warming the back of his legs through his plain brown chausses, and regarded his Prince and his Queen steadily.

"I believe it is true Madame, that the Earl of Warwick has taken Edward of York captive and is holding him somewhere in the north of England." He flicked a glance toward Jasper Tudor, the newly arrived Earl of Pembroke, for affirmation.

"Yes Madame, it is true. Her Grace of Burgundy received a message from the Duchess of York confirming that Edward was with Warwick in the north of England and that they were awaiting the outcome of his stay there. It seems that he was outwitted Madame and taken with no resistance." He grinned triumphantly.

"Outwitted, you say?" Marguerite raised defined eyebrows over still beautiful eyes. Pembroke nodded.

"It seems that he underestimated his cousin and the depth of the hatred which had sprung up between them. He never believed that Warwick would turn against him and so did not arm himself against the possibility. Hence he was captured with only Hastings and Gloucester at his side."

"Are they held with him?" Beau was curious.

"No, Warwick let them go, which I think is a mistake for they are as loyal followers of York as we are to our Prince of Lancaster." Pembroke nodded towards the Prince.

"And loyal to my husband, of course," Marguerite murmured, as she always did when they forgot that the imprisoned King Henry was still alive.

"Of course." Both men nodded their heads in mutual assent.

"But what is Warwick going to do with Edward of York?" Prince Edward looked puzzled. "He can't keep him prisoner forever. So, what advantage will it have to hold him now? As soon as he releases him he will go back to London and turn on Warwick. That's what I would do;

drive him from my kingdom or kill him for such a flagrant flouting of royal authority."

"Indeed Edward, you are right." Beau smiled fondly at the boy, pride gleaming in his eyes. "Unless he deposes him, but who would he put in his place; Clarence?" He snorted mirthlessly. "Jesu', I hope not! I recall Clarence that day at Ludlow; he was brave but very obviously stupid!"

"He lacks York's charm as well, so is not loved by the English as York is." Pembroke shook his head in obvious wonder. "Though quite why they love York so much is beyond me!"

"Because he is a hand span above six feet, undeniably handsome and has the physique of a God, perhaps?" Marguerite laughed at Pembroke's evident bewilderment. "Women admire him and men want to be him. It is helpful in the game of politics to have that kind of advantage."

"You sound as though you admire him, ma mère?" Edward stared at her coolly and she laughed again.

"There is nothing wrong with recognising your opponent's strengths, my son, and admitting the impact they have," she said.

"Madame your mother is right Edward." Beau smiled at the boy. "It is always good to understand how someone like York keeps his kingdom." He grinned suddenly, "Or not as the case may be!" They all laughed and he continued, "When I was at court, first with my father and then with my brother, before the old Duke of York tried to claim the crown, I remember Edward of March as he was then, very well. He may be lazy and like his pleasures, but he is a good-humoured man with intelligence and wit and is good company. Men like that should be willing to follow an easy-going, generous man far. But the flip side of that coin is that he has become complacent and failed to retain the loyalty of great political men like Warwick and so he finds himself in this predicament. If he does not learn from his mistake then he may well find himself without a kingdom and at Warwick's mercy."

"You think Richard Neville is a great political mind?" Marguerite's voice was hard with dislike at the remembered Earl of Warwick.

"Yes Madame, I think that is irrefutable."

"I agree." Pembroke smiled at her expression, his tone somewhat patronising as it always was when dealing with women.

"I am not denying that he has risen high under York but do you not think that if a man thinks he can take a king prisoner, he sees himself as above any law of the land?" Marguerite was curious as to how these men did not see that if a nobleman felt he could do this then no one was safe from his actions.

"But if the King was a true King, Madame, then none would be able to do this, for he would not put himself in that position." Beau shook his head adamantly with his words.

"My husband is a prisoner, my Lord. Was that because he is not a true king?" Her voice was silky and he coloured rapidly at her tone. Pembroke looked from one to the other, his expression slightly bemused.

"You are twisting my words, Madame," Beau said softly, his expression remaining bland, and she raised a cool eyebrow.

"If you say so, bien aimée." He flinched at the term that she had once used in affection but now used in sarcasm, and not for the first time he wondered if he should have just overcome his ideals and bedded her when she had offered herself to him. At least now she might not be this bitter, difficult woman she had become.

"I do say so, Madame." He smiled and then turned back to Edward. "So you see why it is good to know the strengths of your opponents?"

"Yes, my Lord."

"And that you can admire someone without it meaning that you support them?"

"Yes, my Lord." Edward nodded, his face thoughtful. "And you can learn from both their strengths and weaknesses, what to do and what not to do."

"Exactly." Beau's eyes glowed with pride at the boy's astuteness. "It pays to study your enemy, son." Edward responded to Beau's expression with a glow of his own and they began to animatedly discuss the merits of politics versus soldiering.

***

"Will you walk with me, Madame?" Pembroke offered his arm, as he noted with satisfaction that Edward was benefiting from having a man like Somerset as his paternal role model. He could tell, though, that Marguerite did not like the boy's closeness to the young Duke, in fact sometimes he would swear that she did not like Somerset at all, but he could not imagine why that would be. Somerset was a great Lord, who had proved himself serving Duke Charles and fighting in Burgundy and who was ideal to tutor the boy in politics and warfare; and for all his volatility and his intensity, his devotion to the boy was absolute and returned in equal measure. The Earl could not help but think that Somerset was a better father figure to the boy than his brother the King would ever have been, not that he would ever have voiced such an opinion to Marguerite, or anyone for that matter. He smiled at Marguerite and gestured for her to walk with him away from Edward and Somerset who were now deep in discussion and had forgotten the existence of their companions.

"The boy is doing well, Madame," he said softly. "Somerset is good for him."

"It would seem so." She shrugged indifferently.

"Is there a problem, Madame?"

"A problem, Jasper?" She looked at him in astonishment.

"Between you and Somerset?" He flushed as he spoke. "There seems to be friction between you." He was taken aback when she laughed bitterly.

"What do you expect, Jasper. My son idolises him and no longer listens to me."

"A boy needs a man at his age, Madame." Pembroke was surprised at her reaction. "It is unusual for a boy to be with his mother for as long as Edward has been in your care."

"Are you saying that I have not raised him well?" Her eyes were suddenly very cold, but Pembroke was unfazed. He had known her since she was fifteen and still thought of her as that strong-willed, lovely young girl who had come and shaken up his brother's life.

"No, I am saying that you must let him go, Madame; Let him go and become the man that he will be." He caught her hand and kissed it.

"I don't want him to end up like Somerset." Her voice was hard.

"There are worse men he could become." Pembroke smiled, his heavy face softening. "I know Somerset has his faults as did his sire, but he has talent and the boy admires him."

"Aye, and probably admires his arrogance and his philandering as much as his soldiering skills. I will not have my son thinking it is fine to bed any woman he wants and then desert them." She shook her head. "That is not the role model I want for him."

"Boys will be boys, Madame." Pembroke could see nothing wrong in bedding a few women. Good luck to the lad if he could follow in Beaufort's footsteps with women; all knew Somersert's looks and magnetism paved the way for his conquests just as Edward's charm and his crown would do for him but what was the harm in that; if he had had the same opportunities as Somerset he would have blazed the same trail. "You must let him grow up, Margaret." She smiled at the Anglican pronunciation of her name.

"Must I?" She looked up at him sadly.

"Yes, you must." He squeezed the hand he still held. "It is the lot of all mothers to let go of their sons."

"That's easy for a man to tell a mother." She extricated her hand and looked down at her wedding band. "But it is never the man that must relinquish the child."

"He loves you Margaret and he always will," he said softly and she looked up into his kindly blue eyes. "But it is time to stop coddling him and let Somerset have his care."

"I know you are right, Jasper, but I just wish it was not Edmund Beaufort who was to be his tutor."

"I know, Madame, I know, but we do not have much choice and he is the best man you will find to teach him to be a knight." He patted her shoulder knowing that he had won. "And it is not like he will be going anywhere. Somerset's knights and household are here so he will still be close to you."

"Alright Jasper!" She laughed ruefully at his clumsy platitudes. "You can stop appealing to the Queen, the mother is won over."

"You will not regret that decision, Madame, of that I am sure."

"I do hope you are right." She looked across at her son and Somerset still deep in discussion and her eyes narrowed. "I really do hope that you are right."

Middleham
June 1469

Fire blazed in the great hearth in the centre of the chamber, casting billowing clouds of smoke out into the air so that it hung like a second ceiling above them. Torches burned in their holders high up on the walls, casting shadows like grotesque caricatures on the stone. Pages already scurried to and fro, carrying pitchers filled with warm mulled wine, to revive even the weariest traveller, and trays of tankards of frothing ale that would quench their heavy thirst. Stephen's stomach gnawed hungrily at the tempting smell of roasting meat which wafted up from the kitchen underneath, and he realised suddenly just how long it was since he had had a good meal. At the end of the hall the Earl of Warwick laughingly fought off the attentions of the over excited dogs, whilst attempting to issue orders to his men. It looked very much like an ordinary homecoming and Stephen found it difficult to believe the figure still veiled in his heavy travel cloak was in fact the King of all England and prisoner of his father–in–law. Taller by a head or more than every other man in the room, and so powerfully built that his shoulders seemed to fill the doorways as he passed through them, Edward was naturally a focus for all eyes, standing, occupying space almost at the centre of the hall. Slowly he threw back his hood, revealing the glinting goldenness of his Plantagenet colouring, and the iridescent blue of his coolly incurious eyes surveying what he saw without obvious expression; but there were tell-tale furrows about his mouth, and a pallor to his skin which gave indication to his fatigue, and though he strove hard to control it, a nerve twitched along his rigidly contorted jaw-line. Stephen could not help but feel some admiration for this man, thrust into a situation never before experienced; he had coped remarkably well, treating his stay at Warwick castle as though it were merely part of a royal progress, never losing his natural regality and treating Warwick as if he were indeed his greatest friend and ally, throwing the Earl off balance with his easy affability. Stephen guessed it must have been hard for a man so used to being acclaimed the darling of all, to suddenly have to take commands from another, but he had complied with all his captor's wishes without complaint.

He removed his cloak now, handing it nonchalantly to one of the men close to him, as if he were part of his own household and not wearing the distinctive Bear and Ragged Staff of Warwick, and it said much for his authority that the man took it without question. His tunic shone almost the same shade as his eyes, once again attracting all eyes to him. He knew well how to take advantage of all the physical perfections God had given him, and he had somehow escaped much of the mud splashes and grime that caked his companions. But it was not the brightness of his clothes which caught Stephen's attention, it was the sudden change of expression from feigned boredom to alertness, a stiffening of those wide shoulders and a sharpening of his features. Stephen followed his gaze across the hall and saw his father-in-law being greeted by his wife and children. His heart jumped at the sight of his own wife, vibrant in emerald, her hair escaping from the confines of her pretty headdress in curling tendrils about her face. He watched her intently, detachedly admiring, not for the first time, her simplicity of dress which always seemed to be the height of elegance. In some respects, she was appealingly French and her sense of style was one of them. Warwick was laughing, enjoying the attentions of his family, enjoying commanding the respect in front of his cousin. Stephen watched as they made their way across the stone floor, through the melee of scurrying servants and hungry men to where Edward stood, regarding them with sharp eyes. He wondered how Edward would react, wondered if he would still carry on the charade of the visiting monarch, or whether Warwick's tactics of close confinement and deprivations of certain comforts had broken his somewhat battered spirit.

Francis Lovell was presented first and Stephen remembered Kate telling him that he was a good friend of the King's youngest brother, and Edward, renowned for his extraordinary feats of memory, would doubtless know that. He was not close enough to hear what was said but he could see, as Francis stepped away with a low bow, that there was admiration in his eyes and a smile about his lips. Edward had one friend in the castle at least. It was the Countess's turn next, and Stephen saw the frosty Lady thaw under his blatant flattery, and respond to it, whilst Warwick watched her with a mixture of pride and irritation and seemed glad when she excused herself to attend to the arrangements. Edward turned his attentions to Anne, who was pushed reluctantly forward by her father toward the towering figure. Anne's frailty appealed to Stephen's protective instinct, like most men, and her sweet nature added to her dainty charm, but unlike many men he could see no beauty in her save her luminous green eyes which were too big for her small piquant face. He could see that Edward watched her curiously, perhaps recalling how actively his brother had pushed for her hand, studying her face with surprise, and Stephen guessed that she was not the sort of lass to appeal to Edward's overriding sensuality. As she made to kneel before him he had to bend almost in half to lift her to her feet, so small was she in relation to his great height, but he caught her easily and drew her towards him in a cousinly embrace. Anne's reaction was instant and instinctive as she recoiled violently, scalded by his touch, her face flushing crimson as she jerked out of his arms. Then as Edward looked on in somewhat bewildered amusement she executed a perfunctory curtsey and bolted from the hall, turning her back on him in a flagrant breach of etiquette.

Stephen could not help but allow himself a quick grin of satisfaction that for once the famous Plantagenet charm had failed to make its mark. Edward shrugged and murmured something to Warwick who shot him a quick look and then grinned. The two men's eyes met for a second and they laughed, another flash of the old camaraderie catching the rift between them, and men in the hall glanced at each other and muttered softly, not sure what to make of this strange relationship.

That left only Kate to be presented to her cousin, last as always because of her birth. Once Stephen had felt sorry for the stain of bastardy which besmirched her, but now he saw that it had its advantages; at least she had the example of the others to follow at her first royal presentation. She kept her eyes demurely downcast and hands clasped before her as she walked forward, and he moved closer to them to see if he could hear what was being said. As with Anne, Edward caught her before she could kneel, but with Kate he did not have to bend so far since she was tall for a woman, as tall as a number of men in the room. But instead of drawing her into an embrace, he cupped her chin with long fingers, tilting her head up so that he could look into her face. He seemed to stare for a long time, then suddenly he smiled, a different smile from the others, for this one lit up the cool blue eyes, crinkling them appealingly at the corners, rubbing away the fatigue etched there. Letting go of her chin he said something with a wry twist of his mouth and Stephen saw Kate give a pert reply. The King gave a snort of laughter and turned to Warwick, remarking something which caused the Earl to smile with pride. Stephen had guessed that this encounter would be different for he knew Edward would not have forgotten her, in fact he had been in Warwick's company when the King had asked after 'little Kate'. He just wished he could see her face, to see how she reacted to his attentions and he felt the sharp pang of jealousy in his gut. Edward leaned forward and spoke quietly again, Kate responding in like fashion, and then they both broke into laughter which could be heard around the hall. There was a lessening of noise, as all tried to hear what a young girl could say that would be so amusing the King. Unable to bear it any longer Stephen shouldered his way forward through the crowd to a better vantage point, suddenly resenting that this man could monopolise his wife's attention and there was nothing he could do about it. But the resentment altered to another stab of jealousy as he saw Kate's face for the first time during the encounter. Her cheeks were flushed and her eyes sparkled with laughter, and something more, an appealing coquettishness which Edward was responding to with the ease of a natural philanderer. Stephen's heart lurched sickeningly, bile rising in his throat, as he was forced to watch them.

"And has time been as kind to me as it has to you, sweet Kate?" Edward was asking with a spark of vanity behind the amusement in his voice.

"You do know it has, your Grace." Kate glanced sidelong up at him through thick lashes. "Why, almost every man in this room does wish he did look just like you...and every wife is wishing he did also." It was a jest designed to flatter and provoke laughter and it succeeded, but Stephen felt the sharpness of the barb as though it were a personal insult, even though it was not aimed at him. He knew he was as little like Edward as any man could be, for he was not tall, only average height, nor was he fair, and for the first time in his life he was conscious of this as a defect. As he watched with narrowed eyes, Edward held out his hand for her to kiss, a gesture of dismissal, but just as she leaned forward to do so, he caught her and pulled her to him, softly kissing her lips before whispering something in her ear. Kate flushed scarlet but laughed as she backed away, dropping another deep curtsey. Edward did not take his eyes off his comely Neville cousin. There was that in his look which chilled Stephen to the heart. A mirror of his own desire perhaps, but more than that, a spark of interest that was just as dangerous as the desire, for Edward's palate was jaded and anything that interested him enough deserved to be pursued as unrelentingly as possible. Once more, jealousy rose from the pit of Stephen's stomach, surging through his veins until he felt physically sick.

"Is there aught wrong, my Lord?" Kate's warm, slightly accented voice broke into the bitterness of his thoughts. He swung round and saw her stood behind him, her lovely face wreathed in a smile of welcome.

"Did you have to play the coquette to such effect?" he asked harshly, avoiding the hurt in her eyes at his tone.

"I was not, my Lord." She looked uncertain, the smile still hovering at the corner of her mouth.

"Well it looked like it to me." He caught her wrist roughly and pulled her towards him. "I will not brook that kind of behaviour, lady, so best we make sure that you know that now."

"I can assure you, my Lord, that I would not behave in any way which would cause you hurt or embarrassment." She regarded him steadily for a moment, her cheeks aflame with colour, her eyes suddenly veiled and cool; a different face from the one which had so enchanted Edward. "I am disappointed that you think I might."

"Aye, well I know what I saw and I didn't like it." He leaned forward and kissed her cheek, aware that he was being watched by his father-in-law, dropping his hand from her wrist and lacing his fingers instead through hers. His grip was firm and uncompromising. "And you will learn Madam that if I do not like something then you will not do it." She stared at him for a moment and then smiled a breathtakingly dazzling smile.

"It seems to me, my Lord," she said, leaning into him, her voice low, "that you do not like anything I do." And oblivious of anyone else in the hall she challenged his gaze until he was the first to look away.

Chapter Four

Middleham, September 1469

Kate was sitting on the settle on one side of the fire, embroidering as the King and Frances Lovell played chess at the table on the other side, looking up and smiling occasionally at their competitive banter, quite accustomed after a fortnight to having the King as their special guest.

"I swear if you delay much longer, your Grace, cobwebs will begin to form around those pieces." Edward raised startled eyes at the sound of Francis Lovell's gently bantering voice, and grimaced.

"I'm sorry, Francis, my head seems to be wandering freely and not staying in one place today!" He leaned across and moved his knight. Francis grinned and slid his castle over the chequered board, knocking the knight from the wood and slipping it into his belt.

"Check, my liege," he murmured.

"Jesus wept," Edward swore softly. "I have not played so badly since I was a lad." His evident dislike of being beaten at any game made his voice sharp and then he laughed. "I concede the game. I will give you your moment of triumph but I will beat you tomorrow lad, mark my words!"

"Of course you will, your Grace." There was something in Francis' smile that indicated that he was not so sure and Edward grinned, slapping the boy across the back. But he was serious almost at once, the now familiar furrows of discontent lining his mouth as he got up, stretched and walked over to stare out of the long narrow window. His movement was reminiscent of a caged animal.

"Is there aught I can get for you, your Grace?" asked Francis.

"Aye lad, some wine if you please." He did not turn round, his eyes seemingly fixed on the bleak, barren hills ahead. "And plenty of it at that."

"Perhaps some food also?" Edward shook his head.

"No Francis, I'm not hungry."

Kate looked up from her window seat at the far side of the room, her embroidery needle poised in mid-air.

"You should eat, your Grace," she said softly. "It's not good for you to go all day without food." Edward smiled at the sound of her voice and turned slightly to look at her, his grin briefly banishing the harsh lines of his face.

"Ah! Kate. The Lady caring for my welfare," he teased with gentle sarcasm and Kate dropped her lashes.

"I am caring of your welfare, your Grace, however much you may mock me, and I say that to drink a flagon of wine without food will make even you greensick and you know it."

"And now you are the nagging wife." He laughed and she blushed furiously at the warmth and affection in his voice. "Still Francis, it does not do to gainsay a lady, so if you would bring me a platter of something tasty, and perhaps only a small jug of wine and then at least she will cease to carp at me." Francis bowed and made for the door. Left alone with Edward, Kate suddenly felt a flutter of apprehension in her stomach but Edward seemed to have almost immediately forgotten that she was there, turning back to continue his futile staring from the casement.

Kate could well understand his reasons for the long silences and wayward thoughts, which had led to him conceding the game of chess. Only two days after his arrival at Middleham, his brother George had returned to the castle with his new Duchess, making a grand entrance into the village, displaying a splendour, which outdid even the flamboyance of the Earl of Warwick. All had come out of their homes to see the handsome Duke and his lovely Lady, astride the showy stallion, ducal coronets on fair heads, bodies swathed in crimson velvet. Their entourage was large and well-armed, a show of power not lost on those who watched and more suited to a king than a Prince of the Blood. Clarence had sat his stallion with proud arrogance, very aware that he created a perfect vision, but he lacked his brother's easy charm which had won him so many hearts, and did not relate easily to the common folk of the village. His reception was muted, for although they admired his looks and they loved the Duchess, they did not warm to him as they had their beloved Warwick or their friendly handsome King, but watched him quietly.

Anne and Kate had watched them arrive from the window of their chamber, for Anne had avoided Edward's company since his arrival like one would avoid 'the sweat'. As the cavalcade pulled into the courtyard the Earl of Warwick had come out of the castle to greet his daughter and his new son-in-law. Clarence had swung himself out of the saddle offering a boisterous slap on the back to Warwick before shaking his hand, and then reaching up had swung Isabel high into the air and set her ostentatiously down at her father's side. Both girls had had an uneasy feeling that the rumours raging the castle about what their father intended for both Edward and George might possibly have a ring of truth about them. Neither girl could credit that their father would be capable of anything evil but then neither would have believed that he would execute a man without fair trial until they had heard it from the Earl himself. So Anne had asked her mother if her father did indeed mean to depose Edward and set Clarence on the throne, and had been rewarded with a sharp rebuke and a resounding slap. Anne had been shocked by her mother's reaction as she had never before raised a hand to her. Kate had consoled her but neither girl had been reassured by what had happened.

"I think you should put down your needlework and talk to me." Kate looked up from her reverie and saw that Edward had turned from the window and was watching her, an odd expression on his face. She smiled.

"I would, your Grace, but my sister Isabel will not have her new gown if I don't finish the stitching on this under gown. And you know how difficult Bel can be when she is disappointed"

"I could make it a royal command, I believe I am still at liberty to do that." He said it lightly but she sensed the tautness behind his easy façade. Captivity sat ill on a man of his nature; the confines of a few rooms curtailing the freedom he had always taken for granted and needed so much, grating harshly on his already frayed nerves. As he leaned back against the window embrasure, his assumed nonchalance and light smile did not quite belie the drumming of his restless fingers and the deep edged furrows at the corners of his mouth. He had aged she thought, in the few weeks that he had been there, still handsome but no longer boyish, a ruggedness about his face which somehow made him even more appealing.

"If you put it like that, Sire, then of course I would be happy to relieve your boredom, though how my inane chatter will help, Jesus alone knows!" She laid the gown over the arm of her chair and looked up, meeting his gaze. The smile he gave her melted her heart, and the warmth in his eyes sent another telltale flush up her throat and into her face. She dropped her eyes, uncertain that she liked the feelings he roused in her but somehow she could not keep away from his presence.

"You have known Francis Lovell for some time haven't you Kate?" he said after a while. She nodded

"Yes, your Grace, I have known him since he first came to Middleham and we have always been the best of friends." She paused and then grinned. "Well, he and Richard are best friends and I am very fond of both."

"I am grateful to both you and Francis for being my companions these last few days," He smiled, "The feelings of this household are not the warmest but I am thankful that you and Francis have shown me kindness and that you have made my stay here a more pleasant one." She smiled back at him, still uncertain what to say. Restlessly he moved away from the window, stopping by her chair and looking down at her. "I would have been half mad with boredom if it hadn't been for the pair of you amusing me all the while."

"I am glad that we could be of help to you, your Grace."

"When you were at Calais you used to call me Ned." His eyes were soft, and he smiled. "You were my friend then too, wee thing that you were. You made us laugh with your antics and we adored you; your father especially; in fact your father has always loved you well."

"And he has always loved you well too."

"Aye, he did once...I remember when we were inseparable..." he trailed off, staring distantly and then, "Where the hell is Lovell with that wine!" And she jumped at the rawness of his voice.

"I'm sorry, your Grace, I will go and find him." She got up swiftly to head for the door, but he reached out and grabbed her arm in an unintentionally vice like grip.

"No!" He looked, for a brief instant, like a hunted animal, before swiftly pulling himself under control. "No," he said more evenly, letting go of her, "I would not have you running around after me, he will be here soon enough."

"Are you alright, your Grace?"

"I'm fine" His voice was stilted and strangely hoarse "I just need a damned drink."

"Then let me go and find you some wine..."

"No, don't go," softly, pleadingly, "I am alone so much already."

"Are you sure you are alright?" She had never before seen him in anything except complete control and this vulnerable side to his character was unnerving, yet she felt the desire to protect him and to shield him from discovery, help him regain the equanimity he seemed to have so suddenly lost. He stared down at her sightlessly.

"Aye I'm fine, the world has gone mad but I am fine! Sweet Bleeding Christ!" He spat viciously, making her take an involuntary step back. "For six miserable weeks, I have been held prisoner by a man I used to call a friend, a man I would never have credited with disloyalty; six interminable weeks of signing papers to order, being docile for fear of arousing my Lord's awesome temper, living in two rooms and being watched wherever I go. I cannot even go to the privy in peace without some hairy arsed henchman standing at my side. I suppose they think I may jump down the shaft and escape from the cesspit." He walked away to the window, leaning his head against the cold stone surface of the embrasure, rubbing a distracted hand across his eyes. He stood there for some minutes, and Kate hovered uncertainly behind him, not sure whether to go to him or to leave the chamber and allow him some peace with his anguish. Then all at once he righted himself and swung back to face her. "I have even been civil to my dear brother George, congratulating him on a marriage I expressly forbade, in the hope that this may all be a nightmare and that tomorrow I will wake in my own bed." He flung himself down into the window seat and managed a brittle smile, "But, alas, it is not so. Instead I find myself believing that the man closer to me than my own brothers now plans to do away with me and set George up in my stead, and all because I would not sign my crown over to the French as he wished. Do you think that this is justice for my sins?" He bit down hard on his bottom lip as though the pain somehow helped him keep control. Misery overwhelmed Kate but she dare not move, uncertain if he really knew that she was there, not wanting him to notice the daughter as he railed against the father. He trusted easily and could not credit that trust ever broken, finding it difficult to reconcile himself to the betrayal of a man he had loved so well and for so long, never believing that their disagreements could have led to such violent disaffection. "He knows my weak spots so well: he knows that I find it hard to be denied warmth in my bed and so he tempts me with beauty but ensures that it is unattainable; he knows, too, how I hate to be caged, to have not the freedom to go where I will, and so he locks me up in two rooms; he knows how much I need to know what is happening in my realm and so he keeps all news from me hoping to break my very soul; and, Christ Jesus, I fear he will soon succeed." He leaned forward, elbows on knees, his head in his hands. No longer able to contain herself at the sight of such dejection Kate ran forward and knelt at his side.

"I'm sorry," she whispered, tears catching at her voice and breaking it, "I'm so very, very sorry." The sound of her voice brought him back to reality, dragged him away from the edge of self-despair and reaching out he touched her cheek gently with his forefinger.

"For what, sweet Kate?" he asked softly, "for being my companion in adversity, for bringing sweetness to my captivity or for having the fairest face a man could wish to look upon day after day?" He gave a faint smile. "I have not yet lost the will to fight for what is rightfully mine, and when my time does come again I shall not forget you or Francis and what you have done for me whilst I have been here."

"I don't want your gratitude, Sire, I don't care about that. I just want you to resolve your differences with papa and for things to go back to the way they were."

"I wish it could be that easy, sweetheart, but I can make you no promises." He leaned back wearily against the window, his voice bitter. "Your father is a traitor; to me, to himself and to everything we worked so damned hard to build."

"No!" Kate gasped at the implication of his words. "Papa would never hurt you, he just wanted to…to…"

"To what, Kate? To invite me to stay for a while? To get my attention? Well he certainly has my whole undivided attention now." His sarcasm was brutal.

"I don't know what he wanted to do but he would never hurt you, he loves you as he would have loved a son…"

"Aye, as long as I was an obedient son, but as soon as I gainsaid his plans he ceased to love me." He leaned forward and took her face in his hands, forcing her eyes up to his. "Only time can tell what the future may bring to us and I must wait and see what I have to do but I promise you Kate, I do not expect you to gainsay your father but I will make sure you never suffer for the sins of others."

Angry at his words, Kate pulled her face from his hands and jerked herself to her feet.

"I should hope that York does not wage war on women and children, my liege," she said stiffly

"No, most assuredly York does not, however York does punish traitors by death and confiscation of all goods to the crown and that usually means that their families are condemned to a life of poverty and exile," he said dryly and the edge in his voice did not belie his irritation that she should challenge him so readily. "I would not see that happen to you."

"I am grateful for that consideration." Her tone was clipped, her voice wooden and he stood up suddenly, towering over her, her head only level with the silver button at the neck of his tunic. Catching her arm as she tried to turn away, he pulled her none too gently round to face him.

"I cannot promise peace nor can I promise leniency but I will not exact unnecessary punishment on those who have committed sins; I have no thirst for bloodshed unless it is absolutely necessary. Your father cannot keep me prisoner here forever and at some point there must be an end for I am no man's puppet and he knows that. It does just depend on how it ends..."

"What will happen to my father?" Her voice was trembling and he noted with some satisfaction that it did not occur to her that the outcome would be anything other than his freedom.

"I don't know Kate. As I said, much depends on how this all ends. There must be a punishment but as yet I don't know what. I have no proof of his treachery, I have only my enforced stay here at Middleham to hold him on but I do know that neither you nor your sisters will suffer for his sins." They stared at each other for what seemed like an age, neither able to look away. His finger traced the line of her cheekbone with a butterfly touch. "Oh, Kate!" His voice was hoarse with a hunger that sent tremors down her spine and she felt his fingers trembling against her cheek. "I would that we could have met again under better circumstances." Blue eyes drank her in thirstily, his mobile mouth hovering for a fraction over hers and she knew he was about to kiss her. For some reason she could not react. Her head told her to pull away, to get away from the turmoil he caused in her stomach, yet her body would not obey her and she was held in the thrall of his starving gaze. It was as if he could see right through her and she shivered, then his lips touched hers and she felt her own lips open like a flower to the sun, taking his tongue into her mouth. His arms pulled her close and she was held against the hardness of his body; she could feel his erection pressed against her stomach, rock hard with long denied female release and instinctively she wound her arms around his neck, entwining her fingers in his thick, tawny hair, and his breathing quickened to ragged harshness. She heard herself moan softly and then his answering groan and felt his hand on her breast, fingers seeking her nipple through the softness of her gown, his other hand in the small of her back pressing himself against her, pushing his hardness into her. She felt her loins flood with the sweet sensations she had felt that first night in Stephen's bed and her thighs were sticky with moisture. Stephen; the thought of him shattered her pleasure and brought her back to reality.

"Jesus!" Edward breathed. He slid his hand down her thigh, pulling at the wool of her over-gown, attempting to find a way in so that he could touch her bare skin.

"No," she whimpered, trying to pull back from his embrace.

"Oh Christ." He was lost in her, his need overcoming all his senses.

"No, Ned!" She started to struggle against him, but he held her tightly, his mouth seeking hers once more. She was pushing hard against his chest now and trying to pull out of his embrace, but he had twined his hand in her braid and was holding her by it as he kissed her. She tore her lips away from his, breathing heavily. "I cannot," she gasped. "No!" She pulled away from him again and this time he released her, but so abruptly she nearly fell. It was only when she regained her balance that she realised that he was no longer looking at her but gazing at the door behind her.

"Are you trying to rape our little cousin, brother?" Clarence's voice was maliciously soft, his words heavy with delighted venom. "That would not be a good way to repay my Lord Earl's hospitality." Kate whirled round horrified.

"No!" she breathed, "No, he would not do that..."

"So you were playing the whore then sweet cousin?" Still silkily soft, he was like a cat playing with a mouse,

"No, it was not like that...oh Jesu'!" She was sickeningly jolted by the sight of her husband standing just behind Frances and George, his eyes like glittering pieces of jet in his pale face. Hot colour flooded her skin and she turned to Edward in a mute desperate plea for help, but he was not looking at her, his eyes were fixed on his brother and her husband and his mouth turned up at the corner in a small sardonic smile. The enormity of the scene suddenly washed over her in waves of nausea. "Oh Jesu'!" she whispered again, her hand coming up to her mouth to stem the tide of sickness. Stephen walked toward her, his normal confident gait jerky and ungainly in his anger, his expression one she had never seen before on his face. Catching her wrist, he flung her none too gently toward the door.

"Get out!" he snarled, his voice hoarse with anger. She recovered her balance quickly and turned on him imploringly.

"Please, my Lord, 'tis not as you think!" It was a mistake, for he reacted more by blind instinct than knowledge in what he did, the force of the blow knocking her to the ground, her nose bursting into crimson flow. Gasping in shock she staggered to her feet, aware of movement around her and from the corner of her vision caught sight of Francis lunging forward but Edward was quicker, moving his large frame with surprising agility, placing himself between Francis and her shaking husband, one arm across Francis' chest.

"I said get out." Stephen's voice shook, the pain in his eyes visible, and she realised that it was not merely righteous wrath he felt. But she could not make her legs move.

"You have my leave to go, Lady Thevenot." Edward's voice cut quietly into the tension. Her misery was completed by his total lack of emotion, but she managed a jerky curtsey, unable to look at him, cut to the bone by his betrayal. He had not even attempted to defend her and then he had dismissed her as if the scene meant nothing to him at all. Blindly she left the chamber, oblivious to Clarence's amused smirk, or the fact that her husband moved to follow her. She ran as fast as she could, tears of humiliation and anger fringing her lashes. The anger was directed at herself, unable to believe that she had been such a fool and placed herself in such a position, compromising her virginity.

Now it seemed that she would pay the price for that stupidity; one look at Stephen's white angry face had told her that, and he had every right to be angry with her, for she had insulted him in front of every person present in the chamber and cast aspersions on her fidelity.

"Katherine!" Stephen Thevenot's icy voice behind her stopped her in her tracks, a cold prickle of fear creeping up her spine and into her neck. She turned, giving him the full effect of her battered face, but he did not flinch; instead he grabbed her arm and hauled her along the passage, shoving open a door and dragging her into a small store chamber. Roughly he pushed her against the wall, bruising her spine on the jutting stone, holding her there with the strength of one hand round her neck, blind-angry eyes looking into hers, a need to inflict hurt showing in every movement he made.

"My Lord," she whispered, cold sweat breaking out under her arms and sliding down her sides under her gown. "Please."

"Why?" he asked softly. "Why do you hate me so much?" He reached for a tendril of hair with his free hand and wound it round his finger. "All this time and you have never looked at me like you look at him; never smiled at me the way you smile at him. I have been kind to you Kate and yet you have humiliated me every way you can!"

"My Lord, please, it is not like that…"

"What is it like then?" His voice was still silky soft but his eyes were cold and hard. Whatever she said would cut no ice with him so she tilted her chin, met his gaze and said nothing, an act of defiance she was to regret. "You cannot tell me can you?" He yanked on her hair roughly. "You cannot tell me because you know that if I had not come upon you with him you would be his whore by now. Well lucky for you I came by when I did."

Deliberately he began to unlace his chausses, his eyes never leaving hers, and as she tried to struggle, his hand tightened on her throat so that she choked and coughed. "Because I saved you from that fate, and instead you can play whore to your lawful wedded husband." He pulled up her gown, and kicked her legs viciously apart with a booted foot, again scraping her back against the wall, and jamming his knee between her legs, maneuverer his body so he could push himself hard into her, three agonising thrusts before the barrier broke and he could enter her. She bit down on her bottom lip against a cry of pain, refusing to show him fear, keeping her eyes on his, anger shining as the tears rolled down her face. He held her hard against the wall, the force of his body's movement jarring her against the roughness of the stone.

"Whore," he said jerkily as he thrust into her. "Fucking bitch of a whore." He grabbed the bodice of her gown with one hand and wrenched it downward, tearing the fine material and exposing her right breast, his hand grasping it roughly, leaving bruising fingerprints in the soft skin around her nipple. "This was all I ever wanted and now it's soiled." He looked into her eyes, his own ice cold. "You tried to take away my manhood but you didn't succeed." He kneaded her breast viciously, and thrust hard into her, cracking her spine on the stone.

"No..."Her voice was a whisper against the fingers choking her throat.

"Shut your mouth, whore." He spat in her face. "Dirty, filthy whore." He closed his eyes, each hip movement causing jolts of pain in her back and buttocks and then after what seemed like an age, he tensed, growled and jerked against her, his hand tightening for an instant on her throat, his breathing raw and ragged. For a moment, all was still and then he pulled away from her, releasing her, fastening his chausses as he looked her up and down, contempt and disgust written across his face. "You will attend our chamber this night and every night hereafter and be a proper wife to me. You will let me take what is mine and you will never refuse me or you will suffer the consequences," he said coldly and then he turned and walked silently out of the chamber without a backward glance. Kate slid down the wall, wrapped her arms around her knees, her face pressed against them, sobs wracking her violated body.

***

Sometime later Isabel opened the chamber door and stepped inside.

"I was walking past and I heard noises, I wondered what it was," she said in a puzzled voice. "Mother of God what happened to you, Kate. Oh God, Kate, what has happened?" Isabel tipped Kate's head back and examined her closely. "Jesus, the state of you. Who the hell has done this to you?" Roughly she pulled the still sobbing girl into her arms and cradled her against her breast.

"Stephen." Kate's voice muffled against the fabric of her sister's gown.

"Stephen?"

"Yes."

"Oh dear, sweet mother Mary, I have to get papa!"

"No!" Kate pulled back. "I don't want papa to know."

"For God's sake Kate, you have to tell him."

"No!" Kate clutched at the folds of her sister's gown in panic. "No."

"Why on earth not?"

"He will be angry with me." Kate hiccupped and swallowed against the tide of her tears.

"Angry with you?" Isabel looked incredulous

"It's all my fault!" Kate burst into body-wracking sobs. "It's all my fault."

"No!" Isabel caught her sister's shoulders and looked into her face. "No, it is not. No one deserves to be…deserves this, whatever they have done."

"It was punishment for my sins," Kate answered wetly, still not sure if she was glad Isabel had come or not, but definitely glad she wasn't Anne.

"What sin could you have committed that would deserve something like this?"

Kate briefly and reluctantly explained what had happened in the solar, humiliated by her own stupidity once more, and realising as she spoke how very bad it sounded.

"Oh, Kate!" Isabel said again. "It was just a mistake, a moment of madness. It did not deserve this." Kate made to move away but Isabel grabbed her arm and pulled her reluctantly to her feet. She cried out at the pain in her back and felt the blood run down the inside of her leg.

"Come with me and let's at least get you out of this damned room." Isabel led her along the passage to her chamber and once inside, bolted the door and sat her on the coffer at the foot of her bed. "I cannot ask for water for a bath without bringing half the castle," she said ruefully. "So you will have to take off your clothes and we will clean you up as best we can." She sloshed all the water from a jug into a basin and carried it carefully to the coffer. "Come on." Kate slowly undressed, each movement causing pain in her sore muscles and bruised back.

When she was naked Isabel turned her full circle, her hand over her mouth in horror.

"Jesu'!" she whispered and Kate looked down at the bruises on her breast and the blood which caked the inside of her legs as Isabel said softly, "Your back is a mess, sweeting. The man is an animal." Together they washed her sore skin and cleaned her up so that Isabel could lend her a chamber robe and then Isabel gently bathed her face until all the blood was gone. "I'm going to take you to your chamber, Kate, and then I'm going to get you a sleeping draught; I will just tell everyone that you are not feeling well," Isabel said softly, touching her cheek briefly and even in her grief and pain Kate was touched by what her sister had done for her.

"Thank you, Bel, for helping me," she said, equally softly.

"That's alright, darling." Isabel gave a shaky laugh. "I know we do not always see eye-to-eye but I would never want to see you hurt, and never like this." She gave her a lightening hug. "Come on, let's get you to bed."

***

"Katherine." The door of her bedchamber opened and her father's head appeared around it. "Katherine, are you awake?"

"Yes, papa." Kate's voice was strained and tearful even to her own ears as she tried to sit up, wincing against the pain of her bruises. Richard Neville walked uncertainly into the room, his face a picture of uncomfortable concern, and sat down on the edge of the bed.

"I made Isabel tell me what happened," he said quietly, taking her hand in his and looking searchingly into her face. Tears welled up in Kate's eyes and splashed down her cheek.

"I asked her not to."

"I know, but I made her so don't blame her. I knew something had happened. You could cut the atmosphere in the solar with a knife; Isabel and George are not speaking because she blames him."

"It was not George's fault, papa, it was mine."

"No Katherine. It was not your fault. It was Ned's and Thevenot's and mine, but mostly mine for being stupid enough to encourage you to keep Ned company. I know he is capable of working his charms on even the most cynical of women so it should be no surprise to me that he would be able to charm an innocent and vulnerable girl." He lifted her hand and kissed it. "I have sent your husband away, Katherine, with my displeasure evident in the bruises on his body and I swear to you that I will personally make sure that he never touches you again." He stroked her hair back from her face. "I would never have thought him capable of doing this to you. If I had ever thought that, I would not have wed you to him, I swear."

"Oh, papa." She burst into tears and he gathered her into his arms, holding her tight against him, his head resting against the top of hers, tears in his own eyes as he let her break her heart against his shoulder.

"Kate, Kate, my little girl, my golden child, I am so sorry that I was not there to protect you," he whispered. "I love you so much and I would do anything to protect you from this hurt, anything at all. I am sorry that I left you alone with Ned. I was a fool to think that he would not use his charm on such a beautiful girl as you. I am so sorry I have failed you, my darling." He stroked her hair gently, as her sobbing ceased, rocking her in his arms like she was a child again. Shifting his weight, he moved further onto the bed so that he could rest his back against a pillow and still hold her. "I remember when you came to me, such a sweet engaging little thing you were and we all loved you, even Anthony Woodville." He snorted a quick mirthless laugh. "And as you have grown up you have taken every challenge that anyone has thrown at you and come out triumphant. You have won over your cousins, your sisters and even your stepmother to your side. I am so proud of you Kate, so very proud of the woman that you have become." He kissed the top of her head, and hugged her closer. "Don't let this bastard beat you. Take the challenge, my darling, as I know you can and be brave and strong."

"He said I was a dirty whore," she whispered brokenly. "I am not a whore, papa."

"Of course you are not darling." Warwick kissed the top of her head again, outrage in his heart and voice. "You are a beautiful young woman who caught the attention of the King. It was a kiss, Katherine, nothing more than that."

"But it was wrong!" She started to cry again.

"Yes, it was wrong but wrong of Ned to take advantage of you. He is an experienced man of twenty-eight and he should know better."

He sighed heavily, his heart aching against the wrong done to this, his favourite daughter. "I should not have deprived him; it is as much my fault as his."

"Papa?"

"Yes, sweetheart?"

"Did I deserve it?"

"Oh dear God, no child!" His involuntary response was emphatic. "You did nothing wrong. George told me you were fighting him off when he came into the room and even if you had not been you would not have deserved that."

"Why did he do it?" She lifted her head from his chest and looked at him through blackened puffy eyes. Richard Neville considered the question carefully, aware that how he answered it was important.

"I think for possession and for power," he said after a moment. "Possession because a man hates to think that another man has had what he considers to be his, and power so that he can show he is still a man when he feels he has been unmanned. He felt that you had cuckolded him, made him look a fool and he needed to show you and himself that he was still a man. He needed to make you afraid enough never to refuse him what he wanted from you."

"Do all men feel like that if they think their woman has been...?" She struggled for the word but could find none to fit. Her father nodded.

"To a certain extent I expect probably yes although I can't speak first hand. But I can say that I do not know many honourable men who would take a woman by force, not in the way that he did to you."

"He was so angry that I don't believe he could actually see me." She shuddered and leaned back into his arms and he pulled her close again, giving her a warm feeling of being well-loved and secure.

"Anger can get a man like that sometimes," he said ruefully. "I may not have been blind with anger but I certainly made Thevenot feel your pain this evening. And Ned, although that was with words not fists!"

"Ned did not even defend my honour." Her voice was small and forlorn.

"That's because he is a fool and an arrogant fool at that!" He leaned his cheek back against her hair and sighed. "Kings never seem to apologise, sweetheart. They always assume the right of it and are never wrong!"

"I thought he was my friend."

"Aye, love, I know." He hugged her. "But I have learned that friends come and go, are never reliable and sometimes let you down. Do not raise your expectations too high and then you will never be disappointed."

"Is that what you do, papa. Just rely on yourself?" She leaned back and looked at him again.

"Yes, that and the love of my family. To know you are loved is a special thing." He smiled at her, his brilliant smile an echo of her own, his green eyes soft. "I am lucky that I have beautiful daughters who love me and a good wife who sees to my household and to my comfort and makes it easy for me to go about my business with confidence." He kissed her forehead. "Always know that you are loved Kate, by your sisters and even your stepmother, but most of all you are loved by me. Just remember that you are the child of my heart."

"Oh, papa." She hugged him close to her, her arms tight around him, clinging to the comfort of his presence. He hugged her back.

"Come, sweetheart, you should get some rest." He moved off the bed and nestled her back into the covers, leaning down and kissing her cheek. "You hold my heart Kate," he whispered.

"I love you too, papa." She looked up at him for a moment. "I won't let him beat me," she said softly.

"Good girl." He touched her bright head briefly and turned away to hide the tears that sprang to his eyes at her courage.

"Goodnight, papa."

"Goodnight, sweetheart."

Anjou, France
November 1469

The river was a swirling black mass of foaming water, cascading over the weir and racing along its bed, swollen with the rainfall of the last two weeks. Edmund Beaufort stood on the bank staring sightlessly into its rushing depths, his fur-lined cloak pulled high around his neck, his head uncovered, his boots seeping moisture through the grass under his feet. Uncaring of the icy wind, his dark hair blew back in the breeze, away from the high cheekbones and brooding gold eyes, his lips drawn into a thin white line of anger. The news coming fast and often from England had made him realise how futile this life was, how impossible the situation and how dire. The unrest and the capture of Edward of York by Warwick would have been the ideal opportunity for them to capitalise on and yet there was no support, no means of taking advantage. Marguerite could not bring herself to let him have his way; had called him untried and untested and laughed at his impassioned plea to go to England and rally supporters. Every time she opened her mouth she made another assault on his confidence and every time she called him to account for his father's failure and his brother's folly, she killed a little piece of the respect he had for her. He felt tears of frustration fill his eyes and let them come; he was alone and away from prying eyes, he had no fear that any would see his weakness. Exhausted and worn down by the inactivity and futility of having no ambitions or goals to aim for, no reason for being, no domain to oversee he felt like he was nothing; just an appendage of an exiled Queen who fulfilled some small purpose in tutoring the Lancastrian Prince. Yet somehow even that seemed futile as he could see no future for his prince, except one of poverty and exile, tied to his mother's apron strings.

He picked up a pebble and skimmed it across the water, watching it bounce over the surface before dropping beneath the darkness. He often found himself looking back over the last five years and wondering how they had come to this. He had arrived at Marguerite's court a still idealistic young man of twenty-five, who had lost his father and his brother to the Lancastrian cause, but who believed more fervently in it than either of them had and who was prepared to work tirelessly to keep their campaign going and get the support of powerful men like Charles of Burgundy and Louis of France. And so he had travelled extensively between their courts ensuring that the Queen's profile was kept high, and that he raised money for her, but he could get no substantial offers of support from either, just murmurings of the time needing to be right for a major campaign, or that they should wait to see Edward display weakness and then Burgundy had allied itself with York and he had found himself at odds with his patron for the first time. In the meantime, Marguerite had turned into a bitter woman who railed against the events that had led her to exile. She had castigated him over his brother's failed campaign which had resulted in his death and she had taunted him with lack of judgment for not being by his side in Hexham. The esteem in which he had always held her, tarnished by the night she had tried to seduce him, had been slowly eroded by her bitter behaviour since, and she had wilfully drawn and drained every ounce of emotion from him, tormenting him and abusing him with the sharpness of her tongue and with her bitter sarcasm. Slowly she had reeled him in and then wrung him dry so that he felt like an exhausted, emotional husk, using him as a vent for her anger and bitterness, using her son and the love he bore him as emotional blackmail to make him do as she wanted. He had loved her once with the idealistic, courtly love of a knight who hankered after the old days of the tourneys and the troubadours, and now he alternated between pity and hate as she controlled him. He had no life outside of her and Edward; no Dukedom except the title which he had never officially been given; no marriage; no children of his own; no future that he could see other than this relentless coldness.

"Sweet Mother of God!" he said softly, his voice lost against the sound of the river. "What have I done that is so bad that I am punished like this?" He ran his hand across his face, the tired gesture of a jaded man, his stubble scraping his palm where he had not shaved this morning, and sighed. This was not like him to feel so defeated; he had to snap out of it.

"My Lord! My Lord!" He swung round at the faint sound behind him and saw his squire Gethin Rhys racing along the bank toward him, horse's mane and tail flying in the wind. "My Lord, you must come quickly!" The young man pulled his mount to a showy halt in front him, panting with his exertion.

"What is it, Gethin, that brings you here at such speed?"

"The Prince, my Lord, he has had a fall from his horse. Madame is frantic. You must come at once."

"Is it bad?" His heart flipped a somersault at the thought of the boy being badly injured, and he moved quickly for his mount.

"He has not opened his eyes, my Lord, and they could not wake him."

"Fuck!" Beau swore crudely which would once have shocked Gethin but after a twelvemonth in his service he was used to the Duke's mercurial temperament and colourful language. He waited as his Lord grabbed his stallion's reins and vaulted elegantly into the saddle and then followed him at breakneck speed towards the castle.

"What happened?" Beau shouted as the lad drew alongside him.

"The horse was spooked by something, reared up and fell backwards. The Prince threw himself clear but hit the ground head first. Lord Jack at first thought he was dead, but his breathing is firm and the heart pulse in his neck is firm. It is just he has not woken."

"And the horse?"

"He is fine, my Lord. A little shaken but he will be all right. It is Madame, though, my Lord, she is frantic and blaming you for buying the horse in the first place."

"Is she indeed?" Beau's mouth set in a grim line They rode on in silence until some half an hour later they were clattering into the stable yard, Beau vaulting off his mount before it had come to a stop and throwing the reins to a groom. He ran at full speed into the hall and took the stairs two at a time up to the great chamber; Marguerite met him at the door, her face white and her eyes huge.

"He is awake," she said shakily, and swayed on her feet. He reached out to steady her but she slapped his hand away. "No thanks to you," she hissed.

"Please, Madame." He ignored the jibe, his eyes imploring her. "Can I see him?" She stepped aside.

The boy was sitting up against a pile of soft white pillows, his face ashen and his eyes blue smudged, but he smiled when Beau approached the bedside.

"Sorry," he said softly, flicking his dark glance towards the door and his mother. Beau pulled a wry face.

"It's alright, lad," he said. "How's your head?"

"I'm alright, my Lord. Ebony is not injured, is he?"

"No, I'm told he is fine; a little shaken but fine. What happened?"

"He was spooked by something, just came up and lost his footing. I did as you said and flung myself sideways but must have hit my head. I remember nothing else until waking up and seeing ma mère crying at my bedside."

"Let me see." He reached behind the boy and looked at the back of his head, shifting his hair over the cut and touching the skin around it. "It looks clean enough. The doctor has stitched it I see."

"Yes." The boy bit his lip ruefully. "It hurt!"

"I bet!" Beau grinned. "There is not much skin on the head, so it hurts more."

The boy smiled wanly and stifled a yawn.

"I'm sorry," he said again.

"It's alright, lad." Beau touched the top of the dark head briefly with his palm. "You get some rest and you will feel better tomorrow." Impulsively he dropped a kiss on Edward's forehead, something he had not done since he had entered his teens and the boy smiled shyly as their eyes met in their mutual love and understanding. "Call me if you need me."

"I will." The boy snuggled under the covers, his eyelids already dropping over his dark eyes. Long lashes hovered over his pale cheeks for a second before settling. Beau felt a surge of tenderness for this beautiful boy who, if gossip was true, could be his brother, but felt much more like his own son. He turned away and looked up to see Marguerite waiting for him by the door. Suppressing a sigh he moved forward to join her. Once in the anteroom he took a deep breath and said very quietly.

"It was an accident which could have befallen any boy, Madame."

"But he is not any boy, is he, bien-aimée?" He refused to acknowledge the use of what had once been a term of endearment but was now always used in sarcasm or anger.

"No, Madame."

"He is my son." She stared at him, her expression unreadable. "And you would have been responsible had anything serious befallen him. He will not ride that horse again."

"Madame," he kept his voice low and calm, "you cannot wrap him in soft wool. He will not thank you for it."

"And of course you know my son better than I do." Her brows arched and her voice took on an all too familiar edge. He steadied himself with a deep breath.

"No Madame, of course not." And herein lay the crux of the matter; her jealousy stemmed from his relationship with Edward; a relationship she had fostered and encouraged when he had first joined them, knowing that Edward needed a male parental figure, a man he could look up to. But it had been a more successful pairing than she could have hoped for and somehow she had begun to feel excluded. He understood, but there was nothing he could do or say which would convince her that he had not set out to steal her son's affection. "But we must not delay him on his journey to manhood."

"Must is NOT a word you use to your Queen." She stared at him still, with that unnerving black stare. "Do not presume that my son loves you so much that he would condone your insolence."

"It was not my intention to be insolent, Madame." He bowed his head, hoping that for once he could head the scene off by being completely contrite and acquiescent. "And I would never presume. I am sorry."

"But you are presumptuous, Somerset. Presumptuous in that you think you can trade on the love I bore your father to gain my patronage; presumptuous in that you think that you are some kind of hero in waiting who can win back our fortune and most presumptuous in that you think you can take the affections of my son and make your fortune by them!" Her voice rose gradually until she was finally shouting. He stiffened, met her gaze and lifted his chin defiantly.

"I need no one to assist me in making my fortune, Madame."

"Really?" She laughed unpleasantly. "And doing right well for yourself, aren't you?" She gestured around her. "You use a title that belonged to your dead brother but to which you have no right; you have no money except that which is given to you in charity; and you spend your days aimlessly flitting from court to court trying to drum up support for a cause that is dead and buried!"

"I have given up my life for you, Madame. If I had gone to Edward of York on my knees he would have pardoned me, as he did my brother and I would be Duke of Somerset in truth. But I chose to come here to you." He strode forward and caught her shoulders. "It was not the boy who drew me here but you Madame. I wanted to serve you; to help you; to do something to win back the throne for my King. I wanted to serve Lancaster and you were the symbol and rallying point of Lancaster." Marguerite shook off his touch, her eyes glittering and murderous with rage.

"Do not touch me!" she spat. "Do not presume that we have such a special relationship, my Lord, that you may lay a hand on me. You are nothing to me!" Beau flinched and stepped back.

"Madame, please?" he said hoarsely. "For the sake of my father's memory, at least."

"And why should that mean something to me?" She met his gaze defiantly.

"Because you loved my father, can you not at least tolerate his son?" His voice was soft, almost pleading.

"No, I cannot. You are right, I did love your father, but not in the disgusting way the gossips thought. He was my friend and he helped me when my husband, the King, was ill; he safeguarded my son's inheritance and paid for it with his life." She backed away from him, putting distance between them. Beau stood looking at her for some moments.

"All I want is to follow in his footsteps; to fight for the honour of my King, my Queen and my Prince," he said quietly.

"You are nothing like your father." Her lip curled. "He was a talented man. I cannot even imagine how you would hope to fill his boots."

"I would never imagine that I could be a great man like my father, but I believe he taught me enough to ensure that I am at least an able and competent soldier, strategist and politician."

"Perhaps you are, Somerset, perhaps you are." She sounded weary suddenly. "But there is nothing to fight for any more. My son has no inheritance to safeguard and we have no kingdom to return to. We, that is I, do not need you and you are only tolerated because my son loves you and to send you away would cause him pain, but do not ever presume that you hold my favour as your father did, my Lord." The look she gave him was contemptuous. "Or that you could ever fill his position as my most trusted advisor or my friend." Beau swallowed and pulled back from saying that which he might regret. Thinking of the sleeping boy in the bed in the room next door, he took a deep breath, and pushing his pride away he dropped to his knees and looked up at her imploringly. "Please, Madame, I beg you, let us stop this battle between us. We should not be fighting like this. For the sake of our Prince, can we not show him a united front and go forward in a semblance of unity?" For a moment she softened, looking down at his hard, handsome face, her hand reaching out for his cheek and stroking it softly.

"You look so much like him, you know, so much like your father as a young man. You were such a beautiful boy, Edmund, and showed such promise and he was proud of you. Hal was always his favourite but he knew you were the most talented soldier and your mother doted on you. We had such plans for you, he and I, such great plans and to watch you waste your life like this would have broken his heart. You should have stayed in England, gone cap in hand to York and bided your time; it would have served our cause better. It is such a shame that you have never fulfilled your potential as we all would have wished." She turned away and walked toward the door, leaving him on his knees. "I accept your truce, my Lord. You are right, Edward will not benefit if we are at each other's throats and I do not want my son to be unhappy. But do not think that I have forgotten, my Lord, your arrogance and insolence all those years ago, or that I ever will."

Chapter Five

Peterborough, February 1470

"Well?" Richard of Gloucester gazed at his brother's broad back impatiently. "What does it say?" Edward turned his head slightly, his brow almost connecting with the beam, which ran across the low ceiling of their lodging, and favoured the boy with a wry half smile.

"It says that George is on his way to join his father-in-law and that together they wish to raise a force that will come to my aid over Lord Welles' rebellion." He turned back to the letter in his hand and scanned it rapidly. "It would seem that he feels my need to be greater than Isobel's, and instead of travelling to be with her he has gone back to Cousin Warwick and won him over to stamping out the lawlessness that has 'beset this realm.' How kind of him to suddenly care so much!"

"And do you believe those really are his intentions?"

"What choice do I have lad?" Edward queried, carrying on without waiting for a response, "I can't tell him that I don't trust him, nor can I tell him to rot in hell in case he speaks the truth. For then how would I salvage his twisted pride, eh?" Richard raised straight dark eyebrows anxiously.

"Do you think he's twisted, then?" he asked quietly. The older man shrugged, evading the sinister portent of the question.

"I think he believes everything he says when he says it," he replied with a short mirthless laugh, "I just wish to Christ that I did."

"So what do we do now then, Ned?" Richard looked at his brother's thoughtfully-frowning face, framed greyly by the window behind him, and wished, not for the first time, that he could glean something of what he thought from his expression.

"We carry on as we planned, my lad." Edward grinned easily. "I shall give George and dear cousin Warwick permission to raise their force and tell them that I am duly grateful for their aid. And if that is what it actually is then all is well and good; if it is not then we are still well prepared to take on whatever is thrown our way."

"And if Warwick and George intend to assist the rebels, what then, Ned?" The question was matter of factly put but no less a test to his brother's nerve for that outcome. Richard had been badly shaken to see the man he had revered all his young life as a hero give way under pressure of the violent turn in the disaffection of his cousin and now he needed to be certain that Edward had indeed regained his old fighting spirit.

"Then I shall be well prepared, Dickon, have no fear of that." It was the answer that he sought, given with the conviction that he needed and their eyes met and held for a moment. Richard smiled, lighting up his pale face. Edward turned quickly back to his letter, but Richard caught a flicker of emotion in his eyes, a flash of something he did not understand and he was struck suddenly that for all this close companionship with Edward, he knew nothing of what went on behind those ice blue eyes, nothing of what he thought or felt; he didn't even know if Ned trusted him. He shivered slightly, and stepped toward the fire, ostensibly to warm himself but in reality, needing the movement to rid his head of the dark, crowding memories.

As Richard thought back to before his brother's capture by Warwick, the memory of Edward's face on that fateful day in Newark was one which would haunt him for the rest of his days. The sudden pallor and the look of sheer blind panic which had flooded it at the messenger's news had shaken him to the very marrow of his bones and he had silently thanked Christ that he was the only one present in the chamber at that moment, for had anyone else seen him, their faith in this man with his vice-like hold on their loyalty, would have been destroyed. He had managed to get the messenger out of the chamber before he noticed the blank despair on the face of his sovereign, or his odd jerky movements as he groped blindly for a chair. Richard had tried to get him to take some wine but he had seemed unable to hear or comprehend what was being said to him, and just sat still, staring sightlessly ahead of him, his lips moving rapidly as though in prayer, and it was not until the boy had caught his arm and cried helplessly,

"For Christ's sake, Ned, what shall we do?" that he seemed to come back from the dark place he had gone. But still he had refused to do anything except send them all away, not wanting them to be captured with him. Will Hastings and Anthony Woodville had mistaken his numbness for his usual easy calm in alarming situations, but neither could have guessed the real truth behind the façade, neither knew that this confident man had lost his iron nerve and was about to throw himself solely on the mercy of his cousin and rely on the support of his friends to spring him from the trap.

Richard had waited patiently for more than two months, hoping that soon the message would come, sure that Warwick could not hold him forever, but he worried that with every day that passed the strain of captivity would tell on one such as Ned, and he had been anxious that it would not take further toll on his mind. But once they had gone to him in York he had been relieved to find him almost back to his old self, save from a nerve which jumped along his jaw line at odd moments and a slight tremor in his hands. But in his manner and his spirit he had regained all his arrogance and although he spoke little of his time at Middleham Richard had gleaned that this was largely due to the companionship of his own faithful friend Francis who, with his devotion, had kept the king's flagging spirits alive and given him hope through the isolated weeks of imprisonment. He didn't much like to think of Middleham; it reminded him too much of happy memories and tugged at his heart as he thought of Anne. He had long ago stopped broaching the subject of a possible marriage with Anne, knowing that if he pushed Edward too hard he would give him a final refusal and forbid him to speak of it again. He sometimes wondered what she thought of his defection from her father's side but knew in his heart of hearts that she would never blame him for siding with his brother, just as he would never blame her for her loyalty to her family, but he still felt guilty as though he had abandoned her to her own fate without a thought for her. He knew that she had understood it was not like that, that his love for his brother and his strong sense of moral justice bound his actions completely but he still felt that he had let her down, still thought perhaps if he tried harder, Ned would have consented to their betrothal.

"Ned?" he said suddenly, his voice loud in the silent stillness of the chamber.

"Mmmmm?" his brother did not look up, his tone absent with concentration.

"If you have to attaint Warwick what will happen to his family?"

"What do you mean?" Edward looked interested then, his eyes meeting Richard's with wry speculation.

"What will become of...Anne." Richard dropped his eyes self-consciously and began to studiously examine the back of his hands.

"Ah." Edward's voice was soft in reply. "Perhaps a spell in the tower and few hours on the rack will wring a confession from her." The boy snapped up his head and met his brother's eyes once more, catching the humour behind the cool shade of blue.

"Ned!" he cried, flushing scarlet with embarrassment at his brother's laughter. "I'm serious!"

"And in a way so am I, Dickon. Don't pin your hopes on that girl, for though it is not my intention to make her suffer for her father's sins, neither is it my wish that you should have her. As the daughter of a suspected rebel she is not fit to wed with royalty." He sighed sadly and shook his head. "I had hoped you had grown out of this folly, Dickon. You must know as things stand there is no way you will have Warwick's daughter."

"I'm not talking of marriage, Ned." Richard's tone was defensive. "I just need some guarantee of her safety. We have ever been close and I could not bear to think she may be harshly treated."

"You should know better than that, little brother. Anne will not be held to account for the things that Warwick may have done, but nor can I say that she will be welcomed with open arms at court. I will do my best for her when and if the time does come. You never know, my Lord of Warwick may redeem himself with aid against Welles. Does that set your mind at ease?" Edward gave him a coaxing smile.

"Yes."

"And I can deduct from that that you no longer harbour the foolish notion of wedded bliss with the girl?" Richard coloured and looked away, leaving his brother to snort with an exasperated oath. "Jesus, lad, you would try the patience of a saint with this odd devotion of yours, and a saint is something I am not. There are scores of women you could have with my blessing but you must go for the one you cannot have. I don't care to deprive you of anything, Dickon, but this time I must. I am sorry but the answer will always be no and you must cast your eyes elsewhere."

"I see." The boy looked stubborn suddenly. "'Tis alright for you to wed where you will but not I!" He had not meant to speak so frankly but Anne was one subject that tore beneath his cool armour of self-control. Edward's eyes froze instantly.

"If you wanted her so much then why did you not follow your brother's example and tuck yourself under Richard Neville's wing?"

"That's not fair, Ned, and you know it!" Richard was stung by the unaccustomed barb of Edward's tone, and struck once again by the fear that his brother did not trust him. "I wish to Christ I had never raised the subject. Let us just forget it, shall we?" Edward seemed to visibly shake himself and gave the boy a grin

"I'm sorry Dickon. I should not have said that." They looked at each other for a moment and then Richard took a deep breath.

"There is just one other thing I would know, Ned." Edward looked wary immediately

"What is that?"

"What of Kate. What will happen to her?" The guarded look did not leave Edward's face, but he looked uncomfortable for a second and a suspicion came to Richard, which he could not quite shake off.

"She is close to Anne and will remain with her I suppose. Her husband is no friend to me, that much I do know."

"But you will not hold that against her?" Richard found himself staring at his brother closely, trying to read his expression.

"Of course not! We shall just have to wait and see. As with George and the lovely Isabel, a great deal depends on what happens in the next few weeks." He moved from the window and sat down at a small table "Now enough of this fruitless chatter, lad. I must answer this letter. So if you would not mind sending my secretary in on your way out, and then if you would instruct someone to fetch Will Hastings and tell him that I would see him in my chamber after supper. You too, Dickon, I want to go over the planned route for tomorrow."

"Of course." Richard moved toward the door and turned back hesitantly, one hand on the door latch. "Think you that this will all turn out in our favour, Ned?" he asked, a little need for reassurance in his voice. Edward smiled indulgently.

"Yes I do," he said with his natural optimism. "It cannot fail to. After all I have those I trust doing their best for me, haven't I?" It was the comfort the boy needed, an avowal of trust from the man he loved so much. He grinned.

"I'll send in your secretary," he said, lifting the latch and swinging open the door of the small chamber, slipping out into the larger smoky atmosphere of the inn.

Empingham, Lincolnshire
March 1470

The armies of Sir Robert Welles' rebels and the loyal soldiers of York were drawn up on horn field, facing each other, almost symmetrical in their formation, yet enough distance apart for it to take one man a full five minutes at full speed on horseback to reach the other side. In the space between them, two men confronted each other beneath the white flag of truce, their mounts shying away from each other as though smelling the odour of hatred which separated them. After a few more moments of fierce argument, the stallions swung round and returned full tilt to their respective factions. The talks had failed and action must be taken.

Richard shifted uneasily in his saddle and glanced at this brother, and catching the sideline look Edward smiled tightly, before moving down the line of his men towards the speeding form of Will Hastings. The two men conferred quietly for a few seconds and then Edward swung back, looking for the first time at the man who knelt, divested of his armour, his head resting on a makeshift block, his hands tied behind his back.

"Execute him," he said flatly. There was a stunned murmur from the men, unused to such a display of cold brutality from the sovereign, silenced quickly by the movement of the axeman. Richard closed his eyes, his mouth moving in silent prayer, unable to watch the execution. The last few days had been an enlightening experience for Richard, though not altogether a welcome one. He had always believed that warfare was a glamorous business, which made heroes of ordinary men and discountenanced the cowards, yet in reality it was a sordid affair. Every man who fought a battle was afraid and there was no such thing as a truly brave and fearless man, for he had seen by Edward's pale face and the shadows in his blue eyes that he was just as fearful as any man, and he had fought in battles since he was less than eighteen. He was beset by the same demons as all, the spectre of death and defeat, unsure of which was the worst evil, the loss of life or the loss of his kingdom.

On their arrival at Huntingdon, Edward had sent for the recently pardoned Lord Welles to be questioned, and the man had given full confession of his activities against the crown. Edward had then sent a message to Welles' son, requiring him to submit himself to the Royal Authority or be responsible for his father's execution. Robert Welles had ignored the summons, choosing instead to bring his rapidly increasing army to face the King rather than surrender. Richard could little believe the man's audacity but realised that Warwick's success in capturing Edward had tarnished his brother's military reputation. Few understood the full circumstances of Edward's capture, the shock of Warwick's betrayal, which had temporarily stunned his brother into inaction. Now Edward was back to his best, and Richard knew that Welles had little chance of winning this one. He opened his eyes slowly, avoiding looking at the bloodstained grass, or the twitching form of Lord Welles being bundled into an old sack. He had learned long ago that few men actually chose to watch an execution, and the only man he had known who was able to look unmoved on the violent death of others was his cousin Warwick but then there was little that moved Richard Neville save his own quest for power.

Edward had moved back to his side, his visor up, blue eyes surveying his young brother critically. He looked magnificent; unashamedly the King in his polished armour and surcoat emblazoned with the Rose en Soleil. There would be few who did not know who he was yet he cared little for that, knowing he was a match for the finest soldier when it came to battle, and it was strong motivation for his army to be able to see and recognise their King wielding his sword in the thick of the fighting with the rest of them.

"All right, Dickon?" he asked softly. The boy nodded, feeling suddenly very young and inexperienced for his seventeen years. Seventeen; the same age as their brother Edmund when he had been killed. Richard saw his brother swallow and knew that he too remembered. "No heroics, eh lad?" he said, still in the same soft voice. "If I need you, I will send for you. Otherwise you wait here. Understand?" Richard nodded again. He did not need to be told twice for it was suddenly not so glamorous to be caught up in the thick of the fighting, and he was afraid; afraid to die before he had lived, afraid of defeat.

"May God be with you, Ned," he whispered, and the older man smiled

"And you, little brother." He swung his mount away and galloped back to the forefront of his army and suddenly he raised a hand and the royal artillery sprang to life, making Richard jump even though he had expected it. He knew his brother's plan by heart. The element of surprise was in the firing of the cannon, for Robert Welles would have no choice but to counterattack at once, yet he had not the artillery to do it and therefore would have to sacrifice his horsemen, hoping that they would reach their opponents and engage them in man-to-man warfare before they were picked off by the huge gun. What he had little expected was the cry that went up on the other side, an unmistakable cry even in the noise of the battle going on around them; he heard it plainly in the air, 'Warwick! Clarence.' He wondered if Edward had heard it too, wondered if it was a ruse by the rebels to make the King believe that his brother and cousin had finally declared against him. He guessed he must have, for if it had carried all the way up to him then it must be quite loud in the midst of the field.

He watched the battle as though a spectator at a tourney, half wishing that he and his men were in it and yet relieved they were not. It was an easy thing to raise a force to aid the King but it was another matter to lead it into battle, and he sensed that they were as relieved as he that they did not have to fight. for as yet their commander was an untried youngster, and though their loyalty was not in question, his judgement may as yet be lacking.

Edward was obvious to all in the centre, his flailing sword crashing about him at twice the speed of others, and though his armour fast became dulled with splatters of blood and mud, his physique was such that there was little doubting who he was, head and shoulders above the rest, bearing down on the enemy like a demon riding the devil's own charger, destroying all in his path with consummate ease. The superiority of his artillery and the ingenuity of his attack had left his enemy in tatters and it seemed that before the hour was up he had what was left of Welles' army in retreat and that the field was littered with the bodies of the dead and the dying. Edward's army pursued the fleeing rebels some distance before accepting their victory and returning to the scene of the battle.

Richard felt numb, unable to believe that it was all over so quickly, that victory had been so easy. He felt a surge of pride in his brother, and the fact that he fought for the house of York, the house that his father had so struggled to set upon the throne, which he saw as his right. He guessed that if Richard Plantagenet, Duke of York, could see how his son had fulfilled his dream then indeed he must be very proud, because for all his faults, and there were many, Edward was a fine example of Warrior Kingship. He moved his mount down the bank of the hill, cantering toward the blood-spattered stallion of his brother. Edward was moving back toward his camp, intent on learning the news of casualties and the extent of the victory. By the time Richard reached him he had already swung himself from his labouring mount and was lifting the tent flap to go inside.

"Ah, Dickon, "he said slightly wearily but managing an encouraging grin. "A neat victory, I think, don't you?" Richard grinned back.

"Indeed, my liege, especially from my vantage point." It was a wry admission that he was glad he was not in the thick of it, and one that Edward appreciated.

"I'll wager you had the best view, little brother," he laughed, standing slightly bent as his squire reached up to unbuckle his armour. "Though the fun was to be had on the field. It is a mighty odd thing fighting men who wear your own brother's arms, and on more than one occasion I wondered if I was attacking my own men!" He pulled off his helm revealing damp tawny hair plastered to his head, and a slightly fatigued, mud-splashed face. He eased his neck and puffed out his cheeks in an expression of thankfulness.

"Do you think George and Warwick were involved in this, Ned?"

Edward shrugged in an attempt at nonchalance but Richard saw that he was perplexed.

"I don't know, Dickon. Welles didn't mention them in his confession and I would have wagered that to save himself he would have told us all he knew and fabricated some if need be. Most men will talk if they think they are likely to live longer for it. So it could all be a plan on Welles' behalf to make me think that George is involved; perhaps he imagined it might make a difference to the way I would fight. Perhaps he even thought that I might give in gracefully rather than fight my own brother." He smiled bitterly and Richard knew that it still rankled with him that he had caved in as he had done at Warwick's open animosity.

"I hope you're right, Ned," he said softly. "For I really didn't ever think that they would conspire to open rebellion." Edward eased off his gambeson, assisting his squire as much as he could, giving the young lad an affectionate smile as he stood, finally free of the cumbersome steel and thick jerkin, the cool March air drying the sweat which trickled in tiny rivulets down his broad chest.

"I don't know what to believe any more, Dickon," he said as he stretched his back luxuriously "In fact I have given up making judgements on people. I shall just wait for proof that they are implicated and if none surfaces then I'll be forced to believe that they are innocent of this conspiracy." He shivered suddenly and accepted the shirt that the boy held out for him, slipping it over his head and cinching it tightly at his waist with a wide leather belt. Richard watched with real envy, wishing not for the first time that he had been blessed with a physique like Edward's. There was no fat on his big frame, just muscle and power and an aura of masculinity, which commanded the respect of both men and women. Richard himself had not inherited the appetites of his brothers as far as the women were concerned, though he enjoyed female company as much as any, he preferred his relationships to be linked with some sort of personal involvement, but he wished all the same that he had a body women might admire from afar, and that men might be drawn to him as a leader. "Are you going to spend the night in that armour?" Edward's voice was soft and amused, breaking the spell Richard had woven around his thoughts.

"What?" The boy looked startled and then grinned. "No of course not, I was just anxious to talk to you and I couldn't be bothered to take it off first." He glanced about him and caught sight of a soldier at the tent flap. "Go to my tent and fetch Tom Parr, tell him to bring me my clothes." The man nodded and sketched a bow.

"Your Grace." His squire arrived less than five minutes later, carrying an armful of his clothes, slightly overawed to be in the presence of the King, yet not entirely unused to his royal connections. It never ceased to fill Richard's friends and retainers with pride when they heard him refer to the King as Ned in his familiar fashion, and when they heard them talking together in the way that all close kin bantered and argued, it seemed strange, for they revered the King as some far off figure; yet Richard knew him as brother first and King second.

Edward threw himself into a chair, pouring a goblet of wine and drinking from it deeply, before offering the jug to Richard, and when the boy nodded he poured him a cup from it.

"Is there any news from the field yet, Gethin...any word of casualties?" The young squire shook his head.

"No, your Grace, though it does seem that they lost many more than we did." Edward nodded.

"I did think that as I rode back here. I could see only a few wearing my arms and many wearing even more familiar arms but who didn't fight for me." He smiled, glancing up at the tent opening. "Ah Will, my friend, you survived then?" It was a gentle rebuke that he would have expected to see his friend before now, and one that would normally have provoked a quick retort and laughter, but Will Hastings looked uncharacteristically serious.

"I'm sorry, Ned, I was taken up with one of my men. I think you should come, there is something you should see." The older man's eyes were nervous and oddly humourless. He looked over at Richard, by now almost dressed. "And you too, Dickon, I think that you will wish to see it." The two brothers exchanged glances and Edward grimaced and shrugged.

"What is it, Will? You look like a man who has won at tables and forgot to place his wager," he said softly.

"Aye, well..." Will looked at him. "If you come with me it may be that you will feel the same way." Realising that his friend was indeed deadly serious and that his demeanour was not the set of an elaborately planned jest, Edward stood up, and jerking his head to Richard, followed Hastings from the tent. Richard hastily finished lacing his tunic, not having the benefit of fighting to make him warm, and feeling the need for more than a mere linen shirt. By the time he reached his brother he saw that Edward had a box in his hand, and he had extracted a document and was reading it. His shoulders stiffened visibly and then sagged, and listlessly he handed the paper to Richard. It was a letter addressed to Lord Welles, signed by George and bearing the Clarence seal.

"Jesu Ned, I am sorry," he said inadequately, reaching out to tentatively lay his hand on his brother's broad forearm. His brother did not respond and turned instead to Will and said quietly,

"Where did you find these?" Will gestured to the body of a man wearing the Warwick livery, lying face down in the mud. There was something vaguely familiar about the dark hair or the set of his helmless head. Edward walked forward, putting his finely leathered boot under the man's chest and heaving him onto his back. Richard saw him start and gaze at the dead man, his face flickering with undefined emotions.

"What is it, Ned?" he asked softly "or more to the point who is it?" Edward looked up with a strange smile, almost soft in its sadness, and moving away from the body began to walk back to his tent.

"It seems our brother and cousin have indeed betrayed us," he said in a level easy voice, surprising Richard with the matter of fact acceptance.

"That was easy to see from the letters, Ned." Will Hastings found himself almost running to keep up with Edward's long strides. "But who was the fellow with the casket?"

Edward stopped and looked down at him, a taut smile on his lips.

"He is a loyal retainer of my Lord of Warwick, an ardent supporter and an enemy of mine."

"You do know him then?"

"Aye, I know him. His name is Stephen Thevenot and he is wed, or I should say was wed, to my cousin Warwick's daughter Katherine." He turned to Richard, his eyes once more veiled against probing. "It would seem that we now do have our proof. Both Warwick and our brother Clarence are traitors."

Angers, France
July 1470

Jack Beaufort flicked a glance across the hall at his brother, standing on the dais behind the ornate chairs of his Queen and his Prince, his hands behind his back and his face totally impassive, immaculate as always in a plain, dark blue tunic and chausses, long leather riding boots and a sword at his hip. Never a slave to the latest fashion, he always managed to look understatedly elegant. Jack smiled to himself. His brother had coffers of dark coloured tunics and chausses, never wore bright colours, never wore shoes, always favouring the long riding boot over fashionable footwear. He wore the same jewellery every day; his Ducal signet ring on the third finger of his right hand, an ornate band on his right thumb and a gold and ruby ring on the little finger of his left hand. Around his neck, he wore a thin leather lace with their mother's betrothal ring and wedding band, and on his wrist a wide leather strap with an enamel lozenge bearing the Somerset coat of arms. His tunics were always the same style; high collar, fitted waist and stopping at mid-thigh, a white linen shirt visible at the collar and at the cuffs, his chausses always matched and his boots were always black; no slashes of colour, no braid, embroidery or jewels. Even Jack had to admit he was a good looking man; more than a hand-span above average height, shoulders broad and hips narrow but it was his face that drew the admiring looks from both men and women. A strong face, with high cheekbones, an arched, defined nose and those arresting honey-gold eyes fringed by long, thick, black lashes; an austere, hard face, softened only when the full mouth broke into a smile, which these days, sadly was not often. Jack sighed softly, and leaned back against the wall, making himself as inconspicuous as possible as he waited for the proceedings to begin and this historic moment to spark into life. Poor Beau, he thought wistfully, his life's dream was about to come true, though not quite in the way he had expected it to but in circumstances that could only be described as unreal. When the news had come that Richard Neville had landed in France with his family, they had all been mildly surprised that he should have managed to let the position that he had held with Edward of York slip away so badly that he had had to flee for his life. But then to be summoned, as the Queen, Prince and his brother had been, to Louis' court and told that Louis would support them in getting back the throne if they allied themselves with Warwick, had been quite unbelievable. For once Marguerite had turned in anguish to his brother and the Earl of Pembroke, who had both swallowed their pride and urged her to come to terms with the man who had always been hers and their implacable enemy, knowing that they needed him to get Louis' support, and also agreeing that they could deal with him at a later date if necessary once England was won back to Lancaster. So Marguerite had agreed to the terms Louis offered and Prince Edward had been betrothed by proxy to Richard Neville's younger daughter Anne; and today they were all to meet for the first time. Warwick was expected any minute to make his public oath of fealty to Marguerite and Edward, and then his family would arrive shortly after.

"My Lord." A voice spoke softly near him. Jack glanced left and saw Beau's squire, Gethin. He gave a quick smile in greeting and moved up a bit so the lad could stand next to him.

"What do you think of your Lord, Gethin?" he murmured near the boy's ear and Gethin's normally serious face split in a huge grin.

"Magnificent, my Lord," he whispered. "Makes all the others look somehow gaudy and overdressed." Jack laughed. He liked Gethin; had known his family for many years and knew that they boy had been brought up a staunch Lancastrian as were most of the Welsh. After all he would have to be, as not many fathers would want their sons to squire to an exiled lord. He also knew that Gethin adored his brother and would follow him to the world's end if necessary, so his opinion was probably biased, but he had to say that as another biased onlooker, he agreed completely with the boy's assessment. There was a flurry of movement suddenly as the crowds parted and the door at the end of the hall swung open. Jack used his extra height to look over the heads of the people in front of him and saw Richard Neville, Earl of Warwick, enter the hall, his bare head suitably bowed as he slowly made his obeisance with every few strides he took. Jack was struck by how little he had changed in the ten years since he had last seen him; he was still slim, had very little grey in his hair from what he could see and still wore his clothes, not only at the height of fashion, but in rich fabrics and encrusted with jewels. He was an impressive sight. He looked over at his brother, still impassive, his eyes looking straight ahead and not at the supplicating Warwick, the only sign of tension in the stiffness of his shoulders. Jack stifled a grin as an image of the peacock versus the hawk came into his head and the hawk was looking decidedly predatory. The hall was very quiet as all waited for Warwick to reach Marguerite on the dais and you could have heard a pin fall as he dropped to his knees, head bowed and made the statement of loyalty and fidelity to the Queen and then to the Prince. Marguerite watched him, not taking her eyes from his bowed head, not giving anything away in her pale oval face and Edward, taking his cue from his mother and the Duke of Somerset, waited, not moving at her side. After a full five minutes of him kneeling there, Marguerite rose and held out her hand for him to rise. They looked at each other for a moment and then exchanged a stilted kiss of peace.

"My Lord Warwick," cried Marguerite in ringing tones. "I welcome you to Angers."

"Your Grace, it is an honour to be here." Warwick's voice was warm and rich and carried no less than Marguerite's for all its depth and softness.

"My Lord Warwick." Edward stepped forward and kissed his future father-in-law on each cheek, and Warwick smiled a warm smile which so took the boy aback that he responded with a quick flash of a grin.

"Your Grace."

His brother had not moved and Jack wondered if he was thinking of Hal, who had been put to death by this man on the orders of Edward of York. He knew that Beau was not sentimental and that he would not jeopardise their new status by making Warwick an enemy but it had to be hard to now make of him a friend. They surveyed each other quietly for a moment, each uncertain of the other and then Beau's face broke into a wry grin and he came forward, his hand outstretched to clasp Richard Neville's in a soldier's handshake.

"Warwick," was all he said.

"Somerset." Warwick responded likewise.

All the onlookers in the hall sighed collectively as Warwick and Beau shook hands and everyone began to talk at once. Jack caught Gethin's arm and they made their way through the crowd toward the dais, Jack hoping that his brother would call him up to meet Warwick. He was interested to see this man close to, he looked such an unlikely man to have such a reputation as a soldier; a politician yes, but not a soldier. They got to the front of the dais just as Marguerite was asking Warwick about his family and Jack was struck by the unreality of such normality of conversation between these people who had been such enemies until less than a sennight ago. He looked up at Beau and was pleased to see him beckon him up onto the raised platform and turn to Warwick to introduce him.

"My brother Jack, Warwick. You remember him no doubt."

"Aye, I remember." Warwick grinned and shook his hand. "You were a hellion, lad, when you were younger if I remember rightly?"

"Still is!" Beau dead-panned and they all laughed. Close to Jack realised that Richard Neville looked older, fine lines around his eyes and a slight salting of grey at the temple giving away his age, but his green eyes were still as startling and nothing about him seemed faded or jaded.

"Good to meet you, my Lord." Jack shook his hand warmly, deciding that if they had to be allies, they may as well be friends. That seemed to be the tack his brother was taking anyway, only Madame looked as if she had had to suck a lemon. Edward appeared somewhat in awe and Jack guessed that this was the first time he remembered meeting a real life soldiering hero. Marguerite moved to Beau's side and smiled up at him and then at her son, giving a good impression of complete unity.

"I was just asking my Lord Warwick if his family was joining us?" she said softly. "I'm sure Edward would like to meet his future bride." She included Warwick in her blanket smile, even though she could not bring herself to meet his eyes.

"Yes, Madame. They should be here any minute; a page has gone to fetch them." Warwick inclined his head deferentially. "I hope, your Grace, that you will like my daughter. She is very young and needs a good, kind young man to take care of her."

"Is she pretty, my Lord?" Edward asked shyly.

"I think so, but then I am a biased father." Warwick smiled fondly. "Ah, here they are." They all turned and looked toward the front of the hall where a flurry of activity and the removing of cloaks and hoods was taking place and again the people in the room made way for the party to walk forward. Jack saw that there were four women in the group, the older one must be the countess and the very young one, fourteen or less, must be his prince's betrothed but the other two seemed of an age and both so stunningly pretty that he was for a moment at a loss.

"Fuck me!" murmured a soft voice at his side and Jack bit back a snort of laughter as he recognised his brother's predatory tone. He glanced up but Beau's gaze was riveted and for a moment he thought he heard him breathe the name 'Katherine' under his breath. Warwick had moved off the dais to take his countess's hand, a pretty woman, hard to age but probably late thirties if not forty, fair skin and china blue eyes. Anne Beauchamp curtseyed low, first to Marguerite and then Prince Edward, and Marguerite smiled her first genuine smile of welcome.

"Anne, my dear," she said, leaning down and raising the woman who had once been one of her ladies, to her feet. "It is good to see you after all this time."

"Your Grace." They hugged and exchanged kisses. "These are my daughters, Isabel, the Duchess of Clarence and Anne, the Prince's betrothed." The two girls curtseyed also and Marguerite inclined her head, studying the younger girl carefully and Jack was minded of a market trader weighing up a cow, so keen was she to look over every aspect of her.

"Edward," she said and the girls curtseyed before him. He raised both at the same time and smiled at each, making easy conversation with them and Jack felt a surge of pride that he was so at ease in his role. Anne was pretty but painfully shy and kept looking up at him through her lashes but Isabel was already laughing and at ease and he saw that close up she was indeed a beautiful girl, but there was a fragile brittleness about her gaiety and Jack thought he remembered vaguely that she had recently lost a child. He was aware that his brother had not moved, was still staring, not at Isabel but at the other girl who had not come up onto the dais but was now talking animatedly to the Earl who was smiling and trying to coax her forward.

"Beau?" he said softly.

"I am lost," his brother said, equally softly, his eyes still not leaving the girl.

"She has to be the most beautiful living creature I have ever seen in my life!" Jack looked at the girl again and conceded she was indeed lovely, though hers was an earthy loveliness, all russet and honey tones, not the fashionable cool fair beauty of Isabel.

"Who is she?"

"I don't know, but I am going to find out."

"How?"

"I'm going to introduce myself." He made as if to move forward.

"Beau!" Jack hissed, but was too late as his brother was slapped none too gently on the arm by Marguerite.

"Somerset, you have not greeted our guests."

"Madame, forgive me, I was..."

"I know exactly what you are about, my Lord." Marguerite looked at him sharply. "And it can stop now. We will retire to the solar while dinner is laid and you will escort the Countess."

"Yes, Madame." He manfully hid his disappointment and moved forward to smile at the Countess, his practiced charm suddenly coming to the fore as he introduced himself, offered her his arm and complimented her on the colour of her gown. The Prince had taken Anne's arm and Jack offered his to Isabel who captured his heart effortlessly with one smile. They did not hear Warwick speak quietly to Marguerite, nor see him introduce his other reluctant daughter to the Queen, who remembered Veronique de Roet and the scandal the love affair had caused at the time.

***

"Jesu', the Duke of Somerset looks like he wants to eat you for dessert, darling!" Kate started at the sound of Isabel's voice hissing in her ear. She turned and frowned at her sister.

"What?"

"Somerset. He can't take his eyes off you. Has been like that since you walked into the hall and all through dinner and now he is leaning on the wall over there just staring at you." Isabel grinned. "And damn me if he is not bloody gorgeous!"

"Isabel, for goodness sake, you see suitors around every corner!" Kate whispered, feigning exasperation, and then smiled sheepishly. "Which one is he?"

"The one who is at this moment pretending to talk to papa but really willing you to turn around so that he can catch your eye."

"No. Which of the men is he?" Kate didn't want to turn around and make it obvious they were talking about him. "Is he the younger one with the brown hair who escorted you into supper or is he the one who looks like a hawk?"

"The hawk."

"Looking at me?" Kate blushed at the thought, her face suffusing with a delicate rose pink but she could not resist looking across to where Beau leaned by the fireplace, ostensibly in conversation with a group of men who included the Prince and her father, but constantly glancing across at her. She met his gaze briefly, and felt her stomach flip as the corners of his mouth lifted in an intimate smile.

"See!" Isabel was giggling.

"Oh Lord!" Kate's cheeks flamed scarlet and she started laughing. "I have heard much about him but I didn't expect him to be quite so handsome!"

"I know. He is a dish isn't he?"

"Yes, although what type of dish I am not sure. More savoury than sweet, I think."

"Yes, something with beef perhaps." Isabel giggled.

"Yes, he looks meaty." Kate grinned. "Although lean meat."

"He's quite old."

"Not that old, just mature."

"And beef is supposed to be better if allowed to mature for a while." Isabel winked and giggled again.

"Bel!" Kate feigned shock and joined her laughter.

"Well I definitely wouldn't say no to a little flirtation with him, you lucky girl."

"I think he is a seasoned campaigner in the game of flirtation. I am not sure I could pit my wit against him. Anyway Bel, don't be wicked. What would George say if he could hear you now?" George had been diplomatically left at Louis' court supposedly on a special mission. Isabel's face softened for a moment at the mention of her absent husband.

"He would say exactly what you have just said and then tell me off in that indulgent way he has adopted recently." She laughed, but Kate saw the sadness in her eyes and knew that she missed him. George had redeemed himself in Kate's eyes during that awful crossing to Calais on the ship, when Isabel had gone into labour and given birth to a still-born baby. It had been a truly terrible time for all of them but George had risen to the occasion and been a tower of strength in the crisis. He had directed the crew with an authority of a much more mature man, and when the Countess had despaired of Isabel's life he had come into the cramped birthing chamber, where no man was allowed to enter and had braced her as she gave birth to their dead baby, giving her his strength and coaxing her through the heart-breaking process with fortitude and love. He had been at her side as she had recovered, reading to her, holding her as she cried and crying with her at the loss of their child. Kate had seen a new George emerge from the trials that they had faced, a less arrogant, softer George who loved his wife to distraction and who would have done anything to take her pain himself, just to spare her. In adversity, the family had pulled together as always and had emerged stronger and closer for it. Kate and George had buried their animosity and become better friends, and Anne had grown stronger and more assertive as she had had to fend for herself more, taking her betrothal with surprising calmness, not once referring to her lost Richard, and putting her shoulders back and looking forward to the new life that they were to have under Lancaster. Kate felt sorry for Anne, as it was harder for her since she really loved Richard and had always believed they would marry, her allegiance to York being based on that one thought and now she had to change her views and marry a man she had not met until today. Kate looked over to where Anne was talking with her mother and the Queen and wondered if she would appeal to Edward. She was a pretty little thing, but she looked much younger than fourteen even if she did have quite a womanly figure, and was so very shy. She caught her eye and smiled encouragingly and Anne smiled back.

"How do you think it will work out between Anne and her Prince, Bel?" She asked softly. Isabel shook her head and pursed her lips in a moue.

"I don't know. Papa wants her bedded, but I think she's too young."

"Me too." Kate grimaced at her sister. "Although I can't say I know much about a proper bedding." Isabel touched her arm briefly in sympathy.

"What a family of trials and tribulations we are," she said sadly, "Whatever could go wrong has done so for us, hasn't it?"

"Then we should be in for some luck I say." Kate grinned and lifted her chin.

"I'd say you were!" Isabel glanced towards Somerset and both girls laughed, giggling so much they had to hold onto each other for support, not because it was so funny but for the need to release pent up emotion. Isabel sobered first, conscious of her mother's disapproving glare, and then dissolved again.

"Stop it, Bel," Kate wheezed, breathlessly. "My stomach hurts." They took deep breaths and sobered gradually, avoiding eye contact. "We should join your Lady mother I suppose." Kate said once they had calmed themselves and there appeared to be no chance of another outbreak of giggling.

"I dare you to go over there." Isabel smiled wickedly and flicked her head towards the group of men.

"Bel, don't."

"Go on, I dare you. I dare you to take that flagon of wine over there and offer everyone a drink, Somerset first and then before you leave you have to wink at him without anyone else seeing you." Isabel's voice held a threat of more laughter.

"Bel, please..." Kate jigged from one leg to the other, fighting to resist the challenge. "How will you know if I have done it. I'll have my back to you if I wink at him."

"I'll be able to see by his face. Even men like him can be surprised." Isabel cocked her head to one side. "I'll give you my silver link girdle if you do it." Kate pretended to consider for a moment but they both knew what the outcome would be.

"Alright that seals it. I've always liked that girdle!" She grinned, straightened her shoulders, reached for the flagon and took a deep breath. "Shameless hussy, here I come!" Isabel snorted a laugh and moved quietly and quickly to her mother's side to watch the proceedings from safety. Kate walked determinedly over to the group of men by the fireplace and after curtseying low, offered Beau her most dazzling smile, proffered the flagon and said quietly,

"Would you like some more wine, my Lord?" Beau's pupils contracted visibly at her smile and his gaze met hers in sharp interest, an answering smile turning his mouth up at the corners, his beautiful eyes caressing her face so intimately that she blushed. Close to he was even more handsome than she had first thought, and looked younger. He held out his cup and she poured, surprised at how steady her hand was.

"Thank you." His voice was deep and husky, as if he had somehow worn it out and she felt gooseflesh on her arms as he spoke. Her heart pounding, she turned to the rest of the group, offering each wine from the flagon, aware that her father was looking at her, an amused gleam in his eyes, and aware also that Beau was still watching her.

"Papa?" she said finally and poured for him.

"Thank you, Katherine," her father said softly, catching her eye with a knowing look and a slightly wry raise of his eyebrows. Smiling demurely she turned away, and meeting Beau's avid gaze, winked at him, taking him so completely by surprise that he gagged on his swallow of wine and choked, coughing and spluttering as she walked triumphantly back across the room to face the icy disapproval of her step-mother and Isabel's admiration.

***

"Well Beau, that's the first time I have seen you left breathless and speechless by a mere slip of a girl!" John Courtenay, Earl of Devon, grinned at Warwick as Jasper Tudor battered the still spluttering Somerset ostentatiously on the back. Beau gave Courtenay a fierce look, somewhat spoiled by the tears brimming over his black lashes and onto his cheeks as he jerked away from the heavy hands of the laughing Pembroke.

"Enough, for God's sake!" He growled hoarsely and Jasper Tudor laughed all the more.

"Ah look he's crying," Courtenay jibed again and Beau glowered at him.

"Bollocks," he snarled and Courtenay laughed while Jasper Tudor frowned.

"You will get used to our friend Somerset's midden mouth, my Lord Warwick," he said, noting Richard Neville's amused expression. "He can be as common as a foot soldier."

"When you fight in the guts of the army, my friend..." Beau flicked a cool, if watery, smile at Pembroke.

"Well it might be alright in Burgundy's company but you can refine your language at least for our guest and the ladies!" Pembroke sighed and rolled his eyes at Richard Neville who was still watching the by-play with silent amusement.

"I will give you credit, Warwick, you breed beauty." Beau glanced guardedly at the older man. "Especially that one." His eyes drifted again to where the girl was standing, head bowed, next to the Countess of Warwick, his aroused interest a palpable thing in their midst. "She is quite exquisite."

"Lock her up and quickly." Courtenay murmured from the corner of his mouth and Beau grinned reluctantly, his bright gold eyes conveying an 'I will get you later' message as he glared at his companion, and Warwick laughed.

"That is my daughter Katherine, my natural daughter, half sister to Anne and Isabel." He gave Beau a smug smile. "She and Isabel turn heads wherever they go."

"Well she's certainly turned mine." Beau murmured softly, and Warwick, the least imaginative of men, was put in the mind of a hawk hungrily eyeing its prey.

"She is just recently widowed and comes with a good dowry."

"But bastard born." Beau took the bait.

"I didn't think that mattered in your family." Warwick deadpanned. "Anyway, beggars can't be choosers." Pembroke and Devon looked at each other warily, never sure which way the mercurial Somerset would take teasing such as this. Beau looked at Warwick levelly for a moment and then smiled, a face-changing smile which softened its hard contours and made him suddenly youthful.

"Fuck off, Richard," he said good naturedly, dispensing with formality and Warwick barked a loud, spontaneous laugh, clapping the younger man on the shoulder.

"It was worth a try."

"Keep her in my vision for long enough and you never know, I may take the bait." Beau murmured, looking over at the girl again, his eyes drawn like magnets. "She really is quite exquisite."

"You are repeating yourself, Somerset," Pembroke said sourly, irritated by Beau's elevation of Warwick from uncertain ally to tentative friend. "And lovely though your daughters are, Warwick, they were not what I envisaged spending our evening discussing."

"What would you like us to discuss, my Lord?" Warwick's expression was amused and Pembroke arched black brows in irritation.

"Well I was rather thinking that we would be spending this evening listening to you convince us that we would benefit from your allegiance to our cause and the resources that you might bring us," Pembroke said brusquely. Warwick's smile did not waver as he looked at each of the men in the group.

"And there was I thinking that you might need to convince me that you have enough of a cause to warrant my allegiance." The atmosphere chilled suddenly and tension hung heavy as Pembroke stared at him in outrage and then Beau laughed, a sharp sound in the surrounding quiet.

"I'm sure we can convince you, Richard," he said softly. "After all, beggars can't be choosers."

Chapter Six

Anjou, France, August 1470

The stone floor of the chapel was cold as Kate knelt before the jewelled statue of the Virgin. She had been trying to pray for at least half an hour without much success, her head racing with thoughts which she could not dispel, and in the end she had given in to silent contemplation of the recent events which had turned her and her family's lives upside down. Her relief at the death of her husband had swamped her with guilt, and then wracked her with dreams that he came to her in the night, white and cold in death, often waking her in a cold sweat expecting him to be beside her. Then there had been the devastating race to France, Isabel in labour and losing the baby and no time for her to take comfort or to mourn his loss before they were here in Angers and expected to take their places in Queen Marguerite's court, with that brittle and volatile Lady watching them with a jaundiced eye and uncertain temper. Prince Edward, always good humoured and cheerful, could usually lighten his mother's mood but the dark and brooding Duke of Somerset seemed to irritate her with just his presence, although she always tried hard in front of her son not to show it. Kate had found herself wondering what it was that made Marguerite so bitter towards her most loyal servant, especially after her father had told her how much Somerset had given up to give her his loyalty. Since that first night when she had winked at him, she had not seen much of him, although he had been spending a considerable amount of time with her father, but when she had seen him she had been conscious that his eyes followed her and, even though they had never really spoken, she found herself being so drawn to him that she now looked for him whenever she went for dinner, or if she had to find her father. Then only last night as she was walking from the hall behind Anne to go to their chamber she had looked up to see him leaning on the wall by the door as they left. He had bowed and wished Anne good night and then as Kate had reached him he had kissed his right hand as if he would blow her a kiss, but instead had placed his palm over his heart and given her such a caressing smile that she had blushed scarlet and raced from the hall like a child, almost bumping in to Anne's back in her desire to get out. She laughed ruefully now as she thought of it; what a ninny this experienced and worldly man must have thought her, yet she knew that even though she liked the idea of flirting with Edmund Beaufort she also feared him, feared any man who might want to touch her. Kneeling up she sighed and, deciding to admit defeat on her devotions, crossed herself and said a quick perfunctory prayer as she stood.

"Oh!" exclaimed a pleasantly husky voice behind her. "Forgive me, I did not mean to intrude." Kate whirled, caught by surprise, and looked straight into the warm, golden gaze of the man she had just been thinking about.

"Your Grace." She swept a deep curtsey, her knees still stiff from kneeling on the stone. "You startled me!" Her heart was pounding in her chest so hard that she thought he must be able to see it and her mouth felt suddenly dry as he stood by the door, handsome in his charcoal grey tunic unfastened to the waist in a concession to the August heat, his shirt immaculately white underneath. In his dark predatory presence, the chapel all at once seemed a very small space and she made a move towards the door, but he stepped inside and shut it, leaning against it as he regarded her with a smile.

"Don't go," he said softly. She moved back involuntarily and her fear must have shown on her face for his registered an immediate expression of dismay.

"Dear God!" he said very quietly. "What have they said about me?" Now it was her turn to be dismayed.

"Oh no, my Lord!" she exclaimed, "No one has said anything about you. It is not you. I have a fear of my own. I..." she faltered then shrugged and tailed off helplessly, not sure what to say without blurting out the truth.

"But you are afraid of me?" His voice was flat and expressionless but his eyes were soft.

No...yes..." she faltered again and then took a deep breath to steady her still hammering heart. "I have not much experience and I may not be worldly but I do know what you are, my Lord."

"And what am I?" He looked nonplussed.

"You are a man who...likes...women and who can be very persuasive." She knew she sounded as if she was parroting something she had been told and she smiled suddenly at the absurdity of the situation. "There is less chance for me to escape from you in here, after all," she said ruefully and he looked surprised for a moment at her sudden laughing candour and then his shoulders relaxed and he moved away from the door, pulling it open by the latch, gesturing for her to walk through.

"Perhaps then you would walk outside with me for a while?" He arched a brow but she hesitated.

"I should get back, really."

"Should you?" His full mouth dropped at the corners giving him such a look of a thwarted child that she almost laughed.

"My Lady stepmother keeps me on a short leash, my Lord; I only escaped her because I wanted to go to the chapel." She smiled again, enjoying the impact it had on him. "So, faced with the decision to walk with you and endure her wrath later, or be a good girl and go back to my embroidery now and be in her good books. You must admit, my Lord, that the path is a clear one."

"I see." His expression didn't lift but he stepped back to let her through.

"But I have never been one to take the easy route." She laughed as her words registered and his expression lifted instantly, his face breaking into a broad and beautiful smile.

"I am flattered that you would face that for me." He gestured again for her to precede him through the door and then fell into step beside her, offering her his arm as they walked along the path down the side of the chapel. "I can imagine that the Countess can be formidable."

"I would not be too flattered, my Lord." Her response was pert, as she slipped her hand into the crook of his arm, subconsciously registering the hardness of his muscular forearm through the soft, light wool of his tunic. "It would have been churlish to refuse you..." She grinned suddenly. "...

anyway if I was always worried about getting into trouble with my Lady stepmother, I would never leave my room!" She pulled a rueful face. "She is not the easiest person to please; at least not if you are me."

"Ah." He flicked a glance at her and smiled. "Is it not the lot of stepmothers to be difficult to please?"

"She has my best interests at heart, my Lord. "She felt compelled to defend the woman they discussed.

"I am sure." He chuckled engagingly, his expression belying the words and she shook her head with a rueful laugh.

"As I have got older I have come to understand that it cannot be easy to find yourself bringing up your husband's bastard child."

"No, I suppose not."

"Especially one that is born well after you were wed to that husband." She shook her head again. "If you think of it like that then she has been good to me."

"I know something of your story." Beau smiled, his eyes lighting at a memory. "Well my brother Hal was the one involved at the time, not me. I was too young. You see my brother had a fancy for your mother, in fact thought she was the loveliest girl he had ever seen and wanted to woo her; he was eighteen so only two or maybe three years older than her but it was your father she was most taken with, much to Hal's disgust especially as your father was only a few years younger than I am now."

"As old as that?" She looked up at him through her lashes, her face straight. He flashed her a glance.

"I am not that old!"

"That's what papa says," she teased, her face still straight and suddenly realising that she was enjoying herself. He grinned.

"Anyway, we were not talking of me but of your father who has at least ten years, if not more, on me. Your father's love for your mother caused some scandal at the time because the Countess was very unhappy about it and left him and went back to her castle at Warwick. It was a good six months before your father went back to her, so I can imagine that when you came to live with them she was not best pleased!"

"I didn't know that; it must have been awful for her." Her voice was slightly wistful. "Did you know my mother, my Lord?"

"No, not then, although Hal told me she was very beautiful as a girl."

"Not then?" Kate looked at him sharply, taking in what he had said. "But you have met her since?"

"Yes, she has been one of the Queen's ladies on and off over the years. Did you not know that?"

"No. I did not." She was not sure how she felt about the information he had just given her; in fact, she wasn't quite sure what she would do if she suddenly bumped into her mother. "She is not here now though?"

"I don't think so. I haven't seen her for some weeks although I'm not always here." He stopped and looked down at her. "Have I said the wrong thing?"

"No not at all." She smiled up at him, suddenly conscious of his height; although he was not quite as tall or as powerfully built as Ned, he was imposing enough. "It is good to be forewarned. You see I haven't seen my mother since I was seven years old and have not heard from her either so it would be quite a shock to see her now." She started to walk and once again he fell into step beside her.

"I'm sorry, I didn't know."

"Oh no, don't be sorry, how would you know?" She shook her head. "I'm sure a man like you doesn't involve himself in the intricate tangles of a life like mine."

"Perhaps not but I am thinking that I might like to." His voice was soft and throbbed with so much warmth that she blushed prettily, again flashing him a look through her lashes, flushing deeper at the expression in the eyes regarding her steadily. "Katherine, I have a confession to make. I didn't accidentally come across you in the chapel; I knew you were there and disturbed you on purpose. I have been waiting for a chance to talk with you since that first time I saw you in the hall."

"Have you?" Her cheeks were a delicate shade of rose and she stared at the path self-consciously.

"You took my breath away...quite literally if I remember rightly."

"My Lord." She met his gaze, her smile belying the hammering of her heart.

"Your reputation as a...a..." She searched for the right word. "...courtier precedes you even into my small world and I am not so simple that I will be taken in by your flattery." She lifted her chin in such an appealing mixture of coquetry and defiance that he smiled, but the hungry expression in his eyes didn't change.

"Do you know the story of Katherine Swynford?" he asked, changing the subject suddenly, taking her off guard

"Why yes, my Lord!" Her eyes lit up. "It is one of my favourite stories of history. She married John of Ghent after being his mistress for many years and bearing him four children. She is my father's great grandmother… and your's too of course!" An expression of enlightenment crossed her face. "That would make us cousins of a sort, my Lord."

"Yes it does; just as we are all linked, the Yorks, the Nevilles and the Beauforts, by the Lady Katherine Swynford. My family is very proud of our ancestry as we are the direct descendants of the first Beaufort son, so the story is much told. But far more importantly than that, did you know that Katherine Swynford had red hair?"

"Did she, my Lord?"

"Yes. She was supposed to be a very beautiful red-haired girl who captured the Duke's heart when his wife, Blanche of Lancaster, died and she cared for his children." He stopped again and looked down at her intently. "My grandmother told my mother about her; she had met her, you see, when she married my grandfather and even in her forties Katherine was a very beautiful woman. I imagine that as a young woman she looked very much as you do now."

"Me?" Kate was taken aback but he nodded.

"Yes, you." He smiled at her disbelieving expression. "'Beautiful red hair and so very fair to look upon,' my grandmother said, and that sounds very much like you, to me." He caught her hand and brought it to his lips, his mouth soft and warm on her knuckle. "Ever since my mother told me that story, when I was but ten years old, I have had a partiality for redheads…" He shook his head and let go of her hand, conscious of how young she was and not wanting to intimidate her with his intensity.

"I always thought blondes were fashionable at court," she said, taking back her hand with a smile, the imprint of his kiss still warm on her skin.

"Fashionable perhaps, but not to my taste." His smile was like a caress and her spine tingled as she flushed once more.

"And if I was a brunette would you have a pretty story for that too, my Lord?" she laughed up at him but he shook his head, genuinely offended.

"Contrary to what you may have been told of me I am not that crass, Katherine!"

"I am but teasing, my Lord!" She giggled and he relaxed with a rueful smile.

"It is just that when I saw you in the hall that first time, it was as if you were my mother's Katherine brought to life." He laughed. "You probably think I'm completely mad..." He shrugged and she smiled shyly, stepping back from him, her heart once again hammering in her chest, only this time it was a sort of terrified excitement that coursed through her veins and not crippling fear.

"I should go, my Lord," she said softly. "My stepmother..."

"Now I've scared you off, haven't I?" He shook his head. "It was not my intention. I really just wanted to tell you how very fair you are."

"No, my Lord, you have not scared me and I am flattered by your compliments. I very much enjoyed our walk and our talk, my Lord."

"Did you?" He smiled. "You're not just humouring me?"

"Now you are just fishing for compliments." She laughed, the ground feeling firmer under her feet, "But no, I am not just humouring you. And I wouldn't go if I really didn't have to get back."

"But you will walk with me again sometime?"

"Perhaps." She dropped a curtsey, hiding her smile. "My Lord."

"My Lady." He inclined his head but as she walked away she heard him call her name, his voice caressing it in a way that sent shivers up her spine. She stopped and looked back over her shoulder as he kissed the fingers of his right hand and placed them over his heart and this time she didn't blush but gave him a sidelong flirtatious smile and then, laughing, gathered up her skirts and ran across the gardens back to the hall.

***

In an upstairs chamber, Richard Neville watched his daughter racing across the grass, his expression enigmatic. As a father, he was alarmed by Somerset's interest in his daughter, an interest that he had seen from the minute they had arrived. Yet the politician could see that this could be used to their advantage. There was no doubt that Katherine was a beautiful girl but Somerset's interest was more than just being taken in by beauty, the attraction for him was obviously very strong and Richard Neville knew that he could use that to his benefit, but as a father it worried him that a man as worldly and predatory as Edmund Beaufort should have designs on his best loved child. He didn't want to warn him off but he needed to let him know that he was aware of it and that he expected Somerset to behave himself. Kate had not yet recovered from her ordeal with Stephen Thevenot, the last thing she needed was to face it again with Somerset. He sighed and moved away from the window; when the opportunity arose he would deal with it, but right now he had more the pressing matters of a campaign to attend to.

Anjou, France
August 1470

Richard Neville looked up from the table where he was working and raised his eyebrows at the young page who had disturbed him.

"What is it?" he asked curtly.

"Forgive me, my Lord, but there is a lady who wishes to speak with you?"

"A lady?" The boy nodded.

"A lady from the Queen's household, my Lord."

"Did she state her business?" He had hoped that once he finished the letter he was writing he would be able to retire for the night, for he was weary to the bone and he well knew that he needed all the sleep he could muster, for at forty-three he was no longer in the prime condition needed for heading such an important campaign.

"No, my Lord, just that she wished to speak with you urgently."

"Then you had best send her to me, lad," he sighed tiredly, stretching cramped fingers from the quill. The boy bowed and swiftly left the chamber, whilst Warwick looked down at the letter, scanning its contents rapidly, hoping that it said all he wanted of it, for he would have not time to finish it after this interruption, unless he chose to work all through the night. The journey to France and the alliance with his old enemy of Lancaster had taken more out of him than he cared to admit, even to himself, and he had not foreseen how wearying it would be attempting to convince his sceptical new allies that he intended to work assiduously for their cause. He had no conscience about opposing his cousin, though he was sometimes a little regretful to lose such a companionable friendship, but he had little sentiments where friendships were concerned. He still admired Ned as he had always done, but it was not the man he was opposed to; it was Ned the King he hated and to him that was enough to justify such cynical and self-seeking action.

The about-face of his loyalties had brought him more than he anticipated, and he was more than just pleased with the negotiations for Anne's marriage to prince Edward, and Louis' promise to see the couple publicly bedded, for it was imperative to his survival that the union should be consummated or their fortunes would be little less precarious than at present. He had thought little of Anne's feelings, dismissing her tears at the news with the brusque observation that women were emotionally turbulent, and telling her bluntly that she should reconcile herself swiftly to her fate as her weeping and wailing would do naught to halt it. As a father he was distressed to have to inflict such pain on her but he saw it to be for her own good, and anyway she reminded him a little too much of his wife when she was weeping and he found himself becoming less fond of her. He had been vaguely aware of Isabel's chagrin that Anne was to be the one who would be Queen of England when she had been convinced that that particular honour had been reserved for her, and he had begun to feel slightly uneasy. He knew that George would quickly see the futileness of his position and that Isabel, under no illusions about her father and blessed with his own unsentimentally, would not think twice about encouraging her gullible husband to see the slight inflicted on him by his father-in-law's action, even if it meant arranging herself against her own father to do so. But he relied on Edward's anger toward his brother to prevent him from returning to the Yorkist fold; he had after all been there to witness Edward's words when he confronted George at York before he left to return to Westminster; the only way that Clarence would be returning to court would be over Ned's dead body, his cousin had so publicly stated. Richard Neville smiled ironically. Have a care, cousin, he thought silently or that may be exactly as it will be.

He reached across the table to pour himself a cup of wine, and it was only then that he became aware that he was not alone in the chamber.

He smelled the scent first, the soft fragrance of roses dragging his senses back in time as he struggled to recall why he knew it so well. As realisation came to him he jerked his head up and looked into a pair of golden brown eyes, their expression at once fearful yet warm, apprehensive yet excited. He put his cup down with a jarring crash, oblivious that some of its contents splashed onto the table leaving rose red stains on the heavy parchment of his carefully crafted letter.

"So, Madame," he said tightly, in a voice completely unlike his own quiet tone. "Once again you do surprise me!"

She dropped a deferential curtsey, taking her cue from the unmistakeable coolness of his reception.

"My Lord," she murmured "Forgive such an intrusion but I had to see you before you left for England." Warwick raised his eyebrows in sardonic surprise.

"Indeed, Madame?" He gestured impatiently for her to rise from her knees. "And what is it that could be urgent enough to bring you to my presence, when you have shown little inclination to see either me or our daughter for the last ten years?"

"Please, my Lord...Richard...it is hard enough that I come without you make it impossible." At one time, he would have smiled at the way she spoke his language but now it only served to irritate him, his normal assurance shattered by the vision of this woman before him, who had meant so much to him, the mother of his best loved child.

"Jesus wept, Madame," he said bitterly. "What did you expect from me?" He slipped without thinking into flawless French, making it easier for her to understand him. "It's nigh on seventeen years since you left to return to France, and in that time I have seen you but once, and only then so that you may abandon your child into my care. You can scarce expect me to be pleased to see you!"

"I had hoped you would have found it in your heart to forgive me Richard, and if not forgive then come to understand at least why I was forced to commit such action." She stared up into his still attractive face, but saw nothing in the vivid green eyes to comfort her, nothing in his belligerent stance, which gave her confidence to continue. "But I see that I have made a mistake in coming here, forgive me." She turned disconsolately away, tears in her eyes, and made to head for the door. He watched her, his heart softening at her misery, and memories of their love flooded back to him. She had scarcely changed in all those years, her body was still slender though more curved perhaps with maturity, her hair still thick and honey gold, nor had he seen any obvious signs of aging in her face. He took a deep breath,

"Veronique," he said hoarsely. "Wait!" She halted but did not turn back to him. He tried to offer an apology, but it was not in his nature to humble himself, instead he merely gave a harsh laugh "I would never wish it be said that I was an unjust man, least of all to the plight of women. I am willing to hear you out." She turned to face him once more, but he could not meet her eyes for fear he gave himself away. Instead he gestured curtly to a chair by the fireplace and poured her a cup of the fine white wine he loved so much. "Here." He thrust the cup into her hand, trying to ignore the touch of her fingers on his. "Now what is it that is so imperative that it brings you to my presence?"

"I only came back to Madame's household yesterday and only learned this morning that you were here, and that you had brought…your family with you. I have never ceased to think of you Richard, nor Katherine either, but it seemed to be so futile too long to see a child so far away and to long for a man when I was wed to another so I tried to push all thoughts of both of you from my heart. But finding that you were so close, I could no longer resist and so I am here." She came to a faltering stop, her voice catching with tears. She was desperate for some show of warmth from him but coldness was his only defence against the feeling she stirred in him and he continued to avoid her eyes.

"I can offer no comfort as far as your daughter is concerned Madame. She was much bewildered by your desertion and I doubt she found it in her heart to forgive you for it. As for myself, I hold no illusions. After you cast me off in such callous fashion, I was unsurprised that you should inflict the same pain on your own child."

"Cast you off, my Lord?" She looked incredulous. "Your memory of the event is somewhat flawed I fear. As I recall, it was you who abandoned me!" What he had long suspected was now brought into the open, yet he could not stop the anger and could not halt the flood of words fighting against his teeth to be released.

"Of course, you would lay the blame for our separation at my door Madame, for it is against your nature to accept that you hold responsibility for anything. Did you think, when I have always shown such willingness to acknowledge any babe born to me, that yours would be different? Could you doubt me so much when I have raised her as one of my own family for all these years, when you were content to leave her in my care in Calais. Surely you know that had you confessed your pregnancy to me I would have cared for you and the child?" He had worked his anger high enough to risk a glance at her face, his startling eyes cool and appraising as they looked into hers. "Did you have so little faith in me then?" he asked softly. She flinched, and drew a swallow from her wine cup.

"They were stronger than me," she murmured after a while. "They had the power to command me hither and thither. How does a child resist the pressure placed upon her by a Queen? How could I know whether they lied or not when you were gone from London and I had no way to contact you. If I had written to you I would have found none to carry my letter, and if I had found a courier by the time you returned I would be in France and you would have lost me anyway for you would not have come to France for me." He gave a mirthless laugh, and moved away from the fire towards the table, pouring himself another draught from the jug.

"Do you think not?" He raised the cup top his lips, but met her eyes over the rim. "As Captain of Calais, France is not so far and in those days, I would have gone to the land of the Saracen had I thought you would come back to me." He hadn't quite meant to give himself away but somehow the words slipped from his tongue before he could stop them. She dropped her eyes from his and flushed, disconcerted yet thrilled by this rare show of emotion. She could remember everything about him so vividly; his wry humour, his lust for power which seemed to match if not surpass his lust for women, but most of all she remembered how she had cherished their time alone together, when he would tell her he loved her and show her a softness he showed to no other, and for that she had always been grateful that she had a part of him that few had witnessed, let alone possessed. Was there a glimmer of hope that he still cared for her?

"Why did you not tell me of the child?" His enquiry was conversational.

"Because I thought you would be displeased." A simple truthful response.

"Yet you told the Queen?"

"She had guessed with the intuition borne of women. She said you would not acknowledge the babe and would seek to make a whore of me. She said she would try to get you to admit that the babe was yours and then she called me to her and said you did not acknowledge paternity for my child. I believed her. Why should I not?" She had dropped her voice almost to a whisper. "I supposed I was just a dalliance and I accepted her offer to send me back to France. I realised after coming to you at Calais that I was mistaken, that she had lied to me but by then it was too late. You had hardened your heart to me. I could not bear it, that is why I left without saying farewell."

"And broke your daughter's heart." The anger in his voice brought her eyes to his.

"Does she hate me so much?" she asked at length and he nodded.

"She does not understand why you did what you did."

"And I suppose you have done nothing to make her understand that what I did, I did for love of her!" Her voice was sad, but without bitterness.

"No!" His voice was sharp, then he checked himself. "No I have never sought to turn her against you. She has chosen herself never to speak of you and the only time that we have, I have sought to help her understand."

"I brought her to her father because he could give her so much more than I could." He noticed that her hands shook as she clutched her wine cup.

"No, Veronique," he said softly, "you brought her to me as some sort of revenge, thinking you would shock me, hoping that you might inflict hurt on me with the knowledge that you had withheld her from me for all those years." He saw her shoulders sag and knew he had hit the mark. There were tears in her voice when she spoke.

"Yes, you are right. I really wanted to hurt you for the pain you had caused me, for the ultimate punishment of childbirth I endured as your parting gift to me. I thought you had deserted me. I was barely sixteen when she was born, the stain of bastardy on her from the first so none would have aught to do with us, leaving me with, I thought, no hope of ever marrying. I do not deny that I resented her but Jesu', after I left her with you I missed her every day that passed me by and the hurt has not diminished in time. I believe that to be my punishment and one that I must live with for the rest of my days."

"And what of Kate, Veronique, must she live with your punishment; a punishment that she deserves so little, for a sin she never committed. Must the child suffer for the sins of her mother and father?" He had moved closer, looking down at the soft gold of her bent head, wanting to touch her but not daring to.

"No, Richard, that was never what I wanted. It was you I wanted to suffer not Katherine, but I did not understand what I had done until the task was complete and there was nothing that I could do to alter it."

"And now you must convince Kate that you regret your actions, and that you do truly care for her, or you will have no hope of claiming her love and forgiveness." He was so close to her that she could see the intricate stitching on his soft Italian leather boots, winding its way round the toes like a finely worked snake. She wanted to look up at him but she could not bring herself to. She could not bear to think that he might despise her when she so desperately wanted him to still love her. She had not realised, until the Duke of Somerset had told her that Warwick and her daughter were in the chateau, just how much she still cared for this man, and she knew this was her only chance, for once he was in England there would be no way for her to see him. She felt the tears well in her throat and finally gave into the sobs which had long been threatening to overtake her.

"Will she never forgive me Richard? Must I always be punished for what I have done?" Her shoulders shook, tearing at his heart but he held back the impulse to pull her into his arms, and crouched before her instead, taking his kerchief from his belt and giving it to her to dry her eyes. He did not answer her question, knowing that he could offer no comfort for he knew not whether Kate would forgive her mother and in that moment he cared little, he was just glad that Veronique had chosen this night to come to him. For these last nights, would be when he was more vulnerable to his own needs and when his wife, who had never been his love, had spurned his advances and made it clear that she had no interest in his lusts or his bed. He wondered if it was too late, after seventeen years, to start again, to pick up the threads of the love they had once shared, and knew that if that was what she wanted then he was prepared to meet her more than half way. But he did not wish to push her into anything and for the minute he was content to discuss their daughter, a fine bond between them which had brought them together after all the years that had passed them by.

"Kate is a beautiful girl," he said softly, the tone of his voice changing as he thought of his daughter, seeing her as a child and not the woman she had become. "She reminds me of her mother, though hers is a wilder beauty not to the taste of all men, but believe me, if it ensnares then it enslaves. She has had a hard time of late. I wed her to the wrong man but he is dead now, the devil take him, and I hope that she can learn to be happy. I have done my best by her and am proud of her, though she is a little spirited perhaps, but that cannot be so bad can it?" He was trying to peer into her face, a smile still playing on his mouth. She felt her heart skip a beat, not sure if the message she read within his eyes was clear, afraid that she misunderstood what they were trying to convey to her.

"Perhaps if I had had more spirit I could have withstood them when they sent me away," she whispered, fighting to control her tears, aware that red swollen eyes would not add to her beauty.

"But then you would not have been the woman that I loved as I have loved no other, and perhaps we would not be talking as we do now." This time she was sure that she did not mistake the tenderness in his voice, but she held herself still waiting for him to make his move. "I will speak with Kate before I leave and ask her to see you." Hope leaped in her eyes, as at last she raised them to his and he felt a warmth flood through him as he once more took in the soft familiarity of her loveliness.

"Oh, yes please! But how can you be sure that she will listen to you." She could not believe that it could be so easy, but he smiled, his almond eyes crinkling at the corners.

"Because I will tell her you and I are reconciled and as she is a good, obedient girl, she will do as I ask but the rest will be up to you." He spoke very softly, knowing that his feelings showed in his eyes but caring not. He wanted her and there was nothing he was going to put in his way to prevent her coming to him if that was what she wanted. He thought he saw an answering need in her tense expression and he felt gauche of a sudden, like a shy boy, so afraid of rejection yet aware that he must lay his pride on the line if he wanted to win her.

"Oh Richard," she murmured, touching his cheek with a soft hand. "I know not how to thank you"

143

"Damn it Veronique, I have been such a fool!" He stood abruptly, startling her, walking away from her toward his desk. "I should have followed you when you left me instead of bewailing my woes. We could have had happiness and yet I let it all go for the sake of my godforsaken oversized pride!" She was behind him now and he could smell her scent, feel her warm presence at his shoulder.

"It is not too late to salvage some of that happiness, my Lord." She spoke very low, breathless almost and he turned to face her keeping his hands to his sides, still afraid to touch her just yet. "But your husband..." he murmured but she cut him off with an abrupt gesture of contempt.

"I care naught for him nor he for me. Twas always my wealth he craved and never my person."

"Then he has done me great favour, for your wealth I care nothing for but your person I do want more than I have ever wanted anything else in my life." He reached out and caught her hand, drawing her to him in a tight embrace. "Oh Veronique," he breathed, "God help me but I want you." Her mouth opened sweetly under his, and her slender arms wound tightly around his neck in a response which sent rich floods of desire coursing to his loins, and as he slowly drowned in the honeyed beauty of her kiss, he thought fleetingly how fitting it should be that he should spend the last nights before a long campaign in the arms of the only woman he had ever loved.

***

Kate, late in coming to say goodnight to her father, opened the outer door and saw him locked in the arms of a woman she knew, viscerally, to be her mother. Giving a low moan of horror, as the implication of their reunion sank in, she stumbled blindly away.

Anjou, France
August 1470

"My Lord." Beau started as the chamber door opened and a tousled fair head looked around it. "My Lord Warwick, there is a groom outside who needs to speak with you urgently."

"Did he say what about?"

"Yes, my Lord, something to do with the Lady Katherine."

"Send him in." Warwick rolled his eyes and turned to his companions apologetically. "Sorry gentlemen." The groom entered, twirling his cap through nervous fingers. "What is it man?" The Earl looked impatient.

"It's the Lady Katherine, my Lord. She went out on her mare this morning and it's coming in twilight now and she is still not back."

"Who escorted her?"

The man moved from foot to foot and grimaced nervously.

"She went alone, my Lord."

"What?" Warwick's voice rose. "What do you mean alone?"

"I begged her not to but she would not listen. She was desperate to go and saddled the mare herself in the end and flew out of the yard like someone was chasing her."

"What time was this?"

"Early, my Lord, before nine on the clock."

"Jesu'! It is an hour from dusk. Why did you not alert me before now?" Warwick's face was a mixture of horror and rage.

"I did not want to get her into trouble, my Lord. She's such a lovely lass and…" The man looked thoroughly miserable and Warwick softened.

"Alright. It's alright; at least you have told me now." He turned to his companions again. "I'm sorry gentlemen but I need to…"

"We'll help you, Richard, won't we, Jack?" Beau came gracefully to his feet, directing his next question to the groom. "Any ideas which direction she went in?"

"No, your Grace, but I do know that she sometimes goes to the river and sometimes the other way towards the forest." The man went red as he realised he was breaking a confidence.

"She's done this before?" Warwick looked incredulous.

"She often goes for rides alone, my Lord, but never for more than two or three hours; not like this but she looked like she had the wind right on her tail this morning…"

"Very well. Jack, you and Richard go towards the forest and Geth and I will head to the river." Beau cut him off, giving his orders with the natural authority of his rank. Warwick stiffened for a moment and then recognised the wisdom of what he was saying. These men knew the area far better than he did and could find her more quickly.

"Thanks Edmund." He looked up at the younger, taller man. Beau smiled.

"What are friends for?" They moved for the door as one, taking the stairs two at a time. "Jack, take a light in case we are out after dark and take Saracen, he will help to sniff her out. I'll take Loki."

"All right." Jack headed the group across the inner courtyard and out through the gate to the stables, whistling for the alaunts who came bounding round the corner, tails wagging, wolf like faces alight with joy at being summoned. Their horses were already being saddled as they got there.

"And come and find me if you find her, I'll be along the riverbank somewhere!" Beau vaulted into the saddle as Gethin came racing on foot across the yard. "Come on, Geth!" And scattering dogs and stones behind him he galloped out of the gate leaving the boy to grab his own reins and swing into the saddle as his horse was already moving. Jack grinned at Warwick.

"Such a show off," he said fondly, as they followed at a more sedate pace.

An hour later there was still no sign of her and darkness was creeping in steadily. Beau was beginning to worry that they would not find her before it was dark or worse still that something bad had happened to her. He chewed the inside of his lip absently as he watched the dog in front of them, his nose down and tail wagging as he hunted for a trail.

"What do you think, Geth?" He glanced at his squire. "Do you think she'll be this far down the river?"

"She certainly could be, my Lord. She could be in Jurvadeil by now, she's had enough of a head-start." He considered for a moment and then his face cleared. "Where's the place with the otters?" he asked suddenly.

"About half an hour that way." Beau pointed further west along the bank. "Why?"

"It's the sort of thing that would appeal to a lady, my Lord, the otters tumbling about and swimming like they do. You said that she had been this way before?"

"Good thinking, lad, let's head that way." He spurred his stallion forward, and whistled the alaunt. "Loki. Come!" he shouted. The dog changed direction and raced along the bank just in front of his master's horse. Some half an hour later they were walking the horses along the edge of the bank when Loki stopped and sniffed the air, one front paw raised and then let out an enormous howl, making the skin on the back of Beau's neck crawl with apprehension. The dog howled again and Beau began to shout.

"Katherine?" He stared at the dog which was slowly walking forward now, his hackles up. "Katherine!" Suddenly Loki yelped excitedly and ran forward, his tail wagging, but stopped again, uncertain. Beau strained his eyes into the twilight and saw what the dog had already seen; a figure and the prone body of a horse. "Katherine." Beau leaped off his horse and ran forward then came to an abrupt halt as he took in the true horror of the scene before him. "Jesus wept. Katherine!" The girl was sitting on the ground, covered in blood, a knife next to her, and the horse was dead, it's throat cut cleanly.

"She broke her leg," she said flatly. "We were on our way home and she dropped a leg down a rabbit hole and broke it. I had to kill her."

"Mon Dieu!" Beau swore quietly, "My God!", his tone a mixture of disbelief and admiration. He found himself quite unable to believe that this young and somewhere underneath all that blood, lovely creature had had the cool nerve to cut a horse's throat. He had always thought women were supposed to be hysterical, squeamish creatures who could not look at blood or gore. Gethin came forward and exclaimed softly, before igniting the lantern with a flint and tinder and putting some light on the gory landscape.

"Jesu'," the youth said, taking in the state of her clothes and the fact she still sat in the pool of blood. "We need to get her home, my Lord." He took the lantern closer, lighting up her face which was tracked with tears. "Was it a bad fall, my Lady? You are not hurt, are you?" The girl looked up at him blankly and then shook her head.

"No. I landed in front of her and was able to keep hold of the rein. When she couldn't get up I realised she had broken her leg so I did what Richard taught me and used my knife across her throat and then held her head while she died."

"My Lord?" Gethin turned to his master who was still staring at the girl. "Will you take my Lady up with you? Shall I head off and tell my Lord Warwick that we have found her? I will be able to travel faster than you with two-up."

"Yes lad, good idea." Beau came out of his trance and walked towards the still immobile Katherine. "Come Katherine." He held his hand out to her but she looked at him blankly and he saw that her eyes were huge black pools of shock. He hesitated a moment, looking down ruefully at his tunic, and then shrugged, and leaning forward swung her up into his arms and set her on her feet. Her gown hung heavy, sodden with blood, soaking his sleeves as he did so.

"We'll have to get this off you," he said tersely, tugging at her sleeve. "Do you have riding chausses on?" Kate nodded silently. "Turn around." Obediently she turned her back and he flicked a glance at his squire. "Geth, get your tunic off." Beau then slipped his knife out of his belt and in one swift movement cut down the laces at her back and then further through the material so that he could drag the gown off her shoulders and drop it into a pool at her feet. Carefully averting his eyes, Gethin handed over his tunic and Beau slipped it over her head. Dutifully she slipped her arms in the sleeves and let Beau turn her around and lace up the front, steadfastly avoiding looking as he did so. The garment drowned her, the sleeves hanging well below her hands and the hem coming almost to her knees. In spite of the seriousness of the situation Beau found himself smiling as he swung her up into his arms and carried her over to his big stallion. "Can you ride astride?" he asked and she nodded again. "Good girl." He flipped her onto the horse's back in one easy movement and swung up behind her, the saddle, made for a man in full armour, easily taking both of them. Gethin threw her small saddle onto his stallion's neck, hitched the bridle over his arm and cantered over to them.

"I will see you back at the hall, my Lord?" he said softly, the white linen of his shirt bright in the moonlight.

"Aye, tell the Earl of Warwick we should be back within the hour and tell him not to be angry." Beau's voice held a caress that made Gethin's mouth quirk speculatively but he knew better than to say anything.

"Yes, my Lord." He cantered off into the ensuing darkness as they followed at a more sedate pace, no light but the moon to guide them.

"Are you alright, kitten?" he asked her gently and felt her nod. Her back was straight as if she was afraid to touch him and she shivered. "Lean back against me, you must be exhausted and it will be warmer."

He felt her relax into his chest and he shifted slightly so that she was effectively in his arms but he still had his hands on the reins. That way she could fall asleep and not worry about falling off. "It is a shame about the mare, she was a lovely animal."

"Yes." Her voice broke slightly. "She was my wedding gift when I was but thirteen. My late husband bred her himself and I loved her."

"I'm sorry lass, she must have had great sentimental value to you."

"Yes she did, but not for the reasons you think; she was my freedom. You see, for the first time I had my own horse that I could ride whenever I wanted and did not have to beg, borrow or steal a mount." He could hear the tears in her throat and it caught at his suddenly soft heart.

"Ah, kitten," he murmured sympathetically. "I remember the first stallion I ever owned. My father got him for me when I was fifteen and he was beautiful, I was very proud to own him and you are right it is good to be able to just take your own horse out of the stables and ride whenever and wherever you want."

"I learned to ride the quintain on Sable."

"The quintain?" He leaned round and looked at the side of her face, not quite sure he had heard right.

"Yes and the rings. Richard, Francis and I used to have mock tournaments against my father's other squires." The tears in her voice had been replaced suddenly by wistfulness.

"The same Richard who taught you to cut a horse's throat?"

"Yes."

"He has progressive ideas, this Richard, when it comes to the education of women." Beau laughed suddenly. "I'd like to meet him."

"I think it unlikely, my Lord, unless it is on a battlefield, you see Richard is my cousin, the Duke of Gloucester." There was sudden, wry amusement in her voice too. Beau laughed again.

"Ah, that Richard; well actually I have met him. In fact, he sat exactly where you are now about ten years ago, when I picked him up off a crowded street in Ludlow. But that is another story for another day!" He pulled her closer with his forearms and she snuggled back into his shoulder, relaxing more, and he allowed a feeling of contented enjoyment engulf him. "You still haven't told me about the quintain?"

"Papa always let me ride with the squires, he would have let Anne and Isabel too but the Countess would not allow it. Papa believes that women should see the hardship that comes with being a man, so he always encouraged me in my riding and swordplay, in fact he bought me my own knife when I was ten, the one I carry with me today. I cannot hold a battle sword very well but I can fight with a dagger, am good at the quintain, or at least I used to be and I can pick up the smallest rings with a lance; except I have to have a special light lance as I can't carry a man's one." She turned her head slightly so that she could see his face from a sideways glance. "I can also ride a destrier and put it through its battle paces."

"Well I'm damned!" Beau shook his head in wonderment. "You, my little kitten, are full of surprises!" She turned her face back and changed her position to get more comfortable, leaning completely into him. Casually he let go of the reins with one hand and slipped it around her waist, as if holding her on the saddle but actually drawing her into him. She didn't pull away and he allowed his arm to stay there, encircling her in his embrace, and he dropped his chin to rest on the top of her head, inhaling the scent of jasmine from her hair.

"Do you hunt?" he asked after a moment.

"Not much. We rode out on the moors in Yorkshire and took rabbits and things but I haven't really hunted properly. The boys used to sometimes when papa was home." She yawned widely. "Sable can… could jump high hedges. We used to do that for fun." Her voice caught again and he squeezed her waist sympathetically.

"I will ask Madame if you can have a mount from the stable, one that is just for you to ride when you want to."

"You would do that for me?" she sounded surprised.

"It's not such a big thing." He was puzzled.

"I have seen the way Madame looks at you and talks to you. If I was you I wouldn't want to ask her!" she said emphatically, stifling another yawn. He laughed.

"That's just her way."

"Mmmm." She didn't sound convinced. He felt her hand over his at her waist. "Thank you, my Lord, for being so kind to me."

"I am not being kind, kitten. You undervalue yourself." He laced his fingers into hers and they rode on in comfortable silence until he realised that she was asleep in his arms, breathing regularly, her head resting in the crook of his shoulder. Gently he put his mouth to her temple and kissed it softly, a feeling of warmth in his belly, his heart beating faster against her shoulder blade. His strong feeling of peace and wellbeing astonished him and he realised that the feelings he harboured for the young woman asleep in his arms were different from any he had had before. This was not just lust; there was much more to it than that. He would have been quite happy to ride like this for the rest of the night, just holding her close to him and breathing in her scent, something he would never have imagined possible. So when, some time later, the walls of the keep reared up in the darkness he felt a huge sense of loss and disappointment.

"Katherine," he murmured, his mouth still against her temple. She stirred in his encircling arm and her eyelashes flickered, but she snuggled closer making his heart melt. "Katherine." Long lashes swept up from her cheek and she looked up at him.

"I liked 'kitten' better," she said sleepily and he gave a soft snort of mirth.

"We are home, kitten, look." He pointed to the gates ahead.

"Shame." She swept her lashes back down over her cheek. "I was enjoying myself." He laughed softly and pulled her in tighter, tracking soft kisses from her temple to the corner of her mouth. Her lips curved upwards in a smile.

"That's not very cousinly," she said, not opening her eyes or moving away.

"No?" He let go of the reins and turned her chin towards him, claiming her mouth in a soft and gentle kiss. "What about that?" he asked.

"Nor that," she murmured and he grinned, gathering up the reins again and shouting to the gatekeeper.

"Open the gates. The Duke of Somerset is without!" He felt her laugh against him.

"Without what?" She giggled. "Sounds like you are lacking something, my Lord." He smiled.

"For the first time in my life I think I am," he said softly as they cantered through the open gates and into the bailey where her father and his brother waited

***

"I need a drink." Beau had changed out of his bloodstained tunic and had joined his brother in the hall. Jack gestured to a page but his brother stayed his arm. "Not here, let's go into town." Jack grinned.

"I'm up for that." He grabbed his hat, contemplated his cloak and then decided not as the night was still very warm. Within fifteen minutes they were sitting in the inn, at a table in the corner, a flagon of red wine in front of them and some bread and cold meat. Beau was spinning his eating knife on top of the table and looking at his brother, his expression troubled.

"I'm lost, Jack," he said at last. Jack raised his eyebrows quizzically.

"Lost?"

"Lord Edmund." A girl with a tangle of dark hair and her breasts spilling out of her dress slid her arms around Beau's neck from behind and murmured something in his ear. He smiled briefly at her and patted her hand.

"Not tonight, sweet." She moved away disconsolately before looking back at Jack hopefully who winked and shook his head. Beau was spinning his knife again. "Aye, lost," he said as if they had not been interrupted. "I have lost my heart and I know the precise moment it happened." He looked back up at his brother and shook his head, disbelievingly. Jack grinned at his bewilderment.

"And you're sure it's not just your cock talking?" he asked. Beau shook his head again, this time ruefully.

"That's just it. You know me lad, I know when my cock is talking and right at this moment it's not talking much at all. Oh, don't get me wrong I want her; she is the last thing I think of before I sleep and the first thing I think of when I wake up." He smiled a lopsided smile. "But today I could comprehend for the first time in my life what a wonderful thing it was to have a beautiful woman just sleeping in my arms and if someone told me I could never have her in my bed I would still be quite happy if I knew that I would see her face every day."

"I'm really sorry, Beau." Jack laid his hand on his brother's forearm, his face set in mock sympathy. "But it sounds to me like you are well and truly smitten." Beau gave him a look and then spun his knife once more across the wooden surface of the table.

"The question is, what do I do?" He stopped the spin with his forefinger and met Jack's gaze. "After all, this is Warwick's daughter we are talking about, not some low-born girl who would be happy to sacrifice her honour just to be my mistress, and I can't offer her anything except that can I?"

"No, I suppose not." Jack squeezed his arm and smiled. "But you could just enjoy it and see what happens. Mind you I wouldn't want to be in your shoes if Warwick thought you were bedding her; he thinks the world of that girl."

"I know."

"Did you know her Mama is back?"

"No I didn't. When did she get back?" Beau thought of Kate and the conversation they had had about her mother.

"Yesterday."

"How do you know?"

"Warwick told me. From what I could read on his face I think they might have rekindled their passion, he certainly looked somewhat fond."

"Shit. Madame won't like that!" Beau laughed harshly. "Madame won't like me much either if she catches me."

"Be discreet, Beau. You know how she is and she made your life a misery last time with what happened with Segoline de Crecy!" Jack leaned forward. "She hates Warwick and if she knows that you have a fancy for his girl she will make your balls into a purse."

"Aye, I know." He sounded weary. "I will try to be discreet but I feel like it's written all over my face, even Warwick keeps looking at me oddly."

"Talk of the devil."

"What?"

"Warwick. Just come in and he's heading over here." Jack grinned and Edmund snorted.

"Of course he is." His brother shrugged, still grinning.

"Jack." Richard Neville's warm, rich voice broke over Beau's head. "Edmund. I had thought you would be here."

"Richard." Beau tried to muster an enthusiastic smile and gestured, "Join us, please?" Warwick smiled and sat down and the dark haired girl brought another cup, looking briefly at Beau then, getting no response, smiled seductively at Jack.

"Actually gentlemen, if you don't mind, I think I'm on a promise." He got up from the table with a wink and a grin. "I won't be long." The other men laughed watching appreciatively as the girl sashayed ahead of him up the wooden stairs. The two men turned back to each other still smiling; as always Jack could be counted on to lighten the atmosphere.

"You've made quite an impact on my daughter, Edmund." Warwick took a swallow of wine and looked at his companion speculatively over the rim of his cup. Beau met his gaze steadily, trying to decide exactly how much to tell him before smiling quizzically.

"Have I?"

"She seems quite taken with you." Warwick put his cup down and leaned forward. "As a father that concerns me."

"I can assure you…"

"Please let me finish." Warwick held his hand up, cutting the younger man off, ignoring his irritated expression. "I am aware that you have a certain reputation for bedding and discarding women and that concerns me for at least two reasons." He stopped and considered for a moment. "One reason is that I could not accept that for any daughter of mine and the other is because Katherine herself is very special." He met Beau's gaze earnestly. "I need to take you into my confidence, Edmund, regarding Katherine, but if I do you must never let her know that I have told you what I am about to discuss with you." The younger man nodded warily.

"Alright."

"Katherine has had a difficult life, she was left with me by her mother when she was seven and never saw her again…"

"Yes, she told me, although she did not seem overly affected by it."

"That's because she hides things well, as you will learn if you come to know her better. She made friends with her sisters quite quickly, although she and Isabel often fight, but my wife was not always kind to her and does not like it when Katherine shows her spirit. So, she spent more time with my squires than perhaps was ideal and was great friends with her cousin Dickon."

"Gloucester…yes, she told me that too." There was an element of challenge in Beau's gaze but Warwick smiled.

"As I said, she is somewhat taken with you," he said quietly, "or you would know nothing about her. Anyway, that's how she learned, amongst other things, to cut a horse's throat but you should not be fooled by that spirit, Edmund, for she is a fragile and vulnerable girl. The reason she ran away like she did was because she saw me with her mother last night and she cannot understand why I would forgive her and take her back into my life after what she did." Warwick sighed and rubbed his hand across his face tiredly. "How does a father answer a question like that?" He shook his head and then looked up. "But that was not what I wanted to say. What I wanted to say is that when Kate was eleven I wed her to one of my retainers; a young knight of good birth and temperament as far as I knew and who wanted to join my family. Then early last year, when my cousin of York was staying with us at Middleham, Thevenot decided that he was paying too much attention to Katherine and that she was making a fool of him, so he beat her and took her by force." Warwick shuddered. "She was terrified, bruised and battered, and he almost destroyed her spirit." His eyes were like green ice and Beau found himself clenching his fists, his stomach churning at the picture so vividly set before him.

"What did you do?" he asked softly.

"I did what any self-respecting father would do. I beat the shit out of him until he begged for his life." Warwick flexed his hands in remembrance, his face like granite. "I should have killed him, but he was useful to me. Anyway, she picked herself up and forced herself not to be set back by it, but I have heard her crying at night and I have seen the fear in her eyes sometimes when she is faced with men she does not know."

"Yes." Beau's voice was very soft. Warwick took a large swallow from his cup and then looked back at the younger man steadily.

"I could not bear it that she should suffer so again," he said quietly. Beau was taken aback.

"Jesus man, I would never hurt her!" he exclaimed. "I have never forced a woman in my life!"

"I know that you would not intentionally hurt her, but what I am saying is that she is very taken with you. I talked with her before I came here and she told me how kind you had been to her, was glowing in her praise of you." He sighed and rubbed his face once more. "I know not how to put this except in the bluntest of ways." Beau arched his brow in question and waited. "I would not warn you off my daughter; I want her to be happy and I am not blind to the advantages of your attraction to her, however I would ask you to think very carefully about what exactly you want from her before you embark on any ploy to win her. I will not have her turned into a whore because you want her in your bed for a night but I would not be averse to sanctioning something more long-term and respectable. I would expect her to occupy an honourable position in your life and be treated with respect." He reached across and laid his hand on the other man's broad forearm. "Just think about it, please, before you act," he said softly. Beau met the emerald gaze with a steady gold-flecked one.

"It is not my intention to hurt Katherine in any way," he said, equally softly. "But I do not know at this moment what I can offer her. There are many things I have to contend with, not least of which is Madame. What I do know, though, is that she has captured me and riding home with her tonight was the most enjoyment I have had with a woman either in or out of bed for a very long time, if not ever. For the first time in my life I am not just thinking of my own pleasure." The expression in his eyes softened as he spoke. "But I don't know what promises I can make to you, Richard, other than that I care very much about her and I would never dishonour her." Warwick closed his eyes for a moment and then smiled tightly, the father at war with the politician.

"Thank you," he said, squeezing the younger man's arm before leaning back and draining his cup. "My other daughters' futures I have already assured but I may not be here to guide Katherine and she has no one else. I have to trust her to make the right decisions but I need to know that you will not take advantage of her youth and lack of protector. She is the child of my heart and I could not bear to see her hurt again." He leaned forward again, sentimentality pushed aside and his expression once more intent. "Yet I also cannot ignore your position and, if I am being bluntly truthful, my daughter could do worse than be the Duke of Somerset's mistress."

"You flatter me, Richard."

"No I don't." Warwick regarded.him levelly. "I do not underestimate your position with our Prince and I am not unaware of the debt I owe you in fostering our friendship. This venture could have been a disaster and I know that it is down to you that Prince Edward has accepted my daughter, and the Queen has grudgingly accepted my aid." Beau inclined his head but did not say anything, his calm expression belying his distaste at the ease with which Warwick could sell his daughter for political gain. Warwick's lips quirked up ruefully, as if he had caught a thread of Beau's thoughts. "Well I am glad we understand each other and I should go, I am encroaching on your evening." Warwick pushed back the bench and stood, smiling down at Beau. "I promised Veronique I would not be long and it does not do to keep a Lady waiting." With a cheerful wave, he ducked his head under the beams and through the door and within a few minutes Jack was in his place, his face eager.

"So what did he want?" he asked quietly. Beau began to laugh softly, shaking his head, and his brother looked at him in puzzlement. "What?"

"Believe it or not I think he just gave me permission to bed his daughter."

"You are jesting?" Jack's face was a picture of wonder and Beau laughed harder.

"Nope. He said she could suffer worse fates than being the Duke of Somerset's mistress."

"Jesus!"

"I almost could not keep a straight face and he was so serious."

"Bloody hell, Beau." Jack burst into laughter. "The man is a consummate politician who is not averse to sacrificing a child in the name of power; first one daughter and then another!"

"And, obviously, a less honourable fate for the less politically important daughter." Beau spat into the rushes, a sour taste in his mouth all of a sudden. "And Katherine thinks he loves her!"

"He does love her, dotes on her in fact, but the politician will always win over the father. Anyway look on the bright side, it leaves your way clear."

"Yes it does but I will not take her because he says I can." Beau smiled suddenly at his brother, his face softening, white teeth shining. "But if she is willing..." He held his hand out palm up and his brother slapped his own down. "...then so am I."

"I'll drink to that." Jack laughed and after a moment Beau joined him.

Chapter Seven

Anjou, France, September 1470

The Queen was speaking in low and rapid French to her son who was seated on her right. From the seat on her left, Beau followed their conversation with the easy familiarity of having been in her service for so long, but was not really listening with any interest. He had just got back from Barfleur where they had seen Warwick off on his venture and he was feeling the frustration of Marguerite's refusal to allow them to go to England with him. He had considered going anyway but in the end two things had stopped him; the fierce, ingrained loyalty he had always shown for his cause and Warwick's beautiful red-haired daughter. He sighed and looked across the hall from his position on the dais at the girl who was so instrumental in turning his emotions upside down. She was young for him perhaps, but Jesu' she was delightful, laughing as she was at something his brother was saying, and he felt a pang of annoyance that he could not be down there to listen to what they were talking about, to join a conversation that looked far more entertaining than anything that was being said up here on the dais.

"Do you not think so, my Lord Somerset?" Marguerite had turned to him, one eyebrow raised enquiringly.

"Forgive me, Madame?" He turned back to her smiling half apologetically and half quizzically. "I heard not what you were saying."

"Your attention was elsewhere, I fear." The eyebrow was still raised but the voice turned cool.

"I was but thinking, Madame." He smiled his most charming smile, lighting up his austere face.

"I could see that, my Lord. But I would suggest that you don't think, at least not in the direction of that girl." Marguerite refused to be placated.

"Girl, Madame?" He feigned innocence.

"Yes that bastard chit of Warwick's. Don't deny it for I have seen you with her and see you watch her even now. Take some advice and do not be so foolish, my Lord, as to philander with Warwick's daughter; it would be a mistake to involve yourself with her." She kept her voice pitched low so that her son could not hear, but conveyed no less feeling for that.

"I am not an idiot, Madame." He kept his voice devoid of all emotion, his smile still in place, but not quite reaching his eyes

"Good!" She tapped his arm with her fingers. "I do not need Warwick breathing down my neck because he thinks you have defiled his daughter's honour, nor do I need you distracted at this time, chasing some little strumpet." She smiled then, and touched his face lightly. "We need your full attention, my Lord, as always to get us through the times ahead."

"You always have my full attention, Madame." The response was automatic, but she accepted it and did not detect the flatness of his tone. She turned back to her son and said lightly, "I am going to retire, my son, so I will bid you goodnight." She leaned down and offered her cheek for the boy to kiss.

"Perhaps you, my Lord Somerset, will escort me to my chamber." Beau stood and pulled back the Queen's chair as she also rose and held out his arm which she took, but risking a glance back he saw that Katherine Neville was talking animatedly with a number of young people, including her sister Isabel, his brother Jack and, now that his mother was retiring, his Prince and the Princess, Anne Neville, were joining them. Marguerite tapped his arm again to regain his attention. "The young people are better left to have fun, my Lord."

"Yes, Madame." He forced his attention back to her.

"Edward seems to quite like his little Neville wife?"

"Yes, Madame."

"Let us hope he does not like her too much. I am not sure the marriage is destined to be a long one."

"Madame?" He looked at her sharply.

"Well, Warwick's girl was not what I had in mind for him." She looked up at him through her lashes.

160

"No, Madame." He was non-committal. It had not been his idea of a great match he had to admit, but Anne Neville was a sweet and lovely girl and his Prince seemed quite delighted with her. He could see Marguerite having some trouble if she thought to prise Edward away from her.

"I would prefer an alliance with the French royal house." They stopped outside the door of her bedchamber and he hoped that she was not going to ask him to come in to continue the conversation. He wanted to go back down to the hall and get roaring drunk and forget all his frustrations and troubles in the bottom of a flagon of wine.

"The French royal house would be a perfect match for him. He is a fine lad and he deserves a fine wife, although the Lady Anne is a pleasant girl, Madame." He opened her chamber door for her.

"Hmmm," she snorted, turning in the threshold and facing him. "She is pathetic and insipid...and bear what I said in mind about Warwick's other little slut. Do not shit on my doorstep, my Lord, for it will not be tolerated."

"Yes, Madame."

"I will not clean up another mess like the one with the de Crecy girl."

"The child was not mine Madame."

"Really?"

"It was born seven months after I first bedded her and was as fat as a nine-month babe. She was already with child when I had her, of that I am certain." His face was stony and his tone flat.

"So you said, my Lord." She gave him a sharp look. "However, that you put yourself in that position was bad enough and I will not tolerate it again."

"No, Madame."

"I need you to be focused on my son and ensuring that Warwick does what he says he is going to do. You wanted this friendship so you manage it."

"Yes, Madame."

"And I will not have you losing your wits over some ginger haired little chit."

"No, Madame." She held out her hand for him to kiss in a gesture of dismissal.

"Take this as my last warning!" And with that she slammed the door behind her.

"Madame." He pulled a face and parodied a bow at the closed door and then allowed himself a grim smile. He would either just have to be careful or go ahead and call her bluff, after all she needed him as much as he needed her. He took the stairs two at a time, making his way back into the throng that gathered as always in the hall. His time away had given him space to think and he had thought mostly about Katherine Neville. Seeing her today had merely reinforced his feelings; he did not think even Marguerite's disapproval and warnings could stem that tide, but he was not about to push the girl into something she did not want so he had decided he was going to enjoy any time he could spend with her and see what happened. Almost colliding with a page as he took the last step, he grabbed a flagon from the boy's tray and took a long draw directly from it, choking as it hit his throat, his eyes stinging, and then drank again long and hard. The wine was red and rich and slid down his throat into the pit of his stomach, instantly warming and very welcome, and he took another long swallow as he felt the familiar feeling of relaxation start to envelop him.

"Jesus, Beau, steady." His brother was beside him, laughing. "Save some for me!" Beau shook his head.

"Sorry, I needed that." He grinned ruefully and wiped the back of his hand across his mouth.

"Madame?"

"Aye, Madame. When is it ever aught else."

"What now?"

"She is still harping on about Segoline de Crecy."

"That old chestnut?"

"And a sharp warning not to distract myself with Warwick's 'bastard chit'."

"Jesus, she has eyes in the back of her head...I warned you to be discreet!"

"I know, lad, but somehow she always finds me out!" He took another swallow and blinked rapidly. "Anyway, I don't want to talk of Madame or to think of her, let's just get drunk."

"Well actually Edward sent me for you, he wants you to join us in the solar." Jack Beaufort gestured to the stairs at the other end of the hall. "He says we need some ancient wisdom!"

"Great!" Beau grimaced. "That makes me feel good." Jack laughed.

"The 'Bastard chit' is up there," he said softly and his brother grinned.

"So what are we waiting for?" Laughing with wry self-mockery at his sudden excitement, he grabbed Jack's arm and half dragged him across the hall and up the stairs. As they walked into the solar, Beau swiftly scanned the room and stopped at the settle to greet his Prince. "Your Grace, you asked for me?" He looked around as if searching for somewhere to sit and the girl sat on the settle unfolded her legs, making space for him next to her with a smile of welcome, just as he had intended. He inclined his head with thanks and a return of her smile, and dropped his long, lean frame gracefully into the seat opposite the fire and his Prince.

"Ah, Somerset, I have not had chance to formally welcome you home, my Lord. We have missed you."

"Thank you, it is good to be back."

"Really?" Edward grimaced knowingly. "So you are not wishing you could have gone to England then?"

Beau smiled.

"Perhaps, but then there are some compensations for being home, after all I wouldn't have the chance to spend the evening with you if I was in England, would I?"

"Somerset, you always say the right thing. Jack, you could learn much from your brother." Edward laughed and winked at Jack Beaufort.

"So everyone tells me all the time, your Grace." Jack grinned.

"Anyway Somerset, we have been discussing whether we will be in England or France for the Christmas festivities. What thinks you?"

"I know not, your Grace. I would say that much depends on my Lord Warwick and your Lady mother. If my Lord Warwick is successful quickly then we may well be in England, however your Lady mother does not wish to commit herself to your return until England is securely in our hands and Edward of York has been defeated."

"If I could have had my way it would have been my preference to join my father by marriage in England." Edward grimaced again and Beau smiled indulgently.

"Your mother is rightly cautious, your Grace. She does not want to take unnecessary risks with you or the men that we can raise in your name."

"I know Somerset, but it is frustrating all the same."

"Aye lad, it is, but as with games of chess it is important to get the strategy right to avoid a check mate."

"Still, it is hard to wait."

"I know, lad, but wait is what we have to do so we had best make the best of it." Beau smiled again. "I'm sure we can think of many things to occupy us for a few weeks." He winked again at Edward who blushed and glanced at his new wife, laughing.

"You are right, there are better things to discuss than where we will be for Christmas. More interestingly, let's talk about what we can do for the festivities?" Edward glanced at Anne again, touching her hand gently. "What would you like to do, love, Lord knows we could do with some fun?"

"Perhaps we could plan a Christmas celebration with music." Isabel Neville stretched her slippered feet towards the fire and rested them on the metal rung of the hearth. Edward grinned and Anne Neville brightened immediately.

"What sort of celebration?"

"I don't know. We could write one...we can all play something." Edward caught Isabel's idea and then they were all talking at once, each clamouring to be heard for what the celebration should be about and why they should have a role in it. Edmund Beaufort leaned back on the settle and raised his eyebrows to his silent companion, offering her a refill with the flagon he had put on the little trestle next to him. She held out her cup and smiled at him.

"Missed me?" he mouthed and she laughed.

"Yes," she mouthed back.

"How much?"

"This much." She held her fingers a small distance apart

"Charming!" He pretended to sulk and she laughed again.

"You went without saying goodbye."

"I know, I'm sorry, there was no opportunity." He raised his voice to a whisper.

"I know." Her smile was wistful. "I'm just teasing, I really didn't expect you to."

"Tell me again that you missed me." He leaned closer, his voice a breath in her ear, bringing gooseflesh out on her arms.

"I missed you," she whispered back as he turned his ear to her. He looked at her and smiled a sudden and tender smile which crinkled his eyes and softened his mouth.

"I want to kiss you," he murmured and a delicate flush of colour suffused her skin. She giggled and glanced up at him through thick burnished lashes, at once innocent and gut wrenchingly seductive.

"Stop that!"

"Stop what?" he grinned.

"Your courtier's flattery!" She rolled her eyes, but she was still laughing.

"It is not courtier's flattery, it is but the truth!"

"It's flattery by whatever name you call it."

"Perhaps but I still want to kiss you." He did not bother to hide the longing in his voice. She blushed once more.

"You are only saying that because you know you can't," she said confidently.

"Are you challenging me?" He arched his brow enquiringly, keeping his voice low, still smiling.

"You wouldn't dare!" Her eyes danced with fearful anticipation, her mouth quirking with suppressed giggles.

"Try me." He leaned in towards her, his mouth against her ear and she instinctively moved into him so that his lips caressed her lobe softly as he spoke and he felt her shiver. He flicked a glance across the room, aware that they may be being watched but everyone was still engrossed in the Christmas celebration and their role in it, not taking any notice of the quiet couple on the edge of the group. He sat back in his seat, giving the impression of propriety but surreptitiously lacing his fingers into hers and squeezing her hand. His stomach flipped as she squeezed his back.

"I take it you are not putting yourself forward for a role in the celebration?" he inquired softly, attempting to carry on a normal conversation whilst his thumb stroked her hand and his eyes caressed her face.

"Lord no!" She laughed. "I leave all the acting and playing to my sisters, they are much better at it than I am. It is not my idea of fun and it was not something I excelled at in the schoolroom."

"Nor mine. I would rather stick hot needles in my eye." He laughed with her. He could feel her hand trembling in his and was not sure if it was excitement or fear.

"I had heard, my Lord, that you play the lute right well." She glanced up at him again through dark red lashes.

"Whoever told you that was lying." He stretched out his legs nonchalantly and relaxed his thigh so it lay alongside hers, their hands sandwiched between them, gratified that she did not pull away from the touch. "I am a competent player perhaps, but I have no real musical talent." He reached out and claimed her other hand, pretending to examine the long white fingers and then the callous free palm. "I would say these hands are possibly the hands of a musician."

"Then you would be wrong, my Lord." She did not pull her hand free, but looked up at him with an amused expression, seeing straight through his ploy. "I play nothing well."

"Nothing?" He raised dark brows over hawk eyes, crinkled at the corners by his smile. He looked down at her hand again deliberately turning it over and assessing it. "Are you sure they have never caressed any kind of instrument to pleasurable effect?" This time she blushed scarlet at his innuendo before dropping her eyes and laughing silently.

"My Lord!" she admonished and he grinned.

"What?" His face took on a mock innocence.

"You know what!"

"What did I say?" He shrugged, still feigning innocence, his stomach swooping at the laughing look she gave him through her lashes. "So what do you do well then, Katherine Neville, other than be incredibly beautiful?" The wine had taken enough effect on him so that he had lost his courtier's impersonal mask, but had not yet affected his speech or his movements. He knew he was showing her how much he wanted her, how attracted he was to her and that his easy informality was drawing in the young and lonely girl at his side.

"Nothing except that I ride, or at least I used to."

"Of course, forgive me, I forgot; the quintain no less." He raised his eyebrows and grinned.

"Now you are mocking me." She pulled a face and poked out her tongue and warmth flooded through him again. "I am an excellent rider."

"I never said you weren't." His gaze was riveted on her, his voice soft and warm.

"I ride as well as any man."

"Do you now?" His eyes roved her face in blatant admiration, causing her blush to deepen but she still did not look away. The girl had courage, he had to give her that, and a streak of mischief which was very appealing. He already thought her beauty was unmatched but the more time he spent with her and the more he learned about her, the more he wanted to know. This was new to him; he had never cared a fig about his victims before and had never wanted to know anything about them. "I assume that we are talking about horses, Katherine?"

"Of course, my Lord." She made her eyes into huge round black orbs and her face took on a look of contrived innocence. "Whatever else?" and then they were both laughing, not because it was particularly funny but because it felt good and it added to the crackling atmosphere between them.

"I promised you a mount, didn't I, when I brought you home that night?" he said after their mirth had subsided. His words set her off again.

"Yes, my Lord," she said, trying unsuccessfully to suppress her giggles and he found himself grinning just from the sheer pleasure of making her laugh. It wasn't helping his lust much and he had been, at the very least, half hard for the last ten minutes, but he had to admit that he was enjoying himself immensely.

"I am sorry. It is not that I forgot, it is just that my time is taken up..." He gestured toward the Prince and shrugged with a disarming smile.

"I know, my Lord. My father was ever thus. Promising too much when he was too busy to honour those promises."

"I hope you do not see me as a father figure!" he said in not entirely feigned horror. She giggled again.

"No, my Lord, I definitely don't see you as a father figure," she said drily and he laughed also.

"What do you see me as then?" he murmured, shifting so that the whole of the left side of him touched her.

"I see you as a man, who is teasing me for his own amusement." She gave him a sideways glance

"I am a man enjoying the company of a very beautiful woman."

"You are an outrageous flirt, my Lord." She giggled. He gave a rueful smile.

"I see I have a reputation that I will never shake off."

"I suspect you may have earned it!"

"Perhaps, and you are right, I am flirting with you but I mean it when I say that you are the fairest creature I have ever seen in my life and that I really do want to kiss you." He dropped his voice to a murmur and for a moment as his eyes met hers he saw an answering flare of need in their depths and her hand tightened involuntarily on his. They stared at each other for what seemed like an age before the spell was broken by Jack Beaufort's soft voice at his brother's side.

"If you don't stop looking at her like you are going to have her for dessert, Beau, someone is going to notice." Kate's skin suffused yet again with colour and Beau glared at his brother.

"Jesus, Jack!" he said, equally softly. Unperturbed, Jack sat on the arm of the settle, smiling benignly at Kate and then his brother.

"Did you not want a part in the celebration, Kate?" he asked.

"No, my Lord. I was just telling my Lord Duke that it is not something I ever excelled at in the schoolroom. I play no instrument," her mouth quirked wryly, "of any kind. Nor do I have much of a singing voice. I'm alright in a choir but on my own the dogs join in!" Both men laughed.

"I don't play anything either, although I can sing," Jack said. "But Beau plays the lute right well."

"Ah, he just told me he didn't!"

"I don't. I have no flair, I can just follow a tune."

"Well that's more than either of us can do." Jack looked at Kate in mock exasperation. "He's always better than me at everything, and such a show off."

"If you've got it, flaunt it, I say." Beau winked at Kate and they all laughed.

"Can I ask a question, my Lords?" Kate looked at both of them in turn. "Why Beau, is it just short for Beaufort?" Jack shrugged.

"I don't remember anyone in our family calling him anything else," he said, and Beau smiled.

"My Lady mother always called me Beau. Apparently when I was born, I was 'her Beau fils,' and then Hal just called me Beau as he couldn't pronounce Edmund and so it stuck. Even my father used it except when he was wrath with me!"

"Trust a mother to call a son 'beautiful'!" Jack shook his head. "Humility was never going to be part of his makeup, was it?" His open face was free of envy but Katherine guessed it must be hard sometimes growing up with two brothers who were so much older, more experienced and better looking than you.

"You are quite alike though," she said, which was true in essence for although Jack's eyes were a dark brown and his face was rounder he had his share of good looks; he was just not as astonishingly handsome as his brother.

"Yes it's just he has cheekbones." He pulled a face and Kate laughed.

"What are you gossiping about over there?" Prince Edward peered over at them, a smile hovering at his lips.

"We were discussing how my brother got the looks but I got the brains, my Lord Prince." Jack grinned and everyone laughed. Beau leaned back against the settle, shrugged and smiled, his body once more stretching along Kate's.

"Ah yes, brother, but I am sat on the settle enjoying the company of a very beautiful woman and as usual you are perched on the edge of my chair trying to bask in my glory." He winked at the Prince who grinned and started relaying a story about Beau and his brother Hal and their boyhood call-sign for beautiful women. Using the conversation as cover he leaned in and murmured, "The stables, after breaking your fast, if you dare."

"Dare what?"

"Dare to meet me."

"I dare."

"Good. Wear your riding gear." He squeezed her hand. "We are going for a picnic."

***

The sun was just coming over the horizon as Kate washed swiftly and dragged on her clothes as quietly as possible, conscious of not waking the sleeping girl on the pallet close to her, or her sister and Edward asleep in the big curtained bed. Once dressed and her hair braided she ran down the stairs and through the hall to the kitchen, her stomach drawn by the smell of baking bread.

"Morning, Jacques," she said softly. The big man at the table looked up and smiled a beatific smile.

"Morning, my Lady. Going riding?"

"Yes. Could I have some bread and honey, I'm famished." She grinned back at him. He laughed.

"I don't know where you put all the food you eat, my Lady, reed slim as you are." He bustled about cutting a chunk of bread and smearing it with a thick layer of butter and then runny golden honey. He adored this daughter of the Earl of Warwick, not least for the reason that she spoke real French fluently, but also for her ease of manner and friendliness; there was nothing haughty about her, not like the Earl and his wife. He handed her the bread and poured a frothing cup of buttermilk from a jug. "You're not riding out on your own are you, my Lady?" he asked sternly. She laughed through a mouthful of bread.

"No...I am riding with my Lord Somerset!"

"Jesu' forfend, my Lady, I hope you are to be chaperoned, what with his reputation!" He looked horrified and she laughed harder.

"You sound like my father." She grinned. "It's alright, I will be quite safe."

"Do not be so sure. After all, I have known him longer than you, my Lady, and he has worked his way through many a lass in this kitchen, let alone Madame's household!" Jacque pursed his lips prudishly. "I would not want you to be taken advantage of." Kate softened and patted his arm.

"I will be fine, I can look after myself, you know," she said. "And anyway he is a chivalrous man and I know he would not want to offend my father. I had better go for he will be waiting for me." She handed him her empty cup, blew him a quick kiss which brought a rush of colour to his rough cheeks and scampered out of the kitchen door into the inner bailey, cramming the last piece of bread and honey into her mouth. The sun was still low over the horizon, but there was a promise of warmth even though it was late September, and the sky was cloudless. She slipped out of the inner gate and across the outer bailey to the stables, smiling and waving at the keeper on the gate who was leaning over the wall to see who was about; the man waved back with a grin.

Beau was already there, dressed today in dark green, immaculate as always and emanating the familiar clean citrus smell of bergamot. Hercules was saddled and waiting, and he was running his hand down the stallion's fetlock and over his hoof, checking his feet for any stones. He looked up as she leaned over the door and put the horse's hoof down.

"Hey," he said softly, smiling and coming over.

"Hey." She smiled back, her voice equally soft.

"This hour suits you," he murmured, brushing her lips with his. "You look ravishing."

"Flatterer." She laughed but did not resist when he claimed her lips again, this time deepening the kiss, their mouths clinging together with soft sensuality as he explored briefly with his tongue.

"Now that was what I wanted to do last night," he said lightly as he released her and stepped back, undoing the stable door and beckoning her in. She laughed again, her outward composure belying the hammering of her heart and the warmth that had assaulted her body as he kissed her.

"Good, at least we've got that out of the way then," she countered, stepping into the stall and glancing up at him sideways. "So where are we going for our picnic?"

He smiled, undeterred, slipping his arms around her waist and looking down into her face, his hawk's eyes glowing with warmth. She rested her hands on his shoulders, not sure if she was planning to resist or fling her arms around his neck if he kissed her again.

"As I only have the morning I thought we could go along the river; I know you ride along there often but it has the best places for a picnic and it is not too far away to get back just after dinner." He brushed a curling tendril of hair from her face with one hand, his calloused palm rough against her cheek. "And I want to see these riding skills for myself." She was conscious of watching his full mouth as he spoke and reliving its softness as it had covered hers.

"So I take it I have a mount then?" she murmured, not taking her eyes from him and the air between them seemed to crackle with intensity.

"Yes." His voice sounded even huskier than usual and his lips hovered just above hers as they formed the words. "Christ, Katherine, you are beautiful!" Her arms slid around his neck just as his moved from her waist and closed around her, his mouth taking complete possession of hers. She sighed softly as warmth flooded her loins and she met the gentle invasion of his tongue with hers, her body melting against him fluidly. She heard his breathing quicken and he made a soft appreciative sound in the back of his throat, his arms tightening about her and drawing her into him.

"My Lord?" Footsteps sounded along the corridor outside the stalls. "My Lord Duke?" The couple sprang apart, Kate catching her arm on an old hook sticking out of the stable door as she swung away from him. She made a soft strangled sound and Beau grimaced in sympathy, snorting a rueful laugh through his nose.

"Shit!" he whispered and then laughed again, shaking his head. Involuntary tears stung Kate's eyes as she blushed furiously and turned towards the stallion still standing patiently at the back of the stall, stroking his nose with a shaking hand just as Gethin appeared at the opening of the stall.

"The grooms and the horses are all ready, my Lord, and the Duchess of Clarence is just coming across the bailey with demoiselle Lucia."

"Alright Geth, take Hercules, we are ready." He smiled as the youth took the stallion's reins and led him out of the stable. "Katherine?" Beau held out his arm to her and she took it, the blush on her skin subsiding. "Are you alright?" he whispered.

"Yes, I think I tore my sleeve and it's a new riding gown."

"Let's see." He looked at the back of her arm. "Yes but its only a small tear, easily mended I should think, and just a bit of a scratch, hardly any blood," he said. "I can kiss it better if you like." She shook her head with a wry laugh.

"I feel enough like a naughty child who has just been caught out in a mischief, thank you, my Lord!" She pinched the inside of his arm none too gently as she spoke. "And I can't believe you have invited my sister; I don't know whether to be angry or grateful!" She giggled suddenly as she walked beside him.

"I thought it only proper." Beau laughed shortly. "Better Isabel than the Princess Anne; I'm not sure I could spend a whole morning under that disapproving glare!"

"True." Kate mirrored his expression. "Oh well, at least I shall be safe I suppose!" He glanced down at her, his hurt showing in his eyes.

"I am somewhat offended that you might think you are not safe with me," he said softly but she laughed again.

"I was thinking more about being safe from myself!" She looked up at him, her own eyes dancing and he grinned.

"You really are delightful" he murmured warmly as they walked out into the bailey and the melee of horses, dogs and people. He led her towards a sleek black mare which she recognised as being one of Marguerite's and, cupping his hands, boosted her into the saddle himself. "This is Noisette and I chose her especially for you."

"She is beautiful, my Lord." Kate patted the glossy neck.

"And she has a courageous spirit." He looked up at her. "Just like you." Their gaze held for a moment and Kate's heart lurched and beat faster in her breast.

***

Isabel, already mounted, watched with unashamed interest until Beau moved away to mount Hercules, calling the two capering and barking alaunts to his side.

"Saracen, Loki, come."

Kate waited warily as her sister sidled her mare alongside her, her lovely face expressionless.

"So?" Isabel's voice was soft.

"So what?" Kate met enquiring blue eyes with a raised eyebrow.

"Is he a nice kisser?" Isabel grinned.

"Bel!"

"Oh don't play innocent, lady!" Isabel glared at her and then dissolved into giggles.

"Yes he is, if you must know!" Kate grinned and quickly glanced over at where Beau was gathering Hercules reins and then back at her sister. "He scares me though…he's hard to resist."

"Don't resist him then." Isabel followed her gaze as Beau and his brother swung their horses round, ready to leave, appraising him unashamedly. "I wouldn't."

"Bel!" Kate hissed, genuinely shocked and then laughed at her sister's disarming shrug. "Anyway I have no intention of ending up as another notch on his bed post, however good a kisser he is!"

"Coward."

"No, not a coward. I'm just not prepared to be yet another conquest to brag about." Kate smiled benignly at her sister and then jumped at the sound of Beau's voice at her side.

"Will you ride with me?" he asked, smiling down at her. She blushed and nodded and he transferred his smile to Isabel. "And you, my Lady?"

"Of course, my Lord." Isabel favoured him with her best smile but he was already turning away, trotting to the head of the group with her sister so that she had to urge her mount into a canter to catch up.

***

The day was proving to be as warm as its promising start and as they made their way along the riverbank, with the sun shining brightly down on them and the lovely early morning smells of late summer wafting on the breeze, Kate got her first taste of Somerset the practised courtier, entertaining them with tales of the old English and Burgundian courts, making light conversation and eliciting laughter with his stories. Learning to be a courtier was part of the training all men of rank received, beginning at home and then continuing, along with the soldier's training, as they moved to be squires in another noble household, but she had never imagined that a man who was so driven and intense could be such an effortlessly entertaining companion. Last night he had flirted with her with the consummate ease of a man who knew how attractive he was to the opposite sex and had easily reeled her in with his compliments and his teasing but this was a different side to him and she found herself being drawn to much more than just his exceptional good looks. He smiled and laughed a lot more than she had ever imagined and though his conversation was inconsequential and light-hearted, she sensed a keen wit behind it.

"I don't suppose you go to Burgundy much now that Duke Charles is married to cousin Meg, do you, my Lord?" Isabel asked suddenly.

"Yes I do when necessary, but I don't stay as long as I used to and his Duchess and I do tend to ensure we keep out of each other's way." Beau smiled diplomatically. "She doesn't like me much though I can't imagine why!"

"Neither can I." Isabel laughed and then shook her head. "But Meg was always Ned's staunchest supporter!" She turned to her sister. "I can remember when we were all waiting for word from papa after St Albans; Mama was frantic and all Meg kept saying was that Ned could not possibly lose. She was right of course but Lord she could be so annoying with her blind faith in her brother!" She smiled at Kate. "You of course were not with us then."

"No I was still in Calais with just Anthony Woodville for company." Kate looked thoughtful, trying to remember the Queen's brother as more than just a tall, blonde blur.

"Woodville!" Beau snorted. "That upstart turncoat popinjay!"

"If I remember rightly he spoke very highly of you too, my Lord!" She flashed back and he laughed.

"I'll wager he did!"

"He was very good to me considering he was papa's prisoner and I remember thinking he was very handsome. He used to read to me and helped me with my letters, although I think he fancied my nurse." She shook her head in a kind of wonder. "It is quite funny that he ended up being Ned's brother by marriage; papa and Ned mocked him mercilessly and I am surprised he was ever able to forgive either of them."

"I'm sure the rise in fortune made up for it," Beau said drily. "I must admit I was never a fan of the Woodvilles, especially after Rivers married Jacquetta, the old Duke of Bedford's widow. He was just a knight then and not a very prominent one and she married well beneath her, much to her family's disgust. But Harry being Harry, never one to slight his uncle's widow, welcomed Rivers into the fold and up they rose. I have to say Anthony was very much like his father, always looked the part of the dashing hero but never delivered the goods. His mother, Jacquetta, was a beauty who quickly became one of Queen Marguerite's ladies, as of course did the lovely Elizabeth as soon as she was old enough." He laughed softly. "And she turned more than a few heads, I can tell you."

"Papa said she is very beautiful but there is little warmth in her," Isabel volunteered. Somerset nodded slowly as if trying to recall the young Elizabeth Woodville.

"I only knew her when I was young, sixteen or so, and then not very well for she was wed to John Gray by that time, but she had the palest silver hair I have ever seen in my life, and white skin; she looked almost fey." He shook his head. "I never fancied her myself but I can see why York was taken with her, though I was stunned when he wed her."

"Papa said she was clever enough to hold out where all others have given in and so Ned being Ned, never one to let anything get in the way of his pleasure, married her to get what he wanted." Isabel glanced at Kate as she spoke, conscious of the potential Pandora's box. "I think he hoped she might keep quiet."

"Fat chance of that!" Kate responded derisively, having successfully blocked her emotions regarding Edward and stored them safely away. "Who in their right mind would keep quiet about being married to a King?"

"Especially someone raised high from relatively humble beginnings!" Beau agreed. "I think also he underestimated her and her family."

"And now he's stuck with them." Isabel laughed. "All twenty of them or however many there are."

"Ten I think." Beau frowned. "Or is it twelve?"

"It's a penance, however many it is." Isabel grinned.

"A penance of Woodvilles." Kate giggled. "How appropriate." They all laughed and Beau's gaze glowed with a blatant, admiring tenderness. They rode on for a while, Kate listening to her sister's and Beau's reminiscences with interest, learning about people whose names she knew but who had only ever figured on the periphery of her life, until Beau suggested that they should stop in the next clearing and set up their picnic. A flurry of activity from the two grooms, Gethin and the maid Lucia as they tied up the horses, and shooed off the dogs. They laid out the blankets and flagons of ale and then a spread of cold capon, cheese, white wheaten bread, hard boiled eggs, honeyed wafers and crisp apples which forestalled any further close conversation. Instead there was much light-hearted joking and laughter as they ate, the sun shining on them warmly and the river drifting past them.

Later, after they had sated their hunger and the food had been cleared back into the panniers, Isabel made a point of wandering off along the bank to find small flowers to make a garland. Once she had drifted off Beau stood up quietly and offered Kate his hand, mouthing 'walk with me' to her. She smiled and nodded and coming to her feet, found her fingers laced tightly through his as they walked along the bank away from the foraging Isabel.

"I've always loved the river," he said softly when they had walked for a few minutes. "No matter how fast it flows it always seems somehow peaceful here."

"I love the sound of water," she agreed.

"I come here when I need to think."

"I always used to feel that when I was on the moors at Middleham." She smiled wistfully, glancing up at him and he squeezed her hand.

"You must miss it."

"Yes, I do, although I lived in Anjou and then Calais for almost as long as I lived in England, but somehow Middleham is my home."

"I had forgotten you were brought up here."

"I hadn't," she said dryly. "We lived here in Angers for much of the time, although my grandfather also had lands at Jurvadeil. I did not remember though, until I came back and recognised some of the town, that my grandfather's house had been here. It is surprising how much you forget when you are just seven."

"Your grandfather was a knight in Duke Rene's household, was he not?"

"Yes he was; that's how my mother became one of Queen Marguerite's ladies."

"Do you remember much of your life before you went to live with your father?" He sounded genuinely interested but she was conscious that her childhood must be a dull subject for a man such as he.

"A bit...my mother was not always easy...she had a difficult life." She smiled sadly. "My grandparents were embarrassed by my existence."

"So you did not miss France when you left then?"

"I missed my mother but Middleham always felt more like home than anywhere I had ever lived before. It has its own kind of beauty and whenever I could I would climb up to the top of the moor to look down over the village and sometimes I would imagine I was watching little people in a toy town." She gave a soft laugh. "I must have been such a child."

"We are all allowed childhood fantasies, sweetheart. If my memory serves me correctly, mine was that I was Sir Lancelot, using my skill as the greatest Knight to help Arthur keep his kingdom." He surprised himself with his admission, grinning self-consciously. "Jesus, that was a long time ago!"

"Indeed it must have been, my Lord!" she said pertly and then grinned at him as he laughed sharply.

"I told you before, in my head I am still twenty-one!"

"That's still older than me."

"Thanks for reminding me." He squeezed her hand none too gently and she laughed.

"Do you miss England, my Lord?"

"I can't remember what it feels like to live in England to be honest." He shook his head. "I suppose Anjou has been as much my home as anywhere since my father died and certainly since Hal was..." He stopped abruptly, conscious that they were straying into difficult territory.

"Killed?" She gave him a sideways glance through her lashes and smiled softly at his startled expression. "My father did not shield us from the...difficulties...between your family and mine, my Lord. He told us all before he made his peace with the Queen."

"Did he?" He sounded taken aback and then sighed. "It is so hard to find a safe subject between us."

"Then why try to?" She smiled again and he frowned.

"Because I want to talk with you."

"No, I mean why bother trying to find a safe subject?" She stopped and looked up at him, her eyes very green against the background of trees and grass. "Our families have been on opposing sides since the trouble between York and Lancaster began, my Lord, and there will be many things that we might talk about that will be difficult or strange at the very least. But perhaps if we agree that we will not blame each other for the acts of our families and our fathers then we can talk without worrying that we will say something that will upset the other." He stared down at her for a moment, his expression unreadable and then he smiled.

"Every time I think I have your measure, you astound me." His eyes glowed with an admiration that sent a scarlet flush speedily up her neck and into her cheeks but she did not drop her gaze.

"It is just that I think we would stumble too much over things we thought would offend." She looked down then at the hand that still held hers, studying the long brown fingers, laced through her own. "I don't want our conversation to be just trivial, my Lord." She looked back up at him, her cheeks flaming again. "I would like you to enjoy talking with me and not think that I do not have an interesting thought in my head."

"I cannot imagine ever thinking that; everything you say is of interest to me." The admiration did not subside.

"The trouble is that now I cannot tell if you are just being the consummate courtier or if you actually mean what you say." She laughed softly and began to walk again, forcing him into step beside her. He brought her hand up to his mouth and kissed her knuckle with soft lips.

"I always mean what I say to you," he murmured, and she laughed again.

"No." She giggled. "I still cannot tell."

"Katherine." He caressed her name in admonishment but she laughed again.

"I have your measure, my Lord, even if you do not have mine," she said and flashed such a laughingly flirtatious look up at him through her lashes that he could not help but join her laughter, squeezing her hand again.

"How can I convince you?" he asked after a moment.

"I am not sure you can, my Lord, I have heard too much about you." She disengaged her hand and bent down to pick up a stick, throwing it into the river and watching as an excited Saracen threw himself off the bank and paddled after it.

"So my cause is lost before it has begun then?" He sounded dejected.

"Perhaps."

"Ah but 'perhaps' is not definite; does that mean I still have a chance to redeem myself?"

"Maybe." She smiled. "A very small chance."

"Then I will take a small chance over none at all." His smile widened, but his eyes were serious.

"I will give you credit for your persistence, my Lord." She jumped out of the way with a squeal as the big alaunt clambered up the bank and shook himself vigorously, showering them both with droplets of ice cold water. He dropped the stick at her feet and looked up at her expectantly, his tongue lolling.

"Look, even my dogs are in love with you," Beau murmured, now behind her, slipping his arms around her waist and pressing his cheek to her temple.

"My Lord!" she admonished, but could not stop herself from leaning into him, her head in the curve of his shoulder as she looked up at him. "We are public here." He smiled and, his arm still around her waist, drew her towards the cover of the trees, away from prying eyes before taking her into his arms and holding her against him, resting his chin on top of her head.

"Whenever I smell jasmine I think of you." He breathed and she could feel his heart hammering a fast rhythm against her shoulder. "In fact you seem to be all I can think about." He kissed the top of her head and then tilting her chin towards him, kissed her mouth softly. "I am completely besotted with you." He ran his thumb along her cheekbone, his eyes devouring her face before his mouth covered hers again in a long and sensuous kiss, sending molten liquid flooding through her and arrowing her loins. She could not resist him, returning the kiss in full measure, her arms around his neck and her body pressing into his as his breathing quickened and she felt him begin to harden against her. "Oh, kitten." He made a soft noise in his throat, his hand sliding down her waist and into the small of her back, as he pulled her even closer to him.

"Beau!" The shout was faint but urgent behind them and Beau stiffened, his arms tightening round her a fraction. "Beau!"

"Sweet blood of Christ!" He let go of her and turned, his shoulders tense, his eyes closed against his exasperation. "What?" he shouted.

"A message from the Queen!" She could not see Jack but it was unmistakeably his voice.

"Shit!" Beau turned back to her, his face a picture of frustration and regret. "I'm sorry Katherine," he said softly. "It seems I am not to be allowed any peace."

"It's alright." She smiled up at him, disappointed yet relieved, slipping her hand into his, and was rewarded with a look that made her heart pound as he leaned down and kissed her cheek gently.

"I will make it up to you," he whispered in her ear. "I promise." He brought her hand swiftly up to his mouth and then whistling the still expectant Saracen he strode across the grass towards his brother.

***

It was dark and the torches were just being lit as Kate hurried across the hall with the big basket of underclothes she had just collected from the laundry. It mostly contained Anne's chemises and underdresses, all aired and dried and which now needed packing into their coffers, but on the top were two or three shirts of Edward's which needed mending and which she had decided to do to occupy her before supper. She walked across the bailey and into the tower which housed Edward and Anne's chamber and trotted up the stairs, her left hand on the wall in the almost pitch darkness, working her way round until she came to the top. She pushed open the bedchamber door and came to a stop as she saw Edmund Beaufort and Prince Edward in close conversation, seated by the fireplace. She had not expected anyone to be there.

"Forgive me, your Graces." She curtseyed, trying to balance the basket. Edward smiled and beckoned her in.

"It's alright Kate, come in."

"I do not want to disturb you, my Lords."

"You won't." Beau added his voice to Edward's, a brief smile creasing his eyes. She carried the basket across to where three coffers were lined up against the wall and, kneeling down, began to methodically fold and put away the garments in her basket.

"How long will it take you to get there?" Edward carried on the conversation.

"I think I can do it in five days in this weather as long as it doesn't rain and the roads stay hard."

"We need to know when he will give us the money he promised us. I know he and my Lord Warwick are in close communication, but we cannot wait for Warwick to hear from him and then send to us. We need to know more quickly than that."

"I think he will wait to see how Warwick fares before he gives us any more financial support." Beau leaned back in his chair and stretched. "But I will take your Lady mother's letters and see if I can persuade him otherwise."

"So you will be gone at least a fortnight." Edward pulled a face and Beau smiled.

"I'll miss you too, lad, but you should enjoy the time with your Lady wife. When we finally get to England there will be little time for that."

"You're right and I suppose at least Jack is staying behind this time. It's just without you I am completely surrounded by women and at my mother's mercy!" He shook his head. "I love her dearly but she tries my patience."

"She has your best interests at heart, Edward." Beau's voice was soothing.

"She tries to coddle me." Edward snorted in irritation. "She still thinks I am a child."

"I was twenty-six when my mother died, and she still treated me as if I was a lad who needed protecting from himself, and poor Jack as if he was a babe in arms. It is what mothers do!" Beau laughed and Edward reluctantly joined in.

"Talking of which, I think she wants to see us both before supper." Edward stood up and yawned. "I need to visit the privy." He glanced over at Beau who had also got to his feet. "I'll meet you in the solar in ten minutes?" Beau nodded. Edward turned to Kate. "Do you know where Anne is?"

"Yes, your Grace, she is in the solar with your Lady mother and the Countess of Warwick." Kate looked over her shoulder and smiled at the dark haired boy. "I believe that Pere Hugo is doing a bible reading." Edward grinned.

"Ah," he said with a wry laugh. "They won't mind us interrupting then?" Kate smiled again. It was well known that Pere Hugo's bible readings were probably the most boring activities that took place in the castle, but Marguerite allowed them in order not to offend the man who was her confessor. She turned back to sorting through the coffers as the men headed for the door, hearing it click as it shut behind them.

"Katherine?" Beau's husky voice made her jump.

"My Lord!" she came to her feet with an exclamation of surprise.

"I'm sorry, I didn't mean to startle you. I can't stay long, I told Edward I had forgotten something." He moved toward her, looking down at her from his full head advantage. "I have to go away again tomorrow, Madame is sending me on an urgent errand to Paris."

"Oh!" the disappointment sounded in her voice

"I will be gone for more than a fortnight." He caught her shoulders and she felt a huge sense of gratification that the disappointment she felt matched the expression that raced across his face. "This time I wanted at least to say goodbye."

"I am sorry that you are going, my Lord," she said quietly. "I enjoyed our time today."

"Did you?" There was an intensity in his eyes that made her spine tingle. "It seems no sooner do I get home than I must leave again." He reached for her and drew her into his embrace, his arms closing around her, laying his cheek against the top of her head. "It would seem that time is not something we are destined to have. That was all

I wanted from today, a little time alone with you, but even that was thwarted."

"Perhaps it is not meant to be, my Lord," she whispered against his chest.

"Don't say that," he said, drawing back from her and staring down at her. "I need to be with you."

"Do you?" She was spellbound in the hypnotic intensity of his eyes, her heart leaping at his words.

"Yes," he whispered and his mouth came down on hers in a kiss that held all the intensity of his gaze, nothing gentle about it, his lips urgent as they claimed hers, his embrace tight as he held her against him. She clung to him for support as warmth flooded her, instinctively responding to his need with her own, pressing her body against his as he held her. She could not say when it changed for her, except that one minute she had her fingers in the hair at the nape of his neck and the next she was pushing against his shoulders, trying to pull from his embrace. Perhaps it was the point at which his hand cupped her breast, or when she felt him hard against her belly, or even when he whispered her name on a harsh ragged breath; whenever it was, suddenly she was afraid; afraid of his intensity, afraid that she was going to be overwhelmed by his need for her, that he would overpower her. She cried out against his mouth and he released her abruptly, so that she staggered backwards, her hand to her lips, catching the wall for support. They stared at each other for a moment and then he gestured helplessly.

"I'm sorry," he said breathlessly. "Jesus, Katherine, I am so sorry." She backed away from him, making her way around the wall towards the door as he watched her, his expression desperate. "Katherine, please!" She placed her hand on the door latch. "Wait!" She stopped, her back to him. "I would never hurt you." He spoke softly, soothingly as if to a frightened animal. "I swear on my life." She shook her head and turned back to him, hazel eyes glittering with unshed tears.

"But you would use me like a cheap whore to satisfy a lust!" A tear tracked its way down her cheek. His expression was horrified.

"I would not..." His voice was little more than a whisper. She said nothing, her eyes not leaving his face as she blinked hard. "Don't assume you know..." He shook his head, trying to articulate his thoughts.

"I was afraid," she said very quietly, "afraid you would not stop."

"Christ." He closed his eyes in mortification. "You cannot think that of me."

"I don't know what to think."

"You don't understand," he said, still very softly. "I...I care for you, Katherine." The tears which shone in her eyes finally spilled over as she shook her head, the hand on the door latch wrenching it open. She backed through the door, her voice catching on her tears.

"Are there no lengths you will not go to, to get what you want?" she said, and whirling round fled down the corridor, slamming the door behind her.

***

Beau stood where she had left him, one hand reaching out to her, stunned still.

"Fuck!" he said softly, "You fucking idiot Beaufort, you stupid fucking idiot." He moved for the door then unable to believe that what should have been a touching goodbye had gone so badly wrong and that he had allowed his feelings to overcome his judgment. But he could not excuse himself, not at his age and not knowing her history, even if his need for her was made so intense by the emotion she aroused within him. There was no sign of her as he walked down the passage and took the stairs two at a time, thinking all the while what he could do. He was leaving tomorrow at dawn which left him almost no time at all to make amends. He had to reach her somehow as he could not imagine coming home in a fortnight's time and finding that she would have nothing to do with him. In fact, the idea that she might reject him filled him with a dread he could not even contemplate and he pushed it to the back of his mind. Catching sight of his brother he hurried across the hall.

"Jack." he called urgently, grabbing the young man's arm and taking him into a quieter corner, not bothering to apologise to the man he was talking to. Jack looked at first surprised and then fondly exasperated at his brother's peremptory attitude.

"At your service," he said dryly. Beau didn't even crack a smile.

"I need your help," he said curtly, never imagining that Jack would not do as he asked. "I've fucked up and I need to make amends but I don't have any time to sort it out; I have to be with the Queen in five minutes."

"Sort what out…what sort of 'fucked up'?" Jack frowned.

"I have…upset Katherine." The granite expression did not encourage any questions.

"That would explain why she came racing through here like the wind then."

"Did she?" Beau grimaced "Shit!"

"What kind of upset?" Jack cocked his head to one side. "Are we talking 'never speak to you again'?" Beau shook his head, irritated.

"I'm not prepared to go into detail, but suffice to say that I need somehow to touch her heart and ask for forgiveness."

"Surely you didn't let her catch you bedding someone else?"

"No!" Beau sighed. "It's complicated but I think I may have…asked too much of her…" he admitted grudgingly, a flush creeping up his neck.

"Oh Beau!"

"Don't 'oh Beau' me, you are not my father!"

"Well, for God's sake, how could you…She's not one of your village lasses or a whore, she needs wooing, Beau!"

"I know but I just never seem to have time to woo her and I wanted her to know how much I would miss her; I just didn't know how to tell her."

"You know, brother, for someone who has bedded half of France you know very little about women!" Jack shook his head and then subsided at his brother's withering expression. "Alright, alright! Jewellery will not do for someone like Kate; she wears nothing other than her wedding band and anyway you need to get to her heart, which jewellery would never do, she'd see straight through it."

"How do you know so much about her all of a sudden?" Beau glowered at his brother and Jack laughed.

"Because I actually like women, Beau, and I listen, watch and learn. I don't have your looks to ensnare them and I don't always think with my cock like you do." His expression softened suddenly at his brother's discomfort and then cleared as an idea came to him. "I think I know what you can do that will work," he said softly, and then looked at him levelly, his expression serious for once. "Kate is a sweet and lovely girl who does not deserve to have her heart broken for a lust, so think first, Beau, and make sure you mean it."

Beau considered for a moment and then nodded.

"I mean it," he said simply.

Light was just starting to dawn over what had been a sleepless night for Kate, laying next to the sleeping Anne, after Edward had for once forsaken his wife's bed to plan with his mother and Beau late into the night. She rubbed her eyes and sighed, slipping silently out from under the covers and dragging her chemise over her head before splashing water on her face and pulling out her night plait for brushing. Anne stirred briefly, turned over and then snuggled back under the covers, and Kate smiled, drawing the curtain around her, not wanting to disturb her peaceful slumber. Her sister's relief at a night's respite from Edward's attentions had been palpable for although the girl was obviously fond of him she did not feel the same physical attraction towards him that he so obviously felt for her. She had confessed to Kate in the dark of their curtained bed last night that she tried to respond to him as enthusiastically as she could but sometimes she found it a strain and the thought of a whole night without having to worry whether she was pleasing him had been a treat for her. That, coupled with being able to share her bed with her favourite sister and gossip and giggle into the night as they had used to when growing up at Middleham, had made it a pleasant night indeed. Kate had refrained from telling Anne of her encounter with the Duke of Somerset in this very chamber and her own embarrassment at what now seemed an overreaction to his passionate advances, or how stupid she had felt by the time she had got back to their room after dodging round the castle to avoid both him and his brother. She felt such a ninny for having run out on him like that, and for how bad she had obviously made him feel, but she had no idea how to make amends or how to get a message to him before he left this morning and now she would not see him for more than two weeks. Still cross with herself she dragged the brush through her hair, her annoyance making her especially brisk and giving no quarter to any tangles, before she tied it back into a thick plait, secured at top and bottom with a long leather lace. That done, she selected a soft, white linen under-dress and a pale blue over-gown from her coffer and dressed hurriedly, lacing herself up deftly and brushing out any creases in the wool as she did so, then slipping her feet into some pretty silk slippers she opened the chamber door and slipped out, aiming to go down to the kitchen and sweet talk Jacques into putting a platter together for Anne to break her fast in bed. As she turned to shut the door as quietly as she could she saw to her surprise that there was a square of parchment pinned to it with her name written in an unfamiliar bold black hand across the front of it. Taking it down and unfolding it she frowned.

"Follow the signs," she murmured and then shook her head, puzzled, and looked around her. She could see nothing that looked like a sign until she looked down and saw that there was a mark like a small arrow on the stone floor, painstakingly scratched so as not to be noticeable to all but there if you were looking for it. Intrigued she walked in the direction it pointed and saw that a few strides further on there was another one and then another, all leading along the passage towards the entrance to the roof of the tower in which Anne and Edward slept. Sure enough, when she reached the staircase the arrows pointed upwards on the steps; someone had gone to a lot of trouble to get her here and excitement began to flutter in her stomach. Slowly she walked up the spiral stone steps, her left hand steadying her on the wall until she came out blinking into the early light, standing for a moment to get her bearings. Next to the doorway, on the floor, was a small basket, the lid closed and a note written in the same black hand pinned to the top of it, 'This is the property of Katherine Neville.' Taking the note off, she unfolded it and stared at the words written inside.

'Forgive me, Beau.'

"Oh," she whispered, inhaling the faint but familiar scent on the paper, before opening the basket and staring at the small white silky ears followed by a button black nose which popped over the edge, a tiny little pink tongue swiping at her fingers. "Oh, who are you?" she said softly, lifting the tiny bundle out of the basket and holding it to her face as its stumpy tail wagged furiously and little blue eyes looked at her with adoration. "And where did you come from?" She kissed the top of the little head. "You are beautiful." She picked up the basket and put the puppy back in it, closing the lid and making sure there was nothing else on the rooftop before going back down the stairs to the passageway. The puppy squeaked unhappily and she made a soft soothing noise in the back of her throat. "It's alright, poppet," she murmured. "It's alright... oh!" She stopped in her tracks. Edmund

Beaufort stood at the top of the steps from the bailey, a long, black fur-lined travel cloak covering his clothes, twisting a black cap nervously through his fingers, his chest rising and falling rapidly.

"I saw you on the roof…I was just about to leave…" When she said nothing, he gestured to the basket. "I see you found him."

"Yes." There was so much she wanted to say but nothing would come to her.

"I hope you like him," he said awkwardly, clenching his fingers around the cap.

"He's beautiful."

"Katherine…" He moved towards her, stopping uncertainly in front of her.

"It's alright, my Lord." She smiled a soft smile which made his heart swoop. "There is nothing to forgive."

"I behaved like the worst boor." He shook his head in self-disgust. "I'm sorry."

"And I am sorry too; I behaved like a child." She took his right hand in both of hers and looked at the long, tanned fingers, adorned only with his ducal signet ring and the band on his thumb. "I am flattered by your attentions, my Lord, and you would know I was lying if I said that I was not attracted to you." She took a deep breath and looked up into those beautiful and arresting eyes. "But it will only end in dishonour for me and I cannot do that to my family."

"Katherine, listen to me." He slid his free hand across her cheek and into her hair. "You may have heard that I am not kind to women, that I have had my share and treated all of them badly and discarded them without thought when I have finished with them. But I have never lied to them; not any of them; not ever. I have never promised anything I was not willing to give and if I have tired of them quickly then I have never strung them along with false declarations of love or told them that I care. So when I said I cared for you I meant it; it was not some ruse to get you into my bed."

"But that is where we would end up." Her smile became sad. "It can be the only outcome."

"I would cherish you." His voice was a husky caress.

"But when you tired of me, you would move on and I would be tarnished forever as a whore." She leaned into the hand caressing her cheek, her heart pulling her one way and her head the other. "I cannot do it."

"Then all I ask is that you promise me one thing." He traced her cheekbone softly with his thumb. "Promise me that when I come home from Paris you will spend some time with me."

"I don't..."

"Please Katherine. I have to leave now, I have no choice, but please do not deny me the chance to talk to you when I come home."

"Alright." She nodded. "I promise."

"Thank you." He drew her gently, without resistance, into his embrace and held her, resting his cheek on her hair and inhaling her jasmine scent. "Have you thought of a name for him yet?" he asked as the puppy squeaked again.

"I thought I might call him Anthony." She leaned back and looked up at him, her eyes sparkling, trying to take the intensity out of the air around them.

"Anthony?" He cocked a brow quizzically.

"A good name for something that is beautiful but has no obvious use." She grinned and he laughed sharply, his eyes taking on that admiring look which sent heat to her loins.

"Katherine..." His gaze roved her face hungrily and she put her hands up to his chest, as if the physical gesture could ward off the assault on her senses.

"You have to go, my Lord," she said quietly.

"Yes." He leaned forward and kissed her briefly, a soft touching of lips which conveyed as much as a passionate embrace ever could have. "Please don't close your heart to me while I am away, darling,...please," he said softly. "Promise me that you won't do that." She looked up at him for what seemed like an age and then nodded.

"I promise." He kissed her again and then let her go.

"I think you should call him Samson," he said, smiling.

"Samson?"

"Small things need a big name." He watched as she took the pup out of the basket and held it up to look at.

"Samson." She tested the name and the stumpy little tail wagged furiously. She laughed. "Samson it is then." She smiled at Beau and he stroked the puppy's head with his forefinger.

"Goodbye little man," he said and then bowed formally to Kate. "Farewell, Katherine, and the Lord keep you safe. I will see you on my return, God willing."

"God grant you a safe journey, my Lord." She dropped a curtsey and they looked at each other for a moment as he backed away, touching his fingers to his lips and placing them over his heart, and then he was gone.

Chapter Eight

Anjou, France, October 1470

Wearily, Kate laid her hot, aching forehead against the coolness of the thick glass, closing her eyes at the momentary relief it brought her. She felt so stunned by the news from England that her eyes had doubted the words coming out of her stepmother's mouth as she read the bold black writing so clear on the letter in her hand.

"True to his word, this time Jack stood by me, no longer able to stomach Ned and his ingratitude. Ned could never believe that anyone might turn against his charm, least of all our Jack, and it seems that once again the desertion of a Neville from his side has unnerved him for he fled without much thought and I understand is residing in ignominy at his brother by marriage's court in Burgundy. But he will wait long if he expects aid from Charles for he was ever one to be loyal to Lancaster and cautious with his coffers."

"So," said the Countess in her quiet voice. "It would seem our cousin of York was afraid to stand out against uncle Jack and that your father has won a great victory so we shall all be joining him soon in England." She did not sound completely pleased by that thought, but Kate guessed no one would be surprised by that for it was no secret amongst Marguerite's whole household that her father had had eyes for no one except Veronique de Roet on the morning of his departure, and it was now very much the gossip of the moment that this lady was also the mother of his seventeen-year-old bastard daughter who was with the Warwick household.

Kate shuddered involuntarily as the memory of her father and mother in close passionate embrace came into her head. She could still see them entwined, as they had been, her beloved father's cool composure destroyed by the naked need Veronique had obviously aroused in him. She could even feel the complete misery, which had welled in her heart at the sight of them, knowing that no longer was she all he had left of his love, the sole reminder of a passion that had passed him by, and she had sensed when he summoned her to his presence only hours before he left, that her mother had replaced her as first in his heart. Quietly and with obvious joy he had told her that her mother and he were reconciled and asked her, if only for his sake, to put her anger to one side and make every attempt to live amiably with Veronique, for when they all returned to England she would be going with them and he expected to see a lot of her. He had said that what he wanted more than anything was for the two of them to be friends so that he could leave France in the peace and knowledge that his beloved daughter and her mother were together, helping each other in their time of need. She had listened to his words without outward expression and obediently agreed to see her mother and to attempt to forgive her, for the last thing she wanted was for her father to leave France thinking that his daughter might try to destroy his love, so newly rekindled and so vulnerable for that. She gave nothing away of her feelings to anyone, least of all the person who had caused her torment, treating Veronique with the same casual politeness she accorded any stranger, not attempting to draw her into the closed circles of her life and yet not repulsing her tentative advances. Her sisters had been curious to know the woman who had given her life and to see what it was about her that had so captured their father's interest, and, though prepared to dislike her because of the humiliation she had caused their mother, they had found that they admired her, enjoyed her amusing conversation and amiable yet sophisticated nature, and so Kate had found herself with only one ally, and this in the unlikely form of her stepmother. Had she been able to be objective, she would have laughed at the irony of the situation; a dilemma which united the Countess with the girl she had once hated with such passion, and when she would have once jested about the jealousy which had become such a bond between them, taunting herself as well as the Countess for their stupidity, she was now merely grateful for the silent support of one on her side, one who did not see Veronique as some kind of angel who had romantically saved her father's jaded soul and captured his elusive heart.

"It would seem, though, that Edward managed to get a message to the Woodville bitches and she has taken to sanctuary to wait the birth of yet another child." The countess was rapidly scanning the page of the letter and this time her mouth turned up in a bitter grimace. "Jesu', the woman's life is a round of being with child and being brought to bed. I suppose her fertility is one thing her husband can thank her for." Her envy was quite understandable.

"What of Dickon, mama, did he go to Burgundy with Edward?" Anne's voice was small and her question tentative.

"Of course, dear, where else would the little lapdog be but trotting obediently at his master's heels?" The tone of her mother's voice belied the cruelty of the words. Anne's lip quivered and Kate sought to intervene before Anne betrayed her still warm affection for her cousin.

"How strange, "she murmured thoughtfully, drawing the Countess's eyes to her as she spoke, "That Richard, who does have such a strong sense of right and wrong, should follow a man such as Ned who does not." The Countess gave a mirthless snort of laughter and ran her eyes speculatively over her stepdaughter.

"Well sometimes the magnetism of a man attracts all sorts of people to his side. Even those who have the morals he lacks. I believe you found his magnetism quite mesmerising yourself, Katherine."

"I was taught my lesson very quickly though, Madame." Kate bristled and then subsided. "Papa understood." There was no point in falling out with her stepmother now that her father was not with them after all, and they all needed to make the best of it. Her father's parting words to her had been,

Should aught befall me, Katherine, never sell yourself too cheaply to any. Your worth is far greater than the value you place upon yourself and it would be well for all who pursue you to remember that. Think carefully child and do not demean yourself for anyone; you deserve only everything that a man can give you whether he is knight, nobleman or king.' Tears sprang to her eyes as she thought of his earnest expression and the love he had so constantly shown her.

"Yes well your father ever-indulged all his children, but he pays the price for that now as they all begin to show their true colours." Anne Beauchamp let her china blue eyes rest on her youngest daughter. "Anne thinks I don't know it but deep down she bewails her fate at being Princess of Wales instead of Duchess of Gloucester; Isabel carries grudges against her father and secrets in her heart and you…well hopefully you have learned your lesson and there will be no further 'dalliances' from you." She carefully folded the letter and tucked it into her girdle. As an exile in France she had cared little for her husband's change of loyalty, foreseeing that it would bring them nothing and lose them all but now that he was once again the power behind the English throne she had decided that he might be worth fighting for, after all it would be pleasant to be fêted as the wife of England's premier Earl once more. "Now I would suggest that we prepare for our summons to England, for surely it cannot be long before the presence of the Queen and her son are required there." And smiling triumphantly she glided from the chamber.

"I'm frightened," said Anne quietly as soon as the door closed behind her mother.

"So am I." Anne stared at her sister for a moment, for never once during this conflict had Kate admitted to fear. She looked at her, seeing for the first time the high spots of colour on her cheeks and the shadows under her eyes.

"Are you alright, Kate?" she asked.

"Just a headache."

"Are you sure?" Anne looked dubious.

"Yes I am fine, honestly." Kate sighed heavily. "Look Anne you have to start thinking about what you are saying. With papa's victory over Ned our lives have altered forever and are now bound up completely with the fate of Lancaster; you cannot afford to keep showing your partiality." She closed her eyes and leaned her head once more against the cool glass of the window, drawing her knees beneath her and resting a slender hand in her lap. "Do you understand what I say, Anne, you must be the model of a Lancastrian Lady?"

"I cannot help it, Kate, nothing that papa or anyone can ever do will stop me from loving Richard and I cannot bear to know nothing of him."

"Then leave me to ask, for they will think less harshly of me if they think it is I who have a fondness for him and not you. After all you are wed to the Prince of Lancaster; you can't constantly be asking after a Prince of York." She reached for her sister's hand. "I'm not asking you to forget, just to hide that you remember. It is for the best."

"I know you're right, but it's harder than you know to keep such love a secret." Kate was saved from answering her sister's exasperating response by the sound of the heavy door opening and Isabel coming morosely into the chamber. She glanced first at one girl and then the other.

"Oh Jesu', you are not still weeping and wailing over Edward's retreat, are you." Anne bristled.

"We were talking of love, actually," she snapped.

"Dickon you mean?" Isabel's tone was biting; Anne's dogmatic devotion to Richard annoyed her beyond reason.

"That's unfair, Bel." Kate leaped to her defence almost immediately and earned herself a wry grin from her elder sister.

"Sorry, nursey, I didn't mean to upset your little charge." She laughed with a flash of her old malice.

"Don't be so hateful!" Anne drew herself up to her full height but was still dwarfed by the average height of Isabel.

"It's time you faced reality, Anne, my dear," she taunted, laughing down at her. "Soon you will be in London being fêted as Princess of Wales so now is not the time to be thinking of others and wishing for what cannot be."

"How can you be so sure that Ned won't come back?"

"I am sure he will try, but because I do still have the sense I was born with, I can see that papa has a good chance of holding out, for many still see King Henry as the rightful King and not Ned." Isabel's voice began to rise hotly. "So for heaven's sake, Anne, face it; you will never wed with Richard, like as not he is already casting around for another bride, especially now he knows you are wed to Lancaster." Anne burst into tears and Kate leaped from her seat.

"Why do you have to be so damned callous?"

"Oh yes, its all my fault, isn't it?" Isabel stamped her foot like a child. "No one cares that my husband is in England at war with his own brother, oh no, they all think I have no sensitivity, not like sweet little Anne. Well, dear Anne will soon be swanning around as Princess of Wales, wearing a crown that should have been mine had papa had the guts to fight for it!" Anne stopped crying and stared at her sister's angry face, horror mingled with disgust in her green eyes.

"So that is it Bel! You are jealous that soon, if all goes to father's plan, I shall be Queen of England. Well it may be of great surprise to you to know that the thought of wearing that crown makes me feel sick, fought for, as it will be in the blood and lives of good men; in truth, I detest the very thought of it, but then I didn't inherit our father's ambition as you did, nor his blatant lack of moral scruples. So, if you wish so much for this precious piece of jewellery which will sit so meaninglessly on my head. Divorce your husband and marry mine, for I want him not."

"Anne!" Kate hissed. "For the love of Jesus, hush. If Edward were to hear you he would be heartbroken!" Even Isabel looked stunned at her sister's outburst. "This fighting is not going to change or resolve anything. None of us are happy with how things are but we have to make the best of it. I love my cousins too but we cannot live in the past; we have to move on!" she faltered, tears springing unbidden. "Papa is in England, fighting for our future, and all we can do is squabble about how hard done to we are!"

"Oh Kate!" Anne looked stricken. "I didn't mean to be thoughtless or ungrateful."

"It doesn't matter." Kate was suddenly too weary to speak. "I cannot think. I need some space; some air." She turned for the door, grabbing her cloak. "But for God's sake if you are going to fight, be careful what you say or you will bring Madame's wrath down on all of us."

***

Outside, taking gulps of cool October air, she felt a sudden sense of loneliness and dread and realised she was shivering; she missed Beau far more than she had ever imagined and wished she could find him and talk to him now. Her arm was throbbing painfully where she had scratched it in the stable and, when she had looked at it this morning, the skin around it was red and puffy as if it had festered a little. She walked across the bailey towards the chapel, resolving to speak to her stepmother tomorrow and see if there was anything they could put on it to help it heal better, and opening the chapel door she went in, genuflecting at the altar, then taking a seat on the bench to the right and leaning her throbbing head in her hands. She murmured a short prayer for her father's safety and then sat for a long time, thinking of nothing, her head swimming and her body shivering before she slowly slipped to the floor, her mind descending into blackness.

Paris, France
October 1470

"So, my Lord Somerset, our friend Warwick won a bloodless victory then?" King Louis, the eleventh reigning monarch of that name, rubbed his long-fingered hands together and gave a wolfish grin. Beau inclined his head with an answering smile.

"Indeed, your Grace. It shows how disaffected the people were with York's rule. I had heard that Warwick raised his army without resistance and was cheered loudly when he entered London."

"You did well to talk my aunt around from her initial refusal of his aid. King Henry would never have been restored without the military help from one such as Warwick. No offence, my Lord, but you would not have had the same success raising a force and gaining the support of all England as he did."

"I take no offence at a true statement, your Grace, and I would consider Richard Neville a friend now; in fact, I look forward to joining him in the King's Counsel." Beau smiled again. He liked Louis and was in awe of his agile mind which wove webs and traps for people to fall into, exactly as Edward of York had done with Warwick, but he held no illusions that the support was for Warwick and not for the Lancastrian cause; he had no allegiance except to the alliance that would bring him the most gain.

"I would advise you to get Madame Marguerite to England as quickly as possible and parade young Edward on the streets of London so that he can win over the Londoners. He is a handsome boy and that little wife of his is a comely piece; they could win much in support, especially as York's Queen is so disliked." Louis indicated Beau to a chair by the fire and sat down himself, a page serving them fine spiced red wine from a flagon. "Is the marriage successful Somerset?"

"I think so, sire. He is certainly very fond of her although Madame is less convinced. She wanted a French princess for him. I think perhaps Anne Neville is a little young for breeding just yet but I don't think it will be for want of trying!" Both men laughed slightly wistfully, remembering what it was like to be young like Edward and in the first flush of lust.

"I hear the Woodville woman is with child again!" Louis pulled a distasteful face.

"So I understand," Beau replied drily. "I'll give York his due, he's prolific in his legitimate offspring. Mind you, she is a bold piece is Elizabeth Woodville. I remember when she was wed to John Grey and she served our Queen; she always reminded me of nothing less than a sleek cream-fed cat with very sharp claws and her beauty is fey and cold, your Grace."

"Well, York seems to like her. He obviously visits her bed often enough, along with all the others he frequents."

"Aye, and they are many; his appetite is huge, and I would not consider myself slack in that regard. We are not that far off being of an age, York and I, and I can still remember vying with him over the attentions of women as a lad; he was half a head taller than me and twice as wide, even when he was seventeen and I was one and twenty." Beau grinned. "Hal and I had no chance against him!"

"I'm surprised he let Warwick outwit him twice like he did."

"I think it was John Neville's betrayal that hit him hard. He never expected to lose his loyalty, not after he stayed his hand when Warwick expected his aid before he fled to France."

"Well it should not have been unexpected after the way he treated him, taking the Northumberland title away from him and giving him Montague instead." Louis shook his head. "How to win men to your side and hold them for life, eh?"

"Aye. Mind you, there is no better battle commander than York, your Grace, even if his governing leaves something to be desired. I have seen him fight and he is a demon at the front of his men in his white armour for all to see; the man believes he is invincible and for that reason he generally is. I have seen him in the centre of the fighting, on foot, alongside his men and there is no greater motivation than having a man like York fighting at your side." Beau was reluctantly admiring. "I think the main reason we lost at Towton was down to York and nothing else. He rallied those men like I have never seen before and he was right at the forefront through all of it."

"You sound envious." Louis looked at Beau closely.

"I'm envious of his chance to gain such a reputation when I have not been able to. I was always in the shadow of my father and my brother and never a commander on my own. I would have given anything for opportunities like he has had to lead men as he has and to win the battles that he has won. I know that in his shoes I could have done it, but as it is I have won nothing and achieved very little in my life." Beau looked up and met the cool blue eyes of his host. "Sorry, I'm being a little maudlin."

"Your loyalty to your cause is to be commended, my Lord Somerset. I know how difficult a mistress Marguerite can be and I know that you have had to strive to cleave to your conscience and stay with her, but that to me is as admirable as winning a great battle. There are not many who can demonstrate that level of loyalty, save the likes of William Marshall or John of Ghent." Louis smiled. "Although I must say that my favourite English hero is a Frenchman, Simon de Montfort." Beau laughed.

"Naturally," he said, dryly. "I read about him in the schoolroom as a lad. He was a principled man and he had a point, I have to say."

"Aye, the nobles must have their say, but the King should rule. But de Montfort understood real government and I have learned a great deal from reading about him and his Oxford Provisions," Louis admitted. Beau was interested.

"So you study the art of governing then, your Grace?"

"Of course. I would never presume that I could rule without study and without understanding the needs of my people. Some men are natural rulers, such as de Montfort or William Marshall, even if they are not born to Kingship, but others are born to it and not fit to rule such as..." He hesitated.

"Harry of Lancaster?" Beau raised his eyebrows and Louis smiled.

"I was going to say King John, whose misgovernment paved the way for the loss of the English throne for a while before Marshall was given the Regency, but yes if you wish we could say the present King Henry is not a natural ruler."

"His boy is different." Beau smiled fondly. "He could be a great leader. He listens and learns all the time and never believes that he knows it all, and he takes direction and has ideas which he asks for input into; I would like to think that I have influenced that and that I have given him some of those principles and that wisdom. I don't know who he takes after but it is neither his mother nor his father." Louis raised his brow sardonically and Beau grinned. "And certainly not my father; he never listened to anyone or took advice at all. My brother Hal was much the same, although a little more inclined to listen I suppose but certainly not to me." Beau stretched out his legs and sighed. "Such a waste of a young life and such a blow to our cause; Hal was but twenty-eight when he threw away his life over a skirmish and now, from the age of thirty-one, I realise how young that was." Louis nodded.

"It's when you look back that you comprehend these things, my Lord. Looking forward is the only way." He smiled and beckoned the page forward again with some more wine. Beau held out his cup and watched the wine pour into it, his thoughts drifting back to Anjou and his departure, watching Kate with the puppy, her sad smile making his heart leap in his chest, needing to stay and talk but having to leave her behind. The lonely feeling engulfed him suddenly and he wished he could just see her for a moment, see her smile and look at him in that way that she had, the way that made his stomach lurch and his heart beat faster. He realised that Louis was watching him.

"Sorry, your Grace. I was away thinking," he said self-consciously. Louis smiled.

Don't dwell on the past, lad," he said misreading Beau's sadness for regret over things that had happened in earlier times. "it is best not to regret but to learn from what has happened and not to repeat the mistake. You will triumph as Warwick already has and when you take that boy across the narrow sea he will win the people over as his father never could and his mother never tried."

"I believe he will, your Grace. He is a handsome lad at seventeen, perhaps not in the same way as York, but how many York's come along in a man's lifetime?" Beau grimaced. "As I said, I have never seen a man as tall as Edward of York or as broad. He is a full half-head taller than I am and I am near a head taller than most, and when I think of Richard of York and Dame Cecily, I wonder how they produced him. Only the boy Gloucester seems to resemble his father!"

"Well there was that story about the archer in Rouen reputed to be York's father, but if the truth be told the Plantagenets have always been tall, right back to Geoffrey of Anjou, Richard Coeur de Lion and all three of the Edwards before this one. I think Richard of York being short and dark was somewhat misleading." He laughed then and winked at Beau. "Although it is more fun to believe that proud Cecily Neville was tupping a lowly archer behind her husband's back!"

"Cecily Neville is another one I really can't imagine tupping anyone!" Beau said with feeling. "I cannot abide that woman, proud as

Lucifer and as cold as an ice block. I wonder what York thinks of those rumours. Didn't my Lord Warwick resurrect them initially when we all thought he was going to aim for Clarence on the throne?"

"Yes, but Clarence would have been a disaster." Louis shook his head. "I cannot imagine what was going through Richard's head. To even consider someone as feckless and unprincipled as Clarence was complete madness. Do you know the boy?"

"I met him once when he was about ten, in Ludlow, when my brother sacked it. I rescued Gloucester from under the feet of a runaway stallion and Clarence was there with his mother. He struck me as fearless and stupid at the time. Gloucester was an appealing little thing then though and showed some real bravery in the face of what must have seemed like the end of the world to him."

"I don't know much about Gloucester except that he was earmarked for your Princess once upon a time and that he looks like his father but that's just hearsay."

"I only know what I have heard in idle chatter from Warwick's daughters, who grew up with him. He excelled as a soldier it seemed in training and was well loved by all of them." He thought of Richard teaching Kate to cut a horse's throat and smiled to himself.

"I had heard tell that Warwick was reunited with his bastard daughter's mother when he was at Marguerite's court?" Louis' question was innocently put but Beau knew that he loved to gossip over the intricate lives of his vassals and retainers. Beau's smile widened.

"Aye, the lovely Veronique de Roet. He apparently never forgot her and they were reunited when he came to Madame's court, but I am not surprised; nan Beauchamp is another cold fish and I am sure a man like Richard Neville needed warmth in his bed."

"What man does not?" Louis smiled, his protruding blue eyes glinting mischievously, and Beau laughed. "So." Louis made one of his mercurial shifts back to business. "What is the plan from here for England then, my Lord. What do you intend to do?"

"Get Madame over there as quickly as possible and in the meantime, I am going to Burgundy to see if I can persuade Charles to give Edward of York up. I can't see it because of his wife's kinship, but Charles also has kinship to me and my house and to my Prince's house so hopefully we can prevail."

"Yes, interesting dilemma for my Lord of Burgundy there." Louis grinned. "I am thinking of exerting a little pressure on him to push him to send York to us." Beau arched his eyebrows in surprise.

"Could that not just push him in the other direction, your Grace?" he asked.

Louis shrugged.

"Perhaps; Warwick and I are prepared to take the risk while you, my Lord will use your friendship, charm and wit to see if you can achieve our desired outcome by diplomacy."

Beau smiled.

"Easier if Charles was a woman," he said laconically and Louis laughed and then rose gesturing to Beau.

"Come over here and I will show you our plans." He led the way to a table with several parchments scattered on it. Beau sighed and grimaced inwardly. This was going to be a long evening.

Some hours and several cups of wine later, as he made his way somewhat unsteadily to his chamber, Beau reflected on Louis' easy and engaging manner which seemed to draw every confidence out of the recipient of his hospitality. He had found himself confiding his fears over his ability to persuade Charles and how Marguerite knew just how to make him doubt himself. No wonder they called Louis 'the spider king'; it wasn't just about the webs he weaved but the fact that he devoured his victims as well. He smiled tipsily at his analogy and sighed; he was exhausted and hoped that Gethin had put some fresh water out for him. He needed a bath really but he could not be bothered to summon the water, which always took an age, and none would be impressed at bringing water at past eleven at night. He walked across the bailey and into the tower where his rooms were, taking the stairs slowly and deliberately and then along the passage to his room. He clicked the latch and entered the warm chamber and then smiled gratefully. Hot water bubbled over the fire and cold sat in a jug on the wash stand, and Gethin was curled up asleep in a chair by the fire, his black hair tousled and his tunic unlaced to the waist.

"Geth." Beau laid his hand on his shoulder and shook him gently. "Geth." The boy started awake and stammered his apologies. "It's alright lad. I wouldn't have woken you but I'm too far into my cups to carry hot water from that fireplace to that bowl." He smiled and the boy grinned. It wasn't often his Lord was ever drunk, but when he was, he was a genial drunk, not an unpleasant one.

"I thought you were with the King, my Lord?"

"I haven't been carousing if that's what you are thinking, my lad!" he said, in mock sternness. "But Louis can sink cups of wine like...like..." He couldn't think of an analogy. "Well he can drink a lot anyway and I realised I am actually a lightweight compared to him."

"You wouldn't think it to look at him would you, my Lord?" Gethin had picked up the pot and was carrying it across the room to the wash bowl. He poured some in and then mixed some cold with it, the ritual totally familiar to him now and one that he followed himself, due to his Beau's fastidious nose. Beau had already unlaced his tunic and was shrugging it off as Gethin reached for it, before pulling his shirt over his head and stripping down to his braies. He took the rough flannel cloth and put it in the water; he wet his upper body with it before picking up the soap, laced with his favourite bergamot scent, and rubbing it over his skin. Gethin took his clothes and laced his tunic up before folding it and packing it into the well-scented coffer, taking the chausses and packing them in their coffer, keeping up inconsequential chatter as he went along.

"I assume you don't want your chamber robe, my Lord, and that you are going to go to your bed straight away; I have warmed it for you and taken the fur coverlet out of the coffer as it seemed quite cold tonight. Would you like a cresset lamp, my Lord?" By this time, Beau was naked but Gethin had mastered the squire's art of looking but not seeing and continued to collect up items and arrange them neatly, aware of his master's need for tidiness and following the ritual carefully.

"I will cover the fire, my Lord, so that I can light it quickly in the morning as we have to be up and ready for our journey to Burgundy. I have packed everything but left your dark green tunic and chausses out for the morning and your fur-lined travel cloak. I have also left out a fur-lined cap in case it is very cold." Nodding, Beau reached for the towel, dried himself and then took a bottle, the contents of which he sprinkled over his hands and rubbed on his neck, chest and armpits; once again the smell of bergamot filled the room and Gethin's nostrils.

***

Gethin could never think of anything except his Lord when he smelled that scent. Beau indicated he had finished with the water and walked naked across the room, his impressive physique on full show, totally at ease with his own nakedness and his body. Gethin covertly admired Beau's lean but muscular frame and strong thighs, and wished, not for the first time, that he was tall like him and had the same long legs. Beau pulled back the covers of the bed and slipped into the warm linen sheets, grabbing three pillows and propping them up behind his head.

"Any messages, Gethin?" he asked, his husky voice blurred, even though he seemed a little more sober after his wash.

"Oh yes, my Lord, a few actually; two letters from England, Lords Warwick and Pembroke, one from the Queen, one from the Prince, oh yes and another from the Duchess of Clarence."

"Isabel?" Beau frowned. "Are you sure?"

"It's definitely her seal." Gethin always made sure he knew everyone's mark so that he could tell his Lord who had sent what.

"Give it to me." Beau's tone was sharp, conveying a sense of foreboding as he sat up crossed-legged under the covers. The boy coloured, scurried to the writing table and hurried back with it, and Beau took the square of parchment and snapped open the seal, scanning it rapidly and biting the inside of his lip as he always did when reading. As Gethin watched, he became suddenly very still, his face drained of colour and the pupils of his eyes contracting to slits.

"My Lord, what is it?" Alarmed, Gethin took a tentative step forward, but did not touch him, aware that his Lord's most natural reaction was to lash out when angry or hurt and not wanting to be at the end of a blow from his big hands. Beau, however, did not move, but the letter fluttered from his hand to the bed. As Gethin leaned to pick it up, he heard the older man make a strange hoarse sound in his throat, and bring his hands up to his face, covering his nose and mouth, his eyes glistening suspiciously.

"Read it," he said, his voice muffled, gesturing to the letter in the young man's hand. Gethin scanned the short note, no more than ten lines or so and gasped.

"Jesu' my Lord," he whispered.

"'Not likely to survive,' it says, Geth." Beau's voice broke on his name and Gethin saw the tears clinging to his lashes just before he dragged a shaking hand over his face, rubbing away his emotion.

"Lady Isabel says it is a blood fever, my Lord, caused by bad humours in a cut on her arm." Gethin shook his head disbelievingly.

"Aye, she did it in Hercules' stable the day we went for the picnic, I remember. She was more concerned with having ripped her sleeve." He snorted a mirthless, shaky laugh that came out more as a sob. "I never thought for a minute…" He faltered and shook his head dumbly.

"It is hard to believe, my Lord, that something so small can cause this." Gethin continued to scan the note. "But Lady Isabel says that she has been delirious for more than a week and they cannot get her to consciousness, even with bleeding." He looked at the top of the note. "This was sent five days ago." He swallowed, realising that that meant Katherine Neville was probably already dead. He glanced up at Beau and knew he was thinking the same thing, still chewing the inside of his lip, his yellow eyes sightless, his shoulders hunched.

He had known his Lord had had a strong fancy for this girl but had not realised that it was more than just a fancy. In the three years, he had served the Duke of Somerset he had come to know him as a man of strong lusts who took what he wanted when he wanted it, never by force and rarely from a woman of his own class unless you counted Segoline de Crecy, and she was hardly an Earl's daughter, bastard or no. But he had never seen him emotionally involved, only sexually charged and even then it was normally over in a matter of days. He never brought women back to his chambers and never stayed the full night with any woman, he just slaked his lust and left. But now, in this unfamiliar moment of pain, Gethin did not know how to react, fully aware that his Lord needed comfort, but also aware that he was likely to get a backhand across his face if he laid a hand on him; not that Somerset ever meant to hurt, but he was not a man to be touched when his emotions were raw or his temper on edge. In the end, he did the only thing he could think of and poured a cup of wine which Beau took with a shaking hand and drained in one gulp, handing it back to the boy and gesturing for another one. He leaned back against the pillow and closed his eyes.

"I should be grateful to the Duchess for sending me word, but I can't even go and see how she fares; I have no choice but to leave for

Burgundy tomorrow and I cannot afford a fortnight detour. I have to carry on as if nothing has happened without knowing..." He took the full cup back from Gethin and held it balanced on his chest, staring up at the canopy over his bed, his drooping eyes blind to anything but his mind. "How will we know if she is..." He faltered and a tear slid from his left eye down the side of his face. Gethin waited uncertainly by the bed for a moment but, when his Lord did not speak again, began his nightly ritual of blowing out candles and making up his own pallet bed, positioned as usual near the fire. When he had banked the fire and finished dousing the candles, he undressed down to his shirt and braies and went back over to his Duke, taking the cup from his slack fingers and putting it on the side table. The steady sound of the man's rhythmic breathing told him that Beau had at last succumbed to the effects of the wine, and he drew the curtains around the bed and went to his own, where he lay awake for a little while thinking sadly of the lovely redheaded girl who was likely to have already lost her life, and his Lord's pain at her passing, and felt his own sense of loss at the end of such a sweet beauty before drifting into sleep. At some point in the night the sound of muffled sobbing penetrated his deep slumber, and he stirred briefly, but when he awoke at dawn the following morning, Somerset was already up, dressed and hungover, his face white, his eyes bloodshot and his mood foul.

Anjou, Frances
October 1470

The piercing scream rang out across the room and Veronique de Roet jerked out of a light slumber and to her feet before she realised she was awake, just as the girl in the bed retched dryly in her delirium. Tears filled Veronique's eyes and spilled down her cheeks as she held her daughter down, trying to minimise the jerky spasms of her wasted and wretched frame. The girl's skin, always pale, was parchment white and her veins tracked blue lines through its virtual transparency, her eyes sunken and her lips bloodless. She had been in a delirious world of her own for more than two weeks, so ill that a week ago they had not expected her to last the night, as the blood fever ate away at her body and infected her mind. Yes, in the morning she had still endured and so it was every day after that. There had been no heat, just a pale, clammy coldness and the gradual wasting of her body as the blood maggots ate away at her insides.

Veronique looked up, conscious of a noise beside her and met the cool blue gaze of Anne Beauchamp. Veronique made to curtsey, but Anne laid a pale hand on her arm and shook her head imperceptibly. Somehow this adversity had brought them to an understanding, not exactly amicable, but an understanding which meant they could function in the sick room together and look after the child that one had borne and the other had raised. Anne had been surprised at the depth of feeling that her stepdaughter's illness had raised in her, not realising that she had learned to respect the feisty red-haired girl, if not to love her, and she had been prepared to accept Veronique's presence because it was obvious that the woman loved her daughter and Anne could identify with that. If this had been Anne or Isabel she would have been beside herself with grief and she thanked God every day that he had seen fit to spare them, but she was genuinely saddened by this child's suffering and had worked as tirelessly as the girl's mother and her own daughters to alleviate it.

"No change?" she murmured and Veronique shook her head, the tears still in her eyes. Anne reached out and touched her arm briefly in a mother's sympathy. "Go and get some rest, I'll watch her," she said softly.

Veronique shook her head again.

"No, I can't leave her."

"Then rest in that chair and I will sit here by the bed." Anne indicated to the stool next to the bed near Kate's pillow. Gratefully Veronique went back to her chair and sat down in it, curling her legs underneath her and leaning her head against the wooden back. Through narrowed eyes she watched the cool, poised Countess take her seat next to the bed and take Kate's hand in her own, whispering a prayer as she did so and brushing the dull, dry curls back from the girl's face. Veronique felt a pang of jealousy that this woman had spent more of her daughter's life bringing her up than she had, and then pushed it to the back of her heart, knowing that she had no right to it, that Anne Beauchamp had been more of a mother to her child than she ever had.

"What was she like growing up in your household, Madame?" she asked softly.

Anne turned her face towards her and smiled.

"A reincarnation of her father," she said dryly. "All his spirit as a lad and all his courage, although none of his temperance. I never understood quite how brave she was until I thought about it these last weeks. She came into my house a stranger in a hostile home and she has never once outwardly disobeyed me; yet still she has managed to do many things that I would not have countenanced." Anne smiled fondly. "She has a strong spirit and I am sure that is why she has endured so long through this illness."

"I missed her more than I ever thought I would." Veronique sighed softly. "It does not do to look back but I wish I had never left her."

"But by doing so you have ensured that she had a life you could not have provided for her, demoiselle. She was ever the child of my husband's heart and yes I resented that once but I can see why he found it easier to love her than to love our daughters. For Anne and Isabel, he has always had to do his utmost to gain them the best marriage and the highest rank, but with Katherine it is always about just him and her. Whatever he does for her it is more than she has ever expected and because of that she ever loved him unconditionally." Anne turned back to the girl in the bed and patted her clammy hand with her cool one. "I cannot say that she will never again exasperate me but I can say that I have learned to love her over these last ten years, more than I have ever realised, even if it is sometimes tinged with enjoying making a lady of a child who does not naturally lean that way."

"You talk as if you expect her to recover." Veronique sounded sceptical but Anne smiled again.

"Yes, because she has endured so long when death seemed likely to claim her, because I know how perverse she is and because I do not believe she will let anything beat her." She brushed the curls once again from the girl's damp, cold forehead as the eyelids flickered and the girl twitched and then subsided, muttering incoherently. "My husband once said if she had been a son then she would have been the bravest, most courageous boy a man could ever wish for and I think he is right. She will fight this to the very end." She leaned over and looked at Katherine's arm, noting ironically that the infection had subsided from that spot and looked to be clearing up, yet her body was wracked with the poison from it. Veronique shifted in the chair and her eyelids drooped as the need to sleep engulfed her. She did not realise that she slept until she jerked awake some while later to the soft sound of Anne Beauchamp reading aloud a passage from a Greek romance, the older woman's gentle voice comforting in the stark reality of the sick room. She leaned her head back on the chair and stared up at the ceiling, already aware of the child that grew inside her, a brother or sister to the girl in the bed and more heartache for the woman who nursed her. Her reconciliation with Richard Neville had been the most wonderful thing to happen to her and something that she had never envisaged, even when she had heard that he had come to France. But now, faced with the cool and dignified composure of his wife, she wondered if she would be able to enjoy a life as the mistress of this most powerful man whilst knowing that his wife loved him and suffered for his infidelity. She sighed softly and then sat up, glancing across at the bed as she stretched. What she saw stilled her movement and she gasped.

"Lady Anne!" Anne Beauchamp jerked up her head at the urgency of Veronique's tone and looked at the bed swiftly.

"Katherine?" Anne's voice was soft. The girl's head turned toward her a little and her eyelids fluttered.

"Ma mère?" Veronique's heart leaped and then she understood the girl was talking to Anne.

"Oh Katherine!" Anne leaned over the bed and touched her lips to Katherine's cold forehead. "You can hear me?"

"Yes, ma mère." Katherine's voice was cracked and breathy through lack of use, but her eyes did not open.

"Oh Jesu', child, you have had us so worried. We thought we had lost you." Anne sat back down on the stool, keeping Kate's hand in hers.

"What happened to me, ma mère?"

"Your blood was poisoned by that cut on your arm." Anne looked up for a moment. "Veronique, get Katherine some wine," she said softly and then moved out of the way so that Veronique could prop Kate up and hold the cup to her lips. "Your mother is here." Veronique smiled gratefully at her lover's Countess and Kate's eyes flickered open.

"Maman?" she whispered.

"Yes my darling, I am here." Veronique smiled at her daughter, tears spilling down her cheeks as she looked at her poor wasted face.

"I am so tired, Maman." The girl's voice was very faint.

"Then sleep darling. Sleep will make you well." Veronique stroked her hair back off her face and kissed her forehead. Kate's face relaxed into sleep and Anne leaned back in her chair and sighed a shaky sigh.

"I cannot believe it, Veronique, I cannot believe that she has come out of it. Jesu', the first hurdle is climbed!"

Veronique nodded her head, tears still streaming down her face. Anne patted her hand sympathetically and Veronique burst into sobs.

"I am sorry, Madame. It has just been too much!" she said as she tried to pull herself together. Anne nodded.

"I know. But this is a miracle and now we have every chance of making her well."

Veronique rubbed her hands across her eyes and then she smiled a tear-filled smile at Anne Beauchamp.

"Can you ever forgive me, Madame?" she asked quietly and Anne Beauchamp smiled wryly, understanding her immediately.

"If it was not you then it would be another," she said softly and shook her head as Veronique would have said more. "We understand each other Veronique and we understand Richard. I think that is enough."

Bruges, Burgundy
November 1470

Jack Beaufort cantered into the town of Bruges after more than a week on the road looking for his brother. Beau had been in Nancy with Charles but he had received word, after two days' heading towards that city, that Charles had moved on and was headed for Bruges so he had changed direction and headed for the town, asking along the way if anyone had seen his brother. Once he had passed through the town gates he had found out quite quickly where Beau was staying and had found out just as quickly that Edward of York was also in the city. He had laughed uproariously at that, at the fact that Edward of York and his brother were in the same city, exiles at the same time and for once Beau was not the one who was dependent on Charles's charity, but York was the one who had been brought low. He pulled his stallion up outside the stables and paid a groom to look after his horse, unsaddling him and pulling off the panniers which carried the limited belongings he had brought with him, throwing them over his shoulder and heading towards the inn he had been told his brother was staying in. The innkeeper greeted him enthusiastically, remembering him from a previous visit as Beau's brother, showing him to Beau's room and sending up food and wine carried by a very comely flaxen-haired serving maid who, when paid a few coins, stayed long enough to satisfy the need of a twenty-two-year-old man who had been on the road for over seven days. He washed and changed after she had gone, conscious of his brother's aversion to smell, and also aware that there was some sense in keeping clean and louse free, especially around the private parts, and then laid down on the bed, intending just to relax for a few minutes but falling into a deep sleep. When he awoke, it was dark and there was still no sign of his brother or his squire, so, rising, he lit the oil lamps and cressets and put some more logs on the fire, pulling a chair close to the flame, poured himself a cup of wine and sat back, soaking up the warmth. He wondered how Beau was, guessing that his brother would have retreated into himself, operating as he needed to without any emotion, and treating all those around him with a callous indifference. Jack remembered how hard it had been to bring him out of that void when Hal had died, and get him to grieve, especially when he had been but sixteen himself at the time, and had had no real relationship with this middle brother. He smiled at how close they had become, but knew well enough that that was because he deferred always to his brother's superior rank and experience. Not that he begrudged him that deference; he loved Beau very dearly and was proud of his stature and standing at the courts of these powerful politicians, but he was very much aware, being the most intuitive of the three Beaufort boys, that his value to Beau was based as much on his easy affability and his obvious admiration as it was on his ability to view situations so objectively. Edmund Beaufort was a complex man and Jack did not even attempt to understand him. His contemporaries would have been surprised to hear him described as emotional as he always seemed to others hard and cold, but Jack knew the cauldron of feeling that bubbled beneath the surface and right at this moment he felt incredible sympathy for Gethin Rhys, who would be bearing the brunt of his Lord's pain. Jack was glad that his mission was essentially a happy one and that he could alleviate some of his brother's angst and ease Gethin's life. At last he heard footsteps on the stairs and he stood, putting his cup down, aware that his presence may be a shock to his brother. The door opened and Beau was on the threshold, his eyes first taking in the light and then coming to land on his brother, surprise dilating his pupils and then fear contracting them immediately, his body becoming rigid and wary, his arm poised in mid-air.

"Jack?" he said hoarsely, the pulse in his throat jumping visibly. Jack walked towards him, smiling.

"She made it, Beau," he said softly. "Kate made it." Beau's eyes flickered for a moment, taking in what the younger man was saying and then he turned blindly towards the window of the small room, a harsh ragged breath escaping him, and his shoulders heaving once. Gethin, coming into the room behind him looked quickly at Jack who flicked his hand in a gesture of dismissal. Not needing to be told twice, Gethin closed the door and fled down the stairs. Jack took a deep breath and came to stand behind his brother, laying a tentative hand on his shoulder, relieved not to be shaken off.

"I had convinced myself she was dead." Beau's voice cracked on the words. "I have been delaying returning home because I could not face it."

"I guessed that when they told me that you had followed Charles back here." Jack squeezed the older man's shoulder and went back to the hearth, pouring wine for them both and bringing it back. Beau turned, his gold eyes glistening with unshed tears, his face drained of colour as he reached for the cup with a shaking hand and took a swallow.

"How does she fare?"

"As well as could be expected under such dire circumstances; she has not yet got out of her bed and none except her mother, stepmother and her sisters have been allowed in the sickroom, oh, and Samson of course."

"Samson?" Beau looked confused.

"You remember Samson, the pup. Veronique says he has much aided her recovery since she was awake and that she loves him dearly." Jack grinned and Beau attempted to return it, but his mouth did not curve upward, instead setting in a thin line against the onslaught of emotion. He leaned back on the sill of the window and rested his head against the shutter for a moment, his eyes closed.

"Jesus, I have been in such a dark place, Jack," he said at length, his voice low and fast. "The nights have been the worst, lying there hour after hour, my thoughts as black as the sky outside." He shuddered. "I could not outrun the black dog."

"Ah Beau." Jack looked at his brother, his face soft with understanding; he had seen those demons before and knew how black the dog was. "You were not going to come home were you?" Beau shook his head, looking out from under heavy lids.

"I really don't know," he said softly. "I had thought of hiring myself out as a soldier to Italy or Spain or going on crusade rather than coming back to Angers or going to England. I could not even bear the thought of seeing anyone or anything that would remind me of her." He rubbed his hand tiredly over his face, blinking rapidly against the tide of tears that threatened again. "If I did not come home I could pretend it didn't matter." He closed his eyes again and sighed shakily. "I have drunk far too much far too often and made Gethin's life a misery with my foul temper; to be honest I am surprised he is still here." He opened his eyes and met Jack's dark brown gaze. "I need to make it up to him somehow. He is a good lad and he has taken the full brunt of this without any complaint."

"I'll go and find him in a minute." Jack smiled and cocked his head to one side. "Are you sure you are all right?"

"I think so."

"I had expected you to be more joyful somehow, happier."

"I am overwhelmed I think." He shook his head. "It feels like the resurrection!"

"Understandable."

"I suddenly feel very tired and somewhat light-headed."

"You probably just need some sleep, Beau."

"Yeah." He moved away from the window and walked to the hearth, dropping down into one of the chairs and pouring himself some more wine with a shaking hand before holding out the flagon to Jack. The younger man shook his head, intuitively seeing in his brother a need to be alone to gather his thoughts and feelings.

"I'm going to go and find Gethin," he said.

"Alright." Beau nodded gratefully.

"I expect he could do with a drink." Jack grinned briefly.

213

"Tell him I'm sorry." Beau's voiced cracked as he rubbed his face again, his lashes glistening and his mouth contorting as his emotions finally overwhelmed him. "I love her, Jack."

"I know you do."

"I did not want to live without her." Beau buried his face in his hands, his body wracked with his sobs.

"Well now you will not have to." Jack laid a hand on his brother's dark head, feeling not for the first time like the older sibling. "Now you can come home."

After a few moments and a few more words of comfort, he slipped out of the door and shut it quietly behind him, heading down the stairs and into the common room. Gethin was sitting at the table, nursing a cup of ale and staring morosely at the fire, his mouth turned down at the corners, his chin in his hand.

"Hey." Jack sat down opposite him and smiled. Gethin looked up but did not return the smile.

"My Lord," he said quietly.

"That bad, huh?" Jack gestured to the barman for a mug of ale for each of them as the young man regarded him levelly.

"Is she dead?" he asked, still in the same quiet, emotionless voice.

"No. She pulled through."

"Thank God!" Jack was surprised at the fervour in his voice. They were of an age, he and Gethin Rhys, and had worked and travelled together for three years, but Gethin always seemed somehow naïve, untouched by the unpleasantness and politics that often went with being the body squire of a powerful man. He was perhaps old for a body squire and still not knighted, but he had already been a competent horseman and soldier, learned alongside his father before he came into Beau's household. They sat for a few minutes in silent contemplation, Gethin staring down into his mug before he made a visible decision to talk.

"The Duke has been black, my Lord, since he received the Duchess' letter about the Lady Katherine, and no matter how I have tried I have not been able to reach him." His fair skin coloured and he blinked rapidly, his eyes glinting suspiciously.

"None can reach him when he is like that Geth, believe me." Jack's response was heartfelt and the young man looked at him with renewed interest. "When my brother Hal was killed, he was in this mood for six months and I was just a lad and had no idea what to do with him. He functioned on wine, anger, vigour and hate. He came out of it eventually but I despaired often and almost left him several times."

"He hates me."

"No, he doesn't; he was hating everyone and you were just the nearest."

"He hit me once, when I dropped a flagon of wine and I could see murder in his face; he has cuffed me before but for the first time in his service I was afraid of him and though he stepped back from the edge I was petrified of firing his wrath after that." Gethin shuddered. "You think I'm soft, don't you?" Jack shook his head.

"No, lad, I don't. It is not soft to be afraid of a man like my brother if he is in a foul temper, I know how strong he is and how dark he looks when anger strikes him, believe me. Because I was so much younger than him he has rarely turned it on me but he and Hal fought like animals. My father twice had to separate them before they killed each other."

"It feels disloyal to talk of him like this. You are not angry are you, my Lord?"

"Christ, Geth, of course not; I think you have earned the right. None knows as much as me how hard he can be to live with. If you had left him then I might have been angry, but I would still have understood, but that you have stayed with him means much to me and it also means that you are as brave as any. I know how fearsome he is when he is like that." He reached across and gripped the other man's forearm. "He thinks the world of you Geth. But unfortunately, we always hurt those we are fond of when we are railing against what life has thrown at us. Believe me if I had been here, you would have been spared and I would be sat here nursing my ale and hoping I didn't have to go back upstairs until he had drunk himself into oblivion." Jack grinned and the other boy laughed reluctantly.

"I did sit in the inn in Nancy a few nights, waiting for him to be asleep before I went upstairs," he admitted ruefully. "I have never seen him drink like this. He is normally a moderate man, but, Jesu', he got through some wine and then in the mornings..." He shook his head remembering.

"I know; raging headache, white face, stopping at the roadside to puke and growling unintelligibly at anyone who spoke to him?" Jack raised an eyebrow, peppering his words with humorous looks belying the harsh reality. Gethin laughed again.

"Exactly that, my Lord." He shook his head again. "A man such as your brother, so…so definite about his clothes and his baths, retching into the bushes when his stomach was so wine-sour he could not even hold water down." Jack grinned.

"That bad? I bet you kept out of the way those mornings." Gethin nodded.

"Indeed I did, my Lord. I put out his wash water and then went down to break my fast. I'd take him up bread a bit later and more often than not he ate it, but some mornings he could not face it."

"Aye, well I know how that feels. I have been there myself on occasion." Jack laughed. The colour was coming back into the lad's cheeks and he was obviously feeling better, but Jack's smile hid his surprise that his brother had been so badly cut up by what essentially would have been the death of a woman he hadn't even bedded. That he was in love for the first time there was no doubt, but trust Beau to fall in love with the same excess that he approached everything in his life; it was all or nothing for everything that he did, excel at everything or don't attempt it. "Well, hopefully that's all over now." Jack stretched, linking his hands together over his head and flexing his fingers, and they were silent for a while, each in their own thoughts, a comfortable silence which gave them both some warmth and fanned a flame of friendship.

"I think we'll be going home tomorrow," Jack said, breaking the silence again after some time. "It is probably not a good idea for us to be in Bruges while Edward of York is here anyway."

"I saw the Duke of Gloucester yesterday. I didn't know it was him but my Lord Duke recognised him, said he looked a lot like his father the old Duke of York. They just looked at each other and then passed by, but my Lord Duke told me about Ludlow and picking Richard of Gloucester up off the street by his tunic and calling him a girl because he snivelled so much." Gethin grimaced. "I know Richard of Gloucester is only eighteen but I could not imagine him snivelling at all. He has such a stern face for a man so young."

"I've never seen him." Jack shrugged. "But I do remember Edward of York a little, I was only ten or eleven when I saw him and he was the tallest man I had ever seen in my life. Made my brother look short." Jack smiled wryly.

"Me short?" Beau's hoarse voice broke into Jack's musings as he sat down next to him and flashed a smile at Gethin, who smiled shyly back.

"Next to Edward of York." Jack slid over and made room for him as the landlord brought a cup. He looked better, although his eyes were red-rimmed and very bloodshot, but his face had colour and he was clean shaven.

"Ah." He ignored the cup and the ale and looked from one to the other of the younger men. "I think we should set off back to Angers tomorrow, I have to stop off with some messages for the Queen and then go on to Paris. I know you have just arrived Jack..."

"I've already told Geth we probably would be going back tomorrow."

"Geth..." Beau looked at the dark-haired boy levelly. "When we get back to Angers, if you want to leave my service I will find you a position in my Lord Warwick's or Pembroke's household if you wish."

"You want me to leave your service, my Lord?" Gethin misheard and his face fell, colour rushing into his cheeks.

"No lad, I don't." Beau was emphatic. "But I would understand if you wish to and I will help you get a good position."

"I don't want to, my Lord." The boy leaned forward earnestly. "If I cannot weather the hard times along with the good then what kind of man would that make me?"

"Your loyalty does you credit, lad." Beau smiled and Jack looked sideways at his brother.

"Perhaps we should take that as our motto," he said. "Weathering the hard times while we wait for the good. Because, thanks to my Lord Warwick I think the hard times are almost over. So here's to the good." Jack and Gethin raised their cups and Beau grinned.

"To the good," he said softly.

Anjou, France
November 1470

"Are you alright, Kate?" Anne fussed around her in the solar, making sure she had cushions behind her and that she was warm.

"Yes, sweet, I am fine." Kate smiled at her sister warmly. Everyone else was in the hall, enjoying a visit from some travelling players, but

Kate could not face it, too much noise made her head ache. "You go and join Edward, I shall be alright here."

"Actually, I am quite enjoying the rest." Anne grimaced ruefully. "You have been a good excuse for me."

"I think it is sweet that he dotes on you so much." Kate yawned and leaned back against the cushions. "I wish I had someone to care for me like that."

"Well you have Samson." As if on cue the puppy galloped over from his exploration of the hearth and scrambled into Kate's lap. She hugged him as his tongue swiped at her face wetly.

"And anyway..." Anne stopped and looked down at her elder sister, noting that she had more colour today and that her hair looked healthier.

"What?" Kate raised a brow.

"I think you have had more than your fair share of admirers." Anne screwed up her nose. "I've had no end of them asking if you are alright."

"But that's not the same as having someone who cares for you."

"No, true," Anne acknowledged. "I think there is one who would like to care for you, well perhaps not care for you but from the way I've seen him look at you I would say he'd like to do something for you!" Anne blushed prettily and then giggled. Lacking both of her sisters' sensual nature and bawdy sense of humour, she was still embarrassed by references to sex, even though she was wedded and bedded.

"Who?" Kate was interested.

"My Lord Somerset."

Kate laughed, a blush creeping up her neck.

"I wanted to talk to you of it before." Anne was serious again. "After that night in the solar when he sat next to you on the settle and was flirting with you, Edward told me that Madame the Queen would be very upset if you..." She struggled for words and settled for, "...dallied with him. I think mama and papa would be upset also, especially after all that fuss with Ned."

"Oh Lord!" Kate started to laugh quietly and Anne looked at her quizzically.

"What?"

"I can't believe that you are giving me maternal advice!"

"I'm not!" Anne flushed to the roots of her hair. "I'm just telling you what Edward said."

"He gave me a puppy, Anne. He didn't ask me to bed with him!" Kate had no wish for her younger sister to know of any of her encounters with Edmund Beaufort and not for the first time she thought that Anne and Richard of Gloucester would have been perfectly matched for their moral attitudes, if not for their love for each other; how her father had bred such a daughter, she could never imagine.

"Perhaps not but that can be all he is after."

"Why?" Kate bristled. "Can a man not be friends with a woman?"

"No. A man either wants marriage or sex." Anne was adamant.

"Is it one or the other then?" Kate grinned. "I thought you were having plenty of marriage and sex?"

"Kate!"

"What?"

"Oh, it's no good!"

Just then the door opened and Isabel came in, flushed and laughing.

"Who's no good?" she asked interestedly.

"No one. Kate and I were just discussing the merits of keeping out of trouble." Anne looked a little irritated by her sister's unceremonious arrival.

"Go down to your husband, Anne, I'll stay with Kate for a while!" Isabel offered.

"No, I'm quite happy to stay." Anne protested but Isabel ushered her sister reluctantly to the door.

"Edward is asking where you are," she said, opening the latch and pushing her outside. "He wants you to go down to the hall." She came back and threw herself into the chair next to Kate by the fire. Kate eyed her warily. Isabel was a great ally in a crisis or when mischief-making, but she rarely went out of her way to be sisterly and helpful once the crisis was over, or the mischief done.

"How are you feeling?" Isabel asked, helping herself to a roasted chestnut and grinning at her sister.

"I feel alright, actually; just really tired." Kate unconsciously rubbed the scar by her eye tenderly.

"That scar looks much better."

"Does it? I haven't looked really."

"Mmm. I think it will be quite presentable." Isabel made a show of studying her.

"What is it you want, Bel?" Isabel looked hurt at the question.

"What do you mean?"

"Well you don't normally come in here offering to be with me, at least not now that I am getting better."

"You know me too well!" Isabel grinned wickedly. "Are you up to another visitor?"

"Depends who it is." Kate yawned again.

"You'll want to see this one."

"Alright, yes I think I can manage another visitor."

"Hold on then." Isabel went to the door and spoke in a low voice to someone outside. She came back in and had just sat back down by the fire and was peeling another chestnut when the door opened again and the long, lean frame of Edmund Beaufort ducked through. Kate drew an audible breath and Isabel grinned.

"Surprise!" she laughed.

"Isabel!" Beau walked into the room, still wearing his long fur-lined mantle against the cold of his journey from Bruges, his hands outstretched and his golden eyes alive with his smile. "Good to see you."

"Edmund." They exchanged kisses on each cheek. "You look well!" Kate was surprised by the warmth of the greeting; she had not known that they were on such good terms. He turned to her as she contemplated getting up from her chair.

"No Katherine, do not rise!" He leaned down and kissed her mouth softly, lingeringly, his lips cool against hers, his composure belying the pulse beating erratically in his throat. "I cannot stay long, Madame is expecting me. I just came to see how you did." He grinned down at her. "You look awful!"

"Thank you, my Lord!"

"How did you cut your eye?"

"When I fell in the chapel, I landed on my face apparently." There was a hint of laughter in her voice and his grinned widened.

"Saved by your hard head then! The scar looks to be healing well." He made as if to touch it, and then dropped his hand self-consciously.

"You can stay for five minutes, can't you Edmund?" Isabel interrupted, moving towards the door, her expression innocent and guileless. "I just remembered that I left my embroidery in my chamber and Kate cannot be left alone. Could you stay with her?" Beau nodded, playing along with her.

"Of course!" He unfastened his cloak and threw it over a nearby chair, and, looking round, pulled up a stool and sat down in front of Kate, so close that his long legs sandwiched hers between them. She was conscious of how good he looked, the stark dark blue and white of his clothes and his day's growth of beard setting off his hawk-like face to handsome perfection.

"You are sure you are alright?" he asked softly, his eyes taking on a new, tender expression, roving over her face. She blushed a little under his scrutiny.

"Yes, my Lord."

"You look much too thin."

"I have lost some weight but then I did not eat much for nigh on a month, my Lord."

"And your arm has healed well?"

"Yes, my Lord."

"And you had no more head pain?"

"No, my Lord." She started to laugh.

"What?" He smiled quizzically.

"You are acting like ma mère!" She tilted her head to one side. "And when did you and Isabel become so friendly?"

"When she realised how much I cared for you. She wrote to me and told me how sick you were." His pupils dilated at the memory and his mouth set in a thin line, as if he was holding back some emotion. "She was the only one who thought of me at the time."

"But why the need for the game and getting rid of Anne?" Kate resisted the temptation to touch his face.

"Because your sister disapproves of me and would not have let me see you, and if Madame the Queen found I had been here before I have been to see her then she would make my privates into an ornament." He grinned and she laughed. "And once I am with Madame then I will never get away to be able to see you. So I thought it best to do it first and I asked Jack to ask Isabel to help me. Hence the reason I cannot stay long." He leaned across and took her hand, lacing his fingers through hers gently. "I just wanted to see for myself that you were alright," he said softly, his thumb caressing the back of her hand.

"Yes, I am fine. I am stronger every day." Her skin shivered under his touch and her large eyes locked into his, not making any attempt to take back her hand or feeling the need to speak.

"I have to go away again tomorrow," he murmured at last, looking at their entwined hands. "To Paris. I am only here for tonight."

"Paris again?" Her voice echoed with a disappointment that made his stomach lurch.

"Yes." He traced the back of her hand with his other forefinger, and then looked up at her sideways, his hair falling appealingly across his eyes. "I have to go and see the King; I'll be gone for at least a fortnight and I needed to see you before I went just to see that...you were well." His voice faltered and he dropped his mouth to the back of the hand he still held. "I thought I had lost you." He drew a sharp, shuddering breath. "Isabel wrote to me and told me they could not wake you from your delirium and that you were not likely to survive. I thought you were dead and I had never got the chance to spend time with you and get to know you, and it seemed such...such a...tragedy. For the first time in my life I had met a woman who interested me beyond the bedchamber and she was being taken from me." She felt the warmth of his breath on her skin. "That last evening, in the Prince's chamber, that's all I wanted to do. I never meant to dishonour you or even to touch you, let alone kiss you; I just wanted to tell you that I love you and to say a proper farewell." She felt rather than saw the tear land on the back of her hand and her heart swooped.

"Oh, my Lord!" she whispered, reaching out and caressing his dark hair as he rested his forehead against her hand.

"When I come back..." His voice was muffled against her skin. "I want us to have time together. I will be here for a while and I want to spend that time with you and get to know you properly; I want to know about your childhood, your loves and your hates, your dreams and your desires. There are so many things I need to know about you that have never interested me about women in the past. I have never met anyone who makes me laugh like you do and who is so fair to look upon that my heart leaps in my chest every time I see you. I am just happy to be with you and that's all I want when I come home."

"You really do mean it, don't you?" Her stomach filled with warmth as she brushed his hair back from his forehead. He had said he loved her; this beautiful, worldly man had said he loved her and she could not keep the wonder out of her voice. He lifted glittering eyes to hers.

"Yes." He nodded.

"Then I would like that, my Lord," she said softly, her thumb wiping the moisture from beneath his right eye.

"I can offer you nothing except myself for I have little to call my own but what I do have is yours," The face turned upward to her was alight with tenderness and feeling. "I am a loyal and faithful friend."

"As am I, my Lord." She slid her hand to his cheek and he leaned into it, closing his eyes and savouring her touch.

"I wish I didn't have to go." His voice was a caress. "I just want to stay here like this. With you I have found peace."

"I wish you didn't have to go either." She traced his mouth with her thumb, smiling as he kissed it softly. "But I am already looking forward to you coming home."

"I do not want to leave you." He rose suddenly, scooping her up from the chair and sitting in her place, settling her against him, his arms tight around her. She slid her fingers to his cheek and turned his face to hers, touching her lips against his, slipping her fingers into the soft silkiness of her hair.

"I will be here waiting when you get home," she whispered, her heart pounding as his eyes devoured her and the air crackled with the intensity of their attraction. He made a strangled sound in his throat and buried his face in her neck, his breathing ragged with the obvious force of his emotion, crushing her to him. She was content to be in his arms and to feel his need, the strength of his feeling sending thrills of power through her and when he raised his head and kissed her, she kissed him back with interest, knowing that in her weakened state she was safe from the lust which was so integral to their attraction. He released her mouth and laid his cheek against her hair, long fingers caressing her as she rested against him and she felt him relax, his lips touching her hair from time to time, his breathing regular. A sense of tranquillity enveloped her as they sat in perfect harmony, the only sound the crackling of the fire and Samson snoring beside it.

The sound of Isabel's voice, unnaturally loud outside the door, finally broke the spell, and then there was the ostentatious clicking of the latch before she entered, still chattering to the boy by the door. Beau stood up reluctantly as her sister entered the room, settling her into the chair, tucking the blanket about her, his eyes warm and caressing on hers, before turning to greet Isabel. "Ah, here you are!" he said, easily as if he had truly been waiting for her. "Now that I know she really is still alive, I should go." He leaned down and kissed her again, a longer kiss this time, full of need and possession. "Adieu, sweetheart," he whispered. "I will try and see you before I leave."

"Oh Lord!" exclaimed Isabel after he had gone, as they burst into convulsive giggles. "Damn you Kate you are so lucky!" Isabel said when they had somewhat recovered. "First Ned and now him!"

"Isabel!" Kate blushed again and sought to look suitably shocked.

"Well you are! All I get is the men who want to worship me from afar. You, you lucky wench, get the downright dangerous ones who want to rip off your clothes and ravish you!"

"Isabel! Stop it!" Kate covered her face, her cheeks scarlet.

"Well it's true. You've had two of the handsomest men in England trying to get your chemise off." Isabel pulled a morose face. "I've not had one offer of anything vaguely illicit since George went to England." She sat on the stool Beau had vacated.

"Don't be wicked, Bel, George is also one of the handsomest men in England. Why would you want anyone else?"

"Because illicit is exciting, and just for once I want to be exciting!"

"But everyone thinks you are beautiful, Bel!"

"Yes but not in the way they think you are. Men want to sit at my feet and adore me whereas they just want to couple with you!"

"Thanks!" Kate laughed "I think I'd rather be adored!" She looked at Isabel, suddenly serious. "Would you truly break your marriage vows for some excitement?"

"Hell yes, if it was someone like Edmund Beaufort!" Isabel pulled a lascivious face and then snorted down her nose. "No I don't suppose I would but more because the price to pay could be too high and the consequences too great than because I think it is wrong." They giggled again and then Isabel was serious once more.

"Don't listen to the killjoys Kate," she said suddenly. "Who knows what will happen to us in the future; take your opportunities and enjoy them." She leaned forward earnestly. "I love my husband but I am damn sure I would find a way to couple with Edmund Beaufort if there was no risk of George finding out!"

"He wants to spend time with me when he gets back from Paris."

"You should and you should enjoy it." Isabel tapped the back of Kate's hand. "Just be careful, alright?" she said softly. "Now would not be the time to get with child."

"I know." Kate's voice was equally soft as colour flooded her cheeks again. "Its just..."

"Just what, sweet?" Isabel cocked a brow and Kate's colour deepened.

"I...don't really know what to do."

"It seems an easy decision to me."

"No, I mean I don't know what to do to please him, you know...in bed."

"Ah, poppet." Isabel laughed from her elder sister advantage and experience of having been wed for a whole year. "The main thing is not to be shy, to touch him and to listen, to watch and learn; his response will tell you everything you ever need to know."

"I tried that with Stephen and he called me a whore." Her words came out much shakier than she wanted them to.

"That's because there was something wrong in his head!" Isabel was quick and vehement in her response. "It was not because you did anything wrong."

"Ma mère will disown me." Kate laughed shakily, deciding not to dwell on the foibles of Stephen Thevenot.

"And I will disown you if you don't." Isabel slapped her arm playfully. "It would be such a waste!" She was serious suddenly. "Just enjoy it, Kate, everyone deserves a little bit of happiness."

"Thanks Bel for being such a friend to me." Kate squeezed her sister's hand impulsively.

"I'm only doing it so you will tell me all about it... You will tell me, won't you?" Kate laughed.

"Who else would I tell?"

Chapter Nine

Anjou, France, December 1470

"Maman?"

Looking up at the sound of her daughter's voice, Veronique smiled.

"Ah, Katherine," she said in her warm, soft voice. "Come to help me?" Kate returned an identical smile. They were in the Queen's wardrobe, and Veronique was perfuming winter dresses to put out to hang, beautiful fur-lined wools and silks, some quite old judging by their style, but all expensive and well made.

"If you like," she said. Her relationship with her mother had warmed considerably over the last weeks after being thrown together during her recovery, and she had heard how her mother had nursed her through the nights and days of her illness. She knew that Veronique was conscious of not trying too hard or being too eager to be her mother and appreciated that she was prepared to settle for building a friendship. They worked in companionable silence for a while, Veronique holding the dresses inside out while Kate rubbed the perfumes into the armpits and around the neckline. They packed herbs into the pockets and around the fur to ward away moths and lice and then hung them up, covered in fabric sleeves, in the large robes which lined the walls.

"Maman?" Kate glanced across at her mother, trying to work out how best to pitch their conversation.

"Mmmmm?" Veronique's face was a mask of concentration and Kate was struck by how young she still was and still looked; there was hardly any sign of age in her lovely face.

"How did it come about that you fell in love with my father?" Veronique looked up and her face creased into a soft smile.

"I was with the Queen in the King's chambers and saw him across a room with the Duke of York. I looked up and he was watching me. He was so handsome, such beautiful eyes and always so well dressed; I was lost the minute I saw him."

"Did he speak to you?"

"No. It would not have been proper for him to do that. He waited at the end of the hall later that night, and then he caught me as I left."

"My Lord Somerset said his brother fancied you." Kate grinned and Veronique laughed.

"Ah, Harry Beaufort?" She pulled a face. "He was a nice boy but he was nowhere near as sophisticated as your father, or as handsome as my Lord Somerset. He was tall and dark, but pretty I would say rather than handsome, and only eighteen, which seemed very young to me even though I was but fifteen myself. Your father on the other hand was a man, twenty-five years old, and a seasoned soldier and courtier. It was easy, at fifteen, to fall in love with him."

"Did papa court you?"

"Yes he did, very extravagantly with jewellery and poetry and flowers mainly. He completely turned my head and everyone told me I was a fool to fall for it, but I knew he loved me just as I loved him." Veronique looked misty-eyed and then laughed at her own sentimentality.

"How did you know, Maman?" Kate was fascinated by the parallel to her own story.

"I could just tell. He was different with me, tender and warm and not like the cool arrogant courtier he was with everyone else, although that was part of his charm." She glanced at Kate speculatively. "As I am sure it is with my Lord Somerset."

"Was it not hard to find time together?" Kate ignored the hint for the moment and steered the conversation gently.

"Yes it was. I'm afraid most of our relationship was made up of hurried trysts in quiet places and only twice did we ever get to spend a full night together." She looked sad for a moment. "If you added up the time we got to spend alone together I don't expect it would make more than a sennight. Perhaps if I had not come back to France he would have got me a house in London and we could have spent more time together, but as it was our time was short"

"That must have been difficult when you loved him so much?"

"Yes it was." Veronique stopped shaking out the dress she was holding and looked at her daughter levelly. "The lot of a mistress is a difficult one. Whilst it is acceptable for a man to have a leman, it is not acceptable for a well-born lady to be one; other women are the ones most likely to hate you and other men think they can have you because you are a whore." She laid the dress on the table and Kate picked up the perfume and began rubbing it into the wool.

"But you are still prepared to be his mistress?" she said softly.

Veronique shrugged.

"He is the love of my life. I cannot resist him and nor do I want to."

"The trouble is, maman, I am not sure if I am in love with my Lord Somerset."

"It would be easy to be flattered by the attentions of one such as he." Veronique smiled. "He is a very handsome man."

"It is definitely more than just being flattered." Kate leaned her elbows on the table and looked at her mother appealingly. "I want him, so much, in fact, that it hurts and that he fills my dreams and my thoughts." She dropped her lashes, her cheeks flushing.

"Your father told me he could see this coming." Veronique sighed. "I confess I was concerned but I am not in a position to preach."

"My father knows?" Kate was shocked.

"Your father sees more than you girls ever know!" Veronique smiled at her daughter's expression. "But he is especially tender of you."

"What did he say?"

"He would not be entirely displeased if you chose this path for there are advantages in it but he wanted you to be sure. He trusts my Lord Somerset to be discreet and to treat you honourably." Veronique leaned forward and pushed a tendril of hair from her daughter's cheek with a gentle hand. "He wants you to be happy."

"Preferably with advantages?" Kate laughed shortly and Veronique smiled.

"Preferably with advantages," she agreed.

Anjou, France
December 1470

It was cold and the sky was dark with threatening snow, the hard ground rutted and treacherous under Hercules' hooves, fit only for a fast walk or at the very most a slow canter. Edmund could not afford to damage the stallion's legs for he was all he had and buying another such would cost money that he was unable to spare. Having his Dukedom ratified by King Henry on his redemption had not brought him any more wealth and would not until he could reclaim his estates, and so he must continue to watch his expenditure. Apart from that he loved the horse, his temperament was fine and he was wonderful to ride, his smooth gait belied by his sturdy build and shaggy legs, and would do nothing to risk him. He pulled the fur collar of his black cloak around him and glanced up at the sky once more. Snow was the last thing he wanted on this the final leg of his journey back to Angers, for there was little in the way of shelter on this road and only a few very dubious inns should he be caught in a blizzard; besides which, he really just wanted to be home after more than a month away, and having spent a fortnight in close company with Louis and Jasper Tudor, he needed his brother's sense of humour to lighten his spirit. He liked Louis and Pembroke but they were not light-hearted men. He yawned and rubbed a hand over his face tiredly. He had not been sleeping well these last nights, his anticipation of coming home keeping him awake and Katherine Neville playing havoc with his dreams when he finally did sleep. He had managed, with force of will, to keep her at bay whilst he had been with Louis but as soon as he had begun his journey home she had begun to fill his head and he had found himself resorting to some adolescent nocturnal habits in order to relieve his needs. He had not been with a woman since some time before the day he had received Isabel's note to say that Katherine was dying, and he had no intention, if everything worked out, of bedding another woman for a very long time.

"My Lord Duke."

"Mmmmmm?" Beau looked across at his squire.

"A rider ahead I think, my Lord. I just caught sight of him against the sky."

"Alone?"

"I think just the one."

"A messenger of some sort then probably." He squinted ahead for some moments, his eyes very gold in the darkness of the day as he watched the speck in the distance become larger and larger, and then grinned broadly. "My brother, Gethin; I'd know that stallion anywhere." He pushed Hercules into a gentle canter, heading for the black-clad rider coming towards them. "Jack!"

"Beau!" Jack pulled up alongside his brother and they clasped arms in a soldier's grip, laughing. "I did not think I'd catch up with you so soon. It is only just past dinner!"

"My Lord Duke had us on the road in the dark this morning, my Lord!" Gethin jibed, grinning shyly at his Lord's brother. Beau laughed and mimed a cuff around the back of his head.

"Mind you, it has hardly been light at all so far today." He looked up at the sky which was lowering ominously. "Have you come out specially to meet me or are you on some other business?"

"I came to meet you but I also promised Lady Veronique I would run an errand for her whilst I was over this way." He gestured vaguely to the west. "I thought I would catch up with you first and you could come with me." He saw Beau hesitate at lengthening his journey home. "There will be warmth and hospitality and a chance to catch up?" He looked up at the sky meaningfully. "If it snows you will regret not taking me up on my offer."

"Alright." Beau was reluctant, seeing another night slip by before he was able to be home. Jack beamed delightedly, swinging his stallion around and falling into stride beside his elder brother.

"So what kept you?" he asked in his usual cheerful and forthright manner. Beau laughed.

"Pembroke," he said succinctly and Jack grimaced.

"Still bemoaning Warwick's government?"

"Aye and more. It is natural for him to be unhappy that Warwick is taking the lead in government but we have no practical experience. Warwick was York's chief minister for nigh on eight years and he knows the mood of the country better than we do. Once we have eliminated our enemies then we can redress the balance of power and redistribute the roles, but Pembroke cannot see that and is chafing against Warwick's authority. Luckily Louis was able to calm him and persuade him that he can add more value going back to Wales and raising an army from his welsh compatriots." He smiled ruefully. "Anyway, Warwick would never have taken the task on any other terms so we have to accept his position for now."

"Is it a problem to you Beau?" Jack was interested in his brother's opinion.

"Not really. I have to admit I know nothing of government and have much to learn, and anyway I feel secure enough in my position with the Prince for it not be an issue when we go to England. I would rather work as friends with Warwick if I am honest; he is an able man and I have learned to trust him. I just hope that Pembroke does not jeopardise that trust."

"He would not be so rash, surely?"

"Who knows. Jasper Tudor is a strange man; conscious of his dignity and status as Harry's half brother. I like him a great deal and respect him even more but I find him hard work sometimes." Beau shook his head wearily. "It is good to see you Jack."

"Have you heard from Warwick?" Jack glanced up at the sky and held out his hand as the first soft snowflake landed in his palm. Beau pulled his cloak around him and his cap down over his head as he nodded.

"Yes, while I was with Louis, a long letter urging me to get Edward to England as quickly as I could. The boy will be the one to pull the people to our cause and if we can get him and his Princess over there then they will charm London, and from there, the rest of the country." He glanced at Jack. "You have to admit, whether she is to your taste or not, Anne is a pretty little thing and they make a fine picture together." Jack nodded.

"Yes they do look fine together, young and full of promise!" He grinned. "Best get them over there quick before they turn into jaded old souls like us."

"Us?" Beau barked a laugh. "You are only twenty-two my lad and Geth is but twenty so that leaves me as the old and jaded soul, I fear!" The boys laughed. "Anyway, where the bloody hell are we going?" He looked about him as they turned off the main track, the snow falling harder now and starting to settle on the land around them.

"I told you to run an errand for Lady Veronique."

"Is it far?" Beau looked up at the sky. Jack grinned and shook his head.

"Half of an hour and you will be in the warm and dry." Beau returned his smile.

"I should count myself fortunate that I ran into you then, the weather turning as it has," he said. "Although I had counted on being home today." He glanced at Jack again and dropped his voice low. "Talking of the Lady Veronique, how is Katherine?"

"She is very well; quite back to her old self," he said innocently. "Radiantly beautiful in fact."

"I had hoped to see her today." Beau's voice was wistful and Jack bit back a smile.

"She's not at Angers at the moment," he said.

"Oh." Beau's face dropped.

"No, she is away visiting family, so you wouldn't have seen her anyway. She will not be back until Sunday I believe. Don't look at me like that!" Jack burst out laughing at his brother's suspicious expression. "I was finding out on your behalf not mine!" Beau looked abashed and then grinned and shrugged disarmingly.

"Sorry," he said.

"You haven't asked after Madame." Jack's expression was once again innocent, but Beau glared at him.

"Do I need to?" he asked. "I can't imagine she has changed much in a month!"

"No, not much. Although she has taken a huge dislike to Anne Neville all of a sudden and is making her life a misery. Edward, give him his due, is sticking up for her but generally they are just keeping out of her way." Jack's expression changed to one of great affection. "Edward has missed you, Beau; missed your support and allegiance, but most of all missed someone who can act as a buffer between him and his mother's excessive affection." He glanced at Gethin who was walking his horse behind them, aware that he was being indiscreet, but reassured by the squire's far away expression.

"Aye, I know poor lad." Beau grimaced but his essential sense of fairness forced him to add, "You cannot blame her for doting on him though; he is the only good thing that came out her life in England. In some ways, I don't blame her for not wanting to go back, but I do think she is wrong when she tries to persuade Edward that it is not his destiny."

"Well, York has not provided a replacement Prince, has he?"

"No, for all his potency he has only girl children."

"Aye and they were mostly born in wedlock. Don't you think it odd that he only has one bastard?" Jack looked thoughtful.

"Well, either he is very lucky or very careful." Beau laughed sadly. It was his biggest regret that none of his women had ever borne his child and although it was a popular concept that it was the woman who was barren, the more he thought about it the more he thought the fault must lie with him. He and Izzy had shared a bed for nigh on seven years on and off and she had never once quickened with his child, yet she had married a year after he had come to France and had dropped a babe within nine months. And apart from Segoline de Crecy, who had falsely accused him of fathering her child, none of his court conquests had ever conceived; not that he was with any of them for long but it only took one time to make a child, as his younger brother already well knew, having at least two bastards to his name.

"He doesn't strike me as the careful type." Jack chuckled.

"Don't underestimate him Jack, he is a shrewd man."

"Lighten up Beau. I was talking about chasing women not bloody politics!" Jack pulled a face at his brother and Beau held up his hands.

"Sorry, lad, I've spent too much time with Pembroke!" They rode on in silence for a while, Jack contemplating his brother surreptitiously from under his fringe, taking in the furrows of tiredness at his mouth and the fine network of lines around his eyes. He was still a relatively young man but his life had taken a toll on him, making him seem older than his years and it was only when he smiled and the cares fell away that he looked young. Yet that did not seem to detract from his looks, his eyes that odd distinctive topaz colour, flecked and ringed with black, his cheekbones razor sharp over a somewhat full and sulky mouth, and Jack knew from experience that his body was lean, well-muscled and as hard as iron; he was a magnet to women, as much for the callous indifference he showed them as anything else, which proved that women preferred a complete bastard to a good man. At this moment, he was chewing the inside of his lip, as he always did when thinking or concentrating, his eyes turned inward, corners creased against the snowflakes fluttering into his face.

"A prayer for them?" Jack smiled.

"What?"

"I'll give you a prayer for your thoughts." Beau smiled back and shook his head.

"Not for other ears I'm afraid." He laughed softly. "I was daydreaming."

"You were leagues away. I presume the day dream had red hair."

"Perhaps." He laughed again. Jack rubbed the wetness from his face, grateful that the wind was not too keen.

"I think this snow is going to set in Beau, we could be here for more than a cup of wine." Beau looked up at the sky which showed no sign of letting up on its thick, heavy greyness.

"Yes, there's a good ground covering in that, I think." They followed the narrow track around a bend and suddenly to their left some walls loomed through the blur of falling snow.

"Here we are." Jack turned left down a track lined with big bare trees which ended in some big wooden gates. "Open up; the Marquis of Dorset is without," he shouted in French, and as they reached them, the huge gates parted and they walked their horses in. Beau looked around him with mild interest, wondering briefly what the errand was that brought Jack here, noting the old-fashioned style of the house, with its big single-storey hall being the main piece of accommodation. He dismounted swiftly, handing over the reins to a groom who had come out of the stables to greet them, quickly unbuckling his panniers and slinging them over his shoulder. Gethin appeared by his side with a smile, and lifted them from him.

"I will take those, my Lord," he said quietly. Beau nodded thanks and followed his brother into the hall. At first glance it was empty and he shot a look at Jack who seemed unperturbed, walking across the floor towards the dais. Suddenly a small white shape hurled itself through a screen behind the platform and careered towards them, coming to a skidding halt in front of Beau, its lips drawn back from its small white teeth, a low growl coming from its throat.

"What the fuck?" Beau stared at the little dog with its white hackles up on its back and its brown eyes on his face. Jack was laughing silently, his hand up to his mouth as he sought to hold his mirth in, and even Gethin was grinning at the puppy's open declaration of hostility. The dog looked vaguely familiar and as realisation began to seep through his brain into his consciousness, he looked sharply at Jack who was an air of studied innocence, and then Gethin who shrugged and shook his head.

"Welcome, my Lord." The gentle voice brought him back to the dais and he swallowed at the vision before him. She was smiling softly at him, her curly russet hair was caught back loosely, hanging well past her hips and her slender body was sleeved in a gown of green wool as she clicked her fingers at the little dog who ran to her side, still grumbling in his throat.

"Katherine?" Beau's husky voice was almost a whisper, as he stared at her. Jack motioned discreetly to Gethin to follow him away from his Lord, taking in the boy's awed expression as he did so with a smile. They moved toward the hearth, leaving Beau with his Lady, Jack's arm dropping around the squire's shoulders, his voice soft in his ear.

"This took some pretty planning my lad," he murmured. "So I am afraid you have two days in my company with nothing but wine, dice and tables to entertain us. Although you have been elected to serve any refreshments to the happy couple so that the rest of the household does not see the honoured guests together in the chamber; I don't think they will be calling on your services often."

"What about my Lord's things?" Gethin indicated to the panniers over his shoulder.

"We will worry about that later." He glanced across and saw that his brother was being led by the hand through the screen and into the great chamber behind. "I don't think he will be thinking much about his belongings for some considerable time.

***

"I cannot believe this." Beau watched as the girl poured hot water from the fire into the big wooden bath which was already steaming. She looked up at him and smiled softly, one hand stirring the water for a moment, before she decided it was at optimum temperature.

"Cannot believe what, my Lord?"

"This." He gestured towards her and the bath.

"I thought you would like a bath, my Lord after such a long time on the road. I am guessing they are not easy to come by in an inn."

"No they're not. I have not had a bath for a fortnight." He looked bemused. "But that wasn't exactly what I meant; I meant this; you; here." He gestured again and she smiled again.

"Ah," she said, turning away and putting the big pot back onto its iron stand in the fireplace.

"Katherine?"

"Yes, my Lord?"

"Did Jack ask you to do this?"

"No, he didn't." She turned back and faced him, her cheeks flushing delicately. "I asked Lord Jack and my mother to help me." His face showed his surprise and she laughed softly, "You see this is my mother's house and I can tell you it took some planning and a great deal of deceit, but between us all we managed it." She looked up at him, her eyes luminous in her pale skin and his heart lurched in his chest.

"So what does it mean?" His expression was still bemused.

"Whatever you want it to mean, my Lord." Her smile wavered, uncertainly. "You said you wanted to spend time with me…that is still what you want, isn't it?"

"Yes." His smile was breathtaking, his reply fervent. "Sweet Jesus, yes."

"So do you want this bath or not?" Relief flooded her and her heart steadied as, moving towards him, she forestalled his next words. "There is no need to call your squire, my Lord, I can assist you." She saw him swallow and then nod in assent, and nervous though she was, acting on instinct alone, she knew that she was on firm ground. He began to unlace his tunic, his fingers shaking slightly, and she helped him shrug it off, laying it neatly over the nearest chair while he untied the points of his chausses and pulled his fine white linen shirt over his head.

"Oh my," she murmured as she took his shirt, her fingers touching the fine dark hair on his chest and trailing down his stomach. He breathed sharply down his nose, his eyes intent on her face, watching as she reached for the cord of his chausses and began to unfasten them, her tongue touching her top lip. He caught her wrist for a second, slipping off his black leather boots and then pulling her to him, his mouth covering hers in a hot kiss, parting her lips, his tongue capturing hers, his other hand at her cheek. She savoured the warm softness of his kiss, her fingers caressing the hard leanness of his waist before she brought her hands up to his chest and held him off, her mouth curving against his in a smile.

"The bath," she said softly, he laughed silently.

"Are you telling me I need it?"

"No, but it has taken me nigh on an hour to have the water drawn; your hair is soaked, you have dirt tracks down your face and your skin is freezing." She smiled impishly and drew away from him, her fingers back to the lacings of his chausses and then finally his braies, pulling at the cord so that they dropped at his feet. He stepped out of them and his mouth quirked in a smile as she stared at him. "Oh my," she whispered again, laughing shakily, her hand reaching out and then dropping self-consciously to her side, suddenly remembering Stephen's reaction to her touch. He caught her wrist again, drawing her back towards him.

"Don't ever be afraid to touch me," he whispered, guiding her hand, his breath hissing through his teeth at her touch. "Not ever." He kissed her again, his breathing ragged as he savoured the feel of her hand on him, stroking his hardness with an exquisite butterfly touch. Once again she moved away from him and smiled, guiding him back toward the bath. He stepped in and sat down, closing his eyes and leaning his head back against the soft pillowed rim, stretching out his legs luxuriously. She removed her gown, knelt beside the bath in just her linen chemise, the tablet of soft soap laced with bergamot in her hand, her firm breasts straining at the sheer material.

"Christ, you are beautiful," he said softly, without opening his eyes. Reaching up into her hair he took a strand and twirled it around his fingers. Then he gasped as she put her hand on his stomach, sliding over its taut flatness and up to his chest, soap in hand, her mouth touching his in a brief kiss and then a longer one, her tongue parting his lips as she kissed him, rubbing the soap over his skin and then down his thighs. He whimpered against her mouth and she smiled, moving back up toward his chest.

"How am I doing?" she whispered mischievously and he laughed.

"Give me the soap or I won't even make it out of the bath." He slipped his hand under the water, still laughing as they splashed about for the tablet, until he reached out with his other hand and, over balancing her, pulled her into the tub on top of him, the water soaking through her chemise and her hair. She shook her head vigorously, drenching him, and he grabbed her, pinning her against his chest, her face above him, her body full length over his. "Last time I saw you, you were too weak to even get out of your chair and now, just over a month later, you are in my bath seducing me." He grinned and then was serious suddenly. "Why the change of heart, kitten?"

"My heart hasn't changed." Her smile was soft. "It's just my head is not ruling it."

"You are sure this is what you want?" He pushed a wet strand from her cheek and tucked it behind her ear.

"It's somewhat late to say no now." She laughed but he did not.

"No it isn't." He stroked her cheek with the back of his hand.

"It's what I want." She leaned down and kissed him, and then leaned back up to look at him. "And I may lack experience but I would say that this…" She rubbed her pubic bone against his erection playfully and he caught his breath. "…means it's what you want?"

"And you would say right." He grinned and kissed the tip of her nose. "Jesus can a man actually be this lucky?"

"I doubt it." She returned his grin in full measure, loving his responses to her caresses and his joyful expression.. "No other man has ever had me in his bath or his bed for that matter."

"I have never had you in my bed either," he murmured huskily, letting his hand slide over her buttocks and pulling her hips into him, his eyes opaque with desire, his pulse erratic in his neck.

"So what are we waiting for?" Liquid seemed to be flowing into the pit of her stomach, making the blood rush faster through her veins, creating a throbbing urgency between her thighs. He pulled her down to him and kissed her hard, his other hand caressing the soft curve of her bottom, and her breathing quickened even to her own ears, desire coursing through her in waves as he groaned in response. He let go of her and she looked down at him for a moment before pushing herself up and out of the bath, her chemise clinging to her, and he caught his lip between his teeth, his eyes on her avidly. He finished washing himself quickly and then reached for the towel she offered him, and stood, wrapping it around his waist, pinning his erection to his stomach before he stepped out of the bath. He reached across and stripped off her chemise, taking the other towel and patting her dry gently, chewing his lip appealingly as he concentrated on his task, each touch making her skin tingle with a need she barely understood. Then he gathered her up in his arms and carried her to the bed and laid her on it.

***

"Do you trust me?" Beau asked softly as he lay down beside her and propped himself up on his elbow. He was touched when she nodded immediately, reaching up and touching his cheek. He kissed her gently.

"Then lie back and close your eyes darling, and just tell me to stop if you want me to; we don't have to bed together if you don't want to. I am happy just to be with you and there is no need to rush anything." He stroked her hair and her cheek as he spoke and obediently she closed her eyes. He could tell that she was tense, even though she was responding to his touch and he guessed that she was much more afraid than she showed. He carried on stroking her face gently, kissing her ears and her neck, moving his hand slowly downwards until he was caressing her breast. He heard her gasp and her nipple hardened under his fingers making him smile, but he kept his touch even, and his breathing regular, letting his palm move wider and wider until he was stroking and kissing across her stomach and thighs. When his hand finally reached the triangle at the top of her thighs they parted instinctively and he let his fingers take an intimate walk between them. She gasped and then moaned softly as he found the little nub of her pleasure, keeping his movements regular and firm, allowing his mouth now to travel to her thigh and back over her stomach.. He felt her arch against his lips, and she made soft appreciative noises in her throat, and smiling again he knelt between her legs and placed his mouth where his fingers had been a second before, doing for her what he had never done for any woman. His heart leapt at her response as she cried out at the touch of his tongue, her body tensing and writhing in her pleasure; he felt her hands in his hair, fingers opening and closing to the rhythm of his tongue, and her soft moans slowly reaching a crescendo before she whimpered and then pulsed against his lips, her wild wet hair tossing on the pillow.

"Holy God!" The words were involuntary, forced out by the unexpectedness of her pleasure.

He lifted his head and wiped his mouth with the back of his hand, savouring her taste, and reaching around, he pulled off the towel and entered her slowly, watching her face all the time for any sign of fear. She opened her eyes as she felt him sliding in, her expression full of wonder and surprise before she eased her body into a position to take him right inside her. His breath hissed sharply through his teeth as his eyes met hers, and propping himself up on one arm, he eased the other under her waist pulling her upward so that he could control his movements inside her.

"I am sorry, my darling, but this is going to be over very quickly." He breathed a ragged breath. "I want you so much I cannot hold it for long, I will make it up to you I promise. Oh Christ...!" He broke off as she closed around him, her woman's part sucking him deliciously, making him thrust hard against her. Her eyes widened and then he felt her legs wrap around him, drawing him even deeper inside.

"Oh love!" she whispered.

He groaned at her words and then his body took over, his hips thrusting against her, his head back, his eyes tightly closed, holding his breath.

"Kitten," he whispered her name like a caress, "Oh yes, kitten." And then he made a strangled sound in his throat and softly cried, "Oh, Katherine!" as he jerked hard against her twice, hips and shoulders shuddering, before he collapsed onto her, his face in the curve of her neck, his breathing harsh and rapid. She held him close, her legs still around him, her hands stroking his hair as he clung to her, his stomach fluttering with joy at the pleasure he had both given and received from her, his mind full of the magic that he had wrought within her. Finally he pushed himself up onto his elbows and looked down into her face, his eyes glowing with tenderness and his mouth reaching for hers in a long, slow kiss. He rolled onto his side, taking her with him, still entwined in the most intimate of lovers' embraces, his mouth not leaving hers as they continued their unhurried kissing. Eventually he drew back and looked at her once more.

"This morning," he said softly, "I left an inn in the dark, the sky heavy with snow, excited because I thought I would make it home and perhaps be lucky enough to see you and talk to you." He slid his fingers over her cheek and into her hair. "And then my life turns into a dream and I am here, entwined like this with you, naked and unashamed, feeling like I have never felt before." He kissed her tenderly. "I cannot believe this is happening."

"I wish that I could have truly given you my maidenhead," she whispered, touching his face, tracing his cheekbone and then his lips. "If I could have chosen, I would have chosen you, my Lord."

"Ah, Katherine." He pulled her to him, resting his chin on the top of her head. He was overflowing with an emotion he could not express and did not even intend to try. Having fallen in love with a fantasy and then found that the real thing was so much better than he had ever dreamed it could be, he was struggling with putting how he felt into words.

"He said I unmanned him." Her voice was barely a whisper and it took him a minute to realise she was speaking.

"Who did darling?" He shook himself mentally, coming alert at her words.

"Stephen." Tears filled her voice. "He could not do his duty because he spilled his seed too early and he said it was because I unmanned him."

"Ah, kitten." He did not know what to say.

"When you said it would be over quickly I thought I had unmanned you." She shuddered and he felt tears seep onto his shoulder.

"Ah, kitten," he said again, his heart going out to her. "You did not unman me. I just have wanted you so much for so long that I knew I would not be able to hold back. I am very much a man I can assure you."

"I was afraid."

"I know you were darling." He kissed her hair and then, tilting her chin, kissed her mouth in a long, lingering kiss. "But now you know there is nothing to be afraid of."

"Thank you," she said, snuggling into his neck, her lips tracking down to his collar bone. He pulled her tight against him, unable to think of a suitable response to her strange gift of thanks.

For the first time in his life he was content to lay with a woman in his arms, kissing and talking, and was looking forward to the night when he could hold her and watch her sleep. He never slept much more than six hours and once awake was normally up and out, but right at this moment he could think of nothing nicer than waking in the morning and looking at her sleeping; at least for a little while, before he coaxed her awake with his lovemaking. Slowly he became conscious that his erection had not diminished and that he was still hard within her, and he smiled inwardly; it seemed fitting that she should be the one who could do that to him. He had heard other men talk of being able to continue making love even after reaching their pleasure, but it had never happened to him before and he had never cared much that it should. But now he moved his hips gently and heard her gasp and then laugh softly.

"My Lord!" she looked up at him, her eyes round, and he grinned broadly.

"My Lady?" He moved again, watching her face. She bit her lip and her eyes flared with a need that quickened his pulse rapidly. He rolled onto his back and brought her with him, so she straddled him, riding him like she would a horse, a position condemned by the church as carnal when sex should be for the begetting of children. His stomach lurched at the thought of children; if he could fill her belly then he would be the happiest of men, and thinking of her ripe and full of his child surged desire through his blood. Over the next hour he focused his concentration on her, making her almost sob as he took her to heights of pleasure she could never have dreamed existed, their lovemaking by turns passionate, slow, fast, playful and then at last intense as he finally relaxed his iron control and released his seed inside her for the second time, his orgasm so exquisite that his sharp, agonised cry could be heard by the two young men playing chess in the hall by the hearth. They looked at each other in alarm for a moment and then Jack burst out laughing and clapped the crimson Gethin on the shoulder.

"I'd take supper in to them in about ten minutes, Gethin," he said when he could finally speak. "I should think they've worked up quite an appetite."

***

When Gethin finally plucked up courage to bring a supper tray to them, they were up, Beau in his shirt and chausses and Kate in a long dark-blue chamber robe, both on the settle, sharing a cup of wine, Kate's legs over Beau's lap and his arm around her, holding her into his shoulder. The bed had been roughly made and the rumpled sheets straightened.

"My Lord, my Lady?" he said from the door. Beau smiled and waved him in.

"Come in, lad." He glanced at Kate and raised a brow and she nodded. "Why don't you and Jack join us for supper?" He stretched languorously. "And bring more food, I'm starving." Kate looked at him and then laughed.

"Worked up an appetite, my Lord?" she murmured and he grinned.

"I might have." He kissed her temple. "I have been a busy man."

"I will get Lord Jack, my Lord and some more food and wine." Gethin bowed and backed out of the room.

"Thank you, Gethin."

"That boy is far too serious," Kate said, watching him leave, and swinging her legs reluctantly down towards the floor, although not before she had kissed Beau lingeringly. Her body was still on fire from his touch and she felt like she just could not get enough of him. His arms tightened around her and their kiss deepened, her hand sliding into his shirt before they pulled back and both laughed shakily. He caught her hand and kissed it. "You were saying?" he said, holding her hand to his cheek.

She smiled.

"I said, Gethin is too serious."

"No, what you actually said was 'that boy is too serious,' which I find odd because he is a few years older than you!"

"He just seems like a boy to me; an earnest and eager to please boy." She smiled at him and he laughed.

"Is that because girls mature faster than boys?"

"No, because Jack doesn't seem so young. Jack is worldly at least but Gethin just seems naïve somehow and too quiet and polite, or perhaps the squires I knew were just hellions." She laughed.

"Maybe, but Gethin is a good lad and he is very efficient, better than any I have ever had including Jack!" Beau smiled fondly, just as Jack appeared, his face round the door, his hand over his eyes.

"Is it safe to come in?" They both laughed.

"Quite safe." Beau grinned and Kate made to get up and get some wine, but he laid a hand to her arm. "Darling, you have no need to wait on him, he can get the wine himself, can't you Jack?"

"Of course." Jack walked over to the table and grabbed the flagon and two more cups while Kate silently acknowledged her elevation in status to Beau with a heartfelt and radiant smile. At that moment Gethin arrived with a small trestle which he set up. He then came back with a huge tray perched on his shoulder, laden with cold chicken and ham, bread, cheese wafers, butter, raisins, dates, figs and a bowl of oranges. Kate's eyes lit up; she loved oranges, the fact that you had to peel them to get to the fruit, the tangy sweetness of them and that they were expensive in England because they were rare, all adding to the pleasure. Gethin disappeared again and this time returned with a flagon of wine and one of ale in one hand and a lute in the other.

"We found this in the chamber at the other end of the hall, so I dusted it off and I think I have tuned it, my Lord, but we hoped that you would play it after supper and Lord Jack could sing." Gethin flushed lightly and Kate realised that that was the most she had ever heard him say. She smiled at him and his colour deepened, his fair skin showing the rose tinge to its full effect. He had a nice face, she thought, still somewhat boyish but a nice shape, a strong jaw and wide, full mouth, a neat nose and long dark lashes over sea-grey eyes; not exceptionally striking like Beau but very nice to look at all the same.

"I think that's a lovely idea," she said, turning her smile on Beau who looked remarkably reluctant.

"Perhaps." His face softened at her expression. "For you."

"I am flattered." She looked up at him through her lashes, laughing, and he grinned.

"You should be."

"I think we should drink a toast." Jack said suddenly, looking at them all expansively, "A toast to snow, good food, good company and the lute." He grinned and they all laughed, and raising cups chanted, "Snow, good food, good company and the lute."

***

The evening passed pleasantly in laughter and fun, sharing family information and past exploits and Kate making them laugh with impressions of her father, the Countess and the Queen. She was a gifted mimic and her impressions were remarkably accurate but heavily caricatured to elicit laughter and Beau found himself once again admiring his own good fortune in having not only found this beautiful, spirited, gifted girl but somehow having ensnared her into his life and into his bed. When finally they persuaded him to play the lute it turned out that he was more than a competent musician and that he could play particularly well, but for some reason it was not something he enjoyed very much. Jack told the story of his brother always being asked to play the lute when his mother and father brought exalted guests to the house, clearing the floor so that he sat alone in front of the dais and played, sometimes with someone singing with him, at others alone; and how much he had hated to be singled out for that talent, while Hal was being lauded for his military prowess. Beau took the tale in good part but pointed out that that was the reason behind his dislike of playing the lute, for as soon as he began to play he experienced all those awful feelings of inadequacy all over again.

"You look good the part though, my Lord." Gethin ventured as he strummed the strings with his long fingers. "The lute is definitely an instrument that suits you."

"Well, enjoy it Gethin because I doubt that you will ever see me do this again," Beau replied with a lightening smile. "I have no intention of suddenly turning into anyone's hearth musician."

But the surprise of the evening was Gethin with his beautiful baritone outstripping Jack's nice but unremarkable voice, bringing everything to a halt, and then all three of them bombarding the boy with questions as to how they had never known he could sing. Gethin coloured furiously, but grinned with pride that he was able to show his talents and they all found themselves looking at him afresh.

"You are a dark horse, my lad!" Beau said, shaking his head. "I can't believe that you hid that light under a bushel!"

"How come we have never heard you sing?" Jack was obviously aggrieved.

"There has never been any need, my Lord." Gethin was laughing, coming quite visibly out of his shell at the attention. "It was not that I hid it, it was just that I was never asked."

"If could sing like that I wouldn't wait to be asked, that's for sure!" Jack laughed suddenly. "I'd be wooing every beautiful girl I could find with it!"

"I will bear that in mind, my Lord." Gethin joined Jack's laughter.

"You could learn a lot from him." Beau said with a grin.

"Like you haven't learned from the master already!" Jack shot back.

"Well we'll certainly know who to call on when we need some entertainment in the lady chamber," Kate said and Beau looked at her with mock sharpness.

"There'll be no dalliance with my squire, my Lady," he said sternly. "Poor lad would never come out of there alive with that lot of wolverines!"

"You can play the lute to keep an eye on him if you want?" Her eyes danced as she met his and he laughed.

"God, no!" He put the lute down and stretched his shoulders and cramped fingers. "I cannot think of anything worse than being in the lady chamber and playing my lute. If ever anyone wanted to punish me for a sin that would be a good one!"

"My brother does not like his lute or women overmuch." Jack said with a grin. Beau snorted.

"I cannot abide the gaggling that women do when they get together, no." He pulled a face and Kate laughed and stuck out her tongue at him.

"I'll have to make sure I remember not to gaggle then won't I or I shall find myself at the back of the long queue of women who once 'knew' my Lord Somerset!" Gethin grinned and Jack barked a laugh.

"It's a bloody long queue too!" he jibed but Beau just shook his head and smiled.

"What else do I need to learn, my Lord, to keep one step ahead of my rivals?" She winked at Jack as she spoke, but Beau still refused to rise to the bait.

"You have no rivals, darling, for none could compare with you." He deadpanned and she laughed.

"Smooth, my Lord, very smooth," she said admiringly.

"He is not considered a fine courtier for nothing." Jack laughed.

"I but speak the truth." He kept his expression bland but his eyes were focused intently on her.

"You certainly have a skill, my Lord," she said very softly, smiling at him and their eyes caught, understood and answered the need in each other. Jack, catching his brother's expression, nudged Gethin and flicked his head towards the door, just as Beau said quietly, "I think it is time to call it a night," not taking his eyes from hers. "Leave the food, Gethin, it can be cleared away in the morning." He stood, taking her hand and helping her to her feet, and as Gethin turned to close the door behind him he saw her robe drop to the floor in a swirl of blue wool and a flash of a perfect white bottom before her hair swung to cover it and the door closed in front of him.

***

"Did you know that it was the Romans who brought stinging nettles to England?" She flicked the page of the book she had in her hand and then slid her fingers back into his hair. "They used them to beat their skin with to keep out the cold. Apparently even in winter they went sleeveless and bare-legged, wore those shoes that had no toes in and strapped around their legs so the frost and cold and the snow really was hazardous for them. They kept their blood warm by beating themselves with the nettles."

"Mmmm?" He smiled lazily, his eyes closed, savouring her touch. "Why didn't they just wear more clothes?"

"Pride I think, in their race and their dress." She flicked some more pages. "Oh my!" She started to laugh.

"What?"

"This is lewd!"

"Why?"

"Listen, Love's climax never be rushed, I say, but worked up softly, lingering all the way. The parts a woman loves to have caressed, once found, caress though modesty protests.' Someone called Ovid wrote that." She giggled.

"What *are* you reading?"

"The history of Rome, I think. I found it on the shelf over there." She passed it to him and he looked at it.

"You can read Latin?" He looked up at her admiringly.

"Yes."

"Impressive!" He passed the book back. "And your sisters?"

"No, they could never be bothered much. Papa believed in education for all of us, although ma mère was not a fan so we were educated with my cousin Richard and Francis Lovell, much to their tutor's disgust." She stroked his hair once more, looking down to where his head was pillowed in her lap. "I enjoyed it so I learned but my sisters never felt that they would need it."

"I did not much like lessons." He wrinkled his nose. "I can read French, Latin and English and I can do mathematics but I hate writing with my own hand and I use a secretary wherever possible. Swordsmanship was my forte."

"And the lute," she said innocently.

"And the lute." He poked his tongue out at her. "But of course, swordsmanship was your forte too."

"But not the lute."

"Oh shut up about the bloody lute!" He closed his eyes, smiling broadly. He could not ever remember being this happy or feeling so contented in the company of someone other than his family. Last night was only the second time he had shared a bed for a full night with a lover but the first time he had shared it with a woman he loved, and he had woken up this morning to find her curled up in his arms, her head on his chest and her arm around his waist. He had lain for an age just savouring the feel of her close to him, his arms around her, so touched by her trust and seeming fragility that the surge of protectiveness that had swept over him had taken his breath away. Finally, he had caressed her into wakefulness and then made love to her with a tenderness that had left them both clinging in its intensity, holding each other for a long time after their climax, neither able to speak or find the words to express how they felt. Now, as the grey sky yielded yet more snow, he, a man with normally such restless energy, lay on the carpeted floor with his head pillowed in her lap, the fire roaring beside them, listening to her read extracts from the books she had pulled off the shelf in the solar, and thought that life could not ever get better than this.

"The Romans brought rabbits to England, too, because they breed quickly and therefore were a quick source of food."

"The same could be said of peasants!" he murmured and laughed as she pulled his hair.

"That's mean."

"Was it Julius Caesar who conquered England?"

"No, Julius Caesar came to England but did not finally conquer it; someone called Claudius did, who came quite a long time after Julius Caesar as far as I can make out, and then changed his name to Claudius Brittanicus."

"I have never been interested in history, but you make it sound fascinating." He smiled as he spoke and flinched as she poked him in the ribs.

"Liar. Anyway you have been interested in history; it was you who told me about Katherine Swynford and John of Ghent."

"Ah, but that's my own history." He turned and leaning over her threw another log onto the fire, poking it into place with the iron poker and stoking the remaining logs to greater heat. "Are you warm enough, darling?" he asked softly, turning back and nestling back into her lap. She slid her hand over his forehead, brushing his long fringe out of his eyes, and nodded with a smile, positioning her cushion more comfortably against the settle, her legs curled under her. She put her book down beside her and slid her other hand into the open slash of his shirt, her fingers entwining in the fine hair across his chest. She could feel the steady thud of his heart through his ribs.

"Yes thank you." She tugged gently at a tuft of hair. "Tell me about the Beaufort history, my Lord." He frowned.

"Can I not just be 'Beau' or 'love' or 'darling' when we are private, love?" He caught her hand and held it to his cheek. "I hate it when you 'my Lord' me. It is impersonal."

"Tell me about the Beaufort history, love." She made the correction self-consciously, but was rewarded with the kind of smile that melted her inside. She stroked his cheek with the hand he held there and he closed his eyes contentedly.

"Where shall I start?"

"Tell me about your mother and father and your brother Hal. You have met my family but I know little or nothing about your family except that maman told me that Hal was pretty." She laughed and he grinned.

"He was, and women loved him. He was about my height and dark like me but he looked just like our mother, had her fine bones; whereas I am like my father, although papa was shorter and broader than me."

"And Jack?"

"Jack is a combination of both my parents. He is my father's build and height but looks more like my mother's family."

"What was your father like?" She stroked his fringe back from his eyes again and looked into his face. "As a man?"

"Well." He thought for a moment. "He was hard and uncompromising and never listened to advice from anyone, but I loved and respected him, as did many. He loved my mother and they understood each other, but he loved Marguerite too. I am not sure if he was her lover because no one would ever tell me, but I know that she loved him and that she saw him in me which was nearly my downfall." He grimaced. "But Jack told you about that?"

"Yes."

"I thought he would."

"He told me a lot about you."

"Did he now?" He smiled, his eyes still closed.

"Yes." She laughed but said nothing more on the subject, instead touching the leather lace around his neck. "Are these your mother's rings?"

"Yes. She gave them to me when she died, for my bride, she said." His smile was soft. "She was a beautiful woman, my mother."

"Was she?"

"Mmmm. Glossy, black hair to her knees and eyes like jet. I remember her coming into our chamber when I was a lad, ready to go down into the hall for some celebration or another, and she looked like a Saracen princess. I remember my father coming to find her and the pride in his face as he looked at her." His voice throbbed with warmth at this memory of his mother, of a childhood long ago and almost forgotten; a happy childhood with parents who had loved and been proud of him. "I was her favourite son. Hal was papa's and I was hers and poor old Jack was the late edition who got lost in the family somehow. My sisters were different; they were coins in the dynastic field, making great marriages and ensuring their futures, but we did not have much in common or much to do with each other. I missed my father when he died when I was sixteen but Hal missed him more and was, I think, lost without him. He tried to live up to him with Madame but he could not and lost his life doing something really stupid against an opposition he could not beat, and so ended our hopes until your father came to our rescue." He opened his eyes and smiled up at her. "I have more than once railed against that loss of our hopes but now I find myself strangely grateful that my brother was a fool as it has brought you into my life!" She returned his smile in equal measure and reaching over touched the ring on his thumb.

"Where did this one come from?" she asked, lifting his hand and examining the ornate pattern around it before kissing his palm and putting it back on this stomach.

"That was papa's wedding ring."

"Wedding ring?" She picked his hand up again and looked at it closely. "Jesu', how big were his hands?"

"Huge." Beau laughed. "He could hold a man's head in one hand. When I was a lad it was a recognised punishment in our house to have your head grabbed in a vice of papa's hand, and it bloody hurt as well."

"Did you get punished often?"

"Not that often. I was quite a good lad really; the only time I really got punished was for fighting with Hal. We argued and came to blows often for we were both strong willed and papa ever took Hal's side, teaching me my place as the younger brother to the heir of Somerset. He never really hurt me though."

"My father is not very good at punishment."

"Really?" He was surprised.

"No. Oh he could mete it out to Richard and Francis and the other boys but not to us girls. Ma mère punished Isabel and Anne, and no one punished me much. I am mainly confined to my room or given extra household duties, even now!" She grimaced. "But no one ever laid a hand on me." She smiled fondly. "My father is a soft man at heart when it comes to his daughters."

"You love him, don't you?" He felt a surge of tenderness and hoped that one day she would love him as much as she loved her father. He reached up and stroked her cheek.

"He has ever been good to me and loved me tenderly, sometimes above the love he has given his legitimate children." She kissed his hand. "Did you know he talked to maman about you?"

"About me?" He quirked a brow in surprise.

"Yes. He told her he thought you had a fancy for me and that I was taken with you." She blushed, touchingly embarrassed at revealing her feelings for him.

"No I didn't know." He met her gaze. "He did talk to me, though."

"About me?" She stared at him, unconsciously echoing his own surprise.

"Yes." He smiled. "He came to the inn in town, Jack, and I were in the night I brought you home after Sable broke her leg."

"What did he say?" She had stiffened, her expression wary.

"That he wanted you to be happy and that you were free to choose your way in life, and if I was going to woo you he would not stand in my way as long as I treated you with respect and honour." He kept his hand on her cheek, his expression soft. "I told him that I cared for you greatly, would never treat you with anything other than honour and respect." He twirled a strand of her hair through his fingers. "He also told me about your husband and what he did to you."

She did not flinch but kept her eyes locked to his, their expression veiled.

"Did he tell you all?"

"All?"

"Why it happened?"

"He said that your husband thought that York was paying you too much attention." He sat up and faced her, his legs crossed and his eyes alive with interest.

"My husband and George came in to the solar where Ned was kissing me. I was trying to fight him off but he was too strong for me." She looked at him levelly. "But I confess there was a moment when I nearly gave into him. Ned is a very persuasive and very handsome man and for a moment I wanted him."

"I know how persuasive he is. He convinced my brother to renounce his loyalty to Lancaster and move over to York and they spent a good year in each other's company." He reached out and pushed her hair back from her face. "I spent time in his company as a young man and I know how charismatic he is, and how women love him. I can see how you found yourself in that position."

"Can you?" She looked surprised. He nodded, thinking how badly she had been treated by all the men in her life.

"Yes I can." He kept his hand in her hair. "If your husband had not been dead already, when your father told me, I would have killed him if I could have."

"I think it was more than just the kiss that drove him to his action. I think he wanted his revenge."

"It has more to do with bending you to his will, I think." He shook his head disgustedly. "I don't know how a man can so treat a woman," he said softly, resenting that she had had to suffer so much at the hands of those who professed to love her. "I would never treat you like that."

"No, you would just kill me." Her mouth flicked up in a wry half smile.

"No, I would not; not for a kiss!" He was mildly shocked that she thought him so extreme. "If I had found you in his bed, urging him to his pleasure, then maybe I would think about it, for I would not be able to understand why you would need that from him when we have what we have, but not for a kiss, darling; especially not a kiss like that. Christ, most men have more sport than that with the bride at weddings!" He leaned forward and touched his mouth to hers softly and then longer and deeper, his hands sliding into her hair, the spark of sexual frisson always just under the surface. He heard her breathing quicken softly, his stomach lurching in response, and with an effort he drew back and smiled, running his finger over her lips. "Although I might kill for a kiss like that," he murmured before turning and laying his head back into her lap. "How did we get to this?" he asked, smiling up at her. "We should be talking about sweeter things." He took her hand and kissed it and then touched his cheek with it. "This ring," he said, holding up his left hand and showing the ruby, "was given to me by Isabel Harcourt who was my first lover."

"Was it now?" She smiled and pretended to bristle jealously. He grinned fondly.

"Yes," he said, softly. "I was but seventeen and she was fifteen when we first bedded together and we saw each other for seven years after that. Her father hoped that we would wed but it would not have been right. She was a good friend and I desired and liked her, but her family was no match for mine and my mother and my brother would never have forgiven me." He looked up at her. "I also did not have much of a mind to wed; too many furrows to plough!"

"Did you love her?"

"No; or at least never enough to be faithful or to see her as often as I should have." He sighed regretfully. "Even though I was hurting her and left her without a backward glance, she helped me escape to France and she gave me the ruby to aid my passage, but I did not need it as the captain was sympathetic to my plight and carried me as a favour, and so I have worn it ever since as a symbol of my escape and my freedom."

"She must have been a good woman."

"Yes she was and I will always be grateful." He smiled. "Because if I had never made it to France, then I would never have met you." She laughed as he had hoped she would.

"So it all leads to me?"

"It would seem so." He grinned and held out his wrist. "And this was my father's. He had it commissioned when he first came to his dukedom by an Italian jeweller who had settled in London. So I wear it as he did and as Hal did before me, on the same strap so far." He met her gaze with his. "Can I ask you a question now, love?"

"Of course." She smiled

"Why do you still wear your wedding ring?" She shook her head and then looked down at her hand.

"I don't know really." She frowned. "Because there is no escaping the fact that I am a widow I suppose and because I have worn it for nigh on four years. I was wed at thirteen."

"Take it off," he said quietly.

"Take it off?" She looked surprised.

"Yes, take it off. You have no need for Stephen Thevenot's wedding band." He held out his hand expectantly. She stared at him for a moment and then slipped the ring off her finger and gave it to him. "I will have something made that you can wear instead; something that is between you and I." He threw the gold band into the log fire and then looked back up at her. "It is time to be free of the past and look to the future."

"I don't want to look beyond today." She looked sad for a moment and he quirked his brow in surprise.

"Why not?"

"Because tomorrow we must go back and this will be but a memory." She swept an all-encompassing gesture. "And I will have to once more content myself with watching you from afar."

"Ah, kitten," he said softly, and held out his arms to her. "Come here and let me hold you."

***

Kate slid the cushion that had been behind her under his head and then lay down, her head on Beau's chest, his arms tight around her, not able to resist sliding her hand under his shirt and across his iron stomach as her heart lurched at his indrawn breath. He was the first man she had really ever seen naked, for although privacy was something of which there was little in everyday life, she had not been exposed much to male

255

nudity. She had once or twice helped an honoured guest bathe but had never really looked at them, her natural curiosity dampened by her modesty and embarrassment. But the man in whose arms she lay was the first man she had seen completely naked and she knew, by instinct alone, that it was unlikely she would ever see a man who was more beautiful. He was lean and muscled, and his skin smooth and creamy, unblemished except for two battle scars, one down the inside of his forearm, and a long white line across his stomach, which he said had only been a scratch and looked much worse now it had healed than it had when it had been a wound. The light covering of dark hair across his chest continued down his taut stomach in a long, thin line and disappeared into the top of his chausses, which, when he was laid on his back like this, barely hid the treasure that was contained there. His long legs were strong and well-muscled, slightly bowed from the knee, his walk supremely masculine, his body carriage proud and arrogant. The sexual attraction between them was a tangible thing, something that had a life of its own and existed outside their control; a touch or a kiss igniting the flame and fanning it until it turned into a furnace, leaving them shaking and breathless with its intensity. They could not keep their hands off each other, touching and caressing constantly until eventually they made love again, their climax abating their desire and the cycle of kissing and caressing beginning all over again.

"Beau?" she whispered, trailing her fingers over his stomach between his hip bones, the erratic beating of his heart against her ear.

"Mmmm?" She could hear the haze of sensuality in his voice and her stomach lurched again.

"I don't want this to end." Her throat was tight with tears at the thought and she knew then that she was falling in love with him.

"I don't want it to either, but we have to go back to Angers at some point." He slid his hand into her hair, stroking it back off her cheek, his callused palm rough against her soft skin.

"No, I mean you and I." She felt a tear slide down her nose. "I don't want it to end." He rolled her over so that she was on her back and he was looking down at her, his expression at once tender and vehement.

"Ah, darling." He kissed her hard. "It is not going to end, not ever." He licked the tear on her cheek with the tip of his tongue before claiming her mouth once more. "This is just the beginning, I promise."

"But when we go back..."

"We will manage."

"I don't see how..."

"Then you have little faith in me." He looked hurt for a moment. "Have you any idea how I feel about you?" he asked softly, brushing a tear from the corner of her eye with his thumb. "You are the only woman I have thought of for more than four months now and the only one I have lain with for nigh on three, and if you knew me well then you would know that for me to go without a woman for three months is no mean achievement." He smiled and kissed the tip of her nose. "But since I saw you across the hall that first night, you have invaded my dreams and other women have lost their allure for me. I have been happier with you this last day than I have ever been in my life before; not only do you set my body alight with every touch, but I love just being with you, like we have this afternoon, talking and laughing and fooling around; it has never been like that for me before, I have just flirted and flattered, got what I wanted and then gone." He kissed her lips softly, and then again, lingeringly, unhurriedly. "But no one has given me the pleasure in bed that you have and I have never felt the way I feel with you, never felt so sure of what I wanted before. I feel like I fell in love with a dream and then the real thing turned out to be better than anything I could have ever imagined."

"Oh Beau!" The tears spilled out of the corners of her eyes again and one hand slid around his neck, pulling him down to meet her kiss. "Please say we don't have to leave tomorrow," she whispered against his mouth, her other hand straying across his stomach, down the fine line of hair. "Please can we stay one more day?" She slid her hand inside his braies and he groaned softly.

"Whatever you want, darling." He hissed a ragged breath as her hand grasped him firmly and he lost himself in the pleasure of her touch. "Whatever you want."

***

By the time they left on Monday morning the snow had stopped its flurries and the sky had lightened, freezing the ground hard for their journey back to Angers. Samson, thoroughly sick of Jack's company, had hurled himself delightedly at his mistress when she had emerged from the solar, stopping briefly to growl at her companion. Beau had roared with laughter at the little dog's jealousy and swung him up into the air so that their faces were level.

"You had better get used to it, my boy," he had said sternly at the animal's grumpy expression, "for I am going nowhere." Samson had just looked at him, the tip of his tail wagging uncertainly, and then gambolled off as soon as he was placed on the ground, grumbling from a distance.

They had decided that Beau and Jack would set off an hour or so ahead so that it looked like they had sent Gethin to collect her from her visit to her mother's family on their way back from their enforced stay at an inn due to the weather. He did not want to leave her but they had all agreed it would avoid any suspicion or gossip and Gethin would look after her. They had been awake at dawn and had lain in each other's arms for a long time, just enjoying their closeness before they had to get up and face the world, and then Gethin had come in with water for washing, and their time together was over. Kate had sat on the bed in her chamber robe, leaning over the bed end, watching fascinated as Gethin shaved his Lord and then helped him to dress, until finally the transformation from lover to courtier was complete, dressed from head to toe in dark green, padded shoulders accentuating his narrow waist and hips, white shirt cuffs and collar visible, black jewelled cap and black fur-trimmed cloak the final touch.

"How do I look?" He had turned to face her, smiling.

"Edible," she had said, keeping her face straight. His smile became a grin as their eyes locked and memories merged and his expression told her everything she needed to know about the pleasure she had given him last night. She had returned his grin and got up off the bed, padding across the floor in her soft slippers, curtseying with mock formality.

"Now you look like the Duke of Somerset," she had said a little wistfully. He cocked his head to one side.

"Why, who did I look like before?"

"Just someone who was mine." She had smiled at him and he had laughed.

"I like that," he had said softly, reaching for her hand and pulling her into his arms in a last tight embrace. "Because I am yours." It had been time to go then and she had followed him from the solar and watched him and Jack exchange identical smiles of greeting as she had fussed the excited Samson. They had conferred for a moment and then Jack had headed for the door and Beau had turned to her, inclining his head briefly.

"God willing, I will see you tonight, my Lady," he said quietly.

"God keep you, my Lord," she returned, dropping a quick curtsey. He turned away and walked across the hall before stopping and turning back. He walked backwards for a moment, just looking at her, and then kissed the fingers of his right hand and placed them over his heart. She watched him leave, cloak so long it almost trailed the floor, dark hair swinging over his collar, and her stomach dropped sickeningly. Grabbing the folds of her robe she ran to the door.

"My Lord!" He turned at the sound of her voice and seeing the expression on her face came back.

"What is it?"

"I just needed to tell you..." she faltered and then said, very lowly, "I love you." The smile that he gave her arrowed straight to her loins, and taking her hand he kissed it fervently.

"You hold my heart, darling," he said, equally softly. Their eyes locked and then he bowed once more and walked across the yard with a jaunty swagger.

Feeling suddenly very lonely, she walked back through the hall and into the solar where Gethin was tidying the room, picking up cups and plates. He looked up as she entered.

"Are you alright, my Lady?" he asked with a shy smile.

"Yes, I'm fine." She bent down and picked up her puppy, kissing his head, her expression turned inward, and then she shivered. Gethin looked at her for a moment before he spoke, as if uncertain whether he should be talking to her.

"Would you like a nice hot bath, my Lady, you look a little cold?" He said finally, chivalry overcoming his uncertainty.

"That is a wonderful idea, Gethin," she said, her face lighting up. "Do you think they'll mind?" She was conscious of not imposing too much on the goodwill of those few servants looking after the house.

"It is not for them to mind, Madam. They should be honoured to serve the Duke of Somerset's Lady," he said earnestly.

"Well if it is not too much trouble…"

"It is not too much trouble at all, my Lady, I will arrange it." He walked to the door, still talking over his shoulder. "I hung your gown and under-dress in the hall, my Lady, near the fire to get the creases out from where they were packed into your panniers. I'll get them for you."

"You would make a good ladies maid, Gethin," she said with a quick grin, and he blushed but smiled gamely. She wandered around the room restlessly and then sat in the window seat, throwing open the opaque glass casements and letting the cold in, staring out at the snow and breathing in the clear air. She shivered for a moment and then closed them again, picking up the book left lying on the cushion beside her and reading the page at which it was open and then putting it down again, thinking of Beau's face when she had been reading to him and how beautiful he had looked laid with his head in her lap, his lazy, contented smile smoothing away his cares. Her stomach lurched and she drew her legs up and hugged her knees, smiling into them as she thought about the time they had spent together, and her mood soared to euphoria and then plummeted back to anti-climax in an instant. Hearing the commotion outside, she rearranged herself more decorously on the window seat and watched over the edge of the book, as two men brought in the bath, glancing curiously at her, neither having known her before she had left her mother and curious about the young woman who had come here with her powerful paramour; they might have been kept out of his way but all knew who he was and that he was here with the young woman who was their Lady's daughter by the great Earl of Warwick. Gethin came back with her clothes and hung them on the side of the bed, watching the men critically as they filled her bath, testing the water for her and adding more cold once they had finished. When it was done he slipped quietly out of the room and stood guard outside the door, ensuring that no one entered by mistake. The warmth of the bath seeped through her bones and the feel of the soap on her skin was good as she washed, holding her hair out of the water, conscious that it would never dry in time if she was to get it too wet. She lay back against the padded rim, shaking her hair out over the edge and closed her eyes, yawning quietly as she luxuriated in the water. She thought of the last three days and smiled; they had done so little and yet it had been such a memorable time, just being together, making each other laugh and making love. She knew that he had been delighted with her response to him and thrilled when she had made her own advances to initiate lovemaking, and she in her turn had been entirely overwhelmed by the way he had made her feel and the intensity of the pleasure he had aroused in her. She was not sure how they were going to manage when she got back to Angers, how they would keep their hands off each other or how they would keep their feelings to themselves. Jack had laughingly said they lit up the room when they were close to each other, but she was aware that there was some truth in what he said and it would be easy for everyone to realise what was happening between them. Pushing her thoughts away she stretched and opening her eyes eased herself up out of the bath and dried herself quickly, the room cooling now as the fire was dying down and her skin prickling with gooseflesh. She pulled on her chemise and then her underdress, and her thick woollen overdress with its slashed sleeves showing the white of her undergown through it, and she shivered before the warmth of her clothes enveloped her. She unbound her hair and picked up her brush, trying without success to drag it through the tangles.

"Gethin," she called, and the door opened. "They can empty the bath now, and I will be ready shortly, so you may as well get the groom to saddle the horses." She smiled at him as she spoke and he nodded. "Ow!" The brush caught a knot as she spoke and the cry was involuntary.

"Can I help, my Lady?" He stepped into the room and she laughed.

"What, brush my hair?" He blushed to the roots of his own fair hair, but held her gaze.

"I am the youngest of six children, my Lady, all the rest of whom are girls. Brushing hair was something that I got used to doing from a very young age, as my sisters used me mercilessly as a 'ladies maid' whenever they could get away with it." He emphasised the *ladies maid* jibe with a grin.

"Then be my guest!" She laughed again and swung round, presenting him with her back and the tangle of dark russet curls and also the hairbrush. He began to untangle it with smooth strokes, quickly and efficiently as he did everything else, his hands barely touching her, then, splitting it deftly into three, he braided it swiftly and tied it up with the piece of leather that she handed to him.

"There you are," he said with a smile which for once was not shy and which lit up his grey eyes. She smiled back.

"Thank you," she said, turning to pick up her mantle. "We should go if we want to get back before dark. How long will it take us in this ice?"

"About a half day, my Lady so we should be back a little after three if we leave now. We will be back before it is completely dark anyway." He turned back to the door. "I'll get the horses saddled and then we will be on our way. Are you riding astride, my Lady?"

"Yes." She nodded and as he shut the door, pulled on her riding chausses and then slipped on her boots. She found the woollen material to wrap around her head, neck and face to keep out the cold and protect her skin from the raw wind and snow, then threw on her cloak and pulled the hood up so that only her eyes showed. By the time she had completed wrapping herself up, Gethin was back, dressed in his hat and cloak and leather gloves, holding her own gloves out to her, and handing her her riding whip.

"Ready, my Lady?" he asked, dark blonde eyebrow arched in enquiry.

"Yes." She took one last look around the room. "I think so."

"Let's be on our way then." She followed him out of the solar and across the hall, Samson gambolling at their feet as they walked, and as they stepped outside onto the icy ground he held out his arm for her to take so that she did not slip or if she did he could steady her. She realised then that he was a good half a head taller than she was, something she had never noticed before, and his forearm where she held it was thick and firm. Oh Lord, she thought, I am weighing up the merits of every man I look at now, and she laughed softly to herself.

"My Lady?"

"It's no matter." She laughed harder. "Just a private jest between me and myself." He smiled quizzically but said no more and they rode in comfortable silence for sometime, each immersed in their own thoughts; Gethin, used to keeping his own council, and Kate, hugging warmth and love to her breast. Samson, in his basket across her mount's neck, kept popping his head out and looking up at her, eyes bright as jet, little tongue lolling from the side of his mouth as if he was laughing at her. She reached out and stroked him, the image of a darkly clad Beau coming into her mind as it often did when she looked at the puppy.

"Gethin?" she said at last, overwhelmed by the need to talk of her lover.

"Yes, my Lady?"

"How long have you been in my Lord Duke's service?"

"More than three years, my Lady." He smiled. "I joined him just after he left the Count of Charolais' army, just as the Count became Duke of Burgundy, and came back to Angers. My father had just passed away and my mother wanted me to come over to serve the Duke as my father had served his father."

He served in Charles of Burgundy's army?" She was surprised. "I did not know that!"

"Yes, my Lady. I understand he is a fine soldier and was a good military commander and is more gifted than either his father or brother." He smiled proudly. "He and Duke Charles were firm friends until the Duke married Edward of York's sister."

"Oh, of course, I keep forgetting that he had married Meg."

"Meg, my Lady?"

"Margaret of York; she is my cousin as is Edward of York; their mother, the Duchess Cecily, is my grandfather's sister. I did not really know Meg though."

"But you knew Edward of York?"

"A little." She blushed suddenly, grateful he could not see through the face covering. "I know Richard of Gloucester better. We grew up together."

"I have seen Gloucester, my Lady, in Bruges when my Lord and I were there last." His face clouded and she guessed that he had suffered badly from the black moods that had beset Beau at that time.

"You saw Richard?"

"Yes, my Lady. He and my Lord almost met. They stopped and just looked at each other for what seemed like ages and then nodded and moved on." He laughed suddenly. "My Lord told me a story about how he picked Gloucester up from the street when he was a little boy and Lancaster's army was sacking Ludlow. He saved Gloucester from being trampled by a runaway horse."

"I wonder if he remembers." She looked wistful for a moment and then shook her head. "I don't expect I will ever know, now." She smiled at him with her luminous eyes. "Do you like being in the Duke's service?"

263

"Yes, my Lady. He is a fair and just lord and we have weathered some hard times together; I would give my life for him and his." He met her gaze pointedly and she bit back a smile.

"Well I hope it won't ever come to that," she said. "But I am sure he would applaud the sentiment."

"Now you are mocking me, my Lady." He smiled but she could feel his hurt.

"No I'm not." She laughed but not unkindly. "But you are so serious about everything. I am sure you would protect my Lord with your life but I'd like to think that sometimes you find things to laugh at as well as your duty to honour!"

"I do laugh, of course I do, my Lady but I am proud of my service to my Lord Duke and I take my duty and honour very seriously." He glanced across at her. "I would have thought, Lady Katherine, that you of all people would understand how hard it is to find your way in life when you are born to a different path than most of your peers."

"What, because I am a bastard you mean?" She looked at him with renewed interest.

"Yes, my Lady."

"And because you were brought up a Lancastrian in a time of York?"

"Yes, my Lady." He nodded.

"So you would equate your family's staunch Lancastrian sympathies with being bastard born into my family?"

"Yes, my Lady." He nodded again. "I think the similarities are strong. You have to try harder, study harder, be braver or just be prepared to be plain different. You get bullied and laughed at and others think they can treat you badly because you are not one of them." He glanced at her again and saw that she was staring at him. He blushed scarlet.

"My Lord Somerset is right," she said softly. "You are a dark horse, aren't you, Gethin?"

"I didn't mean to offend you, my Lady."

"I'm not offended in the least." Her eyes were smiling again. "I am intrigued."

"Intrigued?" For once he forgot his etiquette.

"Yes intrigued. I had not realised that you had such interesting opinions."

"Because I'm quiet everyone just thinks I'm dim-witted, or dull at best, but I hope that I am neither." He sounded hurt, but he was looking ahead and she could not see his expression clearly. "My father was a knight banneret, knighted by my Lord's father in 'fifty-five just before the Battle of St Albans, and long in the service of that Duke, first as squire and then as a liege man. We came from a landed family but without title, staunch in our support of Lancaster even when the times went against us. I joined my Lord in 'sixty-seven, and the six years prior to that were the worst years of my life. I learned not to speak unless necessary and to keep my own council or suffer the consequences." He looked sideways at her then. "I am guessing, my Lady, that rather than take that route, you were instead a rebel, but in the end it amounts to the same thing; you didn't fit in." Her eyes were startled for a moment and then thoughtful.

"Yes, you are right," she said after a few moments. "And I still don't, I suppose." She looked at him as if really seeing him for the first time, taking in the studied poise, the seemingly natural efficiency and the groomed appearance, and wondered if these were all a façade. "Do you fit in now?"

"I don't know." He smiled at her, his shyness gone. "Do you?"

"No I don't think so." She sighed. "The sad thing is I don't fit with my father's family and I don't fit with my mother. The only person I feel I can be myself with is my Lord Duke."

"Exactly!" He looked thoughtful. "The funny thing is I think it is the same for him too, like he does not fit in either. He is a prince but not a prince; he should be on the King's Counsel but he is not, and he should be a great soldier like your father but he is stuck here with Madame because he pledged his loyalty to her and the Prince."

"Well, hopefully we will all be in England soon and he can realise his ambitions."

"What will you do when we get to England, my Lady?"

"What do you mean?"

"Will you come to court?"

"No." She smiled softly. "I have lands and money of my own so I shall find somewhere in London to lease."

"A home for my Lord Duke?" He glanced at her profile and she nodded.

"If he should want that," she said quietly.

"I have never seen him so content or light of spirit as he has been the+se last days; my Lord is usually a restless man, mercurial of mood and temper who does not suffer fools at all, let alone gladly." He met her gaze. "Yet he has been a different man with you. You take his cares away, my Lady and that for any man is a good reason to come home."

"You don't disapprove then?" She met his glance with a quirked eyebrow.

"No, my Lady; why should I?" He smiled. "I know that you make him happy, which is all that matters to me."

"That's a very diplomatic answer." She laughed, but he shook his head.

"It is not for me to approve or disapprove of my Lord's actions or to concern myself with his immortal soul. Nor would I presume to judge you, my Lady for I think the world of my Lord and can see why you would love him." He looked very fervent suddenly. "And I can assure you that none will speak ill of you or my Lord in my presence without due punishment." She thought about laughing and then saw that he was deadly serious and softened.

"Well that's very kind of you Gethin and thank you for your care of both me and my Lord Duke these last days."

"It has been my pleasure, my Lady. As I said, it has been good to see him so happy." They exchanged conspiratorial smiles and rode on in silence after that, each in their own thoughts: Gethin thinking how lucky his Lord was to have such a beautiful girl so obviously in love with him and she thinking how nice it would be to go to England and lease a house near Westminster so that he could come to her whenever he wanted to. She could not imagine what it would be like having him come home from his business of the day and to eat and talk and sleep together as a matter of course. She realised that he would travel his estates and that sometimes he would be absent on King's business but to be the person he usually came home to made gooseflesh stand out on her skin in anticipation. She refused to think about the fact that at some point he would need to take a wife and get himself heirs, or to imagine what it would be like to be his leman, the other woman in the eternal triangle that marriage seemed to be. She preferred the idyll rather than reality and hoped that it would be some time before she had to compete with a wife for his attention.

Kate looked up at the sky, noting that the light was beginning to fade.

"How far to go do you think?" she asked.

"About half of the hour that's all, my Lady."

"Good. I'm getting cold and Samson is shivering." She stroked the dog's ears. "Can I ask you a question Gethin?"

"Of course, my Lady." He turned and offered a quizzical smile.

"You say that your family is landed but not nobility?" He nodded, his smile broadening.

"We are Saxon, my Lady, not of Norman French descent as you are, and the name Rhys is taken from the place of our origin, meaning 'ford under a cliff'."

"Really?" She was fascinated. "So your family were true English?"

"We were, my Lady. We did not even have Danish blood and we served King Harold at the battle of Hastings'."

"And suffered for it?"

"No, not really, my Lady, except that my forebears were ever overlooked for a rise into the nobility, but we have married well and served some very powerful earls and dukes in our time, and when the Beaufort line was created we aligned ourselves with them and served them generation by generation. My father was first of our line to be knighted, by my Lord's father and I hope that one day I will serve my Lord well enough for the same to happen to me."

"I have never met a Saxon before." She smiled at him broadly. "Though now I look at you, I should have guessed!

"Do I look like a Saxon then, my Lady?" He grinned.

"Yes, definitely; you are fair and I could see you with braids and a beard." She giggled and he laughed too.

"I hope that I am better groomed than that, my Lady." He shook his head. "I have learned much from my Lord and his fastidious nose and I hope that I am not a Saxon when it comes to smell!"

"Indeed you are not, Gethin, for you smell every bit as good the Duke." She reached and touched his arm. "Which, from a woman's point of view, is a really good thing." They both laughed again.

"Look, my Lady!" Gethin indicated forward and she looked ahead and saw the big shape of Chateau d'Angers looming ahead, towers clear against the horizon, golden stone dulled by the gloom. "We are nearly there." She shivered, partly with anticipation and partly with apprehension.

"Yes," she said softly, glancing across at him.

"Are you alright?"

"I think this is going to be much harder than I had first thought." She snorted a mirthless little laugh. "I underestimated the challenge."

"The challenge?" He cocked his head to one side with a quizzical smile.

"The challenge of pretending." She laughed again and shook her head. "Just ignore me, Gethin, I am being silly; I am sure it will be all right." She spurred her mare forward into a fast walk. "Come on!" she said briskly. "Let's get inside and get warm."

Chapter Ten

Anjou, France, January 1471

"We really will have to stop doing this!" Beau leaned back against the wall, eyes closed, chest heaving, his breath coming fast and short. He heard Kate laugh softly and opened his eyes, taking in the dishevelled vision before him, the laces of her dress undone, her hair escaping around her face and her cheeks flushed as she adjusted her skirts. "God, woman, you are beautiful." He pulled her to him and kissed her hard, a fierce, possessive kiss which conveyed the intensity of his feelings. "And I cannot resist you, but sooner or later we are going to get caught."

"I don't care." She met his gaze defiantly and he smiled, kissing her long and hard once more.

"But I do," he said, finally relinquishing her mouth. "I care very much." He reached out and brushed a tendril of hair from her cheek with a gentle hand. "Not for myself as I can assure you it would do me no harm if I was caught in coupling with you, I would be the envy of all men, but you would be tarnished forever as another of Beau's whores and I don't want that." Drawing her into his embrace he rested his cheek on her hair, protectiveness and tenderness overwhelming him. "You are my heart's joy Katherine and I will not have anyone besmirch that with unpleasant talk or make it sordid with their judgements."

"And you are mine." She slid her hands up his back and hugged him closer, her voice muffled against his broad chest. "But I still don't care what they say of me. Why would I care for anyone else's opinion but yours?" He savoured the feel of her in his arms, knowing that soon they would have to go about their business and may not get the chance to be alone together for days. It had been much harder than either of them had imagined it could be in the month since they had come back from their weekend together. Not only was it hard to find time to talk, but they had had to snatch every opportunity they possibly could to make love, each understanding that controlling their desire for the other was not something they found easy. During the Christmas festivities, there had been a few chances more than normal and one afternoon when there had been an array of visitors from the town to see a party of mummers in the hall and dancing, they had managed to slip up to his bedchamber and spent a very sinful afternoon in the bed he normally shared with Jack. Gethin had kept an unobtrusive watch and they had enjoyed the opportunity to spend more than a few snatched moments together, but that had been a full two weeks ago. Since then it had been a few highly charged encounters either in the stables or once in the wardrobe when Veronique had very discreetly exited when he had gone looking for her, having escaped for a few minutes from Madame's watchful eye. But he knew that he was right, for they were taking more and more risks, especially today when he had come upon her alone in Anne and Edward's chamber, and anyone could have walked in on them during their frantic coupling. Not that they had meant to end up like that; they never did, but a kiss led to another kiss and then somehow before they knew what they were doing, he was inside her and she was wrapped around him, almost sobbing with the intensity of the pleasure he gave her. That the pleasure was equal for him, he had no doubt, for he was instantly aroused by her presence and his orgasms were always powerful, often forcing him to bite into her shoulder to avoid shouting out. He touched his mouth to her hair and then her temple and she lifted her face to his.

"I will have to go in a minute," he said gently, his own face a picture of regret.

"I know." She smiled a little sadly. "But I am glad you came to find me. I have had some news."

"News?"

"Maman is with child."

"Is she indeed?" He whistled softly. "Madame will be pleased!" He laughed then. "When did she tell you?"

She looked up at him, her eyes big pools of dark hurt.

"She has not told Madame yet but she told me yesterday that she is nearly five months gone with child; my father's child, obviously, and I don't like it much." She pursed her lips and laughed ruefully. "I know that's childish but I have always been the only child he ever conceived in love and the one he always loved the best. Now I will have a rival."

"Ah, kitten." He kissed her forehead with a smile, understanding but all the same thinking suddenly how young, sweet and unspoiled she was. She never thought to hide anything from him, never thought not to express an emotion or say what she felt about something, and he loved it. There was no artful side to her nature, game playing was not in her make-up and she was completely open and honest; even when they made love she was without inhibition telling him what was good and asking what he liked which he found both liberating and immensely erotic. She was funny and uncomplicated and he could be himself with her, could tell her things he would never tell another living soul without fear that she would ridicule him; in fact, to him she was perfect. "I hated it when Jack was born."

"Did you?" She looked surprised

"Yes I did." He laughed softly to himself. "You see I was my mother's beautiful boy, nine years old and only sisters had followed me, and then along came Jack and my mother was so proud she had produced another boy. Everybody cooed over him and said how much he looked like my mother and I was convinced that she would love him more than me."

"And did she?"

"No." He smiled again. "Oh she loved him, but she was far too long in the habit of loving me best and so it stayed, much to my joy. I feel bad about it now but I hope that I have loved Jack enough to make up for it."

"Well he certainly loves you."

"Yes I know and I hope that I have at least done a little bit to deserve it." He laid the palm of his hand to her cheek. "But what I wanted to say was I don't think your father will love you any less for the arrival of a new brother or sister." He brushed his mouth against hers softly. "But if he should, then I hope that how much I love you will compensate someway for that." She smiled and, reaching up, took the hand at her cheek and kissed the rough swordsman's palm.

"I thank God every day that I am loved by you," she said, her eyes fixed on his. "And I count myself the luckiest of women." They stood in their close embrace for a while, his arms around her holding her into the hollow of his shoulder as he laid his cheek on the soft silkiness of her hair. Eventually he pulled back from her and looked down into her face.

"I have to go," he said softly and she nodded.

"I know."

He didn't let go of her but kissed her lips once more, a soft kiss full of love and yearning.

"I keep telling myself that it won't be like this forever," he whispered, kissing her eyes and then her lips again. "I never thought I would be the man to say it but I need more than this, kitten; more than quick couplings in dark places; more than snatched minutes together. I want everyone to know how much I love you and in what esteem I hold you, but most of all I want what we had at Juvardeil." He sighed and hugged her again. "I wish we could walk down into the hall hand-in-hand and tell the world that we are lovers."

"I could just imagine everyone's faces if we did!" She laughed silently against him.

"Yes, they would be a picture." He chuckled and then was serious almost immediately. "God, I don't want to go!" He groaned in frustration.

"I don't want you to go, but you must or they will be wondering where you are, and Anne will probably be back soon as we said we were going to sort her coffers today." She pulled away from him and looked up, making his heart miss a beat at the soft expression in her changeable eyes.

"We never get time to talk." He sighed and closed his eyes for a moment, and then smiled. "I know, I know; we knew it would be like this, but it is still bloody hard and the chance of it becoming easier seems such a long way away."

"Yes it does and I wish we could have more time together but I am sure Madame will make the move to go to England soon and once we are there I have my own lands and money and can lease a house and none can stop me." She reached up and touched his cheek with a smile. "Then you could come to see me whenever you wanted."

"I would spend as many days with you as I could and all my nights." He kissed her fingers.

"Until you grew bored with me," she teased, laughing. He did not laugh but looked at her, his expression serious suddenly.

"No," he said vehemently. "Don't say that." He caught the hand at his cheek and held it tightly in both of his. "I will never tire of you."

"How do you know that?" She was still smiling mischievously but he could not bring himself to join the banter.

"Because the thought of being able to come home to you each night and to share my life with you, talk over my cares and know that you have no other interests at heart but mine, is the one thing that keeps me from climbing the walls of this castle in frustration. Just to be able to see your face each day and to know that you love me stops me from just getting on my stallion and going to England right now." He laughed then, a short, sharp laugh with little mirth in it. "I have waited nigh on fifteen years for you so don't think after waiting all that time that I am ever going to let you go; you had better hope you don't ever tire of me."

"Why would I ever tire of you?" She kept the smile on her face, her expression soft. "You give me everything I would ever need. You give me love, warmth, shelter and…" She moved towards him and slid her hand down his body and into his groin. "…more pleasure than a girl has a right to." She squeezed gently and grinned as he responded instantly to her touch. He groaned and then laughed, kissing her, one hand at her cheek the other pulling her hips into him.

"You are such a minx," he whispered, pressing himself against her, the swelling in his groin increasing.

"I aim to please." She rubbed herself against him playfully, fully aware, he was certain, of the effect it was having on him.

"And you certainly do that…" He groaned again and their mouths clung, her hand still at his groin, his sliding into her gown and cupping her breast. Their kissing had just begun to take on that particular intensity that normally heralded an ignition of a passion that was unstoppable when suddenly they heard a man's footsteps in the passageway coming towards the room.

"Fuck!" Beau drew back and looked at her quickly, his lips quirking briefly in a grin. "You look a little ravished darling," he said softly.

"And that is a strange place to keep your lance, my love." She looked down at his groin meaningfully and he straightened his tunic, swiftly

273

adjusting himself and leaning back nonchalantly against the wall as she scuttled across the room to Anne's coffers, just as the door opened and Edward stood on the threshold.

"Aha! I have caught you, Somerset!"

"Caught me, your Grace?" Beau's voice and manner were easy, his grin welcoming.

"Flirting with my wife's sister!" Edward grinned and gestured to Kate, who flushed becomingly, trying to look coy. Beau was conscious that if he came to stand between them, he would be able to see that she had failed to lace the front of her gown, and he had an erection which was very visible from the side view.

"Indeed I am, your Grace, and who would not when, having come looking for a prince, I am faced with such a vision of loveliness?" Beau kept his easy grin. "Are you looking for me Edward?"

"Yes, ma mère sent me to find you. A messenger has arrived from England and she wishes us to join her." He glanced at Kate. "A letter from your father I think," he said, giving her a quick smile. She smiled back and turned back to the coffer that she was aimlessly rifling through.

"After you, my Prince." Beau came off the wall and walked towards the door as Edward disappeared through it he turned to Kate and gestured towards his groin with a comical grimace and a shake of his head. She shrugged and laughed and blew him a kiss just as Edward called.

"For God's sake, Somerset, leave the girl alone, you are old enough to be her father!" Kate laughed harder at Beau's affronted expression and waved him away out of the door, their eyes meeting in one last glance of regret and then he was gone.

***

She sighed softly and laced up the front of her gown, pulling her underdress straight and smoothing her hair, the familiar feeling of sadness and anti-climax dropping over her like a cloak. She was young enough to find the relationship with Beau exciting and somehow wicked, but she was mature enough to see that it was no substitute for them being able to spend real time together and she could also see that it was frustrating him immensely, to the point that it was likely he would just make it known that she was his mistress and fight anyone who insulted her. Not that she cared. She would have been happy for it to be out in the open, but she knew that not only would Marguerite make it hard for both of them but that the Countess would be mortified at her behaviour, probably disowning her. It was also likely that she would be shunned by most of Marguerite's little court, some of whom were jealous and some of whom disgusted at her immorality. That was not a great prospect when her life was so bound up in what happened to Marguerite and because she and her family had to live in this suffocating but necessary environment. Her mother was an example of how a woman who was loved by a powerful man had few friends; she lived her life outside the Queen's close circle of women, often discussed behind her back and sometimes in her hearing as if she had no right to be there. Kate pulled all the clothes out of the big coffer and began to sort through them, realising that at the bottom were some of the swaddling and tiny robes that had been made for the babe that Isabel had lost, and tears filled her eyes. She heard soft steps and then the door opened, Anne coming in and looking round for a moment before her eyes alighted on her sister.

"Oh you are here!" she said. "My Lord Somerset said you were and I could not work out how he knew!"

"He was here looking for Edward." Kate grinned. "And he stopped to chat." Anne snorted disdainfully.

"I bet he did!" Anne looked at her sister for a moment. "I still say you should be careful."

"I am quite safe with him I can assure you." Kate laughed and Anne sensed there was more to her amusement than she was giving away, but knowing her sister well enough not to ask.

"Papa has sent messages."

"Has he?"

"Yes." Anne smiled and held out a square of parchment to her sister, sealed with the Warwick signet.

"A letter?" Kate jumped up and took it, her eyes shining. "For me?"

"Yes, one for each of us, maman, you, Bel, Veronique and me, plus one for Edward, my Lord Duke and the Queen." She managed to make the last sound as if it burned her mouth and then shrugged. "I suppose he thought if he wrote to all of us we might influence Madame to head for England. He is desperate for us to go." She watched Kate tuck the note into her bodice and smiled. "Still, it was nice to hear from him for a change instead of having to listen to Maman reading his letters. I did not know until today that he writes to your mother in his own hand but dictates to a secretary when he writes to Maman." She giggled suddenly. "He obviously doesn't want anyone to know what he writes to Veronique!"

Kate was surprised at Anne's sanguinity about her father's relationship with her mother and the triangle within which he lived, but she guessed that Anne, as a woman of her time, accepted that a man would be unfaithful and only judged other women on their behaviour, hence her concern that Kate would respond to what she saw as Beau's predatory interest in her; Veronique only escaped outward expression of that judgement because she was her sister's mother.

"I don't think I would want to dictate personal letters," she said, thinking of how embarrassing it would be to dictate love words to someone else, and then realising that she was implying that her father's relationship with Anne's mother was not a personal one, she added. "And I would guess that a lot of the things he writes to my Lady Countess are practical things and household arrangements. I am sure that he adds something in his own hand." She smiled at her sister but Anne shrugged.

"I don't think they are like that really," she said, shaking her head. "They appreciate each other and Maman understands him but I don't think they have ever been romantic. I don't think many people are lucky enough to love the person who is picked for them in marriage; I think you just have to learn to like them or at least to get along and understand each other."

"True." Kate pulled a bundle of white shirts out of the coffer in front of her and piled them on the floor as Anne knelt beside her and picked one up, bringing it to her nose and breathing in.

"I have not yet got used to Edward smelling differently to Richard," she said wistfully. "He smells of rosemary and lemon and Richard always smelled of cedar."

"It is funny how you think of people when you smell a particular smell. Papa smells of a mix of jasmine and sandalwood and my Lord Somerset of bergamot. I always think of him when I smell that." Kate smiled, unaware of her sister's sharp glance.

"I think my Lord Somerset bathes in bergamot, it's so strong!" Anne said shortly and Kate laughed.

"Better that than to stink," she retorted good humouredly. "You don't like him much do you?" Anne wrinkled her nose and shook her head.

"No, not really. I think he is brash, arrogant and somehow animal; he kind of looms over you when he is talking to you, and those eyes!" She shuddered involuntarily. "I always feel like he has stripped me naked and found me wanting every time he looks at me!"

"He never makes me feel like I am found wanting!" Kate giggled and Anne glared at her.

"Kate!"

"Oh come on Anne!" She touched Anne's arm placatingly. "You know I am teasing. I like him, he makes me laugh and the flirting is just a bit of fun!"

"I can't see anything about that man that could be fun or how anyone could even like him that much."

"Edward loves him."

"That's because he is a man and men love other men who are successful on the battlefield and with women!" Anne shook her head again, this time in a kind of wonderment. "Why prowess in bed should be so important to them I have no idea!"

"Is it not important to you?"

"God no!" Anne blushed furiously. "I can take it or leave it."

"Even if it was Richard?" Kate murmured, casting a sly look at her sister. Anne coloured even more and then giggled unexpectedly.

"Actually…" she started and then stopped, shaking her head. "I can't…"

"What?" Kate was intrigued.

"I can't tell you." Anne covered her face with Edward's shirt.

"Come on, Anne, tell!" She tugged the shirt from Anne's eyes so that she could see her. "Tell!" she said, more emphatically. Anne took a breath, her nose and mouth still covered by the white linen.

"I found myself thinking of Richard last night when I was with Edward and wondering what it would be like." Anne's voice was still muffled in the shirt.

"And?"

"I sort of lost myself in the thoughts and Edward became Richard and…" The flush crept back up her cheeks. "It was nice," she finished lamely.

"Nice?" Kate pulled a face. "Just nice?"

Anne shook her head sadly.

"It was much more than nice," she said and then her big green eyes filled with tears. "But I won't ever find out now, will I?"

"I suppose not." Kate felt her own sense of sadness recede a little as she thought that at least she was lucky enough to be with the man she loved. Poor Anne would never be with Richard now and her future was changed forever. "I wonder what they are doing in Burgundy?" she said suddenly. "Richard and Ned?" She absently pulled a bundle of chemises out of the coffer and started sorting through them for holes and tears. "I wonder if they are alright?"

"Papa said Duke Charles is refusing to meet with them but that Ned is staying with Louis de Gruythuse, you know, who stayed at the Herber with us during the final marriage negotiations?"

"Yes I remember. I didn't like him much for some reason. I always thought he had a bit of a slyness about him." Kate screwed up her nose. "I wonder where Richard is staying then?"

"I don't know but you can guarantee that Ned is alright." Anne looked slightly sour. "That man is like a huge cat; always lands on his feet!"

"I'm sure Richard is fine too." Kate held up a chemise and inspected a big rent across the bodice. "Did Edward rip this one off you?" she asked with a laugh. Anne pushed her good humouredly.

"No!" She laughed as well. "I caught it with my betrothal ring and it just tore." She turned and looked at her sister suddenly. "Do you really think Richard is alright?" she asked softly.

"I am sure he is fine, Anne." She reached across and patted her arm affectionately. "I don't expect he is having the time of his life but I am sure that he is surviving."

"Do you think we will ever see him again?" Anne had turned away and was sorting at the bottom of the coffer, but Kate heard the break in her voice.

"I don't know, sweet," she said honestly, "But I would say that it looks very unlikely."

"Do you think Ned will come back for his crown?" Anne lifted her head back out of the wooden trunk.

"Yes."

"And?"

"I think he will lose." Kate stared ahead of her at the pattern of stone on the wall. "I think he will lose because King Henry has a full-grown son in Edward and once we get over to England the people will support him because he is handsome, and he is almost of an age to rule alone." She looked back at Anne levelly. "Ned only has girl children and so if he were to die then there would be none to rule after him except George, and no one would want that. Therefore, King Henry is the better prospect for the future and for peace."

"Richard would never come to terms with King Henry, would he?" Anne sighed sadly.

"No." Kate shook her head. "Because if he did, one day he would have to accept that Edward was King of England and you were his Queen and I don't think he could cope with that."

"I don't think I could either; not if I was seeing him every day and married to someone else." Anne fingered the intricate embroidery on Edward's shirt. "I still wish I knew if he was alright though."

"Yes." Kate said softly. "I wish I did too."

Bruges, Burgundy
January 1471

"Dickon! Dickon! Where the devil are you?" Ned's voice, slightly slurred, was loud enough to wake the whole neighbourhood, let alone the occupant of the house he was shouting at, "Dickon!" Richard leaned his head out of the upper storey window and looked down at his brother.

"For the love of God, Ned, be quiet!" He hissed. "Wait there, I am coming down." A minute later the boy appeared at the doorway, his dark hair tousled, a shirt and chausses thrown on carelessly. "Jesu', Ned what time is it?"

"Time?" Edward, blinded by the candlelight, looked slightly confused. "I have no idea?"

"Come in." Richard all but dragged him into the hall of the small house and shoved him towards a table and benches. "What are you doing on the streets on your own at this time of night?" He grabbed a flagon and two cups whilst he spoke, although Edward looked like he had had enough already. He poured and then pushed one toward his brother. "How, in heaven's name, did you evade the watch?"

"I didn't." Edward grinned. "They recognised me and let me go. I told them I had to consult with my brother on urgent state business." He rubbed a shaking hand over his face, furrows of tiredness edging his mouth. The exile in Burgundy had aged him, Richard thought, although the ruggedness sat well on him as did everything; Edward was ever the favoured one.

"And is it?" Richard sat down opposite him, cradling his cup in both hands.

"Aye, of a sort." Edward's face broke into a huge smile. "I have a son, Dickon," he said softly and suddenly tears filled his eyes, clinging to his long golden lashes. "Our Lady mother got a letter to Meg and she got a message to me; Elizabeth has given me a Prince, God bless her. I cannot believe it, a son at last after all this time!" And suddenly he was crying, his head cradled in his arms, great racking sobs shaking his powerful shoulders as the emotion overwhelmed him and the wine relaxed his inhibitions. Richard leaned forward and gripped his forearm awkwardly, comforting even as he marvelled at the irony that the boy should be born now when they had nothing, not even the hope that they would ever get back to England.

"Ned, don't," he said softly.

"Don't what?" Edward's voice was muffled in his arms. "Don't break my heart because my son is born to a King with no kingdom; my wife is in sanctuary without much hope of ever seeing her husband again; my daughters are cooped up in one room and have lost their future, and you, my little brother, have followed me blindly into this pit of poverty when you could have been in England with Warwick, married to your little Neville cousin?" He looked up, his bloodshot eyes wet, his mouth set in a grim line of self-pity.

"I have no regrets, Ned." Richard met his eyes squarely. "And neither should you."

"No regrets?" Edward snorted with mirthless laughter. "No regrets that you live in this hovel; no regrets that you did not marry Anne Neville; no regrets that she is married to Edward of Lancaster?"

Richard coloured but held his brother's gaze steadily.

"No, Ned, no regrets. And even knowing what I do now I would never have made any other decision than to follow you." He smiled, trying to hide the intensity of his emotion. "To the very gates of hell if necessary."

"Christ, Dickon!" Edward looked stunned. "You know how to wind a man when he is wallowing in self pity!" Richard laughed and Edward grinned a wobbly lopsided grin. "I cannot believe it, Dickon, I have a son." His grin faded and he thumped his fist down on the table. "I need to go home! We need to go home!" He pushed himself back from the bench and got up, pacing the room in his long, slightly unsteady stride. "You know our brother in law Charles is once again entertaining the great Edmund Beaufort, so called Duke of Somerset, don't you?" He emphasised the 'great' with heavy sarcasm. Richard shook his head.

"No I didn't." He thought of the tall dark haired man on the big roan stallion who had watched him silently from across the square a few months ago. "How do you know that?"

"De Gruuthhuys told me this evening. He was with Charles when our friend Beaufort arrived." Edward gnawed absently at the edge of a fingernail. "Charles likes him too. I remember Meg telling me that she almost made a big mistake in the first month of their marriage when Charles presented Beaufort to her and she made some comment about his Dukedom, and Charles rebuked her in front of him."

"And Charles has remained on good terms with him even though you are here?"

"Yes, that's why he will not see me. Beaufort has come back to ask him to hand me over to him in return for Louis not taking up arms against Burgundy and, funnily enough, if I am unlucky enough to end up in his custody, I don't think Beau Beaufort would make the same mistakes as Warwick."

"Shit!" Richard swore softly. "That's quite a deal.

"It is if you think you can trust Louis." Edward stopped his pacing for a second and regarded Richard steadily. "If I can persuade Charles that he can't trust Louis then we have a chance."

"How do you do that?"

"Because even if Charles hands me over, Louis could still turn his eye to Burgundy and then Charles will need to turn back to me for support, after all, a friendly King in England is of more use to him than an impoverished exile in Burgundy. And at the moment Warwick is proving anything but friendly. That has to be our way in." He started pacing again. "My biggest problem is getting to see him, especially while he is entertaining his friend Beau Beaufort." He threw himself down on the bench again and looked at Richard. "How the hell do I get him to do that?"

"Surely Meg can help."

"Well she hasn't been able to so far."

"What about if you can get Meg to persuade him, in light of Beau's offer, that you have a counter offer which could prove more lucrative for him?"

"Like what?"

"Like trade."

"Trade?" Edward sat forward and looked at Richard shrewdly.

"If he finances you and you win back your crown then you will open up England to full trade with Burgundy, favouring him before any other countries?" Richard shrugged diffidently. "He could finance you secretly. Louis need never know so he could placate Edmund Beaufort saying that he may well hand you over and all the while he could finance some ships for us and a few men."

"I need more than a few men." Edward looked into his wine cup and then back at Richard, his eyes speculative. "But you do have a point, little brother, and this could be the start of a plan. How do I get the men?" He was musing more to himself and was obviously surprised when the boy answered him.

"I have had a letter." Richard got up and went across to a big sideboard, sliding out a drawer. "Here." He tossed it across to Edward who picked it up and, unfolding it, scanned it rapidly.

"Well, well," was all he said, his mouth suddenly set in a grim line.

"Meg gave it to me. George sent it to her." Richard was talking quickly to cover his nervousness. "I think he means it this time."

"I'm sure he does, Dickon." Edward's gaze was cool. "His position after all is somewhat uncertain now, don't you think?"

"Maybe." Richard acknowledged the validity of that statement. "But he has more than four thousand men that we really could do with. And he is our brother."

"He was our brother when he threw in his lot with Warwick."

"You know how persuasive Richard Neville is Ned, especially with George." Richard's midnight blue eyes were pleading.

"He didn't persuade you."

"That's different!" he said hotly and then subsided. "That's different."

"Why?"

"Because you never much liked George, Ned, and he suffered for it."

"Ah! So it's my fault?" Edward laughed silently and shook his head. Richard almost growled in frustration.

"No, I'm not saying that." He kept his voice level, drawing on the last ounce of his patience. "You and Edmund always looked after me, Ned; always took my side against ma mère; always had a kind word for me and time for a youngest child who struggled for attention. But you didn't do the same for George, and papa was too busy and then he was gone. Somehow George never fitted in and I think he resented you for that. When Richard Neville gave him the attention he should have had from a father, he latched his loyalty to it and followed it like a flower follows the sun. But the sun has gone in now and he is lost."

"Very poetic!" Edward's voice was dry, the sarcasm almost automatic, but it was obvious he could see the sense in what the boy was saying. "What do you suggest, Dickon?" he asked softly.

"Write to him, Ned. See how the land lies and see who else he can bring into the fold. Please?" Richard tentatively reached out a slender hand and clasped his brother's huge one, his heart thumping in his chest as he laid it on the line and begged. "Please?" Edward looked at the brown fingers over his own for a long moment and then nodded imperceptibly and Richard let out a long, hurtful breath. He got up from the table and fetched another flagon, since they had emptied the first one.

"I need to see Charles." Edward said, cupping his chin in his hands and pursing his lips. "He has to realise that Warwick is no good to him."

"I am sure he will, Ned. I suppose we just have to have patience."

"I don't want to have patience. I want to see my son!" Edward's voice rose to a shout, more to let off steam than because he was truly angry. "I want to see my son!" Richard poured them both a cup from the flagon.

"I want to see my son, too," he said softly.

"Your son?" Edward looked up and then grinned "You have a son?" He laughed delightedly. "Christ, lad, why didn't you say so?"

"I'm saying now." Richard flushed, naturally reticent, always shy about talking about his private life, but he needed to show Edward he understood.

"When was this?"

"He was born just after we landed in Burgundy. I had to write to ask ma mère to help nan and earned myself a lecture on the sins of the flesh." He grinned ruefully. Edward laughed again, this time in sympathy.

"Ah Dickon!" he said. "A man should never involve his mother in his indiscretions."

"Don't I know it!" Their eyes locked.

"Did you mean it, Dickon, when you said you had no regrets?" Edward was serious suddenly.

"Yes I did." The boy smiled ruefully. "I'm not saying that it hasn't been hard or that I have not sometimes despaired that we will ever get out of here and I have come to hate Bruges with a passion, but I have no regrets and I would do the same again if I had my time over."

"I'm proud of you, lad, and grateful. I promise I will get us out of this mess." He leaned across and grasped Richard's forearm. "And when I do I will give you whatever you want." Richard laughed and shook his head.

"Now why would I want anything when you have given me so much already," he said, gesturing around him. Edward looked at him for a moment and then grinned.

"Damn it, Dickon," he said with a laugh. "You'll do, little brother, you'll do."

Westminster, London
January 1471

"Jack?" Richard Neville touched his brother's shoulder gently. "Are you alright?" John Neville turned from his contemplative gaze out of the window and gave his elder brother a swift smile.

"Yes Rich, I am fine." The smile died almost as quickly as it came in his ordinary face, his brown eyes returning to their natural soulful expression. "I am just finding it odd, that's all."

"Odd?" Warwick raised a brow quizzically.

"Yes, odd. Don't you?" John shook his head and the smile flitted across his face again. "Ah, I see I am being stupid; of course you don't." He laughed suddenly and silently, lighting his features and giving him a fleeting resemblance to the man he spoke to. "You have already moved on into your new life. How do you do it Rich?"

"Do what?" Warwick was still genuinely puzzled.

"How do you manage not to look back?" John glanced behind his brother and looked at the grey haired man seated on the chair of state in this the presence chamber talking with a small group of men. "How do you manage to stand here and never think of Ned?" Warwick shrugged his elegant shoulders.

"What point would there be in thinking of Ned?" he asked, also glancing behind him briefly. "That is done."

"That's exactly what I mean. I don't know how you can just walk forward and never look back." John showed his sadness for a moment. "I stand here and I see Ned sat there laughing at something you have said, or I see him over there teasing some lass." He gestured to a window embrasure as he spoke. "Wherever I look I see him doing something and I find it hard not to dwell on that." He pushed old memories from his mind, even as he spoke, avoiding the cloud of nostalgia that always seemed to hover close.

"You are cursed with sentimentality, I am afraid, brother." Warwick grinned and Jack nodded.

"Aye, I guess I am. I wish I could be like you Rich and just switch off but I don't think I can. Still, I will get used to it in my own time, I am sure." He looked across at King Henry VI once more, marvelling that this slender old man could replace the larger than life, blonde giant who had held the throne and his loyalty for almost ten years. "How is he anyway, still with us?"

"He is well and seems quite lucid. He never was an astute politician but he seems happy enough to discuss policy, sign documents and even express an opinion which I find encouraging. He is most looking forward to seeing his son, although I don't think he much relishes the idea of his Queen arriving!" Warwick gave a snort of mirth. "But then none can blame him for that, can they?" Jack nodded fervently. He had found both Henry's and Edward's Queens to be particularly intimidating women, equally for their beauty and for the force of their personalities. Both Marguerite's volatility and Elizabeth's iciness sent shivers down his spine and he more than once had thanked God for his very ordinary, very capable Isabella who had never been a beauty and who suited him exceptionally well.

"Have you heard from France, Rich?" he asked softly. Warwick nodded.

"Yes. I had a letter from nan yesterday and one from Somerset, who is in Burgundy, today. Nan says that Marguerite shows no sign of packing although everyone is exhorting her to get here quickly before we lose our advantage, but with Somerset being in Burgundy they have lost the one person who can drive her to action." He bit his lip thoughtfully. "It's odd though, you know," he said, frowning. "She does not like Somerset over much and I cannot for the life of me work out why, for she doted on his sire."

"Perhaps he is not that likeable." John could not imagine liking any member of the Beaufort family, having been brought up to actively oppose them. He was struggling with the concept of the alliance; another thing that his elder brother had just taken in his stride.

"I like him." Warwick grinned. "I grant you he is an arrogant bastard, but he does have talent and has at least proved himself in Burgundy's army. He made up for all Burgundy's soldiering defects and I think Charles' defeats would have been much worse if he had not had Somerset with him." His smile faded. "It is Pembroke I worry about. Oxford and I seem to have reached an understanding but Pembroke is still opposing me for the sake of it and it is slowing down our progress. I think we are better off with him in Wales right now."

"What was the news from Burgundy?"

"Not great. Charles is thinking about our proposition but Somerset thinks that the lovely Duchess Meg is working very hard on her brother's behalf and Charles is weighing up marital harmony against common sense. He has not yet met Ned, and he welcomed Somerset with open arms but he still got the feeling that he was being fobbed off with delaying tactics rather than any real negotiations."

"Well, I suppose we can hardly blame her. They were always a close family, except for George." John glanced across at where George of Clarence lounged in a window seat chatting to the Earl of Oxford. Clarence had mellowed recently, seemed more relaxed and at ease with himself and less highly strung; John wasn't sure if that was a good thing or not.

"Nice for them that they are all together in Bruges then, isn't it?" Warwick deadpanned and then grinned. "They can play happy families together!" John shook his head and gave a half smile. It never ceased to amaze him that his brother could be so detached, so unemotional about what had effectively been the dismissal of ten years of his life. It had taken John Neville a long time to come to terms with the degeneration of his relationship with Ned and even now he still marvelled at what had happened, and how it had happened. He had not been able to bring himself to confront Ned and had mobilised his army to intimidate rather than to fight when Ned had fled to Burgundy. If it came to an out and out battle he was still not sure if he could actually go through with it.

"So, what is the plan now then?" He changed the tack of the conversation, uncomfortable with dwelling on such matters.

"I have dispatched a number of letters to all who have influence to urge Marguerite to get herself and the boy over here. Edward is well taken with Anne and so she is pushing him to influence his mother, and nan is doing her best with Marguerite but I think it will take Somerset to finally get her to take action. I think he is on his way back to France now so we will see. In the meantime, I will work with Louis to shore up our defences and I have Pembroke in the marches drumming up support from the Welsh."

"And what is George doing?" He glanced again at the bright-haired, handsome lad.

"He has put four thousand men at my disposal, already raised and ready to fight at any time we need so I don't think we need to doubt George. He has behaved remarkably well considering the thwarting of his dreams and the difficult position he finds himself in, and has been completely cooperative. I am proud of him." Warwick gave a fond smile. "I think Isabel's influence on him has been a good one."

"Well he does seem to have accepted things." John acknowledged, but still something nagged in the pit of his stomach. "How is Anne getting on with Edward, you mentioned he was taken with her?"

"Yes, he is. He seemed to take to her from the first moment they were introduced and, I will give her her due as I know she always thought she would wed Dickon, she has made the best of it. I think he was ripe for marriage and Anne was young enough for him to feel at ease with from the first. I cannot imagine that Marguerite gave him many opportunities to spread his wings, although he has been under Somerset's tutelage for the last couple of years so he may have learned something of women!" Warwick laughed and Jack grinned.

"I am sure if he had not, you could have taught him a thing or two, Rich." He clapped his brother on the arm and they both laughed again.

"And Kate?" John smiled at the thought of his favourite niece.

"Oh, you know, making lots of friends and admirers."

Warwick's face lit up with pride and he laughed softly.

"She has fully recovered then?"

"Yes, although Nan's letter said that she is quieter and seems to have calmed down a little since she has been ill, and is more content." He smiled, but kept any thoughts he might have on the reasons for the change in her to himself.

"She'll need a husband soon, Rich; a girl like that needs to be wed."

"A girl like what?" Warwick deliberately misunderstood him and John flushed.

"You know exactly what I mean, Rich. She may be my niece but I am not blind to her charms; she has a beauty which makes a man think immediately of bed and its sport, and I know she cannot help it but a wedding is the only way to solve the problem." Warwick smiled.

"We will see," was all he said.

"My Lord Warwick?" A soft, hesitant voice broke into their conversation and Warwick looked round to see a young page at his elbow.

"Yes, lad?"

"King Henry sent that I ask you to join him." The boy bowed and stepped away and Warwick sighed.

"He's obviously finding Louis' envoy overwhelming," he murmured, glancing toward the King. "Come on Jack, let's go and rescue him." And clapping his brother on the shoulder they both made their way over to their new sovereign.

Anjou, France
February 1471

The tall towers of the Castle of Angers loomed up on the horizon as they cantered along the hard frozen track, the rhythmic metallic sound of hooves and swords matching the pounding in his head. The six men at arms behind Somerset were silent, so obviously conscious of their Lord's foul mood, and his brother and his squire rode ahead just to keep out of his way. The sky was cloudless and the late afternoon sun shone with winter brightness, casting a beautiful golden glow over the brickwork of the distant fortress, but Beau did not see it, was blind to anything but the need to get to the castle and deliver his news. Rage surging through him afresh, he spurred his stallion forward and scattered the two riders ahead of him, giving Hercules his head and letting him stretch his stride until the land was flying past him in a blur and the freezing wind numbed his lips. The men at arms speeded up to try and catch him but Jack and Gethin stayed back, after exchanging identical glances of exasperation, and continued their leisurely canter toward home. Some ten minutes later Beau skidded Hercules to a halt outside the gates and yelled admittance, circling impatiently as men scampered to open the gates at the end of the bridge. Once in the outer bailey, he vaulted from the saddle and threw his reins to a hurrying groom and strode across the yard, through the gate and across to the hall, pausing only to ask where the Queen was before taking the steps at the end of the hall, two at a time, and flinging open the heavy wooden door of the great chamber.

"Madame!" His voice cracked over the word, his eyes seeking her out in the centre of her women, and he made a perfunctory bow as she rose from her chair at the sight of his taut, white face. Her heart swept downward as always at the sight of him, but the sheer anger and menace in his face made her catch her breath audibly before she steadied herself. "Leave us!" He gestured at her startled women dismissively and they all looked in askance to Marguerite, who after a moment's hesitation nodded. He waited, fidgeting impatiently as they gathered their things and curtseyed their way out of the room, taking a seemingly interminable time to go as he paced like a caged animal, chewing the inside of his lip.

"Well?" She raised an eyebrow coolly, belying the rapid beating of her heart and the apprehension in her belly.

"Burgundy has betrayed us!" His voice was raw with rage, hawk eyes glittering with anger and hate. "Betrayed us!" he said again. Her face drained of colour and she continued to stare at him.

"How?" she whispered.

"He is financing York to get back to England." He stopped in front of her and looked down at her, his dark presence enveloping her in his fury. "He told me that he would consider handing him over in exchange for some concessions from Louis. I agreed with him that I was to return here and then go immediately to France and discuss the terms with Louis. And then my man in Bruges caught up with me on the road yesterday and told me that as soon as I had left, Burgundy had secretly met York and given him money to finance ships, men and a crossing back to England." He resumed his pacing, anger pulsing from every movement of his body; Marguerite found herself stepping back and distancing herself from the overwhelmingly tangible malevolence. "I cannot believe, after all these years of friendship, that he has done this; I fought for him for fuck's sake, not just once but many times and saved his arse more than once. I gave him my loyalty and I would have died for him if it had been necessary, and he pays me back like this. I told Louis when I was in France that I was worried, and that I thought this grand plan of threatening war to get York into our hands might misfire, but I never thought it would mean that Charles would choose York over Lancaster!" He spat into the fireplace. "Misbegotten son of a York-loving whore and his fucking York-loving harlot wife!" he snarled and slammed his fist into the stone wall in sheer blind anger.

"Edmund!" Marguerite's voice was clear, cold and crisp, breaking through the white heat which had taken away his senses. "For Christ's sake, Edmund, stop!" She moved forward and caught his arm hard, pulling him round to face her. "You will do us no good with a broken hand!" She broke through his blindness and he stared at her uncomprehendingly for an instant before his gaze cleared. It was the first time she had used his given name in more than five years and inexplicably his eyes filled with tears, forcing him to turn his face from her, cursing himself inwardly for his inability to ever exert any control over his emotions. "Sit down," she said more gently, pushing him towards a chair by the fire. "Let me see." Her hand was ice cold as she took his fingers in hers, her touch bringing his gaze back to her. Their eyes met for an instant and then she looked down at his bleeding knuckles. "Can you flex your fingers?" she asked softly. Obediently, he opened and closed his fist and she smiled. "Good." She dipped her handkerchief in a nearby cup of wine and dabbed it gently over his knuckles, the contraction of his pupils the only sign that it hurt. "Sometimes you are such a fool, Edmund!" she said, but for once her tone was gentle and not disparaging and her eyes were soft.

"Yes." He caught her hand and brought it to his lips fervently. "I'm sorry."

"For what?" She held his gaze

"For everything I have ever done to displease you, but mostly for failing you as I have failed you now." His own eyes were despairing.

"You have not failed me." She touched his cheek briefly and then stepped away, dipping her handkerchief once more in the wine and wiping the blood from his hand. "You have only ever had Edward's and my interests at heart and we are grateful for your unswerving loyalty. It is I who should be saying sorry." She turned back to him, her black eyes resting on his. "I never want to speak of this again, Edmund, but I am sorry for how I treated you all those years ago; I was a foolish woman with too much pride but I hope that you can forgive me."

"There is nothing to forgive, Madame." He looked down at his hand as if surprised at the blood on it and blinked rapidly at this sudden turn in her manner. "I am your most loyal and faithful of friends and always will be."

"I know and I have always known." She leaned down and touched his dark hair gently, smoothing it out of his eyes as she would Edward's. "And I was wrong when I said that you were not of the same mould as your father; he would have been proud of the man you have become." She put her head on one side and smiled grimly. "So let us begin anew, as friends, and let's work out how we are going to counter this new move of Burgundy's." He nodded, his eyes once more glistening with unshed tears, and tactfully she turned from him and began pacing the room in his place. "So, how long will it take York to gather enough ships and men and get across to England?"

"Well, it is only four days since he met with Burgundy and it will take him at least a month, I would say, to get anything like a worthwhile set of men and supplies together and then a couple of days to cross. I think it will be early March before he makes his move." Beau leaned back in his chair and closed his eyes, exhaustion suddenly overcoming him. He felt a touch on his arm and saw that she had brought him a cup of wine. Gratefully he took it and drank a large gulp, leaning back and closing his eyes once more as he thought. He was so glad that she had held the olive branch out to him at last and glad that they could be friends without the spectre of her indiscretion hanging over them. He did not know what had been behind her change of heart but Edward was becoming independent and no longer always listened to her, often stood up to her and refused to automatically do her bidding, but he respected Beau and Beau respected her. Between them all they could make the right decisions.

"We need to decide what to do." She poured herself a cup of wine as she broke into his thoughts.

"I think it is obvious. The time has come." His eyelids flickered as he spoke.

"You need to go to England as soon as possible; to warn Warwick," she said quietly. He opened his eyes and looked at her.

"Just me?"

"Yes." She held up her hand before he could speak and continued. "Edward will stay with me while we pack up and follow you, and we will join you in England as soon as we can get everything together."

"I see."

"It is better that way. You need to move quickly."

"He should come with me. The people need to see him." He did not move but his gaze was compassionate. "I know how hard it is…"

"No, you don't!" It was her turn for her eyes to fill with tears and she turned away, angrily. "You do not know for you are not a mother, or a father either for that matter, so how can you know anything about the fear of losing a child?"

"I don't." His voice was soft. "But I do love Edward."

"I know you do." She turned back then and regarded him speculatively. "It is not the same though."

"No." He took another swallow from his cup and she came and sat down opposite him.

"He is my miracle, Edmund, the one thing that has kept my life alight all these years since I was wed to his father, since all the troubles we went through, and then here in exile is his smile, his cleverness, his love and all the wonderful things he has become." She smiled sadly. "I can't bear to let him go just yet." Her dark eyes pleaded with him to understand.

"Alright," he said softly.

"Thank you." She breathed out hard in relief. "So what will you do?"

"Jack and I will go to England and we will take as many men at arms as we can. We will warn Warwick and then prepare for your arrival. But when you come you must let the people see him for he is the one thing that will bring men to us." He sighed and closed his eyes again wearily. "I hope it is not too late."

"Why would it be too late?" She was alarmed.

"I presume you have heard that York now has a son?"

"Yes."

"The people love a madonna and child." He could picture it now, beautiful fey Elizabeth with the baby boy in her arms being cheered by the Londoners who had ever loved York.

"Not when they can't see her." Marguerite's voice was malicious.

"Trust him to pull the rabbit out of the hat when needed." Beau's voice was slurred with tiredness.

"Yes, and yet another 'Edward' to add to the count of English Edwards." There was a hint of amusement in her voice. "Soon the people will not be able to tell one from the other!" He snorted a laugh but did not open his eyes and she had the feeling that he was almost asleep. "When do you plan to leave, Edmund?" she asked loudly, more to rouse him than anything. She was not sure she could sit and watch him sleep in her chamber, the temptation to touch would be too much. He started and opened his eyes, rubbing a hand over his face in such a familiar gesture of tiredness that it made her heart ache.

"I need a couple of days to get everything together and then we will ride for Harfleur." He shook his head. "What day is it today? I cannot think straight."

"Wednesday."

"We will leave on Saturday then." He yawned. "I am sorry, Madame, I have not slept. We have been on the road long hours from Bruges to make it back in quick time and I was too angry to sleep at all last night; I am paying the price now, for I can hardly keep my eyes open."

"Go and rest, Edmund." She leaned forward and smiled. "You will be no good to anyone if you do not sleep."

"Yes, Madame." He stood, unsteady for a moment, and then stretched luxuriously, his hands laced above his head. For a moment, she allowed herself to look and marvel at his lithe feline grace, and the strong muscles of his thighs exposed under his tunic. She held out her hand and he took it, pressing his lips fervently to her knuckles, his mouth soft and warm against them. She closed her eyes for a moment and then gently withdrew her hand.

"I will see you at supper, my Lord," she said softly.

"Yes Madame." He smiled at her, the first unwary smile that he had given her for more than five years and she felt suddenly very sad for the time that they had lost.

"Go on," she said, giving him a maternal push towards the door. "I want you clean shaven, rested and able to plan with a clear head this evening." He laughed and opened the door, turning back as he stepped through it and smiling broadly.

"I have missed you, Madame," he said, and she raised a dark brow.

"Don't push it." Her voice was sharp as she spoke, but she could not help but return his smile.

***

His first thought as he ran down the stairs was to find Katherine but she was nowhere to be seen. He was surprised that she was not in the hall, for normally as soon as she knew he had arrived home she would make sure she was somewhere he could at least see her and catch her glance. He saw Isabel and strode over to her, greeting her and taking the opportunity as he kissed her on each cheek to enquire after her sister. Isabel shook her head and pulled a face.

"I have no idea, Edmund, and to be honest I am glad not to see her." Isabel shuddered theatrically.

"Why?"

"She has been hideous for the last week; absolute poison."

"Katherine, poison?" He was taken aback.

"Yes. Katherine. Poison!" Isabel gave him an icy glare. "Don't look so surprised. She's not a paragon of bloody virtue, you know!"

"Has she been missing me?" He grinned.

"How the hell should I know?" Isabel was not laughing. "She has barely exchanged two words with anyone, and when she has they have been unpleasant!" She glowered at him as if it was his fault.

"Alright, alright!" He held up his hands and backed away, laughing. He looked around once more and seeing there was no sign of her made his way across the bailey and up the tower stairs to his bed chamber. Gethin was already there unpacking; he looked up warily at his master, a look of relief softening his face as he saw that Beau's mood had improved.

"I am going to get some rest, lad," Beau said, pulling off his already unlaced tunic and throwing it to him, then dragging off his shirt. "I want you to wake me in two hours and then I want a bath." He slipped off his boots and threw himself onto the bed, dragging another pillow behind his head and closing his eyes; he was asleep before Gethin had finished drawing the curtains.

Three hours later he was bathed, shaved and dressed in his best black, a flutter of anticipation in his belly. He had woken up on the cusp of a dream which had left him with a throbbing erection that had given him no choice but to deal with it silently and swiftly, before Gethin had finished filling his bath and come to draw the curtains; but it had only taken the edge off his need.

"Gethin, get me the little wooden box that was in my left pannier, will you?" he said, pointing over towards the dark coffer on top of which stood his saddle bags. The boy duly brought the carved box and handed it to him. He opened the lid and looked at the pendant which lay inside; a little emerald heart set in gold on a fine chain; he smiled, knowing that she would love it and would be touched by the inscription he had had engraved on the back. He snapped the lid of the little box shut and placed it in the pouch at his belt and made for the door, feeling much better than he had ever hoped to feel at the start of this day.

When he got to the hall Marguerite was already seated and there was no time for him to look for her. He was greeted enthusiastically by Prince Edward and less so by his little wife, and then he took his place on Marguerite's right hand, smiling at her as he sat down.

"Did you sleep?" she asked, looking him up and down appraisingly.

"Yes, Madame, and bathed." He smiled again. "I feel much better."

"Good." She turned to Edward. "I have told you all of Somerset's news, have I not, cherie?" she said softly. Edward nodded and leaned across her.

"I could not believe it at first, my Lord," he said, shaking his head.

"Believe it, lad." Beau said dryly.

"Maman says you will go to England on Saturday."

"Yes." He smiled at the boy to take the edge off his disappointment. "To pave the way for your arrival." He turned back to avoid having a difficult conversation across his Queen, catching her eyes and shaking his head as she opened her mouth to say something. She subsided and he smiled gratefully as she started to talk of an incident with PHugo which had the boy laughing within moments and lightened the atmosphere. He felt a little sorry for Edward's princess who struggled to follow the rapid French and was left out of the conversation on the dais for most of the time, for English was her predominant language, He was lucky that Katherine was native French and that it was natural for her to speak both French and English. Beau tended to speak French with her, but sometimes when in company with Anne and Isabel they would switch to English, only dropping into French if they were being particularly suggestive and flirtatious, safe in the knowledge that neither girl could follow their talk. He could not believe how much he had missed her while he had been away; missed seeing her face across a room, missed their easy conversation and her sense of fun but most of all missed the soothing contentment of just being with her, and he felt hugely disappointed that he had not seen her in the five hours that he had been home; even just a glimpse of her or a smile of welcome would be enough. He had scanned the room several times with no sign of her and he was just turning back to talk to Marguerite when suddenly she was there, sitting down at a trestle across the hall, talking animatedly to an enraptured Gethin Rhys, looking so radiant and so beautiful that he caught his breath in an audible gasp. Marguerite looked at him sharply and then followed his gaze and rolled her eyes in exasperation, but she forbore to say anything. It seemed to Beau that in the last two weeks she had regained much of the weight she had lost since her illness and perhaps a little more; her breasts seemed more pronounced through the gown's soft material, the oval neckline showing their soft roundness to perfection, and her face, pale against the magnificent russet of her hair, was set off by the wide slash of her red mobile mouth...a mouth which conveyed every possible pleasure to the man who now followed its sensuous, pouting movement. Beau felt his need surge into his groin and almost laughed at his adolescent reaction to the sight of her, biting the inside of his lip to take his mind off the desire that engulfed him. With a supreme effort he dragged his eyes away from her and back to his companions at the high table. He became aware, from the corner of his vision, that Anne Neville was glaring at him, her large green eyes narrowed as she watched his profile. Avoiding her gaze, he leaned toward Isabel on his right hand and murmured softly.

"She does not look so poisonous to me, darling." Isabel laughed and glanced up at him through fair lashes.

"No, I bet she does not, you old stag, but beware beautiful creatures in bright colours for they are the most poisonous of all," she murmured back. "You could be risking your life, or at least parts you value dearly."

"Less of the old, my dear, and do we mean me specifically or do we mean one in general?" He kept his voice light but the enquiry was genuine.

"To be honest, Edmund, I don't know." She turned her head slightly and met his gaze. "Something has happened over the last week or so definitely. Kate and I fight at the best of times but it is normally me who is the snappy one, who starts the fights, not her. Now I find myself being conciliatory as she takes my head off with one mighty swipe of her tongue." Isabel grinned. "And very vicious she is too; if I wasn't ducking for cover I'd be damned proud of her!" Beau gave a sharp bark of loud laughter, oblivious to the eyes in the hall which glanced his way, or the stony expression of one particular diner who watched him, balefully, from the corner of her eye.

"One of the things I like most about you Neville girls is your spirit!" He grinned at her appreciatively. There had been few times in his life he found himself liking a woman, not for the sake of seducing her but actually liking her as a person, but the elder Neville girls had changed his perspective that all women were objects of desire without a thought in their head. "I have a favour to ask of you." He flashed his most charming smile and she laughed, appreciating the attention even as she saw through him.

"An assignation?" she said laconically.

"I think, my darling Isabel, that Katherine and I are beyond assignations." He met her blue gaze with his own level gold one. "As well you know." He leaned in close like a flirtatious suitor and murmured softly, "I need to see her, Bel. I have been away two weeks and I really need to see her, poisonous or not. When supper is over, I will have to go with Madame so will you ask Katherine to meet me at eleven by the chapel?"

"I don't know, Edmund..." she began to joke and then saw his face and relented.

"Alright." He gave her a radiant smile and impulsively kissed her cheek just as Kate turned to look over at him. He met her gaze for an instant and then she turned away without a smile or an acknowledgement of any sort.

"Ooops," he said, catching Isabel's 'I told you so' look and bursting into laughter. "I see what you mean." But inside he felt a quick nag of worry as he looked back at where Kate was now once again talking to Gethin, smiling and laughing, deliberately ensuring that she did not meet his eye again.

As it was, they did not meet by the chapel. After supper Beau, Edward and Marguerite retired to Marguerite's chamber to discuss plans for the next few days but had only been there a short time when she was taken violently ill, obviously a reaction to something that she had eaten. After calling her women and seeing her settled and looked after, Edward and Beau made their way back into the hall, Edward disappearing in search of his wife and Beau spotting Kate sat in a window embrasure, embroidering by a low cresset light as she glanced up every now and then at the dancers in the centre of the floor. With Marguerite indisposed and Edward and her sisters obviously elsewhere, he felt suddenly elated that they would have this time to themselves

"Hey," he said softly, dropping onto the cushions beside her and leaning towards her to kiss her. She did not pull away but she offered her cheek as opposed to her lips.

"My Lord." Her voice was cool and her eyes veiled as she regarded him steadily, laying her sewing to one side. A small knot of fear started to tighten at the pit of his stomach.

"Is there something wrong?" He caught her hand but it lay limp and unresponsive in his.

"I don't know, my Lord. Is there?"

"Is it because I kissed Isabel?" His mouth quirked in a hopeful smile and he squeezed her hand. "I was asking her to tell you that I needed to see you, that's all. I did not have you down as the jealous type."

"I am not, my Lord. I care not who you kiss." She removed her hand from his and made to pick up her frame, thought better of it and put it back down.

"So, what then?" He craned round to look into her face, trying to coax her to good humour.

"I am not sure what you mean?"

"Aren't you?" He raised an eyebrow, still smiling, still sure he could bring her out of her bad humour. His confidence annoyed her.

"I am not sure what you want from me, my Lord. But if you have finished then I would prefer to finish this cuff than talk with you." She reached for it and he caught her wrist before she could, a firm grip on her arm pulling her attention back to him.

"I have not seen you for two weeks or more Katherine; I expected you to be slightly more pleased to see me than this!"

"My Lord?"

"I did not have you down as a woman who played games," he said quietly, very serious suddenly as the fear settled in a large, cold lump in the pit of his stomach.

"I am not, my Lord."

"Then tell me why you are being so cold to me."

"Am I being cold?"

"For fuck's sake, Katherine!" His voice hissed with anger and she jerked backwards, snatching her arm from his hand, her face startled.

"Don't growl at me, my Lord," she hissed back.

"Then talk to me, for God's sake!"

"Someone told me about you and Segoline de Crecy," she said quickly. He shrugged, puzzled.

"So?"

"They told me what you did to her." She felt him stiffen beside her and his pupils contracted to slits.

"And what exactly did I do to Segoline de Crecy?" His voice was flat.

"You got her with child and then you abandoned her and refused to recognise the child as yours." She gave a snort of derision, shaking her head and he looked at her steadily.

"Did I?" he asked. "And who told you that?"

"Does it matter?"

"No, not really." He sounded resigned and shifted forward as if he was going to get up and go. Her mouth contracted to a thin line of anger.

"You told me you had no children and that no woman of yours had ever quickened with child. When I said we had to be careful that was the line you used on me to reassure me that it didn't matter, that the fault lay with you, and I believed you!"

"I did not lie to you."

"Really?" he snorted again. "It looks pretty damning from where I sit."

"I see that you have tried, convicted and condemned me without even talking to me or thinking that I might be innocent." He stood up slowly. "People are malicious and often tell their own versions of the truth. I had expected better of you, Katherine, than to listen to gossip." He looked down at her, feeling very sad suddenly. "When you want to hear my side of the story, if you ever do, then come and find me." He made as if to walk away and then turned back for a moment. "I really thought you trusted me," he said softly before finally turning and striding quickly out of the hall and into the bailey.

Anjou, France
January 1471

The pale winter sun shone softly and, sitting on a bench, the chapel wall protecting him from the cold early February wind, Beau could feel its gentle warmth through the dark wool of his cloak. He rested his forearms on his knees and stared at the pathway, not seeing the soft yellow stone or the tiny ants which scurried between the cracks, his eyes blind to anything other than the workings of his mind. The small well of worry which had sat at the pit of his stomach had now grown into a great, gaping rent of fear, swirling through his veins every time he thought of leaving, yet knowing that he had no choice but to go. The latest he could put off his departure was Sunday, but even so it seemed pointless to wait as it was obvious that Kate was not going to seek him out; she had managed to avoid being alone with him since the night in the hall. He could not understand why she was being like this and why she would not even talk to him. It was so unlike her to be unreasonable. It was not as if it was some kind of game she was playing or that she expected him to run after her and beg and plead, as she had made it quite clear she was avoiding him at all costs; sometimes, when they were in the same room, he had felt her watching him, but as soon as he looked her way she had turned from him. He rubbed his face with both hands, his throat aching over a well of emotion which kept engulfing him, and once again he cursed his own nature for betraying feelings which most men seemed to be able to control. It would be quite easy for him to cry like a baby if he did not constantly battle against the tide of desolation, and he wished he could just set off for England without ever having to think about any of it ever again. Jack had kept out of his way since that first night, sensing that something was wrong but not wanting to put himself in the firing line of any backlash, and so he had essentially been alone with his thoughts except for the times when he had been planning his mission with his brother, Marguerite and Edward. He and Marguerite had shared a pleasant evening the night before as, fully recovered from her bout of sickness, she had supped with him in her chamber and they had talked of his father and the old days when he was but a boy and Hal was the chosen one. But still he had found his mind drifting to Katherine and eventually he had had to excuse himself, pleading tiredness and a headache, and retire to his bed to be desolate in peace.

"Are you alright, my son?" A rich, dark voice interrupted his thoughts. He looked up and met the warm and worldly grey eyes of his father's old confessor.

"Father Andre," he said huskily, trying to smile but managing just a thin-lipped grimace. "I..." he faltered, and shrugged as his face betrayed him.

"May I?" The older man gestured to the bench and Beau nodded briefly, uncertain whether the interruption was welcome or not. The priest sat down, arranging his robes around him and turning his face to the warmth of the sun. Beau flashed a sideways look at the man and the priest smiled.

"The sun is warm here," was all he said.

"Yes." Beau rubbed his face again and then ran his fingers through his dark hair, pushing it back out of his eyes, leaning back against the wall as he did so. "The wall shelters us from the cold I think," he said, squinting up at the sun. The priest smiled.

"I hear you are off to England Tomorrow?"

"Yes, to meet my Lord Warwick and give him the bad news." Beau closed his eyes against the glare and sighed softly.

"Is that what troubles you?" The question was hesitantly put, for although Father Andre de Lucy had known and loved the old Duke of Somerset for many years, and had known him to be a mixture of the devout and the worldly, as powerful men often were, this man he did not know very well at all. The young Duke, as he still thought of him, was an enigma, so like his father in looks yet so unlike him in temperament. The old Duke had been renowned for his gruff yet unruffled manner and his decisiveness in the face of adversity, yet this young man had a reputation as a volatile man who suffered mercurial shifts of mood; not particularly devout, attending mass but sporadically, and yet somehow a much more sensitive and vulnerable man than his father had ever been. He could sense the raging current of emotion inside him, carefully concealed by the tough, haughty exterior, but there was more than that, there was a bleakness about him which was disturbing. Beau laughed harshly.

"Christ no!" He shook his head. "I admit the betrayal of the Duke of Burgundy was a shock that I had least expected but the reckoning had to come. We cannot win without a final defeat of York and at least we now have time to prepare to fight him." He sat forward and stared out over the garden in front of him, his long fingers raking through his hair once more.

"But I do sense that you are troubled, lad." Father Andre mirrored his forward movement, glancing at him as he did so.

"Do you?" The younger man was non-committal but the priest could see the pulse jumping at his throat and the tension in his shoulders.

"Yes, I do."

"How well did you know my father, Andre?" Beau still did not look at him.

"Well enough to know he would have been proud of you, my son."

"I wasn't fishing for compliments." He turned then and met the priest's eye sardonically. "I knew him as a father but not really as a man; I was just interested to know what he was like."

"Well, I knew him as his confessor rather than a companion but he was a fairly simple man with a simple outlook on life." The priest laughed suddenly, warmly. "He believed in God and vengeance and those were the rules he lived by."

"Aye, and died by!" Beau shook his head. "I wish I could find life that simple, Father."

"Ah, my son, not many people do have the ability to view life with simplicity and if they do it is not always a good thing." The priest looked at the arrogant profile, taking in the long nose and firm jaw-line, and saw beneath that to the young man who sheltered unsteadily within. "In my life as a priest I have found that people vary in complexity. Some, like your father, are lucky enough to find life to be a set of simple choices by which they live, others, like King Harry, see more of the grey than the black and the white and that makes it harder for them to take one side or the other, and then there are some, such as my Lord of Warwick, who look only to serve themselves and see that as a clear direction." He touched the younger man's arm briefly. "And you, my son?"

"Me?" Beau pursed his mouth, thoughtfully. "I find myself either riding high on the crest of the wave or crashing on the rocks below, father." He gave a short laugh. "I never seem to be able to find the calm sea or even just a gentle swell."

"And sometimes, when adversity strikes, things can seem very bleak; black almost when you look ahead?" The priest's voice was gentle.

"Yes, father!" Beau was startled by the older man's insight and stared at him. "Did my brother send you to talk to me?" he asked after a moment, his expression a picture of suspicion. The priest shook his head.

"No, my son," he said softly and then smiled. "Do you know much about your family history?"

"A little." Beau looked puzzled about the turn in the conversation. "My family is very proud of its heritage." He felt a surge of sadness as he thought of the tale he had told Katherine of John of Ghent and Katherine Swynford, and with an effort he pushed it away.

"Did you know that your great-grandfather suffered sometimes from the same feelings of despair and euphoria, or that his brother the Black Prince also had very black times during which he treated people cruelly?"

"No, I didn't."

"That is where his name came from, not from the colour of his armour."

"How do you know this?" Beau was surprised that the old man had such a grasp of a history of more than a hundred years before.

"Because the Black Prince is a notorious legend in France; in the great wars he subjugated much of it to his will from Aquitaine to Normandy, and he was greatly feared by all who encountered him; a giant of a man by all accounts, looked like a god and behaved like the devil! "He glanced at Beau briefly. "He could be a cruel man and waged a bitter war on all who opposed him, yet he cannot have been such a bad man for he waited fifteen years to marry his wife and Princess, the Fair Maid of Kent, all against his father's wishes, and by all accounts they adored each other. Some say she softened him once they wed but he was still known for his blackness of temper in these parts."

"And you think I am the same?" Beau was a bit taken aback that the priest was comparing him to the extreme portrait he had painted of his great-grandfather's elder brother.

"No, my son, I don't, for I don't think you have the extremes of your forebears, but you might have inherited something of this temperament." The older man flexed his fingers and looked at his lined, roughened hands for a moment. "I think many things are passed down to us, not always in its former form and sometimes it may miss one generation and pass to the next, that's all." They were both silent for a time, thinking of the King and the illness which many believed he had inherited from his mother's father, who had suffered bouts of madness for all his life and had often had to be shut away from the world. The quiet which descended was both comfortable and companionable, the warmth of the sun through their heavy winter clothes adding to the peacefulness. Beau was eventually the first to break it

"Father…?" he began hesitantly. The priest looked around at him

"Yes, my son?"

"Do you think a man must always be judged on others' perceptions of his past actions?" Beau leaned his elbows on his knees and cupped his chin in his hands, glancing across at the older man as he did so.

"I think he most likely will be, why?" Andre's smile was quizzical.

"So if it is perceived that a man has committed a sin in the past, then he will be condemned for it forever more, even if he never actually did what he is being condemned for?"

"It is human nature to judge others so. If a man is accused of murdering his best friend, he won't find many who will want to be his friend after that!"

"Even if he is innocent of the murder?" Beau stared at the ground, watching the ants carrying a piece of bread along the stone.

"Even if he is innocent, until it is proven that someone else did it. It is a natural thing. Perhaps it is not right but it is natural!" The priest sensed that they were getting to the crux of the thing that was troubling the younger man. Beau sighed.

"What makes people feel that they can judge others so?" he asked quietly.

"Many things." Andre leaned his head back and closed his eyes, his voice warm and rich as he spoke. "But mostly we judge others because we are afraid."

"Afraid of what?"

"Afraid that whatever it is we think the other person has done, they will do to us."

"And how do we convince the person that we won't?" Beau was still staring at the ground, but Andre had the feeling he was seeing something other than the ants on the stone.

"We persevere, my son," he said softly.

"Ah!" Beau sat up and looked at him. "And if the other person won't let you?"

"Then you have a choice my son, continue to persevere or cut your losses and move on." They regarded each other for a moment and then Beau nodded, his expression closing as he smiled, a lightening smile which ended the conversation and the companionable moment.

"Thank you, father," he said, pushing himself up from the stone bench and holding out his hand to the older man to help him up. Andre hauled himself to his feet but Beau did not let go of his hand. "God willing that I will see you in England Father, and may God keep you."

"May God keep you safe also, my son." The priest returned the handshake. He stood for a moment and watched the tall, troubled young man walk away, before turning and disappearing back inside the chapel.

Beau walked towards the hall, wondering if he could bring himself to cut his losses or if he would pursue the impossible for the rest of his life, something nagging at the back of his mind as he walked, something that he felt he should be grasping but was not. And then suddenly it hit him so hard that he stopped dead, his expression first one of doubt, then possibility and then certainty, and then he was running across the grass and over the rutted courtyard, oblivious of the puddles and the mud splashing his boots, towards the hall, his mind galloping ahead of him. He stopped in the entrance of the hall, looking round, but could see none who could help him so, turning, he ran up the stone staircase to the solar, barging through the door and looking desperately around him. Some of the Queen's women were there, startled and flustered by his unannounced arrival, as was Anne Neville who was regarding him slightly fearfully from her seat by the fire.

"Princess." He bowed swiftly. "Where is your sister?" Anne raised a dark brow questioningly.

"The Duchess Isabel, my Lord?" she asked in her little girl voice.

"No, Madame, the Lady Katherine." He refused to play her game, did not have the time. He was conscious of the women exchanging glances but ignored them.

"Why do you want her?" The girl lifted her chin against her fear of him, and Beau subconsciously admired her whilst outwardly being exasperated. He took a deep breath.

"I need to talk with her before I leave for England tomorrow, Princess."

"I see."

"Please, Madame?" He met her eyes desperately and she softened for an instant.

"I think she is with the Lady Veronique, in the royal wardrobe," she said curtly. He bowed again and thanking her briefly, whirled out of the door and down the stairs before she could think of calling him back. A twitter of voices followed him down the stairwell.

He found Kate checking an inventory of gowns with her mother, as Marguerite, true to her word, began the lengthy preparation to move the whole court to England. Veronique looked up, startled at his unannounced arrival, and then surprised at his curt dismissal.

"Leave us!" He did not look at her but watched Kate who was staring at him warily. Veronique hesitated. "I said leave us!" His voice was low but no less authoritative for that. Veronique glanced at her daughter and then curtseyed deeply and left the room, pulling the door ajar but standing outside it in case she was needed. Once she was gone, Beau unfastened his cloak, threw it across the large oak table and strode over to Kate, standing front of her and catching her arm as she made to push past him. "I am going to ask you a question and I want a truthful answer," he said very low, his hand gripping her arm firmly. She looked up at him, her expression at first wary and then a flicker of fear shadowed the depths of her eyes. He saw it and it hurt him, but he did not let go of her.

"My Lord." Her voice was not more than a whisper.

"Are you with child, Katherine?" The words came out more rapidly than he expected and for a moment she looked at him uncomprehendingly, and then the fear flickered more strongly this time. She did not drop her gaze but she said nothing. He jerked her arm. "Tell me. Are you with child?" This time her eyes filled with tears but still she did not speak. "For Christ's sake, Katherine, are you?" He shook her more roughly than he meant to and she burst into tears.

"Yes!" she shouted, jerking herself out of his grasp and raising her chin defiantly. "Yes, I am and yes it is yours!" He stood looking down at her and then grabbed her by the back of her neck and kissed her savagely, his hand in her hair pulling her head back, his mouth taking full possession of hers. Veronique who had put her head around the door at the sound of her daughter's shouts, now backed out and quietly closed the door behind her. Dragging his mouth away from hers but keeping his hand at the back of her neck, he stared at her for a long moment until he whispered, "I would never doubt that it is mine." And then his eyes filled with tears which spilled down his cheeks. "How the hell did we end up like this?" he asked hoarsely, and she shook her head, tears streaming down her own face.

"I don't know," she whispered miserably. He stepped back, wiping his eyes with the heels of his hands, not caring that she should see him cry, hoping that if there was one person in his life who he could cry with or in front of, it would be her. But the tears would not stop and in the end he just let them spill down his face in salty rivulets.

"Why did you doubt me?" he asked after a few moments, his voice breaking over the words, his mouth contorting and turning down at the corners. "I just don't understand why you doubted me."

"I don't know," she said again, her face a picture of dumb misery.

"I cannot believe you thought I would leave you!" He was angry suddenly, angry that what should have been a wonderful time in their lives was now spoiled. "Do you have any idea what it means to me that you are carrying my child?" His shoulders heaved once and a sob escaped him before he drew a deep, shaking breath, bringing himself back under control. "Do you have any idea?" She shook her head, staring at the floor, a tear dripping off the end of her nose.

"I'm sorry," she whispered.

"You thought I would not acknowledge it, didn't you?" He shook his head.

"Yes."

"All because you believed the person who told you I had abandoned Segoline de Crecy?" His voice broke again.

"Yes."

"Do you want to know why I did not acknowledge Segoline's child?" He leaned back against the big table behind him, folding his arms defensively across his chest, blinking rapidly to see through the wells of water in his eyes. She nodded, still staring at the floor.

"Yes."

"Because. It. Was. Not. Mine." He enunciated each word clearly. "She was already with child when I bedded her; the babe was born seven months after I first had her and was as big as a nine-month babe, a big lusty lad who I would have loved to have called mine but he was not. She told her father that he was because she thought he would not disown her if she was with child by me." He looked at her steadily. "Did your informant also tell you that I visited her after the child was born because I felt sorry for her, and I gave her father some money to help her?"

"No."

"And that when I saw her she admitted to me that she had lied to Marguerite that the child was mine, hoping that it would be small and she could pass it off as a Beaufort?"

"No." She was really crying now, her shoulders shaking and her breath coming in gasps.

"I spoke the truth when I told you no woman of mine had ever quickened with my child." He shook his head slowly, quite overcome with the wonder of it. "That you are with child is nothing short of a miracle, Katherine; a miracle."

"I'm sorry." She ran towards him and threw herself against him, clinging to him, her face buried in his chest, her shoulders heaving with huge racking sobs. He did not put his arms around her but held back, anger still not far from the surface.

"This should have been so special," he whispered, feeling his control breaking. "It should have been one of the finest moments of my life, second only to that moment at Jurvadeil when you told me you loved me." His voice cracked and he breathed deeply, shakily, trying not to let go, afraid that if he allowed the dam to break, he would never stop.

"I love you so much and I thought that you loved me."

"I do." Her voice was muffled in his chest.

"But you don't trust me?"

"I was afraid." She leaned back and looked up at him, her eyes puffy with tears and her face white. "I was afraid you would leave me and I couldn't bear it."

"Why did you think I would leave you?" He was hurt by her doubt.

"I...I don't know." She began to cry again. "Everyone is always saying how badly you treat women. They know that you have been pursuing me and they try to make me mistrust you. I was scared and I listened. When my mother left me I still remember..." She could not continue, her sobs shaking her, her hands over her face, and he softened.

"Who told you all this about Segoline and me?" His voice was gentle. She shook her head. He cupped her chin in his hand and brought her eyes up to his. "Who?" he asked again.

"Ma mère." The words were barely audible.

"Your mother?" He was confused for a moment.

"My Lady stepmother," she said quietly.

"Christ, I always knew she was a meddlesome bitch!" She jumped at the exasperation in his voice and he let go of her chin abruptly. "Did she also tell you I am a woman beater?" he asked sarcastically, and when she shook her head, "So why are you suddenly so scared of me?"

"I don't know." She was still crying, and reaching out he drew her into his embrace, his cheek resting on her hair as she sobbed into his tunic.

"Ah, kitten," he whispered, his own tears spilling again and his voice shaking. "I don't know how we came to this but I hope to God we never come to it again."

"So do I." Her voice was thick and heartfelt.

"Then promise me that you will always talk to me before you believe what people say of me. Promise me you will always give me the chance to explain myself?" He stroked her hair softly and she slid her arms up his back, drawing him closer.

"I promise." She sniffed and then hiccupped against his chest and a surge of protectiveness swelled through him.

"I can hardly believe it," he murmured against her hair, his heart lurching suddenly. "We are to have a child!" He kissed her forehead. "Do you have any idea when?"

"August, I think. I have missed two courses and next week will be my third. It must have happened at Jurvadeil."

"And you are sure?" He knew without asking but had to make certain.

"Yes. My breasts are huge, I eat the oddest things and I have been sick several times in the mornings, although that seems to be easing now." She looked up at him with a watery smile. "I had guessed before you went away but wanted to wait until I had missed my third course to tell you so that I was absolutely sure. I wish now that I had told you before you went to Burgundy and then I would not have believed ma mère when she said all these things to me."

"Why did she tell you all this?"

"I think she wanted to protect me from you; she thinks you are a 'sexual predator' and you will destroy my reputation. Anne told her you were after me and papa obviously did not let her in on the deal he made with you."

"It was not a deal!" He pulled her close again. "We just laid our cards on the table, that's all. Your father would never bargain with you," he lied with a clear conscience. "He loves you too much for that."

"It's alright, I know what my father is like and I don't mind. It was my choice in the end, it just happened to coincide with his." She nestled into his chest and he held her tight.

"I love you," he said softly.

"And I love you." She returned the pressure of his embrace.

"Come to England with me." The words came out of their own accord but as he said them he knew it was right.

"To England?" She pulled back and stared at him.

"Yes." He touched his lips to hers. "I will postpone my leaving until Sunday to give you time to pack."

"You mean it?" Her eyes began to sparkle and she touched his face softly, wiping the wetness from his cheekbone.

"We will go to your father first and then I will take you to meet my cousin Meg."

"Meg?" She looked puzzled and then realisation dawned. "Your cousin Margaret Beaufort?" She laughed, shakily. "Oh Lord. She's supposed to be the clever one, isn't she?"

"Yes she is." He smiled. "But you are well-read, darling, and I think she would like you." He hugged her again, excited suddenly. "Ah,

Katherine, to spend all that time together, just us, as we travel and when we get to England, no more finding late times to talk when everyone is in bed, no more quick couplings in quiet corners; no more pretending that we are not what we are." He kissed her then, a long, gentle kiss, one hand sliding into her hair, the other at her cheek; their tears, still wet on their faces, mingling at their lips. "I have something for you," he said softly after a moment and she laughed against him. "No, not that!" He gave a snort of mirth and pulled away from her, shaking his head as he reached into his belt and pulled out a small wooden box. "When I made you throw away your wedding ring, I promised you something that would be a token between you and I. I had this made for you in Burgundy and was able to collect it whilst I was there." He opened the box, revealing the necklace he had bought and held it out for her. She took it and lifted the heart gently out of the box.

"It's beautiful!" she said quietly, her eyes sparkling. He smiled.

"Read the back," he said equally soft. She turned the locket over and her mouth trembled.

"Oh love!" she whispered. "*In life; in love; in death; my heart. EB*." And promptly burst into tears again.

"Turn around," he said, taking the necklace from her hand and putting it around her neck and fastening it. He slid his arms around her waist, one palm across her stomach, his lips at her temple. "Stay with me tonight," he murmured. "I don't want to sleep without you anymore."

"But Anne..."

"Darling, if you are coming with me to England, it doesn't matter anymore does it?" He pulled her in closer, his heart hammering against his ribs in anticipation. "Please, kitten, I need you." His lips tracked down her neck, making her shiver. She turned in his embrace and lifted her face for his kiss, slipping her arms around his neck, her fingers sliding into the silky softness of his hair.

"Alright," she said softly.

"One day you will know how much I love you," he whispered, his mouth claiming hers, hard and possessive. "One day you will trust my love." He took her hand and placed it on his still racing heart. "I am yours, Katherine; everything you see is yours to do with as you will. I cannot function without you. These last days have been hell but they have taught me one thing: I need you with me and I cannot contemplate going to England without you by my side."

"Oh Beau." She ran her thumb across his lips and then his cheek. "I have been such a fool." The tears, still so close to the surface, threatened again and there was an answering glitter in his eyes as he pulled her to him and they stood in a long, wordless embrace. He could feel her trembling with the force of the emotion between them and marvelled that they could be so vulnerable to love's hurts when they had such an affinity and need for each other. He had never opened his emotions like that to any before, had never felt that he could show himself like he had done this day and trust a woman with his innermost thoughts and feelings. As he held her in his arms he felt light and liberated, exhilarated suddenly and so immensely grateful that God had chosen to give him this woman. The wait for love had been worth it if it meant that he would spend the rest of his days with Katherine by his side.

"My Lord." Veronique's voice cut across their embrace and he stepped away from her, his arm still around her shoulders, holding her against him.

"Yes?"

"Madame, the Queen is looking for you, my Lord."

He inclined his head and she stepped out of the room once more.

"I have to go," he said needlessly. She leaned into him and he bent down and kissed her softly. "I will see you tonight?"

"Yes." She took his hand and placed it on her stomach. "We will see you tonight."

"Oh Christ!" His voice broke and he pulled her into his arms, holding her hard against him. "I still can't believe it!" He looked down into her face, his eyes spilling tears once more but his smile radiant.

"Believe it." She laughed and took her handkerchief from her sleeve, wiping his face and brushing the droplets from his lashes. "And don't walk about grinning like a cat who has stolen the cream or it will be obvious something is going on!"

"Why?" He obediently closed his eyes as she dabbed them, without any self-consciousness.

"Because you are not a man who walks around smiling, love."

"Am I not?" He was genuinely surprised.

"No, not really." She looked up at him, gazing at his face. "Many would say you are darkly handsome." She grinned impishly. "I would say you are just dark!" He smiled.

"And I would say," he said, kissing her briefly and walking towards the heavy door. "I thank God each day for giving me you, for my life will never be dark again." He turned and smiled again, kissing his fingers and placing them across his heart. "I love you." And with that he slipped out of the door.

Chapter Eleven

London, February 1471

It was dark and the snow was beginning to fall heavily as they made their way along the narrow street, Beau and Jack riding at their head. All but six of the men at arms had been left by the city gate to camp outside the walls. Kate and Gethin Rhys were tucked in behind them, with the men on foot flanking them to each side. Kate pulled the hood of her fur-lined cloak further over her forehead to shield her face, the wool scarf, which was wrapped across her nose and mouth, feeling wet against her cold skin. She was exhausted; the ride from where they had landed near Folkestone had been fast and arduous; they had made the seventy-five-mile journey to London in just two long, ice-cold, windy days; stopping only at the Abbey near Rochester for food, a few hours' sleep and then on their way again before dawn had broken. She shivered under her cloak, the cold having soaked into her bones so that she felt like she would never be warm again.

"Are you alright?" Beau had dropped back and was beside her, his expression worried.

"I'm fine." Her eyes smiled at him wearily. "I'm just tired." Her hand strayed unconsciously to her still flat stomach.

"I'm so sorry, love." His voice was so low she could only make out the words from watching his lips, but he caught her hand briefly and squeezed it, his eyes catching hers in a caress full of longing. "I could not contemplate us spending yet another night apart." She returned the pressure on his hand and leaned toward him. He met her half way.

"My father might make us sleep apart," she murmured in his ear and laughed at his horrified expression, beckoning him close again.

"I don't think so; it's more likely he would let you have me in the hall and be at your shoulder urging you on!" He cracked a sharp laugh at her wry acknowledgement of her father's politicking, and in a rare public display of affection, lifted her hand to his mouth and kissed her gloved palm, his eyes still laughing as he winked at her and moved back up to Jack's side. The man at arms on her left cast a quick, curious glance in her direction, and then seeing that she had seen him, flushed scarlet. She had got used to that in the last two weeks since they had left France, surrounded by a hundred men interested in their Lord's choice of paramour, taking it in turns to walk beside her so they could see what she looked like. Few of them got to see more than a pair of green-flecked, almond shaped eyes looking back at them, fringed by long, darkly-burnished lashes, which swept the hint of high cheekbone each time she blinked. Cloaked and muffled as she was against the cold she could hide and leave them curious to see more, but she still found it unnerving that she created such interest.

The two weeks that they had been travelling together had been wonderful, taking the journey quickly but steadily so that they rode around thirty miles a day if they could, less when the weather was inclement, staying each night in an inn; a scout always sent ahead to find the most appropriate place. He had bought her a mount so that she did not have to ride pillion behind him, as that would have slowed them down, and so, sometimes, he rode with her and they talked, and others he rode at the head of his men while she watched his back and chatted with Jack or Gethin, or just rode in silent contentment, muffled against the cold in the beautiful sable-lined cloak her stepmother had given her on her departure.

It had been hard telling Anne Beauchamp that she was going with Beau to England, for Anne had not reacted the way she had expected. Her stepmother had been resigned and saddened that she had chosen to become his leman, but not particularly surprised, and she had found that quite difficult to deal with. Her sister Anne had been distraught and disgusted and whilst Isabel was neither of these, she had been resentful that she was not allowed to accompany them, forced to stay with her mother rather than go to her husband. And so neither sister had come to say goodbye as they left on the Sunday morning which had hurt her, but her mother had given her money and a letter for her father and her stepmother had given her the cloak; even Marguerite had not made a fuss, merely ignored her presence as she wished Beau a fond farewell. Edward had kissed her and hugged Beau and vowed to be in England as soon as he could get his mother moving, and then they had left, leaving behind Angers and then Anjou, possibly forever.

They had talked so much in the nights that had followed, in their various beds, curtains closed against the cold, low cresset burning as she lay, warm and secure in his arms, his long fingers stroking her hair as he told her of his hopes and dreams for the future, of King Henry and of Edward and how he hoped that Edward would be able to assist his father in ruling England so that once York was defeated they would have stability and prosperity. He told her how he hoped that her father would help learn how to govern the kingdom and that they could work in partnership with Henry and Edward and the rest of his Counsel to end the wars between York and Lancaster and to have peace once more. She had experienced a moment of sadness at the thought of Ned defeated but had faced that her life was different now. It was wrapped up with Beau, not York, not even Lancaster, but with Beau and with whatever happened to him.

They had talked of their own future and that of their child but he had gone very quiet when she had teasingly brought up the subject of a wife and legitimate heirs, refusing to play along, saying he could not bear to think that someone else would have claim to him or be at his side when all he wanted was her. She had laughed and told him that she had known from the beginning that he would one day take a wife and that she would never be able to appear in public with him because, as his leman, she was only one step up from a whore. He had become angry then, telling her never to refer to herself in those terms and they had had their first real argument, carried out in hissed and hushed tones behind the bed curtains, and gone to sleep with their backs to each other, anger radiating around the mattress. He had woken her while it was still dark and had made love to her with such searing tenderness that she had cried and clung to him, and as he had held her in his arms afterwards he had told her how much he loved her and had vowed that she would never suffer for her position, that she would always be first in his heart and if she could not be his public partner then in private he would elevate her above all others.

She knew that there were some who would feel trapped and suffocated to be loved with the intensity that he loved her, who would run from his obsession. But for her it was the balm she needed after what had happened with Stephen Thevenot, and to be cocooned in all that beauty, love and sensuality and to know that if he looked at another woman it was only to compare her unfavourably with her, was the perfect antidote. If she knew somewhere in her mind that one day she may wake up and feel like she was held in a gilded cage, she was not yet ready to acknowledge it and the love she felt for him and gratitude for the respect and courtesy he showed her overwhelmed her each time she looked at him.

They had not fallen into any patterns as yet in their lovemaking, still in that first flush of passion where they could not get enough of each other, luxuriating in the joy and pleasure, and she knew it would be no different tonight, for no matter how tired she was she needed him. Their physical relationship was important to both of them but they had not been able to make love for nigh on five days. The crossing on the cog has been delayed after they had boarded board and then it had taken forever to cross the narrow channel because of the wind. During their stay in the Abbey they had, for propriety's sake, slept in separate quarters. She grinned to herself when she thought of the crossing, for he was not a good sailor and had only occasionally come out for some air, white as a ghost, clinging to the rails as he staggered across the deck. She, on the other hand, was not affected by the sea at all and had spent most of her time on the open deck, charming the captain and his crew to such an extent that the old man had let her take the wheel, standing a respectful distance behind her just in case he had to catch it or her. Beau had come out at that point and stood, leaning against the rail, watching her, shaking his head in wry amusement as she had handed back to the captain and come scampering down the deck to see him, her skirts soaked as the decks swam with the icy cold spray which shot over the bow.

"Are you never afraid of anything?" he had asked, holding tight whilst she stood grinning, her sea legs holding her up.

"Of course I am." She had laughed up at him, her cheeks glowing and her eyes shining, the sable-lined cloak and her sheer enjoyment of the sailing the only things keeping her warm.

"You are truly magnificent," he had said before staggering back to his bunk. She laughed to herself and then realised that the man beside her was looking at her again. She winked at him conspiratorially, startling him so much that he almost walked into the man in front, before a huge grin split his face and he turned away.

"Oh my!" she exclaimed softly and suddenly, and the man at arms glanced back at her but Gethin Rhys was at her other side immediately.

"My Lady?"

"We are almost there. Up there, look, it's the Herber!" Involuntary tears filled her eyes at the sight of the gates to her old London home, the place where her father was, and she thought she might cry.

Beau had sent word ahead that he was coming, although not saying that she was with him as they had wanted that to be a surprise and had not wanted her father to forbid it, to be going back to one of her childhood homes felt very poignant and to know that her father would be there was almost too much to bear. Butterflies raged in her stomach and she could feel her heart thumping and her hands shaking. She took a deep breath to steady herself. The idea was that she would hide behind Beau and Jack when they entered the hall and then Beau would reveal her once formal greetings had taken place, but she was afraid she might just shout 'papa' as soon as she saw him and throw herself into his arms.

Once inside the hall she found it somehow comforting to be anonymous behind the two tall men as everyone milled about at the entrance, dogs barking and the page rushing to find her father. Then she heard his voice as he descended the stairs from the solar.

"Edmund! Jack!"

"Richard!" Beau's husky tones responded, and they obviously all shook hands although she could not see from her position right behind Beau.

"Jesus man, you look half frozen!" Warwick must have gestured a page. "Some Hippocras for my Lord Duke and Lord Dorset, lad," he said, and then, "Come up to the solar, gentlemen, it is warmer up there."

"Before we do that, Richard." Beau forestalled him, smiling. "We would like to give you a gift."

"A gift?" Warwick laughed. "How generous; what kind of gift?"

"A gift that I hope you will like very much." Beau stepped aside and Kate pushed back her hood.

"Papa," she said softly, her eyes filling with tears again which spilled down her cheeks. Warwick stared at her for a moment and then did the only spontaneous thing she had ever seen him do; stepped forward and swept her into his embrace with a breathlessly whispered,

"Kate, my darling child." And held her to him so tightly she could not breathe. She clung to him, her arms around his neck, her tears wet on his cheek as she just kept saying "Papa, oh papa" over and over again. After a few moments he stepped back and held her at arm's length, shook his head and then hugged her again. When he finally let her go he looked up at Beau and said,

"I am not sure whether to be pleased or angry, but, Christ lad, you know how to surprise a man!" Beau grinned, lighting his face boyishly.

"I would rather you be pleased," he said, obviously enjoying the success of his gift.

"Are you hungry, Katherine, have you eaten?" Her father looked at her anxiously, noting how tired she looked.

"I am ravenous, papa, and I would give my right arm for a chair!" She slipped her arm through his, glancing up at Beau as she did so with a soft smile. He responded with his own smile and a wink and gestured she should lead them up to the solar with her father.

Later, curled up on the settle in the warmth of the solar, her eyes heavy and her stomach full, she watched the two men she loved talking and laughing with ease and felt a surge of contentment wash over her. It could all have been so different had Beau not been prepared to bury his grievances and offer a hand of friendship rather than convenience, and she felt fiercely proud that he could forgive her father and move on. She marvelled at the strangeness of their world; enemies becoming friends; friends becoming enemies; families torn apart with some on both sides and other families following her father into the gates of hell if need be. She wondered what they would make of Beau and what he would make of them. 'The enemy of my enemy is my friend,' she thought idly, and smiled inwardly at that; it certainly worked that way for her father. She stared into the flame and thought for a moment of Ned and Richard in Burgundy, her stomach sweeping downward at the thought of them, far from home and Ned not even having seen his son. She could not imagine how she would feel if she was separated from Beau when their child was born and he was not able to be there with her. It made her more sensitive to Ned's plight and she felt a genuine pang of sorrow for the first time since he had left Middleham.

"Are you alright, darling?" Beau's voice came softly from behind her, making her jump.

"Sorry, I was miles away." She smiled up at him.

"Yes, you were." His smile was quizzical.

"I'm just tired, I think."

"I'm not surprised." He squeezed her shoulder. "Why don't you go up to bed?"

"Because I want to wait for you." She briefly laid her cheek on his hand as it tightened on her shoulder. His eyes took on a hungry expression as he crouched down at the back of the settle, his face level with hers.

"Go on up, sweetheart," he murmured. "I won't be long."

"I was thinking of Ned and Elizabeth Woodville."

"York and Elizabeth Woodville?" His brows shot up in surprise. "Why?"

"I was thinking how awful it must be for her to be parted from him and him not being able to see his son. I could not bear that!" Her eyes suddenly filled with tears and she blinked rapidly.

"Ah, love." His eyes were liquid gold tenderness. "Don't ever think like that."

"Sorry, you're right, I should go to bed, I am over tired." She leaned her cheek against his hand once more and closed her eyes. "If I am asleep, will you wake me when you come up?"

"You can count on it." He smiled.

"Promise?" Her own need was mirrored once more in his eyes and he nodded.

"I promise."

"Alright." He straightened up and came round to the front of the settle, holding his hand out to help her up, bringing her lightly to her feet.

"Goodnight, papa." She walked over and kissed her father on the cheek.

"Goodnight, sweetheart." He hugged her briefly and then she impulsively kissed Jack as well. He grinned at her and patted her arm.

Beau followed her to the door and through it, closing it behind him for a moment. He leaned down and kissed her lingeringly but as her arms slid around his neck, he caught them and pulled her hands into his chest, kissing her knuckles and laughing softly.

"Oh no, you don't or I shall scandalise the household by making love to you here on the staircase." He dropped a kiss on the tip of her nose. "Do you realise that is the first time I have kissed you for days?"

"I know." She pulled a rueful face. "I have missed you."

"I want you so much it hurts."

"Hurry up and come to bed then." She smiled, her eyes glowing in her pale face.

"Are you sure you are alright, kitten?"

"Yes, I am just tired." She touched his cheek gently. "Honestly."

"Alright. I'll be up very soon, I promise." He kissed her again and then turned back to the door.

"Beau?"

"Yes, kitten?" He looked round with a smile.

"Will you tell papa about the babe?"

"Do you want me to?" He looked surprised but she nodded. She had thought long and hard about this and had decided it would give her father enormous pleasure to hear about his grandchild from the man who had once been his enemy, and Beau was so proud that he would be more than happy to give him the good news without realising what a triumph it would be for her father.

"I think it would be nice if he heard it from you."

"Alright." He leaned down and kissed her forehead and she slipped her arms around him and hugged him close.

"I love you," she whispered against his chest and then she turned away, running lightly up the winding staircase to their chamber.

***

Back in the solar Warwick looked up from his conversation with Jack and arched a brow enquiringly as Beau ducked his head through the door and came into the room.

"Katherine looks exhausted, Edmund," he said quietly. Beau walked over to the table and picked up his cup, dropping onto the settle and taking a swallow of the fine white Rhenish wine that was such a favourite of Warwick's.

"Yes," he said and then grinned. "She is tired, but it is only to be expected I suppose."

Warwick nodded and said, "The journey you mean?" But Jack Beaufort's head jerked up and he looked at his brother closely, understanding dawning slowly in his deep brown eyes.

"You don't mean...?" he said softly, and Beau laughed and nodded.

"Yes. Katherine is with child."

Jack whooped noisily as Warwick blinked for a moment and then grinned broadly.

"Well, well," he laughed. "My congratulations lad; you didn't waste much time did you?" Beau shrugged but his smile was still broad and very happy.

"I am so pleased for you, Beau," Jack said softly, getting up and shaking Beau's hand vigorously, his eyes shining with pleasure. "When is the babe due?"

"August. Late on, I think."

"I still think it was foolish to bring her and even more so now I know this." Warwick shook his head, his lips pursed in admonishment.

"I could not leave her," Beau said simply, and left Warwick to make of that what he would. "And it is only our journey from the coast that has tired her. I can assure you she was full of life on the crossing, unlike the rest of us!"

Warwick laughed.

"She should have been born a lad," he said fondly and Beau grinned.

"I am damn glad she was not!" They all laughed and then Jack stretched, linking his hands over his head and flexing powerful shoulders.

"Actually, Beau, Gethin and I had thought we might go over to Southwark and come back in the morning if that is alright with you?" Beau grinned.

"Can you remember your way?"

"How could I ever forget?" Jack turned to Warwick and pulled a wry face. "I was taken for a night in the stews for my fourteenth birthday, courtesy of my brothers; after five minutes of it all being over before it had begun, I wondered what I was going to do for the rest of the night!"

Warwick laughed.

"We have all been there lad!" he said. "For the first two years of my active youth I did not even know the lass was supposed to enjoy it as well!"

"Are they?" Jack deadpanned. "Well you do learn something new each day, don't you!" Warwick and Beau laughed and Jack grinned at his brother. "I suppose you never suffered the same angst as the rest of us?"

"Of course I did." Beau shook his head, still laughing.

"Really?" Jack raised an ironic brow. "And there was me thinking you were always just good at everything."

"Oh, I can assure you I have had my moments of angst and ridicule!" Beau smiled. "And I was a slow starter; I was sixteen before I had my first woman and she told me I should come back when I had grown up and could last longer than it took for her to count to ten."

"But you have made up for it since!" His brother laughed, standing up as he did so and heading for the door.

"Perhaps, but my whoring days are over." Beau smiled at Warwick.

"Well, mine are not and tonight I intend to prove that tenfold. Adieu, gentlemen." Jack grinned and bowed briefly in the doorway, then chanting, "Bring on the Champion," he closed the door behind him. Beau shook his head.

"I have no idea who he takes after!" he said, slightly bewildered but as always amused by his brother's unfailing good humour. "It is certainly not my father or anyone else I know in my family!"

"He is a good lad though."

"Aye, the best." Beau put his cup down and leaned his head against the back of the settle, running slender fingers through his hair, pushing it back from his forehead. "I would not be without him." He stretched his long legs out towards the fire and closed his eyes contentedly in the warmth. "It is good to be back in London," he said quietly. "I did not realise how much I had missed it."

"What are your plans?"

"Well, I had thought to stay here for a few days if that is alright with you. You and I need to do some planning and I need to see the King and I also know Katherine would like to spend some time with you." He looked at Warwick from under half-closed lids. "Then I thought I would go and see whether we could count on Stafford. As he's wed to my cousin Meg, I had thought a family visit might be a good idea."

"A sound idea I would say." Warwick nodded. "And Katherine?"

"Please don't ask me to leave her with you, Richard, for I cannot." The gold eyes were still half closed, but wary "Or more to the point, I will not." Warwick nodded again.

"Alright," he said. "But will your cousin Margaret accept Katherine?"

"If she has grand plans for that lad of hers then she will accept whatever I ask of her!" He shrugged, it all seeming quite black and white to him. Meg could either like it or not and if she didn't then he would take Katherine elsewhere, but he would always remember his cousin's inhospitable attitude. "Anyway," Beau closed his eyes again and yawned, tiredness enveloping him slowly, "Meg is not the prig everyone thinks she is and Katherine will make sure she likes her. If there is one thing that your daughter can do, Richard, it is charm people and I suspect she gets that from you." He laughed softly, realising that near exhaustion and too much wine was loosening his reserve and he was in danger of revealing more of his self than he intended. Warwick laughed with him.

"I am going to Westminster in the morning to see the King and it would be good if you could join me. He is looking forward to you coming," he said, changing the subject.

"How is he?" Beau yawned again and then rubbed his face, before sitting up and lifting his cup to his lips in a bid to rouse his sluggish senses. Warwick nodded.

"He is well and enjoying being back at Westminster; he seems interested in government and what we are doing and has attended counsel meetings with some enthusiasm. He is also looking forward to seeing Edward, although I am not so sure that he feels the same about the Queen." He gave a quick smile and Beau's mouth quirked at one corner.

"They never were a match made in heaven," was all he said, uncertain himself of the odd relationship between his King and Queen. "Madame is still dawdling about coming here, but I think she realises that Edward will not be held back any longer. He is a man now and he wants to come home and claim his rights as heir to the throne."

"I could not believe it when that Woodville bitch had a son." Warwick made the word Woodville sound as if it burned his mouth. Beau smiled, shaking his head.

"If ever a man had great timing it has to be York." Somehow he could hold no rancour towards Edward of York's past luck, for it seemed to him that it had finally come to an end.

"Tell me about it." Warwick snorted in agreement. "His father claimed the crown to silence and then along comes Ned, just at the right time, and is king on the strength of one battle. Who would ever have thought it?"

"Well, we never believed it until it happened and therein lay our downfall." Beau shrugged. "But my boy is a king in the making and if we can get him here then he will charm London and they will not care whether York comes back or not."

"Your boy?" Warwick grinned and Beau's mouth curved up in a fond smile as he thought of the dark haired boy waiting to come to England.

"Yes, *my* boy. He is as dear to me as my own will be and he will win over London of that I am sure." He felt a surge of affection for his Prince.

Aye, London is the key. I can hold the north but London was ever Ned's." Warwick stretched his legs towards the fire, turning the soles of beautifully worked shoes toward the flame. "I have to say that your letter made me think, but it did not frighten me. I have always believed that I could defeat Ned on the battlefield."

"So have I, if I am given the chance." Beau stretched and rubbed his face hard once more. "Unless you ask me to do it now and then I would have to say that he could blow on me and I would fall down." Warwick grinned.

"You look fit to drop."

"I am." Beau laughed ruefully at his own exhaustion. "Ten years ago, even five years ago, I would have been with Jack in Southwark but right now all I want is a bed to sleep in."

"Comes to us all, lad, comes to us all." Warwick joined his laughter.

"And I think I need to find that bed now." He blinked rapidly. "This wine is strong and, coupled with my tiredness, has taken my head. I am sorry Richard but I am fit for nothing." He grinned. "I learned when I was with Louis that I am a lightweight when it comes to good wine."

"Aren't we all compared with Louis!" Warwick laughed again. "Get yourself to bed, lad, and I will see you in the morning. We will leave after breaking our fast." Beau got up and walked to the door before turning and looking at the older man for a moment.

"You do know that I cherish Katherine, don't you?" he said quietly. "She will want for nothing."

"Aye, I know."

"Goodnight, Richard."

"Goodnight, lad."

***

Richard Neville smiled and as the door closed, he leaned back in his chair and allowed himself a small moment of triumph. Somerset loved his daughter, his daughter was happy and Somerset was beholden to him; how much better could life get?

London
February 1470

"Where is my Lady?" Alice Halston, newly appointed chamber woman to the Lady Katherine Neville swung round at the sound of the man's voice behind her, dropping a deep curtsey at sight of the Duke of Somerset striding across the hall.

"She is resting, your Grace," she said as she came back to her feet, looking up at him through light lashes, trying to look sophisticated and flirtatious at the same time.

"In the solar?" He barely looked at her, already making his way towards the next set of stairs.

"No, your Grace. She took to her bed." Beau stopped and looked back. "Is she alright?"

"Yes, your Grace. She was just tired after our visit to the cloth market and decided, as you were still at Westminster, that she would rest until you returned." She smiled at him shyly, very much in awe of this handsome, dark haired man who was her mistress's paramour.

"Did she now?" He gave a grin which made her stomach flutter and, turning again, made for the stairs, Alice trotting after him uncertainly.

"You cannot wake her, my Lord," she said sharply and he laughed.

"I think you will find I can." He began to unlace his tunic as he climbed the stairs, shrugging it off and catching it at the collar, unbuckling his sword belt in one movement with his other hand. In the absence of Gethin at his side, he threw both to the girl who caught them and staggered slightly under the weight. He opened the bedchamber door quietly and gestured to the girl to put his things down on a nearby coffer as he pulled his shirt over his head and dropped that on a chair next to him. Alice blushed, realising that he planned to join her Lady

327

in bed yet unable to take her eyes off his exposed chest, her cheeks flaming as she stared at him through downcast lashes.

"Your Grace, it is four in the afternoon!" she whispered furiously, and he laughed softly, at the same time unfastening his chausses and stepping out of them and his boots so that he stood only in his braies. Alice was caught between a natural moral horror that he should think of bedding her Lady at this hour and pure green envy that her Lady should be so lucky. She had dropped her eyes as soon as he had removed his chausses but she was still aware of the broadness of his chest and the muscles rippling across his stomach.

"That will be all thank you, Alice," he said in an amused voice and glancing at him she realised that he knew what she was thinking. She blushed to the roots of her hair, scarlet this time as he winked at her before discarding his braies and disappearing into the curtains around the bed in one fluid movement. Alice stared at the bed for a moment and then slipped out of the room, closing the door quietly behind her.

***

Beau slid across the cool sheets and curled himself around Kate's sleeping form, his mouth at her neck, smiling as she stirred and sighed.

"You will have to be quick sir, for my Lord Duke will be here any moment and he will be dismayed to find you in my bed," she murmured sleepily and he laughed quietly.

"Dismayed?" he whispered against her neck. "Christ, I'd be devastated!"

"I missed you this morning." She turned in his arms and slid hers around his neck, her mouth meeting his in a welcoming kiss.

"I did not want to wake you." He punctuated his words with more kisses. "Dawn had not yet come when I left." His hand slid down her back and pulled her hips into him, luxuriating in the feel of her warm skin on his.

"I see you have come fully armed," she murmured, sliding long white fingers into his hair and looking at him with warm caressing eyes. "Lance at the ready." He laughed again.

"My lance was at the ready the minute that your Alice told me you were abed." He surged with tenderness as he kissed her, at first softly and then longer and harder. "I cannot get enough of you."

"I hope that never changes." She smiled against his mouth and pressed herself closer.

"It will not." He tracked gentle kisses down her throat as she caught her breath and dug her nails into his shoulder, arousing his own need further.

"Not even when I am fat?"

"Are you planning on getting fat then?" He pulled his head up from its travel downwards and looked at her, his eyes laughing.

"I expect this will make me fat." She put his hand on her stomach which was still, as far as he could tell, completely flat. An image of her with a big, ripe, rounded belly came into his mind and desire surged through him.

"I can't wait for you to be fat," he murmured, claiming her mouth hotly. "I will not be able to keep my hands off you."

"Truly?" She slid her hand down his body in a soft caress, and he caught his breath sharply, need coursing through his loins so that he pressed hard into her.

"Truly," he said, his eyes half closed with pleasure.

"You must be the only man I have met who thinks a pregnant woman is desirable."

"Not any woman, darling, but you will be. I cannot think of anything more beautiful than you, big with my child, sat astride me." He hissed another breath and pulled her into him, shifting her hips slightly so that he entered her and she gasped, her body melting into his. He loved the fact that she held the power when they made love; the way she responded drove how he performed. If she whispered softly how much she loved him, he was tender and loving, if she moaned and called his name, he was hot and passionate, but if she scored his skin with her nails and cried out then he could not hold onto his control and would come to his pleasure quickly, gasping her name. There was nothing for him now except her and his need for her, and this time he fed his need with hers until they came together, panting hard, their bodies slick with sweat.

"Did I ever tell you?" he asked much later, as he lay on the bed, cup of wine on his chest, his head in her lap, "About what happened to me that day that you walked into the hall at Angers with your sisters and stepmother?"

"No, why what happened to you?" Her hand was soft as she stroked his hair, smoothing his long fringe away from his eyes with gentle fingers. He kissed the curve of her left thigh through the linen sheet.

"You took my breath away." He shifted his head and looked up at her with a smile. "You completely ensnared me as you walked towards the dais, you were a real life, flesh-and-blood vision of my perfect woman and I could not believe my eyes; an instant hard-on." He laughed softly and she pulled his hair, smiling all the same. "And then when you winked at me in the solar, apart from being very aroused by your mischief, I realised that there was much more to you than just beauty and I was suddenly intrigued. That was a first for me, to be intrigued by a woman; I'd only ever been interested in bedding them before." He kissed her thigh again. "But I still had not quite lost my heart."

"When did you lose your heart?" She ran her finger along a crease in his forehead before slipping it back into the silkiness of his hair.

"That night I came and found you when your mare broke her leg, as you sat in a pool of blood with a knife in your hand and matter-of-factly told me that you had cut her throat, as your cousin had shown you, and then held her head while she died. You were such a mixture of spirit and sweetness, bloodied but not bowed by your adventure and then, holding you in my arms as we rode back to Angers, I realised that I was completely lost. When we got back to the castle I told Jack that I had fallen in love with you and he thought it was very funny that at my age, having never cared a jot before, I should suddenly find myself smitten." He caught her hand and kissed her palm. "How I kept my hands off you for so long I will never know, especially after that first kiss in Hercules' stable. I thought my heart would leap out of my chest and that you must be able to see it beating!"

"You just seemed really calm and cool to me; the great seducer." She laughed softly. "I felt like such a child and I could not imagine that such a handsome and worldly man would want a girl like me." He pressed her palm against his lips once more, his mouth soft against the smooth white skin.

"As always, you undervalue yourself, darling." He looked up at the bed canopy embroidered with the Bear and Ragged Staff with a kind of wonder. "But I have to admit I sometimes cannot believe it myself. Here I am in Warwick's house, in Warwick's bed, with Warwick's most beautiful daughter." He laughed shortly and Kate slid down the bed so that her face was level with his, looking down at him.

"You don't regret it, do you?" Her eyes looked very green all of a sudden. "You don't regret us?"

"Dear God, no!" he said vehemently, reaching out and stroking her face. "I was just thinking how strange life, or God, or whoever makes these decisions, was that you should suddenly come along and give my life a purpose. I have had nothing for so long and now I have everything I could ever want; I have to pinch myself often to just to make sure." He laughed again as, smiling, she leaned forward and kissed him lingeringly on the lips.

"I never expected you to be like this," she said, her eyes soft.

"Like what?"

"So tender."

"You did not think I could be tender?" He was surprised when she shook her head. "Do I seem so harsh then?"

"No, not harsh, but hard; yours is not a light-hearted face."

"You have said that before and I don't know whether to be offended or think it is a good thing!" He was laughing again, as he did so often when he was with her. She made him feel light at heart and gave him a sense of peace that he had never experienced before. She grinned.

"When I saw you in the solar..."

"Not in the hall?" He was disappointed that she had not noticed him immediately.

I didn't see anyone in the hall. I felt sick that papa was making me meet the Queen. I had hoped that I could stay in the tower room and not come to the hall at all so I did not look at anyone. So, it was the solar when I saw you, when Bel pointed you out and I thought you were very, very handsome but there was nothing soft about you, not like there is when we are alone together." She kissed him again. "I just never expected you to cherish me like you do."

"You think I'm soft?" He arched a brow, watching her lovely face dissolve into laughter, desire flooding through him at the warmth of her sultry beauty, her russett hair surrounding her in a wild tangle of curls, her eyes dancing mischievously.

"As warm butter." She giggled as he grabbed her and rolled her onto her back, marvelling that his need for her just seemed to grow and grow, not diminish as it had with other women in his life.

"Does that feel soft to you?" He pressed himself against her and she laughed harder.

"Like I said," she murmured, her eyes taking on a smoky haze, "Hard not harsh." She slid her arms around his neck, drawing him down and into her, their bodies merging with sighs of pleasure just as there was a loud knock on the door and it swung open. Aware that he had not closed the curtain when he had got back into bed earlier, Beau moved swiftly as Kate squealed at her exposure, pulling her closer into his body so that he shielded her from the door with his naked back view.

"For fuck's sake!" he snapped and heard Jack's deep but embarrassed laugh.

"Oops, sorry!" The door closed again.

"Do we never get any peace!" Beau growled angrily, rolling onto his back and then sitting up and looking down at her. "Bollocks!" he said with heartfelt regret "I had better see what he wants."

Kate sighed, leaning over and grabbing her chemise off the floor and slipping it over her head. "It's alright, stay there darling." He kissed her cheek softly and then her mouth before getting up and pulling on his braies, grabbing his shirt and slipping it over his head. He smiled at her as he dragged one curtain closed and moued a kiss. "Do you want anything?" he asked and laughed when she raised an eyebrow and looked suggestively at his groin. "Later, darling, I promise."

"Just my underdress then please," she said, pouting with not entirely mock disappointment. Still grinning, he passed it to her and then pulled the other curtain, ensuring her privacy as she dressed, while he went to the door and had a brief murmured conversation with Jack, laughing ruefully and without rancour at his brother's teasing at having caught him abed at this hour of the day; She was emerging through the curtains, shaking out her hip-length hair just as he came back into the room rolling his eyes at her.

"You will like this!" he said, grinning. "Your father is on his way with 'a few friends' and has sent Jack ahead to tell you to prepare the kitchen." He started laughing as he delivered the blow. "He will be here within the hour!"

***

Later, after supper had been cleared away and the trestles moved to the side of the hall, and groups had formed as musicians played quietly,

Beau watched Kate laughing with her uncles John and George Neville, and felt a huge sense of pride that she had made it all seem so easy. None would have guessed the frantic activity which had followed his news as she had greeted guests, calm and serene, in the green gown that she had worn at Jurvadeil. Pages waited with warm hippocras as guests tumbled off barges; supper a fine feast of roasted pig and plump partridges in saffron and nutmeg sauces with delightful little almond custard puddings and soft honeyed pears to follow, all served with finest of white Rhennish and rich red Burgundy wines. And now here she was, the hostess in her natural habitat, working the room, making sure all the guests had what they wanted, easy and assured, at least on the surface, and very much Warwick's daughter. He kept thinking that he could not love her any more than he already did and yet every day, with her self-assurance growing all the time that they were together, she did something which made his heart overflow, and every day he wanted to shout his pride in her from the rooftops; he was already tired of the decorum necessary to protect her reputation.

"Hey." Jack's voice was soft at his side.

"Hey." Beau greeted his brother equally softly.

"Do you know all these people?"

"No." Beau smiled. "The Scropes, I know," he said, nodding towards a woman in her late twenties talking animatedly to a stocky dark haired man. "Alison is warden of Madame Woodville at the moment, and John is Warwick's man; John Neville and his Lady I have met at court and George Neville; obviously I know Pembroke, Oxford and Clarence and I think that tall lad over there is Francis Lovell, Warwick's ward, but the rest are unfamiliar to me."

"I feel like an outsider."

"I am afraid we both are, lad, if we are honest."

"I suppose." Jack looked at his brother. "Are you alright; you looked a bit pre-occupied before I came over."

"Yes I'm fine. I was just thinking, that's all."

"Anything important?" Jack's voice was light but his eyes were interested.

"I was thinking of the future." Beau gave him an oblique look.

"Ours or yours?"

"Both."

"And?"

"We need to find you an heiress."

"Great!" Jack grinned. "A fine-looking wench, as well as one with lands and titles please."

"I'll do my best!" Beau laughed.

"In fact, if I could have Isabel Neville…" Jack's voice was soft and self-deprecating but had a wistful edge.

"You'd have to kill Clarence first," Beau countered, equally lowly.

"I think I could manage that!" They exchanged identical smiles.

"I am sure you could," Beau said dryly.

"What about you?"

"I need to wed too." He glanced across at Kate again.

"Ah Beau, not yet; you'll break her heart." Jack followed his brother's gaze across the room, his expression soft, and Beau smiled. He knew that Jack liked Kate; he was as protective of her as a brother and could not bear the thought of her being hurt.

"Not if it is her that I wed." His voice was very low as he leaned back against the wall, and glanced at Jack again, unable to stop his mouth curving upward at the younger man's slightly stunned expression. "I got Harry's permission this morning."

"To wed?"

"To wed Katherine."

"I see." Jack's voice was flat and expressionless.

"You disapprove?" Beau looked at him, arching a brow defensively, always surprised when his brother was anything other than compliant.

"It is not for me to disapprove." Jack glanced at the girl again and then back at his brother. "It's just…"

"Just what?" Beau's brows rose higher and he folded his arms across his chest in an unconscious gesture of protection.

"She's not quite the heiress you were talking about, is she?"

"No," Beau agreed. "And I know to marry for love is a wild and stupid idea and that if papa was here he would tan my hide for even thinking it, thirty-one or not, but it makes perfect sense to me. She is the only one who was ever quickened with my child, she comes from a house as old as ours and I already have an heir on the way. Anyway I just cannot contemplate being wed to someone else when all I want to do is be with Katherine."

"Getting wed would not stop that."

"I know." Beau shrugged. "I know all the arguments, lad, and I have talked myself through all of them, time and again, but somehow I am not managing to convince myself."

"Have you talked to Warwick?"

"No, not yet."

"But you will?" It was a statement rather than a question but Beau chose to answer it.

"Yes," he said quietly, looking once again at the girl who had so captured him.

"Dear God he will be like a cat that has got the cream!" Jack shook his head in wonderment. "When do you plan to talk to him?"

"I don't know." Beau shrugged again. "When I am ready; he is hardly going to say no, is he?"

"True."

"So?"

"So...I don't know what to say." Jack shook his head again, smiling faintly. "There is no point in saying think about it, is there?" His smile widened and Beau grinned.

"No. I have made up my mind." He cocked his head to one side appealingly. "Do you think you could look past the sheer madness of this and be happy for me?"

"Christ, Beau, of course I could!" Jack laughed suddenly. "But you are right, I do think it is sheer madness!"

"Perhaps, or perhaps I am sane and all the rest of the world is mad." Beau's mouth curved upward softly, lightening his face. "I want her Jack, more than anything I have ever wanted in my life, and though she has never said aught to me about the babe being a bastard, I want to give her the gift of our child being born in wedlock. But most of all I want to spend the rest of my life with her."

"Then go ahead, I say." Jack laid his hand on his brother's shoulder.

"Even though the child she carries will replace you as my heir?" Beau looked at him levelly.

"I am the third son, remember, little Jonny Lackland who until recently had nothing. Now I am Marquis of Dorset, I am likely to marry an heiress and am making my own way in life. So grateful though I am for all you have done for me, I do not need to ride on your cloak hem anymore." Jack squeezed the shoulder he clasped, meeting Beau's golden gaze with his brown one. Beau felt tears sting his eyes as he looked at his brother, suddenly very grateful for the unconditional support and affection that the lad gave him, and then he smiled.

"Thanks Jack." The words were heartfelt and Jack squeezed his shoulder again, and Beau felt, not for the first time, like Jack was the sensible older brother.

London
March 1471

"You two look mightily pleased with yourselves!" Kate said waspishly, looking at each of them from the doorway of the solar, her arms wrapped round a basket of linens. Beau and her father exchanged glances and grinned.

"Do we?" her father asked, his expression a picture of schooled innocence. "Can't imagine why!" Warwick hauled himself off the cushioned settle as he spoke and stretched, before taking the basket from his daughter and carrying it to the trestle, looking regretfully at the fire as he did so. "Well, I suppose I should be off to Jack's for supper. What are you two up to this evening?"

"Well, Gethin and my brother have gone out for the night and I have given Alice leave to visit her mother before we depart tomorrow so I think Katherine and I will enjoy a peaceful and quiet supper here." Beau smiled. "I have some letters from France to read, and some to write before we leave tomorrow." He smiled at Kate as she sat on the settle her father had vacated and stretched her slippered feet towards the fire. "Are we packed?"

"Just about," she said shortly.

"What's the matter?"

"Papa's precious Florin has managed to get into our chamber." She glared at her father as she spoke. "And has chewed a hole in one of my riding boots so now I will have to wear the other pair and they rub my toes." She sighed, feeling suddenly very tired, something that had started to afflict her as she neared the middle of the fourth month of her pregnancy.

336

"Time for me to make a swift exit, I think." Warwick had the good grace to look sheepish as he leaned and kissed his daughter's cheek. "What time are you leaving on the morrow?"

"After we have broken our fast, I should think." Beau stood up, also stretching long limbs and, unlacing his tunic, shrugged it off and hung it over the back of a chair by the trestle. He reached inside the pocket and pulled out some sealed letters and then kicked some of the large floor cushions towards the settle. "It should not take us more than four days to get there now that the bad weather has broken." He flicked one of the cushions with a soft, leather encased toe and then sat down, leaning his back against the wood, smiling up at Kate as he did so.

"Well make sure you wake me if I am not up." Warwick took his cue to leave. "I will see you in the morning."

"Goodnight, papa."

"Goodnight, sweetheart;" He nodded his head at the younger man. "Beau."

"Goodnight Richard." The door closed and Kate slid her hand into Beau's hair, jerking his head back none too gently.

"Beau?" she said, raising her eyebrows and he laughed.

"They all call me it in the end," was all he said.

"You two are up to something." Her annoyance dissipated at the thought of the two men she loved most, and how their relationship had gone from strength to strength, and she smiled. "I'm glad you get on together, though."

"So am I." He took advantage of her relaxed grip and sorted through the letters as he spoke.

"It could have been awful." She grimaced at the thought of the consequences if they had not forged a friendship.

"Mmmm."

"I mean, can you imagine if you had hated each other."

"Mmmm."

"Are you actually listening to me?"

"No." He laughed as she tugged at his hair and pulled out a thick sealed packet, handing it to her with a smile. "This is for you."

"Me?" She took the letter and stared at it, anticipation fluttering in her stomach. "Are these from France?"

"Yes." His smile widened. "Now give me a kiss and then shut up and read your letter while I read mine." She laughed and, leaning forward, kissed him, deliberately deepening the kiss before he could pull away, her tongue capturing his, smiling inwardly as she heard his breath quicken. She drew away, laughing down into his upturned face.

"Like that?"

"Do you think anyone has ever made love in this solar?" he asked huskily, his eyes luminous as they looked up at her.

"I doubt it!" She giggled. "There was not that kind of love in this household. Even if there had been, I cannot imagine for one moment that ma mère would...perish the thought!" She shuddered in not entirely mock horror and then laughed again.

"Well, there will be that kind of love in our household, I can promise you that much." He took her hand and kissed the palm softly. "Now read your letter." They read in companionable silence, her hand inside his shirt, toying with the hair on his chest, peaceful contentment filling her and seeming to fill the room as he leaned against the wooden base, scanning through a number of messages from his Queen and Prince.

"Maman says that progress is still slow," she said after a while, scanning her mother's neat hand for more information.

"Mmmm?" He glanced up from his own missive.

"The Queen is not making much effort to speed up packing."

"Edward says as much here." Beau caught the inside of his lip in his teeth for a moment. "I need to get them to see it is urgent. My man in Burgundy says that York is moving fast." He shook his head. "I just don't understand it!"

"What do you mean?" She caught his chin and gently tilted his head back so that she could see his face.

"Well why would you make such haste if you didn't have an army at your back?"

"Because you think you can raise one when you get here?" She answered without hesitation, relishing that he valued her view on all aspects of his life, even his political one.

"Or you already have one waiting." He frowned and looked back at his letter. "Something is definitely not right with this."

"Surely papa would know if there was anybody raising men here?"

"Unless they were raising them for Lancaster with a plan to turn coat." He stood up and went to the door, speaking in a low voice to the lad who stood outside, before coming back and putting his papers on the trestle. "Like Trollope did at Ludlow in sixty."

"Who?" She vaguely recognised the name, sure that her father had mentioned it once.

"Before your time darling, but Andrew Trollope was one of my brother's cuckoos in the York nest who raised men for York and then turned coat in the middle of the night and took them with him. He was the reason we were able to drive Richard of York out of Ludlow." He shuffled through his papers as he spoke and the memory came back to her. Her father had mentioned Andrew Trollope when Ned had been staying with them at Middleham. It had been one of those shared memories that had been all the more poignant because of the deterioration of their alliance. She shuddered involuntarily.

"Jesu', that could be any one of papa's allies if that was the case: my Lord Wenlock, he was always for Ned; my cousin George, uncle Jack and uncle George have never been on any side except York; my Lord Northumberland...well, no one really knows about him, do they?" She shook her head.

"My money would be on cousin George!" He snorted derisively.

"That's because you don't like him!" She felt compelled to defend her sister's husband but it was only half hearted.

"Maybe, but you also have to consider that it will not be easy for him to take to the field against his own brother." He kicked back the bench and sat down, sorting his papers into order. "I'm damn sure I couldn't." There was a knock at the door and a pale face looked around it. "Come in." Beau smiled briefly at the face and beckoned it forward. "I need you to scribe some letters for me." The young man came into the room nervously and Kate recognised him as one of her father's under-secretaries, still learning his trade.

"My Lord." He bowed to Beau and then to her. "My Lady."

"Before you start, Peter, you wouldn't pass me that basket of linens, would you?" she asked, giving him her best smile and winning herself a lifelong admirer for both the smile and the fact that she remembered his name.

"Of course, my Lady."

"Are those shirts?" Beau craned his neck to see what she was doing.

"They will be when I have finished the final stitching. I've been making them while you were at court." She smiled at him.

"But you hate needlework." He looked surprised.

"I know." Her smile widened. "It must be a measure of my regard for you."

"Then I will have to thank the Earl of Warwick for the care his daughter has shown me these last weeks." His voice throbbed with warmth as he grinned back and the young man at the trestle blushed and stared intently at the paper in front of him.

For a while the room was filled only with the sound of Beau's quiet voice and the scratching of Peter's pen, as he dictated responses to his letters and sent out some messages of his own. Katherine sat under the oil lamp by the fire, her needle flicking in and out of the linen, her stitch-work exquisite, a warm feeling of contentment flowing through her at the unexpected domesticity of these last few days at the Herber. It had been a delight spending this time with him entertaining his allies, or having quiet suppers with her father and her uncles in the evening, warm in the knowledge that later in bed he would tell her about his day and they would talk for a while before falling asleep, his long frame curled around her. Sleep would always come for him first and she would lay there, listening to the sound of his soft, rhythmic breathing, enjoying the peace of having him all to herself for those precious hours before dawn. Yesterday she had woken early and found him sprawled away from her on his stomach, the covers across his hips, the cresset shining softly on his broad shoulders and narrow waist, and she had been overcome with sudden lust, hot and liquid in her loins. Tentatively she had caressed and kissed him into wakefulness, until he had rolled over, taking her with an urgency that made her stomach lurch, just thinking about it, and which characterised their relationship. Suppressed as it had been by expected propriety, the depth of her lustful nature had been a revelation to her, and a delight to Beau, who shamelessly encouraged her to express her need for him, and to discard any inhibition she might have. She wondered if the kind of passion they shared could last forever or if it would settle into something less, the more time they spent together. She shivered suddenly, not wanting to think too much about the future and the uncertainty before them, and, biting off the last piece of thread from her needle, admired her handiwork in the light of the torch above her.

"I think I am done, Master Lownes." Beau said, just as there was another knock on the door and two young lads appeared carrying supper trays. "I will finish this last one in my own hand." The young scribe stood, picking up the tools of his trade and leaving Beau to drip wax onto his missives and seal them with his ducal signet, smiled at Katherine and bowed his way out of the door, hot on the heels of the supper bearers.

"I hope you're not adding love notes." Kate lifted the cover off the first tray and inspected its contents of bread and cold guinea fowl, her face a picture of studied innocence. Beau grinned.

"What, to Edward?"

"I'll let you off then." She grinned back and then lifted the cover on the second tray on which was a pile of dried figs and hot cheese wafers. She put two on a pewter plate and pushed them across the trestle and then poured him a cup of wine from a new jug. Taking it round the table she slid her arms around his neck as she placed it beside him, kissing the corner of his mouth. "What happened to your necklace?"

"Hmmm?" He put his hand up to his throat. "Oh, I broke it this morning. Gethin's supposed to have found me a new one but must have forgotten." He looked up at her, his head against her shoulder. "Are you going to show me my new shirts?"

"I thought you would prefer to finish your letter." She kissed him again. "You can try them on if you like." She withdrew her arms and went back to the tray, picking up a cheese wafer and biting into it. "But I made them to the exact pattern of the one you wear now so they should fit." He stood up and went over to the basket, lifting out the garment and holding it up to the light. He made a soft sound of appreciation in his throat and looked over his shoulder.

"How many did you make?"

"Three." She smiled proudly, knowing that he would appreciate them more for the fact that she hated embroidery.

"They are exquisitely worked." He looked back at the fine linen, obviously touched that she should have spent so much time doing something she disliked just for him.

"Look at the left wrist," she said, coming up behind him. He took the sleeve and examined it, his expression softening and a smile curving his lips at the intertwined K and B, stitched in plain white thread, noticeable only to any who knew it was there.

"Now you will always be with me," he murmured and turning, took her in his arms and held her close. "I have so enjoyed the time we have had together these last weeks, but especially these few days here in London."

"I know. It's felt almost like our own home." Her voice was muffled against his chest.

"This is how it should be." He kissed the top of her head and she felt his heart pick up pace until it was hammering a fast rhythm against her ear. "Katherine…" She tilted her head back and looked up at him, puzzled by his sudden tension.

"What is it?" she asked softy.

"Do you remember when I told you that one day you would understand how much I love you?" He cupped her cheek with his palm, his eyes liquid gold tenderness. "And that you would learn to trust my love?"

"Yes," she whispered, her heart surging with uncertain anticipation. "At Angers…in the wardrobe…when I told you about…"

"My child." He ran his thumb over her cheekbone, his mouth curving up at the corners. "I had come to accept that I would never have children of my own, convincing myself that I didn't need that kind of responsibility, then suddenly I have the woman of my dreams and now I am to be a father in less than half a year." He kissed her gently. "You have given me the greatest of gifts."

"I think you might have had something to do with it." She smiled but his expression did not change and he kissed her again, refusing to let go of the intimacy of the moment.

"Now I want to give you a gift," he said quietly, his eyes black with intensity.

"You have given me so much already…" She took the hand at his cheek and kissed it.

"This one is worthy of you." He caught her face in both his hands. "Marry me, Katherine."

"What?" Her voice was little more than a whisper as she stared at him; she wasn't sure what she had expected but it wasn't this.

"Marry me." He let go of her face and dropped to his knees, catching hold of both her hands and laughing up at her, his eyes sparkling. "Be my helpmeet, my wife, my Duchess." He pressed his lips to the back of her hand.

"Beau..." She shook her head, her heart hammering in her breast, the words he spoke making no sense, and he laughed again.

"I have the King's permission and your father's." He slipped his hand inside his shirt and took out his mother's betrothal ring, holding it out to her. "Say yes, Katherine. Just say yes. Please!" She hesitated still and he looked crestfallen. "You would like to be my wife, wouldn't you?"

"Oh God, yes!" The words burst from her spontaneously and his face cleared as he jumped to his feet and lifted her off the floor, swinging her round before kissing her heartily.

"So?" He set her down and grinned.

"Yes!" She laughed up at him, swept by euphoria and bursting with love. "Yes, yes, yes, I will marry you!"

"Give me your hand." He held out the ring, boyish and beautiful in his joy, and suddenly tears filled her eyes.

"Oh Beau," she whispered as she held out her hand and he slipped the ring onto her finger. He smiled and took her hand in both of his.

"I, Edmund, plight thee, Katherine, my troth, as God is my witness." He kissed the ring and her tears spilled onto her cheeks.

"I have nothing to give you," she whispered.

"It doesn't matter." He shook his head. "Just say it."

"It matters to me."

"Just say it darling. Please." He laced his fingers through hers.

"I, Katherine, plight thee, Edmund, my troth, as God is my witness." And taking a ribbon from the neck of her gown, she wound it around his wrist. "Until I have a ring for you."

"We will do it properly in front of witnesses once this is all over, I promise." He kissed her. "And we will have a proper court wedding with the King and Queen in attendance and a fine London house so I can keep you close."

"I don't care." She slipped her arms around his neck and slid her fingers into the hair at his nape. "None of that matters to me." She touched her lips to his. "I would marry you in a cow byre and live with you in a stable if you asked it of me."

"Would you?" He laughed softly and pulled her close. "Well let's just hope I don't have to hold you to that."

London
March 1471

The pale March sun shone softly on the murky waters of the Thames, catching the ripples and making them dance in the gentle spring breeze as the stream of small vessels continued their relentless parade up and down the great waterway. Richard Neville stared out at them, unseeing, wishing he could keep his mind on the task that was so important to him, but he could not and for once in his life he gave in to his weakness and took the letter from his belt and read it again. He missed Veronique, more than he had thought he would and especially since Kate had been home. Suddenly domestic bliss with a woman he loved and a nursery full of children seemed more than appealing against the constant uncertainty and acrimonious relationships he now endured.

For almost six months he had been in England, his elation at so easily removing Ned quickly deflated by Marguerite's constant prevarication over sending Edward to rally the people to his banner and her refusal to come and place herself at her husband's side. Harry of Lancaster had been given a decidedly lukewarm reception by the people of London, which was not surprising since Ned had always been their favourite son, yet with a little careful manipulation and the flaunting of a young, handsome successor and his pretty little wife, he could have them eating out of his hand. But without Edward, he could not do it, and it seemed that the young man was still loathe to gainsay his mother, or to step openly from behind her apron strings and show his independence. He had had high hopes when Louis had first persuaded Marguerite to come to terms with him, and then had induced her to wed the boy to his daughter. But even with Anne now firmly installed as Princess of Wales, should the boy ever some to England that was, his position did not seem any more stable than it had been at the beginning. Pembroke and Oxford watched his actions with gravest suspicion, and while they could not deny he had a valid point of grievance against their Queen, they could also understand the Lady's reluctance to place her beloved child into the hands of a man who had once been her greatest enemy. He sighed bitterly and refolded the letter in his hand, tucking it back into the tightly cinched belt of his tunic, absently smoothing out the folds of the rich fabric as he did so.

"You are preoccupied today, Rich; what's the matter?" enquired a melodious voice behind him. He smiled and turned slowly, meeting the hazel eyes of his youngest brother, George, the Archbishop of York, and shrugging a little self-consciously.

"Nothing much that has any bearing on what is happening before us, except that I wish Madame would hurry up and make up her mind about leaving France. I have come to the conclusion that she would prefer exile to the chance of seeing that boy of hers become a man. Thank God Louis insisted on a marriage consummation, otherwise she would have been there to pluck him out of bed before his precious maidenhead could be violated!" George Neville laughed at his brother's exasperation, but Warwick knew that he too was aware that their state of affairs could not continue in this state of limbo. Louis had been insistent that they raise an army to help France conquer Burgundy, which Warwick had been only too happy to do in the hope that Ned might be captured and taken out of the process. But then that dammed Woodville bitch had given birth to a son in sanctuary, ensuring Yorkist succession, which had altered Ned's precarious position. And now Charles of Burgundy had got wind of their plans and knew that he had to forsake his Lancastrian partiality or lose his duchy, which meant that Ned's position was strengthened still further, and they knew, from Somerset and his man in Burgundy, that he had been given some finance to help him return to England. Warwick was not altogether too perturbed about that as long as all his supporters remained loyal, but that could not be guaranteed, for it seemed young Clarence was keeping his own council, and their brother Jack was suffering severe guilt feelings about being the cause of his cousin and liege Lord's demise. Then there was dubious loyalty of Henry Percy, Earl of Northumbria, who owed the restoration of his earldom to Ned, not counting the rest of the Yorkist nobility who still sat in on Harry's Counsel. It all came down to a matter of timing. If Warwick could put off Ned's attack until Marguerite arrived with her whelp then they would have a far greater chance of victory than if Ned arrived before Marguerite and charmed his way back into the fickle affections of his people.

"Have you any word from Clarence, Rich?" George asked suddenly. Warwick gave a wry smile and shook his head, chestnut curls lightly flecked with Thevenot swinging as he did so.

"You know I have not, George. The boy skulks away from here, an army ready at his disposal, yet he gives me no indication which way he will go. In fact, I'd wager that even he is unsure who to fight for; after all, even though he knows there is little future for him in a Lancastrian kingdom, he could not bear to be constantly slighted by Ned and his upstart kin. It would have to be complete forgiveness or nothing for George."

"But will Ned be prepared to forgive him such treachery?"

"Ned will do anything to regain his crown, even to the extent of forgiving our George!" There was a small reluctant note of admiration in Warwick's quiet tones as he pondered on the nature of their cousin Ned, and wondered afresh how they had ever managed to quarrel to such epic proportions. He was sure that Ned would give the same fond riposte if asked and yet when together all they seemed able to achieve was constant and bitter argument. He pushed the thought out of his mind, knowing there was no point in going over old ground. The situation had changed and they had to make the best of how it had become, for nothing was about to alter. "Damn Marguerite and her godforsaken prevarications." Warwick suddenly banged his fist down hard on a small table at his right, making his brother jump. "It would be so much easier if she was on English soil. I have petitioned Anne to attempt to persuade the boy to make his mother see that he is needed here, but judging by the reports I hear of them I think there is little hope of her persuading him to do anything he does not want to. It seems he likes her well enough but not enough to gainsay that bitch of a mother. If ever a man was plagued by his kin, it has to me!" His mind went back to Veronique's letter which told him everything he needed to know of his daughter's marriage to Edward of Lancaster. It was apparent that the boy had a lot of affection for Anne and liked her well enough but she would never have the influence over him that his mother had, and even if she had she would not have the sense to use it for her father. And Isabel was constantly at odds with her sister because of her jealousy that Anne was to have the honour she had thought was to be hers, and had more than once incurred Marguerite's wrath with her spoiled behaviour. He sighed heavily, thanking Christ that he had one child who loved him enough to cause him no trouble and had made an alliance which could only be of benefit, although the news from Beau had not been very positive. There was uncertainty around the commitment of Stafford, who needed much convincing to jeopardise his position and favour a cause which was still not tested, and Jasper Tudor was playing hard to get, setting conditions for his support to ensure his own position.

"Perhaps we will hear from France soon, Rich. It's foolish to concern ourselves until we know we have something to worry about." George Neville spoke consolingly in his priest's voice, catching Warwick's attention immediately and firing his famous temper.

"I don't need your bloody comforting manner, George, save that for the confessional!" he snapped. "What I do need is a constructive solution to our problem, not your condescending 'there, there don't worry' speech."

"I was just trying to help." The hurt was tangible in his brother's voice. "I think you worry yourself for nothing."

"Do you indeed?" Warwick's dark eyebrows shot up coolly "And what would you know about that?" He laughed unkindly. "If you had to fight to make them see that your way is far better than anything they can think up. If you knew that as soon as Harry is safely and without opponent on his throne they will be plotting the best way to be rid of you, you too would be induced to worry more than you do. Because fear not, George, if they plan to get me out of the way, you will not long survive me!"

"Aye, and you knew all that when you came to terms with Lancaster, Rich, that you cannot deny." George refused to be bullied by the anger in his brother's tone, knowing that it was Warwick's way of venting pent-up frustration.

"True enough, but I cared less then. I realise that I would quite like to stay alive and see my children and grandchildren grow up." Warwick's voice was quiet suddenly and George was startled out of his composure.

"Jesus God, Rich, that damned woman is addling your wits," he muttered, and Warwick grinned.

"Perhaps," he said softly, "But if that is so then I wish someone had addled them earlier. It would have saved me all this." Then he laughed bitterly. "It's alright George, don't look so horror struck, I am but teasing. I have no choice but to fight and I have not completely lost my hunger for what I can gain from all this. I see no reason if I can continue to command Somerset's friendship and Harry's ear, that any should be able to push me out of the way." He stopped and looked up as the heavy door opened and his young squire stood nervously on the threshold. "Yes, Rob, what is it?"

"My Lord, I found this on a trestle in the hall; just left there. It was not addressed to anyone, but I think it must be for you." He held out a letter nervously.

"What does it say, Rob?" Warwick raised a brow and the boy opened the parchment read quickly, and then looked up at his master, his eyes wide

"My Lord, it does say that Edward of York has landed at Ravenspur and that he has issued a proclamation laying claim to his duchy. He requested on landing that the citizens of York give him entry to the city." George Neville's face blanched visibly and Warwick, all humour jerked out of him, looked dumbly at his squire.

"Fucking hell!" he swore, when he could at last bring himself to speak. "So he has used Lancaster's trick!" The boy stared at him uncomprehendingly and Warwick pulled his emotions back under control. "Get me my secretary, Rob, I need to warn Somerset."

George Neville was watching his brother, his bright eyes veiled in sudden haunted realisation.

"Mother Mary, Rich, if the Frenchwoman and her brat don't get here soon, it will be Ned who rises from this the victor, and where will that leave us?" Warwick answered with a quick mirthless snort of laughter and an elegant shrug, his gaze fixed somewhere above the squire's head.

"I don't think there is any question of where that leaves us, do you?" he murmured softly and the Archbishop's already grey skin paled still further as he was unable to meet his brother's vivid emerald gaze. "Still, I'll have you beside me to administer last rites, won't I?" Warwick managed a rueful smile but George was muted by fear and could only turn his face away as the nausea rose into the back of his throat.

"I never thought I would hear myself say this, Rich," he whispered, "But I hope to Christ Marguerite does get here soon."

"So do I, George," Warwick answered softly. "So do I."

Chapter Twelve

Stafford, March 1471

"I think we can safely say the lad is never going to be a dancer." Harry Stafford laughed softly, glancing at his wife as he did so, and was rewarded with a rueful smile.

"Shut up, Harry." She gave him a good natured shove and he laughed again, his pale green eyes full of mirth as he watched the young woman taking the youth through the steps of the Basse she was trying to teach him.

"He's as stiff as a plank of wood, look at him," he chuckled.

"Must be Jasper's influence." Edmund Beaufort's husky tones interjected dryly and Harry gave him an appreciative grin.

"I told Meg she should keep the boy with us more but I think she thinks I am a poor influence on him, unlike good old upstanding uncle Jasper." He reached out and laid his hand over his wife's affectionately as he spoke, and she smiled again.

"With good reason it would seem after last night," she said, her stern expression belied by the laughter in her dark blue eyes. "Bringing him home after midnight, drunk as a rat, and the pair of you no better."

"A rite of passage when you're fourteen." Stafford winked at Beau.

"And what rite is it when you are four and twenty?"

"The rite of entertaining your wife's famous cousin." He moued a kiss at her. "Anyway, Beau and I were not drunk last night!"

"If you say so." Margaret Beaufort grinned, her little birdlike face lighting up, making her almost pretty. "Talking of which, if you will excuse me a moment, I must see to arrangements for supper." She left the dais and headed for the kitchen in a rustle of blue silk skirts. The two men watched the dancers for a moment and then Stafford snorted another laugh.

"Look at him, he's besotted," he said softly and Beau flicked a glance at him, amused.

"So am I." He deadpanned and the younger man shook his head in mock disappointment.

"I know and I was so looking forward to you coming after admiring your prowess from afar when I was a lad, newly-wed and not allowed off my leash. I thought this visit, at the very least, you might corrupt me." He sighed. "And now I find that you are tamed to the point that you didn't even notice the Danish girl in the tavern last night."

"What Danish girl?" Beau frowned trying to recollect the night before.

"I rest my case." Stafford sighed and shook his head sadly.

"I am a changed man." Beau grinned and Stafford laughed, both men's eyes drawn to the lovely girl in the centre of the hall.

"You're a lucky man, Beau." Stafford gave him a wry smile. "Don't get me wrong, I think the world of Meg but I'd have to be a saint not to envy you a little bit." He looked back at the boy dancing with Katherine Neville; his wife's son by her first marriage. "Thanks for bringing Henry back with you from Wales, Meg was thrilled."

"He wanted to come." Beau dragged his eyes back to the young, fair haired man next to him. "It's good you get on so well."

"I was prepared to do whatever makes Meg happy. You know how she dotes on the boy so I figured very early on that my way to her heart was to dote on him too." He flushed lightly and shrugged. "It seemed a wise philosophy to make the most of my marriage seeing as we were both so young when we wed. I'd rather live in amity with my wife than come home to a cold hearth."

"I must admit, a hearth of any sort never really appealed to me." Beau's eyes were drawn back to the girl like magnets. "Until now."

"There can be much pleasure in a warm hearth and a loving bedmate."

"Well, Meg seems content enough, I have to say."

"I have done my best to make her so."

"No sign of any babes of your own?"

"No." Stafford's eyes were wistful for a moment and then he shrugged. "Not for want of trying I might add, but if it hasn't happened after eight years, I can't see it happening now. Meg was so young when she had Henry; she doesn't speak of it but I think she had a very difficult time when he was born."

"I remember my father was furious when he found out she was with child; he thought Tudor had betrayed his position as her guardian, not only to wed her but to get her with child at twelve. None of us are squeamish but she was just a little girl." Beau shook his head in disgust.

"Why was your father not given her wardship?"

"Because familial Harry indulged his half-brothers shamelessly."

"King's prerogative, I suppose." Stafford shrugged.

"Indeed." Beau's expression was unreadable but Stafford had the distinct impression that he had said the wrong thing.

"Have you thought any more on what you will do now that York has laid claim to his duchy?" He changed the subject.

"I'm waiting to hear from Warwick." Beau yawned and rubbed his face tiredly with both hands, two days' stubble rasping against his palms. "I am expecting that he will hold London while I go to the south coast to meet Madame and Edward, if she ever gets herself over here." He puffed his cheeks out and leaned his head back on the wood of his chair. "If she had been here a week ago, we could have had York on the hind foot and back in Burgundy before he knew what had hit him."

"What happens when Madame lands in the south?"

"We head to London and Pembroke comes from Wales and we take York somewhere outside the city walls." He met the young man's pale gaze with an intense yellow one. "If everyone does what they have promised to do, we will outnumber him two to one at least."

"Well, we will have to see what we can do won't we." Stafford kept his gaze even, determined not to be intimidated by his wife's mercurial cousin. After a moment, Beau nodded almost imperceptibly.

"Thank you," he said at last. "That at least is a step in the right direction."

"Who do you fear?" Harry was interested in who Beau thought was the most likely to let him down.

"I don't fear anyone." Beau looked at him sharply and then sighed heavily. "But I am wary of Clarence, after all it can be no easy thing to take the field against your brother and his position with Lancaster is tenuous to say the least. I would add Montague to that except that I believe his love for Warwick is greater than his loyalty to York."

"I always liked Jack Neville." Meg's voice broke into their conversation as she retook her seat next to Stafford. "I thought he was much more genuine than either of his brothers, especially Warwick."

"I can't say I much liked any of the Nevilles and they didn't much like us Staffords either," Stafford muttered, his memory of the Neville brothers clouded by time and his father's opinions. "Always so proud of themselves especially Warwick's Countess; swanned about like a Queen."

"I like Warwick." Beau ignored Stafford's grumblings and smiled at Meg's disbelieving expression. "Once you get over his consummate political style then you can appreciate his qualities."

"It has nothing to do with the fact you are swiving his daughter then?" Meg raised a sardonic brow and Beau laughed at her crudity.

"No." He shook his head and glanced at Katherine, making sure she was still out of earshot. "It suits me to have him on my side but believe me, if I did not think he was necessary to our cause and an able commander and minister, I would have ensured that he was put out of the way as soon as he had driven York out of England." He cocked his head to one side. "And don't be so crude about the woman I adore. Anyway I thought you liked Katherine?"

"I do, she's lovely." Meg looked over at the girl patiently trying to coax her son through some more dance steps. "She's far too good for you. I can't believe she fell for your dubious charm or that she is the fruit of that man's loins."

"I tell you, he is alright." Beau smiled. "Anyway you can't blame the daughter for the sins of the father."

At that moment, as if aware they were talking about her, Kate looked up and smiled at Beau.

"My Lord," she called, beckoning him down from the dais. "Come and show Henry how to dance the full steps of this Basse." She came over to the dais, her smile softening at his hesitation. "Please." She pouted appealingly and then laughed with delight as he made to rise.

"Excuse me; my Lady commands." He gave his cousin and her husband a self-conscious shrug as he left his seat and stepped out onto the cleared floor, grinning at the young Henry as he did so. "Watch and learn, my boy," he said as he nodded to the musicians and took his place in front of Kate. The music started and they began to move fluidly across the floor, as graceful and rhythmic as cats, their hips brushing and their hands touching in time to the music as they followed the steps of the dance. The couple on the dais watched for a while, mesmerised, and then Meg leaned close to her husband.

"I wish I could dance like that," she murmured, her hand sliding over his thigh under the table.

"That's not dancing, that's fornication." Stafford snorted a laugh as he glanced at her sideways through fair lashes.

"Well I wish I could fornicate like that," Meg grinned, her voice softened with an underlying sensuality that marriage to this good looking man had unlocked.

"I'm game if you are?" Stafford caught her hand as it edged toward his groin, kissing her knuckle as he drew her to her feet. "To dance I mean." He met her eyes, his own gleaming with warmth. "Fornication comes later." Meg laughed and returned the look in full measure.

"I'll hold you to that," she said.

***

"Lady Katherine." The youth blushed furiously as he stepped in front of her to halt her progress across the hall.

"Yes, my Lord?" She smiled at him warmly, disregarding what could be deemed his lack of manners.

"I wanted to thank you for teaching me to dance the basse." Henry Tudor's intense cornflower blue eyes were the one feature he had taken from his father, the rest of his face being very clearly sculpted Beaufort. "I do not get much chance in my uncle Tudor's household."

"That's a shame. At Middleham we had dancing almost every night." Her smile broadened at the memory. "But then your uncle is not wed, is he?"

"No."

"So it is a soldiers' household?"

"Yes."

"No ladies?" She flashed him a glance under her lashes and he blushed again.

"Not the sort you would sup and dance with." The boy dropped his gaze but smiled and Kate laughed. He hesitated for a moment and then said shyly, "Would you care to play chequers with me, my Lady?" Kate grimaced a refusal and then relented.

"Alright, but I'm not very good. Beau...my Lord Somerset beats me every time I play him." She walked with him toward the fire where the pieces scattered on the chequered table. "He reckons that women do not have the brain for board games as they require strategy and we only think with our hearts not our heads. Every time I play I want to prove him wrong but unfortunately I always prove him right." She grimaced, ruefully this time, as she sat down on the low stool in front of the table, lifting her skirts around her.

"You just need to learn the right moves, Lady Katherine." The boy sat down opposite her and smiled, changing his face from its angular lines to an engaging softness which reminded her of Jack Beaufort. He would probably be quite handsome when he was older and had grown into his Beaufort nose, she thought.

"Kate," she said, returning his smile. "My family and my friends call me Kate."

"Kate." Henry's smile broadened with delight at their new familiarity. "In Wales I am Harri but in England I must be Henry or it gets too confusing with ma mèr being wed to my Lord Stafford."

"Harri. I like that." Kate imitated the Welsh inflection perfectly and Henry laughed, his youthful gaucheness falling away under her friendly overtures, and Kate smiled again, thinking he looked very different now to the shy, awkward youth who had arrived with Beau yesterday afternoon from Wales, drenched by the spring showers and very much in awe of the kinsman he was riding with. "Do you come to see your mother very often?"

"Once or twice a year for a month or so. Harry brings her to Wales sometimes to see me too." The boy laid the chequers out carefully, his eyes on the board, long fingers placing the circles with precision into the squares. "I was pleased to have the chance to come with my Lord Somerset for I have heard much about him."

"Had you not met him before then?" Kate was surprised for her own family was close knit and she had grown up with her cousins and visited aunts and uncles often.

"When I was very small but I cannot recall it." He looked at her then, his eyes very blue. "He and my uncle Jasper are very different."

"Yes they are." She bit back a smile at the obvious. "Have you spent all your life with my Lord Pembroke?"

"Pretty much. Maman was only thirteen when I was born and only fourteen when she wed Harry. She lived with his family until he was of an age for them to be man and wife, so she left me with uncle Jasper but she visited me often." He stared down at the board, turning a counter over in his hand. "He and my cousin of Somerset quarrelled the night before we left Wales and Somerset accused him of disloyalty to the King."

"Oh." Kate did not know what to say.

"Somerset is wrong, my Lady." He lifted his gaze once more, his expression earnest. "Uncle Jasper is cautious but he is not disloyal. I tried to tell my cousin that but I don't think he listened to me." A flush crept up his neck but he held her gaze. "When I told my Lord Stafford he suggested I speak with you. He said that my Lord Somerset might listen to you."

"Did he now?" Kate looked over at the dais to where Harry Stafford was seated next to his wife listening attentively, her expression unreadable.

"You are not offended that I have asked this, are you, my Lady?" The boy shifted in his seat uncomfortably. "I was not implying anything improper..."

"No Harri, I am not offended." She cut him off with a shake of her head, before he embarrassed both of them. It was all very well everyone knowing she was Beau's mistress, but it would not do to have it spoken publicly. "But I am not sure I can help."

"But he might listen to you, my Lady." The boy's eyes were pleading. "If you could but try...?"

"I won't add to his cares." Her voice was sharp and then she softened at his crestfallen expression. "Alright, alright. I will test the water and see what he says but I cannot promise anything."

"Thank you, my Lady." The lightening smile softened his face once more. "I will always remember your kindness to me and one day I will repay it."

"Well, you could let me win at chequers." She grinned and he laughed.

"I'm afraid I can't do that." He looked at the board and then back at her. "But I can teach you a few moves which might surprise my Lord Somerset next time you play him?" He held out his hand palm up and she tapped her own hand palm down over his.

"Agreed."

***

"Can you put a couple more logs on the fire please, Alice, I'm not sure what time my Lord will be up tonight and I don't want the chamber to be cold." Kate, sitting on a coffer, smiled at the girl as she tugged at the lace in her hair and shook out her braids.

"If last night is aught to go by, my Lady, he won't much care if it is cold." The girl gave her a pert look and Kate laughed.

"Yes, he was a little worse for wear, wasn't he?" She grinned at the memory. "I guess he alerted the whole household to the fact he was sleeping in my chamber." They had, for propriety's sake been given separate chambers, one above the other.

"I think, once he had walked into the piss pot and kicked it across the room, the whole household was awake. Men in their cups find it impossible to be quiet, no matter how hard they try!" Alice poked the fire vigorously before throwing on some sweet smelling applewood.

"Well, I don't think he will be tonight. He was most apologetic when he finally surfaced this morning." Kate ran her fingers systematically through her hair as she spoke, trying to free any tangles before she brushed it. "Anyway I can hardly fault him; I have known him for more than half a year and I have never seen him in his cups before."

"Men never show their true colours until they think they've snared you." Alice said morosely and Kate laughed again.

"You're so cynical, Alice."

"And you, my Lady, are in the first flush of love." Alice picked up her hairbrush and came to stand behind her, pulling Kate's hair back from her face before she began brushing it in long rhythmic strokes. "You will see in time that all men, even one such as my Lord Duke, have faults."

"I can assure you I am well aware of that." Kate was amused by the girl's impertinence. "But I would prefer to wait until he gives me cause before I judge him wanting." Alice said nothing further, working the brush through Kate's hair until it shone a dark burnished red.

"You have such lovely hair, my Lady," she said at last, laying the brush on the coffer.

"Thank you." Kate glanced up at her and smiled. "I used to hate it when I was a child; all I wanted was sleek fair hair like my sister Isabel.

356

My Lady stepmother used to curse my curls and wet them so she could drag them into tight braids because it was so unruly."

"Do you want me to braid it now, my Lady?"

"No, I don't think so, my Lord likes it loose." She blushed delicately but Alice made no comment. "You can unlace the back of my gown for me and my sleeves, though, if you would please." Kate leaned forward and lifted her hair so that the girl could undo the laces which criss-crossed up the back of her overdress. "Then, if you just light the oil lamp and the cresset, you can get yourself off to bed."

"Yes, my Lady."

Kate undressed slowly, folding her clothes and placing them in the coffer as she did so, while Alice pottered about lighting the oil lamp and turning down the bed. She touched the ring which nestled with the emerald heart between her breasts and smiled. Instinct had told her that they should bide their time and she had eventually got Beau to agree that they would tell no one of their betrothal until England was secure under a Lancastrian reign. It had been difficult to persuade him that this was for the best and she had only managed to do so when she had pointed out that the Duke of Somerset could not get betrothed in secret and that a proper betrothal ceremony with guests and celebrations would be expected of him before he made any announcement.

"Hey." His voice was soft behind her.

"Hey." She turned, smiling, her hair swirling about her chemise. "I thought you'd be ages yet."

"I made my excuses. You know the kind of thing; a late night last night; my age; the fact I need my beauty sleep." He smiled. "Whatever words it took to get me out of there and up here to you." He flicked a gesture of dismissal at Alice and then frowned when she looked first at Kate for confirmation before she curtseyed and slipped out of the door. "That girl's impertinent," he said as he watched the door close.

"Yes," Kate grinned and he laughed.

"Trust you to think that's a good thing." He unlaced the front of his tunic and dragged it over his head, tousling his hair appealingly. "Still, it's good she is loyal to you." He looked around for somewhere to put it and then smiled as she took it from him and hooked it on the wall hanger. "Come sit by the fire with me." He held out his hand.

"Let me get my robe." She made to turn but he stopped her, catching her hand and drawing her towards the roaring flames.

"You don't need it, I'll keep you warm." He dragged a stool closer to the chair already there with his foot and then sat down, pulling her towards him and onto his lap as he put his feet on the stool. "See?"

"Mmmm." She curled her legs up and nestled her head into his shoulder.

"I have missed you." He kissed the top of her head and rested his cheek on it, his arms tight around her. "Even more than I expected if I am honest."

"I've missed you, too." She wound the lace of his shirt around her finger. "It was strange being here without you."

"And I am sorry about last night, I didn't mean to get drunk. It was a lack of sleep, food and my pathetic head for wine that undid me."

"That's alright." She turned her face up and smiled at him but he shook his head.

"It was unforgiveable." He touched his lips to her forehead. "I should have been here with you, showing you how much I have missed you."

"I said I didn't mind, although I will say that next time you can sleep in your own chamber; you kept me awake half the night snoring." She nipped the skin of his throat with her teeth and he flinched, laughing ruefully.

"I would have rather kept you awake half the night for another reason." He kissed her forehead.

"You can keep me awake tonight, if you like." She slid her hand inside the front of his shirt and felt his skin shiver under her touch. "After you have told me what is troubling you."

"What makes you think I am troubled?"

"I can tell, not least because we are sat by the fire talking and not in bed making love." She smiled up at him and he gave a short laugh.

"I do value you more than just for bed sport, you know."

"I know, but we have been apart for a fortnight...unless you have made other arrangements for your needs?" She flicked an eyebrow up enquiringly.

"Of course not!" He looked offended then, obviously realising she was teasing, he visibly relaxed. "I couldn't, even if I wanted to, my body craves only you." He leaned down and kissed her slowly. "I have no plans to change that."

"So talk to me, Beau," she said softly.

"It is nothing especially, darling. I just need the peace of our chamber and to hold you in my arms." He ran his hand over the silky softness of her hair. "All the fears I have for the future fade away when I am like this with you."

"What kind of fears?"

"Perhaps fear is too strong a word." He leaned his head back and closed his eyes. "I am not fearful…"

"But you are concerned?"

"No more than anyone would be when faced with what we have to do in the next weeks. It is like playing a long game of chess; I need to make sure all the pieces are carefully set and in the right place before we move to final check mate." He yawned widely and ran his hand through his hair. "I wish your father would tell us what he is doing."

"When is Jack expected back?"

"Not for another couple of days but I was hoping that he might cross with a messenger. I am impatient for action." He sat up as if to emphasise his words. "We are giving York too much time."

"Do you know where Ned is now?"

"He is somewhere in the midlands with Hastings, we think, and about three thousand men. Montague, Northumberland and Oxford all let him pass."

"Why?" Kate looked up into his face in surprise.

"Because your father wants to take him himself, I suspect." He shook his head. "I understand but I wish he had let Montague finish him."

"Perhaps papa didn't think he would." Kate settled back into his shoulder, her expression sad. "Not because he is not loyal but he and Ned were firm friends and uncle Jack would find it hard to forget that. They have always fought together and he is much more sentimental than papa."

"Well, I hope we can rely on him if comes to it." He hugged her close, his mouth against the top of her head.

"I am sure you will be able to." She caught his hand and laced her fingers through his. "How did things go in Wales?"

"Alright." His tone was non-committal.

"I got the impression from Harri…"

"Harri?" He flicked a brow upwards.

"Harri," she emphasised, unperturbed.

"So close already," he murmured teasingly.

"I got the impression from Harri," she continued, ignoring him, "that 'uncle Jasper' was being less than amenable." She ran her nail over the pattern of his thumb ring. "Is that what is troubling you?"

"We quarrelled and I said some things I shouldn't have and that I regret." He sighed. "But it's not just Jasper; others are being just as difficult. I don't understand why everyone cannot just try to work together to get Harry's throne secure and Madame and Edward over here and established instead of fighting and railing against each other. Jasper doesn't trust your father; Oxford and Montague cannot see eye-to-eye; and no one has heard from Clarence for days. And none of them seem to understand that all the while they are fighting, York is biding his time and drawing more people to his side."

"Perhaps they are uncertain of their own position."

"Perhaps, but it is Harry's position we need to safeguard."

"I know that but it is easy for you love; your position in the King's Counsel is assured." She brought his hand to her cheek and held it there. "You are his most loyal supporter. Maybe if you could think of it from their point of view?"

"I would if I could work out what their point of view might be!" He didn't sound too convinced.

"Perhaps Jasper Tudor thinks that my father will take a position that is rightfully his or that he cannot work in a counsel with his enemy. They have been on opposing sides for more than twenty years."

"So have the Beauforts, and your father was the man who ordered the execution of my own brother. If I can do it, why can't he?" Beau sighed again, this time heavily.

"Because he doesn't have your vision?" Kate kissed the back of his hand and looked up at him, her expression soft. "Because you are a better man?"

"Or perhaps he has the vision and I am a fool."

"Is that what you really think, that you are a fool?" She sat up and looked at him in surprise.

"Sometimes," he admitted.

"But why?"

"Because I can see the things that need to be done so clearly and yet no one else seems to be able to share that vision."

"I know no man who is less of a fool than you!" She squeezed his hand emphatically. "It is just that your perspective is different; no one else has sacrificed their life for loyalty the way that you have. My Lord Oxford, uncle Jack, my father, even Jasper Tudor; all those men are not thinking about 'Lancaster' at all when they have their quarrels; they are thinking of themselves and the impact events will have on them and theirs. To be disappointed that they don't share your loyalty is idealistic but not foolish, love."

He looked at her for a moment and then his mouth quirked up at one corner as his self-doubt ebbed away.

"You're right, as always." He drew her back into his shoulder and held her, his hand once more on her hair. "I should learn to be more like your father."

"No!" She shuddered in mock horror. "Don't!"

"I thought you loved your father?" He tipped her chin back and she grinned up at him.

"I do but I absolutely adore you for the reason you are different to him."

He laughed and kissed her thoroughly, eventually pulling away with supreme effort.

"So what have you been doing while I have been away?" He changed the subject, his eyes roving her face hungrily.

"I have been helping Meg with the household chores. We have been changing the hangings from heavy to light now that it is warmer, and spring cleaning. You should have seen the dust in the bed curtains, we had to open all the shutters to get rid of it; it was like a cloud had descended in the room. I don't think much of Meg's maids if they let it get like that!"

"I don't think Meg sets much store by housekeeping."

"No, she prefers to read." She pushed up his shirt and trailed her fingers over his stomach. "Not that I blame her." She watched as he obligingly slipped it over his head and dropped it on the floor, admiring the beauty of his lean, muscular body.

"What else did you do?" He reached across as he spoke, unfastening one shoulder of her chemise so that her left breast was exposed, round and creamy in the glow of the fire. His long, tanned fingers traced the curve and she watched her nipple harden with interest.

"We packed all winter clothes away and aired the summer ones." She caught her breath as he tweaked the hard nipple between his index finger and thumb.

"Did you?" His voice throbbed with warmth and her loins flooded.

"I have also mended your summer tunics and four pairs of hose." She laughed softly. "Is this exciting you, me prattling on about sewing and cleaning?"

It is actually." He leaned down and claimed her mouth once more, his hand fully cupping her breast. "I am very excited."

"Are you?" She slid her hand down his body and into his groin, closing it around the solid bulge with a soft sigh. "So you are," she murmured as his breath hissed through his nose at her touch.

"Just don't talk about embroidery or I may come before we even start." He laughed and then gasped again as her fingers slid inside the soft wool material and closed around his erection. "Let's go to bed," he whispered. She shook her head, straddling him as she freed him from the confines of his braies, and then shifted her hips to take him inside her.

"Later," she whispered. "First I want to tell you about my exquisite stitching."

Stafford
March 1471

Kate stood on the threshold of his chamber, taking in the chaotic scene as Beau raked through coffers and flung things out and Gethin scurried round collecting them up, piling them on the bed.

"Lord Stafford told me your brother Jack was back, my Lord." She announced her presence with the pre-emptory statement as she dropped her riding gloves down on the trestle, the spurs on her boots rattling as she walked on the stone floor.

"Yes, an hour ago." He gave her a brief, automatic smile but did not pause in the flurry of his activity.

"I assume you are packing?" She looked around pointedly. He stopped for a moment, his hand poised over his hauberk, and glanced at her.

"Yes." He picked the chainmail up slowly, as if giving himself time to work out if he had erred in some way. "The Queen and Edward are about to embark on a ship to Exeter and I want to be there to meet them. I was going to pack and then come and find you."

"I see." She dropped the lid of a coffer and sat down, folding her hands in her lap and looking up at him purposefully, her eyes not betraying the hammering of her heart against her ribs. "I am coming with you."

"No, you are not!"

"Yes, I am." Her expression did not change and she didn't raise her voice, but a curtain of cold intransigence settled in the room. It had been like this since he had come back from Wales, their only solace coming behind the closed curtains of their bed, when actions rather than words conveyed the depth of their emotions. She watched him throw the heavy mail on the bed, dislodging his battle sword and sending it clattering across the stone floor.

"Don't be stupid, Katherine. You cannot ride with me to war." He stooped and picked up the sword, the noise still ringing in the room, shaking his head emphatically, his voice sharp.

"Stop being dramatic. I would not be riding to war; I would be riding to meet my sisters and my mother." She glared at him. "Why should I be left behind?"

"For your own safety." She could see he was trying to be patient and for some reason that made her more angry.

"Because you don't want to be burdened with me, more like!" she spat.

"Christ, Katherine, that's unfair." His voice cracked with hurt and anger. "You have no idea how hard it is for me to leave you."

"Then don't. Take me with you."

"It is not safe."

"Oh, so it is alright for your precious Marguerite but not safe for me!"

"It's not like that."

"What is it like then?" She gripped the edge of the coffer, her knuckles white.

"You are not interested in what I have to say so what is the point?" He turned away, his eyes scanning the room sightlessly, anger radiating from his broad shoulders.

"You promised you would keep me close." She knew she was being difficult but she could not help it. At that moment she hated him and his misguided sense of chivalry, wanted only to push him to the extremes of feeling.

"Within reason."

"And what is the reason you have managed to conjour up that makes it alright to leave me behind now?"

"Because you are five month's gone with child, for God's sake!" The words blurted out involuntarily.

Why don't you just announce it to the whole household?" she hissed, outraged by his indiscretion. It was one thing to be his leman and with child by him but it was another to shout it through the household. "Perhaps they did not hear you in the bailey!" Gethin shifted uncomfortably by the fireplace and she turned her scalding gaze on him. "What are you staring at?"

"My Lady, please..." Flushing scarlet with embarrassment he glanced over at Beau in mute appeal.

"Leave us." Beau flicked his hand at the boy, his gaze never leaving Katherine's stiff, angry form. "I'm sorry," he said softly as Gethin closed the door behind him. She turned her head and looked at him for a long moment, coolly appraising his discomfort and enjoying it, and then slowly got to her feet, leaning down and picking up her gloves in a deliberate action before she spoke.

"I am going to my chamber," she said very softly, "where I am going to pack in order to meet my sisters at Exeter..."

"Katherine..." He put his hand out.

"...Alice and I can either travel with you, or we can ask my Lord Stafford for an escort. The choice is yours, my Lord."

"I would have you obey me in this Katherine." His voice was hoarse.

"I owe you no obedience; I am not your wife, my Lord."

"You are as good as..."

"No, I am not." She smiled sadly. "I am your leman." She ignored his furious expression. "And, as such, still mistress of my own decisions, so if you will forgive me, my Lord." She imbued the formality with all the cold venom she could muster and curtseyed low, the air around them throbbing with raw anger, so that they both flinched as the door flung open and Jack Beaufort and Harry Stafford tumbled in.

"Jack says you need to...oh!" Harry stopped in his tracks. "I'm sorry. We will come back..."

"It's alright." Kate managed a grim smile, turning from Beau's fist-clenched rigidity and making for the door. "You obviously have far more important things to discuss." And before he could say anything else she had slipped out and was gone.

***

"Trouble in paradise?" Harry asked softly as the door closed with a bang. Jack's insides shrivelled with apprehension.

"Don't!" he muttered warningly. Beau turned his burning gaze on his cousin's husband.

"Mind your own business!" he growled. Stafford shrugged and shook his head.

"It's just if she was mine, I'd go after her."

"Well she's not!"

"I'm just saying." Stafford grinned and Beau took a deep breath, closing his eyes against a desire to strike the young man.

"What can I do for you Harry?" When he finally spoke again his voice was curt.

"I think it is more about what I can do for you, isn't it?" Harry Stafford smiled, appearing quite unfazed by Beau's anger, and Jack wasn't sure whether to admire his bravery or rue his stupidity. Beau arched a dark brow.

"In what way?" he asked coolly

"I am assuming you want to ask me for some men, don't you?" Harry sauntered over to the trestle and poured wine for the three of them, shrugging when Beau declined a cup. "Well, don't you?" He looked at Beau levelly over the rim of his cup.

"I had thought you would ride with us, Harry." The skin lay taut over Beau's cheekbones and his lips were set in a hard line but his voice was calm and low. Stafford put his cup down and shook his head slowly.

"No," he said softly. "I don't think so."

"Why not?"

"Because my wife does not want me to."

"Since when did you take orders from your wife?" Beau's lip curled derisively.

"I do not take orders from my wife." Stafford shrugged yet again. "But I do listen to her and I have learned she talks sense."

"And what sense is she talking now?"

"She does not want Henry embroiled in your war." He picked up Beau's battle sword from the trestle and turned it over in his hands, feeling the weight with open appreciation. "If you lose..." He left the sentence hanging in mid-air.

"So much for your fine words!" Beau snorted down his nose and shook his head.

"I am willing to give you men."

"But not join us."

"No."

"Then stuff your men, Stafford!" Beau turned to his brother. "Fetch Gethin and get your things ready. We are leaving this afternoon." Jack nodded, no less outraged than his brother at Stafford's sudden change of heart.

"I'll warn the men."

"Yes." Beau looked at the stuff piled on the bed, clearly calculating the time it would take to pack it all into panniers for the three pack horses to carry. "We will be ready to leave by Sext."

"Don't cut off your nose to spite your face, Beau." Stafford gave Beau his sword hilt first. "Take the men."

"I will take nothing from you or my beloved cousin." The older man spat the words as if they burned his mouth. "And I suggest that you expect no favours from me in return. Now, if you will excuse me, I need to pack." Beau turned back to the bed and began to sort through his belongings. Stafford watched him for a moment and then, sighing with obvious regret, slipped quietly from the room.

***

Kate's back was to him, a dark silhouette against the brightness of the light coming through the open shutter, her hands resting lightly on the sill as she looked out over the bailey. On the bed were three bags already packed and Alice was making a final sweep of the coffers to ensure that nothing was left behind. She dropped into a deep curtsey at his entrance.

"Katherine?" he said softly and she turned, a soft sound akin to a sob escaping her and then she was in his arms, her hands up his back, her face pressed against the curve of his shoulder. He held her tightly, his hand in her hair, his mouth pressed to the top of her head. He could feel her trembling against him and he was rushed by a surge of protective tenderness, all his anger dissipating in an instant.

"I'm sorry, I'm so sorry," she whispered, the words muffled against his tunic. "Please don't leave me. I could not bear it." Gently he cupped her chin and tipped her face back from his chest, kissing her long and hard.

"I'm sorry, too," he said very softly when he finally released her mouth. "I'm sorry that I did not think how it would be for you, waiting in a strange house, wondering if I am alive or dead. You should be with your own family." He pushed a tendril of hair from her cheek, his thumb tracing the line of her cheekbone. "But you cannot fault me for being wary of your safety; you are so precious to me."

"Oh, Beau!" She closed her eyes and tears leaked through her lashes, and sat in wet spikes on her skin. "I was afraid you would just go and I would be left here."

"I thought about it," he admitted. "And then Harry and I had words and I was so angry I could not think at all. But Gethin, always the voice of reason, said it would be unfair for you to remain here when I was at odds with my cousin and that's when I realised that I didn't want to leave you at all. I was afraid I was being selfish to ask you to ride with me and as usual went to the other extreme of trying to forbid it." He kissed her nose, smiling ruefully. "How foolish of me to ever think that I could."

"When you came I was trying to decide what to do." She met his gaze, her own eyes very green. "I was going to come and find you and tell you that I would stay if that was what you really wished."

"Really?" He was stunned. "You would stay for me?"

"If that was what you really wished."

"Well, I'm damned!" He gave a short, wondrous laugh, realising that it had never occurred to him that she would do as he had asked. He had always thought he would have to be the one to compromise or accept that they would part on angry terms.

"Don't let it go to your head." She grinned and then they were both laughing and he marvelled that what had seemed an insurmountable hurdle should suddenly become so easy.

"I won't." He leaned down and claimed her mouth again, his arms tight around her, emotion surging through him. "I love you," he murmured, so lowly she could only just hear him. Then, stepping back, he let her go and looked around the room. "Could you be ready to leave within the hour?" he asked.

"I'm ready now." She glanced at Alice who was waiting unobtrusively by the open shutter. "We are packed aren't we?"

"Yes, my Lady."

"You realise that we will have to ride fast?" Kate nodded and he looked at Alice. "Are you up to it?" he asked.

"Yes, my Lord." She nodded emphatically.

"Tell me now, Alice, if you don't think you can. We will be riding long and hard."

"I can do it, my Lord." The girl's voice was firm.

"Alright." He moved for the door. "Meet me in the yard at Sext." He looked back at them. "Have you eaten?" They both shook their heads. "I will get something sent up for you and make sure you eat; we will be riding until dark."

Chapter Thirteen

Barnet, April 1471

Richard Neville looked at his brother's sombre face and smiled bitterly.

"At least now we know," he said as he crammed his helm down onto the top of his head, his voice muffled until he pushed up the visor. "The men would have come in handy, but I have no illusions about George's leadership. God's bones, was ever a man so ill served by his relatives!" He moved to the tent flap, glancing back to make sure he had not forgotten anything.

"Jesus Christ, Rich, surely you do not still mean to fight?" John Neville looked appalled. "We have lost four thousand men and Ned has gained them. And the fog for God's sake!"

"So?" Warwick fastened his chinstrap and then held his hand out to his squire for his gauntlets, his bravado totally unfeigned, his confidence in his own ability to beat his cousin unshakeable.

"So we should wait for Somerset!"

"What, and give that French bitch the chance to say that we are worthless to her?" Warwick snorted harshly. "I don't think so. Anyway, the fog can help us."

"We cannot wager men's lives on someone's good opinion!" The younger man's normally placid face contorted into outrage. "And a woman's at that. Hell's teeth man, this is Ned we are talking about facing across the field!"

"Who is a man just like us, Jack, not an invincible God!" Warwick was exasperated by his brother's continued reverence of Edward of York, affronted that he did not think they were a match for him.

"He is the devil incarnate in a suit of armour, and well you know it!"

"But he can be defeated. I know his flaws and his strengths and that works to our advantage, George and four thousand men or no George and four thousand men!"

"I say it is too big a risk!" John shook his head.

"And I say we fight." Warwick did not intend to argue.

"Rich."

"We fight." His resolve was implacable.

"Just consider for a moment what you are asking of the men." John's voice was hoarse.

"Take up your command, Jack." The emerald gaze was like green ice. John looked at his brother for a long moment and then swung himself up on his waiting destrier.

"I hope you do not live to regret this," he said very softly and snapping shut his visor, wheeled his stallion and raced towards the centre. Warwick quietly watched him go, before swinging up onto his own mount and gathering up his reins.

"If there are to be regrets then I hope I do not live at all," he murmured and, clapping his spurs to its sides, galloped the horse to the van.

***

"Ned, Ned, what the hell is going on?" Richard Gloucester, taking a moment to get his breath, raced to his brother's side, pulling off his helm and grabbing water from a squire to throw over his head and down his throat.

"Oxford was attacked by Warwick. He must have thought it was me in this accursed fog. Now the Lancastrians think they have been betrayed and they are massacring each other!" Edward laughed suddenly, a wild edge to his humour. "I thought for a minute he had us when Will lost his ground but God is on our side, little brother!" He reached across and clapped Richard on the shoulder, white teeth flashing in his dirt-ingrained face. Richard's stallion shied from the snapping teeth of Edward's blood-caked destrier, and he fought to keep it under control.

"God have pity on them," he whispered softly, shuddering at the horror unfurling before them. "For no one else has."

***

The fog had finally lifted and the sun began to seep through as Richard, Duke of Gloucester, sat on the grass, his helm by his side, his head hanging between his knees. He could not seem to draw enough breath into his lungs and his right arm was throbbing painfully, gashed from shoulder to elbow, a flesh wound but sore none the less. He heard the footsteps rather than saw who approached.

"You alright, lad?" Will Hastings' voice was full of concern at the blood dripping over the boy's hand. Richard half lifted his head and nodded, but when he tried to speak his voice did not work. "Here." Will handed him a wineskin and he drank, choking on the pungent contents and then drinking again.

"Fuck, Will!" He croaked when he could finally speak.

"I know, lad." The older man laid a brief but gentle hand on his bent head.

"It was not what I expected."

"Aye, well it's not romantic like the troubadors sing of, that's for sure. The sounds of bone crunching and the smell of blood puts paid to that." The older man gave a bleak, black smile. "They don't tell you about that in the stories of Richard the Lionheart."

"No, they don't." Richard shuddered and then clambered to his feet laboriously, every muscle screaming in protest. "Or I might not have been so keen to take a command." He grinned lopsidedly at his brother's chamberlain who laughed a sharp, harsh sound.

"Every time I fight I think it might be different," the older man said. "And every time I am proved wrong." Richard was just about to suggest they look for Edward when they heard a shout.

"Will. Dickon!" Edward was galloping towards them, his stallion blowing heavily. "They have found Warwick and Jack." Richard froze and Edward shook his head. "Both dead," he said softly, swinging himself to the ground. "I'm sorry, lad."

"Christ." Richard bit down on the knuckle of his index finger, fighting a sudden tide of emotion. He had convinced himself he hated Warwick but now found that was not true; was not true at all. He felt Edward's long fingers at the back of his neck, a gentle pressure of sympathy, and looking up saw his own mixed emotions in his brother's sky blue eyes.

"Jack was wearing the rose-en-soleil under his armour." Edward's voice caught in his throat and Richard made an odd hoarse sound, turning his head to the side, hiding the moisture that fringed his lashes.

"Jesus," he whispered. "He must have been in such conflict."

"Aye." Edward shook his head. "Poor Jack; he is the true victim in this, that's for sure."

"What are you all beating your chests about?" George of Clarence's voice cut through the air like a sharp knife.

"Warwick and Jack are dead." Edward's own voice was cool and Richard's midnight eyes were pools of anguish as he looked up at his brother.

"So?" George shrugged. "Cause for celebration, I would have thought, rather than sorrow."

"Warwick was your wife's father!" Richard stared at his brother. "And your friend!"

"He was God's own fool." George's lip curled. "Anyway, this is what you wanted, isn't it?" Edward shook his head, looking at his brother like he had just crawled out from somewhere extremely unpleasant.

"I never wanted their deaths," he said coldly.

"What did you want then?"

"My kingdom." Edward shook his head. "No more; no less. I am truly sorry that they are dead."

"Well I'm not." George shrugged, turning away dismissively and Edward gave a short mirthless laugh.

"No, I don't expect you are," he said very softly so only Will and Richard could hear. "But then sorry is a not a word you are acquainted with, is it little brother?"

Exeter
April 1471

Beau finally found her in the churchyard, sitting on a stone bench, her face white under her veil, her shoulders hunched against her misery.

"Katherine?" he said softly, his chest constricting at the grief in the eyes she raised to him. He sat down beside her and took an icy hand gently between both his own. "I am so sorry."

"I have been with my mother." Her voice was flat, but her hand trembled and his heart was assaulted anew.

"How is she?" He rubbed her fingers gently.

"Strong." Her voice caught in her throat. "Stronger than I could ever be." She shuddered a breath. "She is proud of him."

"At least she has the babe to focus on."

"Yes."

"And what about you?" He kept his voice soft.

"I loved him so much." She leaned her head against his shoulder as he slid an arm around her and pulled her close.

"I know you did, darling," he whispered.

"But all I can think is that I am so glad it was him and not you." Her chest heaved and then she was crying, great wracking sobs shaking her slender shoulders. "And he does not deserve that from me."

"Ah, kitten." Tears filled his own eyes, his heart caught by her words and her grief, as he lifted her onto his lap and held her close, uncaring of who might see them. He needed to give her this comfort as much as she needed it from him. They had spent so little time together, their journey to Exeter having been so swift and hard ridden, leaving them no time except for eating and sleeping. Then since they had arrived his time had been monopolised by Marguerite and Edward and the other commanders of the Lancastrian army, so that when the news had come of her father's death he had not even been able to be with her to soften the blow. The feel of her arms clinging around his neck and her naked need for him in her grief gave him no small solace. Since he had returned to Meg's from Wales he had felt that there was a strained distance between them as they waited for the start of what they knew was to come, and he had been sorely afraid that they would drift apart and never recapture their closeness.

"Did you know that uncle Jack wore Ned's colours under his armour?" Her voice was muffled against the damask of his tunic.

"They told you that?" Anger flooded through him; there was no need for anyone to tell her; it served for naught except heartache.

"Yes. And that they were killed by mistake in the fog by their own men." Her shoulders began to steady, but her breathing was ragged and he could feel her tears seeping through his light tunic and into his shirt. "Ned made it clear he would have spared them."

"Christ, love, I am so sorry." He held her tighter, the raw sorrow in her voice sending physical pain through his chest.

"Clarence deserted him." He felt her fists clench at the nape of his neck. "At the last minute he offered his men to Ned, but papa would not flee and insisted on fighting." She started to cry again. "And so now he is dead."

"Clarence has a lot to answer for." Beau's voice was savage in its disgust, even though the young man's defection was not entirely unexpected.

"And so has my father with his foolish pride." She unclenched her fists and slid her fingers into the hair at the nape of his neck. "Ma mère has gone; fled to sanctuary as soon as she could sit a horse, and Isabel has been sent back to George by Madame."

"I heard." He shook his head. "I cannot believe that the Countess would leave Anne like that at such a time."

"No." Kate nestled against his shoulder, her arms relaxing from their grip around his neck, her grief receding in the security of his embrace. He shifted his position to cradle her against his chest and pushed back her veil so that he could kiss her temple. He had not had time like this with her for days and the familiar feeling of warmth and peace began to envelop him. "My mother has decided to stay here to await the birth of her babe." Her hand dropped unconsciously to the curve of her own just swelling belly.

"Probably for the best." He laid his own hand over hers, a jagged surge of tenderness and lust assailing him at the sight of her tiny bump.

"She is too big to ride far or fast."

"We will take care of her I promise, kitten. I will make sure of her care here." He laced his fingers through hers. "And when we are wed she can come and stay or even live with us, if you like."

"Oh Beau." She leaned into him, her tears threatening again. "Thank you."

"Your family is my family, darling." He kissed her hair, inhaling her jasmine scent.

"My family has been destroyed in less time than it takes to hear mass." She leaned back and looked into his face, her eyes bruised in her grief. "You are my family now." She took his hand and laid it on the curve of her stomach, tears on her lashes. "You and the babe." He swallowed hard, his own eyes glistening with emotion and then leaning forward, kissed her gently.

"Forever," he said very softly, "I promise."

***

"For the love of God, Madame, you cannot be serious!" John Langstrother, Grand Prior of the Order of the Hospital of St. John of Jerusalem in England and senior Captain of the Lancastrian army, slapped his weathered hand down on the trestle and shook his head in obvious disbelief. "Go back to France?" he cried, outraged. "Now?"

"I will not risk my son's life unnecessarily." Marguerite's face was set hard, her lips a thin white line. "Warwick has failed us as I always knew he would and I will not let you lead my son to his death."

"But I want to risk my life," Edward said quietly, his own expression mirroring his mother's. "And anyway, you are making the assumption we cannot win!"

"You cannot tie the boy to your apron string forever, Madame!" Langstrother had apparently decided to abandon caution. "He is no longer a child!"

"Perhaps not, my Lord, but neither is he a seasoned battle commander capable of making the right decision. He thinks war is glamorous!" The Queen spat the word at the grey haired man who continued to shake his head vigorously.

"He is not a fool either, Madame!"

"I can speak for myself, my Lord." The boy drew himself up to his full height and faced his mother. "I say we stay and fight."

"And I say we do not!"

"Then it is you who is foolish, Madame!" Langstrother started to turn away but the Queen caught his arm in a claw-like grip.

"How dare you?" she hissed, her black eyes like polished jet. "You forget whom you address."

"I do not forget that you are but a woman, Madame, and as such can have no idea of what you speak…"

"Enough!" Beau's husky voice cut through Langstrother's words as he strode into the tent. "That is enough, my Lord Langstrother!" He walked round behind the Queen to reiterate that his support was for her, his golden gaze seething. "This is not the way to resolve our issues and not at this volume in full earshot of the men!" He closed his eyes for a moment, taking a deep breath, and then, softening his expression, laid a hand on Marguerite's arm. "Will you walk with me a moment, Madame?" he said quietly, "I think we could both do with some air." She looked up at him and then nodded, taking his arm as he offered it. Beau flashed a look at Langstrother and Edward which said 'let me handle this' and led her from the tent. They walked in silence for a while, along the bank of the river away from where the army was camped, the peace of the spring evening belying the tension surrounding them.

"You know that Edward is right, don't you?" he said conversationally after a while. "We have to stay and fight." He felt her hand tense for a moment on his arm and then she nodded briefly.

"Yes."

"He seems to have grown up so suddenly." Beau smiled as he spoke. "It is not so long ago that he was assaulting my ribs with his wooden sword."

"He is still a boy." Marguerite's voice caught and she shook her head against tears that threatened. Gently, Beau drew her towards the cover of the trees on the bank and took her in his arms, comforting her as he had comforted Kate only a short while before, risking an intimacy he had never before had with the woman to whom he had committed his lifelong loyalty. She did not push him away but stood in the circle of his arms, her face against his shoulder as she cried away her fears for her beloved only child.

"Dearest Madame," Beau said softly, "To us, Edward may still be a boy, but that is because we see him through different eyes; you who have raised him from a babe and me who has tutored him since he was a lad. But he is a man full grown who must now begin to make his own way in this world we have trained him for."

"I know you are right." Her voice was muffled in his chest. "But inside I just want to race away with him so he can come to no harm." She drew away and searched up her sleeve for her kerchief, wiping her eyes, self-consciously with it when she found it. "I am just a foolish old woman." She turned her face away, clearly embarrassed by her show of emotion and her own reaction to the intimacy of his embrace.

"Ah Madame." He caught her hand and kissed it tenderly, his beautiful eyes alive with a heartfelt warmth and affection. "You are neither, and well you know it." He tucked her arm back in his, ignoring her embarrassment, and continued their walk along the bank. "I think we should head for Wales," he said after a while. "I have been thinking on it since we had news of Warwick's death and I think we should head for Pembroke."

"And then what?" She stared straight ahead, her shoulders set against her instinct for flight.

"We join up with Jasper Tudor and wait for York in Wales." He chewed the inside of his lip for a moment. "York will be on the hind foot in Wales. With Jasper we would have the advantage."

"Yes." She was still not convinced. "But can we get there before York realises what we are doing?"

"I think so." He stopped and looked down at her, hoping that his certainty could convince her. "It will be a hard and fast ride but with the right decoy and as long as we can keep a good pace, we can do it."

"Do you think Edward will agree to ride to Wales?"

"Yes." He caught her hand again and clasped it between both of his own. "It is in all our interests to get to Wales."

"Alright." For the first time she relaxed and her expression softened. "If you think that is the right thing to do then we will do it."

"I cannot vow to keep him safe from all harm," he said as he kissed her hand fervently, his heart hammering his triumph against his ribs, but keeping his expression neutral. "But I swear I will do my damndest."

"Thank you." She did not withdraw her hand but let him place it on his arm once again, enjoying this rare moment of intimacy with him. "And Edmund?"

"Yes, Madame?" He smiled at her use of the given name that only she used.

"The Neville girl..." It was clear that she could not bring herself to say Katherine's name.

"Yes Madame?" His smiled faded and he stiffened.

"She is welcome to join her sister in my household." She looked straight ahead, her face expressionless, but he knew what it had cost her to say those words and he relaxed.

"Thank you, Madame," he said softly, "You do not know what that means to me."

London
April 1471

Richard was overwhelmed by the noise of the crowd as they passed along the river towards Westminster, shouting his brother's name and throwing petals and rice over the procession, like it was a wedding. Never had he experienced anything like it before, and as he watched Edward laughing and waving he realised suddenly that this man, his handsome, genial, older brother, was King of all England and loved by the Londoners like no king had been since Richard the Lionheart.

"This is incredible!" he exclaimed to his other brother George who rode alongside him. George laughed, enjoying basking in Edward's glory and accepting the cheers as if they were his own. Gallantly he leaned down and took a flower from a girl, kissing her heartily as he did so, ignoring the muted applause for his action. The Londoners had not forgiven his betrayal of their favourite son, but his sunlit beauty went some way to softening the blow.

"Harry didn't receive a welcome like this," he said, tucking the flower into the neck of his bejeweled tunic. "Or Warwick."

"No, I can't imagine he did." Richard shook his head, still shocked that his brother could be so matter of fact about his switching sides. George did not see that he had done anything wrong.

"I told you Bel is home?" George smiled, fondly.

"And she is happy to be back?"

"Of course, why wouldn't she be?" George looked surprised at the question.

"Because her sisters are still with Lancaster, perhaps?" Richard shook his head again at his brother's obtuseness, a pang of guilt turning his stomach. Once more there was little he could do to help Anne.

"Anne was hardly going to leave her husband, was she?" George laughed suddenly, leaning in so Richard could hear him more clearly. "And from what I have heard, sweet cousin Kate is not going to leave Edmund Beaufort either."

"What?" Richard stared at George's laughing expression.

"Our Kate is Beaufort's mistress from what I have heard; left Anjou and came over to England with him in February which I thought at the time was a bit odd. I assumed she had come under his protection to see her papa. However from what Bel tells me it has been going on for some months and there may even be the patter of tiny Beaufort booties in the summer." George shook his head. "I bet Warwick loved that; a foot in every camp!"

"Did I just hear you say that Warwick's Kate is bedding with Beau Beaufort?" They had just turned into the outer bailey at Westminster as Edward dropped back in between his brothers, leaving his Queen to ride on ahead.

"Yes." George nodded. "So Bel tells me."

"The lucky bastard!" Edward shook his head in disbelief. Richard stared at him and George laughed suddenly.

"I had forgot..." He began but stopped too late as Edward made a warning face at him and Richard swivelled towards Edward.

"Ned, tell me you didn't?" He stared horrified at his oldest brother who had the good grace to flush.

"Oh take the rod out of your back, Dickon," he said waspishly. "No I didn't!" Then he grinned engagingly. "But I'd be lying if I said I didn't want to. I still can't decide if it was because Warwick had me cooped up for weeks or if she really is as gorgeous as I remember."

"Apparently Beaufort is completely besotted with her."

"Really?" Edward flicked his brows up in surprise. "She must be a sheet scorcher to keep him interested!"

"Ned!" Richard admonished and his brother grinned.

"It's just the Beau Beaufort I knew had a notoriously short attention span when it came to women, that's all." He shrugged. "I meant no disrespect to Kate."

"She is still our cousin, however misguided, Ned." Richard's lips thinned into a line.

"Aye and you can't get much more misguided than bedding a Beaufort!" George laughed harshly.

"Can we talk about something else?" Richard was uncomfortable discussing his cousin in such fashion, as much for the fact that he too had occasionally had lustful thoughts for her, as for the fact that she was his cousin and someone he had grown up with. Both Edward and George laughed, in harmony for the first time since their reconciliation.

"You are such a prude, Dickon. I cannot imagine how you ever managed to beget a son." Edward chuckled and then obviously realising that the young man was genuinely troubled by the conversation, relented, changing the subject abruptly. "I'm waiting for my man to come from the French bitch's camp and tell me what their movements are," he said as he swung down from his palfrey and waited for both younger men to do the same. "I am wondering if she will take that whelp of hers back to France."

"Surely not." Richard shook his head, landing lightly on the hard mud. "They must realise that this is their last chance?"

"Maybe Dickon, but she was always protective of that boy." Edward looked at the older of his companions who was throwing his reins to a waiting groom. "You didn't meet him, did you, George?"

"No."

"I wondered what he had grown up like."

"Warwick never talked about him." George shrugged disinterestedly. "But Somerset is a cocky bastard."

"Really?" Richard frowned. "I saw him while we were in Bruges and I can't say he looked particularly cocky then. Haunted was more the way I would have described him."

"Haunted?" Edward looked at his brother in amusement. "Haunted by what?"

"How would I know?" Richard laughed self-consciously. "But it's the only way I can think to describe him."

"Well, he'll be haunted if he ever falls into my hands."

"Haunting us more like." George snorted at his own humour but Richard shuddered.

"Don't," he said softly.

"You don't believe in ghosts, do you, Dickon?" George jibed.

"No!" Richard shook his head dismissively. "It's just that Somerset didn't seem that different from us and I remember thinking that there must be good men on both sides of this war."

"True." Edward nodded. "Although I don't know if Beau Beaufort is one of them. However one thing I do know is that I cannot let this opportunity pass." He stopped at the bottom of the steps leading up into the main hall and turned back towards them. "Once my man tells me what they are doing, I intend to pursue them and this time I will wipe out Lancaster once and for all."

Gloucester
April 1471

As the breeze rustled the trees, Kate shivered and rolled onto her side. Beau was laid on his back with his arms crossed over his eyes, his ribs rising and falling rhythmically, white shirt pushed up and creased against his chest. The concave leanness of his stomach glowed creamily in the torchlight, the drawstring of his chausses undone, dragged up for decency's sake but not fastened. She reached out tentatively towards him and then let her hand drop uncertainly. When one of his men had come to the Queen's tent as they were readying her for bed, and asked her to come with him, she had thought that something was wrong and her fears had not been eased by the man's silence or the fact that he was leading her out of the camp and into the trees towards the river.

"Where are we going?" she had asked after they had walked for a while.

"You will see, my Lady." The soldier had smiled, a man known to her although not one of Beau's intimates. "We are almost there." And then suddenly she had been in a clearing on the bank, softly torchlit, with Beau standing with his back to her, looking out over the river. He had turned as the soldier had swept a deep bow and backed out of the clearing, standing guard with an unobtrusive companion some distance away, hidden by the trees.

"Katherine." He had breathed her name and then she had been in his arms, no preamble, no conversation, just need, a desperate hunger and the strong taste of wine on his lips. Her own pleasure had been searing but that had been nothing to the hoarse agony with which he had finally cried out her name.

"Beau?" she whispered then stopped as he shook his head. Sitting up, she reached into the picnic basket propped against the tree behind her and pulled out a wineskin, pouring out a beaker and drinking from it as she watched him. "What is it?" she said at last. He shook his head again.

"I don't know." He moved one arm and looked up at her, the white of the exposed eye a map of bloodshot lines. "I just needed you." Rubbing his face with his palms, he tipped his head back and heeled his eyes hard, his hands coming to rest on his forehead, fingers in his hair. "I hate this."

"Hate what?" She kept her voice low, recognising the intensity of his mood. He didn't answer but rolled onto his stomach, his forehead on his arm.

"Sleep with me here tonight?" His voice was muffled against the blanket. "I hate having to spend my nights without you."

"So do I."

"God I *hate* this!" She could smell the wine on his breath, directed, even as it was, into the blanket.

"How much have you had to drink?" There was a smile in her voice to take the edge off the words.

"Quite a bit." He turned his head and squinted up at her.

"What is it, Beau?" She caught his sleeve and tugged lightly. "This is not like you." He shook his head once more and closed his eyes, burying his face in his arm, and she thought that he would not answer her. Then he sighed hard.

"Sometimes," he said, so lowly that she had to strain to hear him, "It all looks so black and I cannot see the light. "

"Oh love!" She slid long fingers over the solidity of his bicep, knowing how hard he fought the demons which always lurked so close.

"I have sat in Counsel tonight, listening to men who think only of themselves and their glory, trying to work to set a clear strategy for facing the best battle commander England has ever seen, and none will hear me. I seem to bang and bang my head against a wall of stone, getting nothing but a headache for my trouble." He folded his arms across the back of his head as if warding off the pain, his face still pressed into the blanket. "I don't know how much longer I can do this."

Kate shifted across, prizing his arms away and insistently tugging at his shirt until he rolled over and curled into the fetal position, his right cheek resting in her lap. Her hands slid gently into his hair, brushing it off his face as though he were a child.

"It has just been a long, hard few days and you are exhausted," she said softly. "I bet you haven't had more than a couple of hours sleep each night since we landed at Exeter; it is no wonder that you feel like that."

"It's more than that."

"What is it then, love, tell me."

"I don't know why I am doing this anymore." He plucked at the material of her kirtle, picking off bits of grass with restless fingers. "I am just following my father's dream like a child follows its hero and suddenly I don't know why."

"But this is everything you have worked for; given up your life for!" She was shocked at the emptiness in his words.

"I think it may all just be for nothing." His voice disappeared into the folds of her gown, but for a moment, as she looked down on his glossy head, she could see the dark abyss over which he hovered. She shivered suddenly in the cool of the night.

"No," she said firmly. "You cannot think you have wasted your life. If not for King Henry then think of Edward and the fine king that he will make!"

"If we can ever get past York."

"Come on, Beau, this is not like you. What happened to your belief; to the man who was not afraid of Edward of York?" She wound his hair around her fingers and jerked it none too gently.

"He is so very tired of holding back the tide." He yawned widely. "I would just like someone to take the burden of my loyalty and hold it up for me; just for a little while." The wine was taking hold and what made perfect sense to him left her uncertain what to say.

"Then rest," she said gently, deciding after a moment to take him literally. Awkwardly, she manoeuvred herself until she was propped against the base of the tree, his head resting against the gentle swell of her stomach, her arms around him. "I will take your burden and you can rest with me."

"You give me peace," he said and then made a sound of amusement in his throat.

"What?"

"You give me pleasure as well."

"I noticed." Her lips curved in a ghost of a smile as her stomach flipped at the memory.

"Nothing seems so bad when I am with you."

"Then send for me when you need me." She held him close. "Just send for me and I will come."

"Will you?"

"Every night if you want me to."

"Every night," he said very softly, on the cusp of sleep. "Every night until death."

***

When she woke in the half-light that comes before dawn, she found he had wrapped her in his cloak and was sat against a rock on the river bank, watching a family of beavers going about their early morning business. He looked rested, his expression clearer and lighter.

"Hey," he said softly as she stirred.

"Hey."

"We should get back." He stood up and came to her, lifting her to her feet and kissing her thoroughly. "Thank you," he said simply.

"For what?"

"For being there; for understanding; and most of all for not thinking less of me." He fastened the cloak at her throat and then, throwing his tunic over his shoulder, slid his arm around her and began the walk back to camp. One of his men, still on guard, slipped into the clearing and gathered up the basket and blanket, keeping a respectful distance behind them. She nestled into the curve of his shoulder and slipped her own arm around his waist, and he matched his steps to hers, enjoying this rare moment of public intimacy. Ahead of them the camp was a hive of activity as tents were being packed up and wagons and horses loaded, water being taken from the River Avon as they made to move out of Bristol and head for Berkeley. There had been no word on the activities of Edward of York except about his triumphant entry into the city of London, but they were expecting to hear soon if he had fallen for their decoy or if he was pursuing them. Beau was still confident of getting into Wales; his despondency came from the lack of enthusiasm or planning for what to do when they got there.

"Beau!" He started at the sound of his name being called and looked up to see Edward and Anne walking towards them. Kate made to put some distance between them, but he tightened his arm about her shoulders and he kept her close, smiling down at her as he did so, determined not to let anything or anyone destroy their renewed closeness.

"Edward," he said as they got closer, ignoring Edward's grin at his creased shirt and Anne's glare at his audacity, "Princess." The young man looked from one to the other, his dark eyes sparkling with laughter as he realised that Kate was wearing Beau's cloak.

"Ma mère was looking for you. She is almost ready to head out. My Lord Langstrother and Devon will lead the men once the tents are packed, and I and the ladies will ride with them, but my mother wanted to ride on ahead with you." Beau sighed softly; he had hoped to spend some time riding with Kate this morning, hoping that Marguerite would be happy to ride with her son and Devon.

"I am on my way," he said. "If you will give me a moment?" Without waiting for Edward's acquiescence, he turned and taking Kate in his arms, kissed her. Edward, his grin broadening into outright laughter, grabbed his horrified and blushing wife's hand and turned her back towards the camp, giving the couple a modicum of privacy. Kate made to unfasten the cloak but Beau stayed her hand.

"It's alright," he said quietly, "I don't need it. Give it back to me tonight."

"I will." The smile she gave him was dazzling and he realised, perhaps for the first time, that she wanted to be with him as much as he wanted her. She always seemed so self-contained that sometimes he had wondered if she truly needed him but the look on her face now told him everything he needed to know.

"I love you," he moued and was rewarded with another breathtaking smile.

"You should go," she said softly. He nodded and reaching out, touched her cheek with long fingers.

"In the darkness of this life, you are my light," he murmured and then, stepping back, he kissed his fingertips and placed them over his heart before turning on is heel and striding towards the camp.

Gloucestershire
May 1471

"How in God's name has he done it?" Beau stared at the messenger before him, incredulity showing in his very stance. The messenger said nothing, remaining on his knees as if afraid that any movement might provoke a reaction from the notoriously mercurial Duke. "Surely no mortal man can cover such distance with such speed."

"I am afraid Edward of York has, my Lord." The messenger kept his voice level and expressionless, not looking at the Duke or the Queen or any of the assembled lords, keeping his eyes downcast.

"Dear God, then we are lost!" The Queen's voice was almost a whisper as she turned away toward the entrance of the tent. Beau flinched at the defeat in her voice but said nothing, his mind racing. He could not believe that York had discovered their decoy and then managed to turn and cover the ground to be marching parallel to them. They had not been able to cross the river Severn in Gloucester, denied entry into the city by Sir Richard Beauchamp, York's man, and had had to skirt the city and head for Tewkesbury to cross there, but now the news had come that York was beside them and they could no longer out-run him. Getting into Wales and linking up with Jasper Tudor was no longer an option and the day of reckoning was nigh. They would have to face York as they were, with a tired army of only six thousand men, and it was all his fault.

"You are absolutely sure?" His voice came out as a hoarse whisper as he gestured to the messenger to rise.

"Yes your Grace. I saw them with my own eyes; York, Clarence and Gloucester riding at the head of their force. They are unmistakable."

"Jesus wept!" He slammed his fist down on the trestle at his side, and cups and a flagon scattered across the floor. John Langstrother reached out a hand and laid it gently on his arm.

"Easy lad," he said softly. "The day was bound to come and if it has come earlier than we expected then that is God's will."

"Or Somerset's incompetence!" Marguerite turned back to the group, her face white. Beau flinched again but Langstrother looked horrified.

"Madame!" he exclaimed. "How can you…"

"He promised me we would get to Wales." Marguerite cut him off, her black eyes boring into Beau's, seeing, he was sure, the crippling self-doubt that assailed him and the knowledge that he was indeed to blame.

"I'm sorry," he whispered.

"You have nothing to be sorry for, lad. We all decided it was the right thing to do, not just you." Langstrother looked from one to the other. "Madame, please…" Marguerite ignored him, coming forward to stand looking up into Beau's face.

"I should not have listened to you."

"I'm sorry," he whispered again, not knowing what else to say. "I'm so sorry."

"Yet again you fail me."

"Please…" Beau felt sick, his face draining of colour at the look of pure hatred in her eyes.

"Get out of my sight!" she spat, turning her back on him. "You have condemned my son to death!" Beau closed his eyes against the horror which filled him and, ignoring Langstrother's hand on his arm, stumbled swiftly from the tent. He did not hear Langstrother turn to his brother and say softly,

"Find your brother's Lady, Jack, and tell her he has need of her."

***

She found him by the river, staring across the wide expanse of the Severn to Wales. She gestured to Jack to go and leave his men at a discreet distance with their backs to the river; that was as much privacy as they were prepared to give her. Softly she padded to his side, looking up at his grim profile, noting the thin line of his lips and the unblinking gaze.

"Beau," she whispered, slipping her hand into his. He gripped it fiercely in his own, his shoulders heaving once as he fought for control. She looked behind her and saw that the men had moved out of earshot and had their backs to them, but even so she drew him gently towards the cover of the trees along the bank. "Ah Beau, love. It is not your fault." She slipped her arms around his neck and then held him as he buried his head in her shoulder and pulled her tight against him, her fingers in his hair, her lips at his temple, his cheek, anywhere she could place them to give him comfort.

"I should have let her take Edward back to France." His voice rasped against the skin of her neck. "I should not have dissuaded her."

"Have you asked Edward what he thinks?" She pushed him away from her and looked into his bloodshot burning gaze. "Have you asked him if that is what he wanted?" He stared at her for a moment and then shook his head.

"No."

"Why is this always about her?" Kate caught his face in her hands. "There are ten other men on the Prince's Counsel and always it is about her."

387

"She said I had condemned him to death." He seemed dazed, shaking his head as if to clear it.

"Jesus God, what a bitch!"

"Have I condemned him to death?"

"No!" She shook her head vehemently. "Of course you have not. You are not responsible for the decisions made for Edward. The Counsel made the decision and she chose to listen to them. Anyway who can know what the outcome of this will be?"

"No." He looked confused for a moment. "I suppose not."

"What is it about her that unmans you, Beau?" The words were harsh but the tone was very gentle. She could see that he was shaken to his core, that he was close to giving in to the blackness that always lurked so close and that she needed to shock him out of it.

"I don't know." To her surprise he answered honestly. "But she has ever had the knack."

"Talk to Edward, love. See what he has to say before you take all the blame of the world on your shoulders." She let her hands slide off his face in a caress. "Stop listening to Madame and see what your Prince and his Counsel think." His eyes cleared as she looked at him, came into focus and looked down into hers, glowing in their tenderness.

"You are right," he said softly, reaching out and tracing her cheekbone with his thumb.

"I know." She smiled at him, gazing up flirtatiously through her lashes and suddenly he laughed, the black demon receding from the gold of his eyes, banished for the moment.

"How did I ever manage without you?"

"I don't know." She slid her arms around his neck and pulled him down to claim his mouth in a long and tender kiss. "You will go and see Edward?"

"Yes." He kissed her again as if tasting her mouth for the first time, his hand sliding to her breast, his breathing quickening.

"Beau!" She tried to draw away from him albeit half-heartedly. He drew her back, his mouth insistent, his hands urgent.

"Be sweet Katherine, I need you," he breathed, pulling her down onto the grass, "I need you."

Tewkesbury
May 1471

Kate knelt before the altar as father John said a blessing above them, her stomach lurching at the audacity of what they were doing, her excitement running swiftly through her veins. When Gethin Rhys had asked if he could escort her to mass for Vespers as Beau was with the Counsel, she had been completely unsuspecting. Even when he had asked afterwards if she minded accompanying him on an errand he had agreed to run for the Duke and taken her to the small chapel of St. John inside the Abbey church, she had not grasped what he was doing. It was only when they had gone through the wooden door and she had seen Beau standing by the altar with his brother and the Prince of Wales, had any suspicion that this might be a wedding crossed her mind. Beau had taken her hands and drawn her to the altar, gently explaining that Father John had agreed to marry them without the banns being posted, and that the Prince had agreed to stand as witness, but that no one apart from this group knew that they were getting married. He wanted, he said, to do this because he could not wait any longer to be her husband and to give their child his name and that he wanted to do this one thing before he faced York on the battlefield tomorrow. In a daze, she had knelt with him before the priest and he had commenced the marriage ceremony and blessing. He had placed his mother's wedding band on her finger and said his vows, never once taking his eyes from hers as he recited them after the priest. She had had nothing to give him so she had taken off the betrothal ring he had given her and placed that on his little finger as her token of the marriage.

"You may kiss your bride, my Lord." Father John was saying now, and, smiling, Beau leaned across and kissed her softly. Then she was being heartily hugged and congratulated by the Prince and Jack Beaufort, who both took full advantage of the tradition that everyone should get to kiss the bride quite thoroughly at a wedding, and was given a very shy but very sweet kiss on her lips from Gethin who went bright red in the process.

When finally they had walked out of the chapel into the abbey grounds, Beau's arm around her waist, Edward bowed to them both and smiled.

"I am going to go and spend some time with my wife," he said, addressing all of them. "And I would suggest we allow Somerset to do the same." Jack and Gethin took the cue and made their excuses so that they were left to walk the abbey grounds alone.

"Happy?" he asked softly, after a while.

"Yes." She leaned into his arm, smiling up at him. "And afraid." She kept her voice light, not wanting to sour the mood. His arm tightened round her.

"I wish I could tell you it will be alright but I cannot, and I know that you would think I am a fool to say so." He kissed her temple. "But you can believe that I will do everything I can to stay alive."

"I know." She laid her hand over his at her waist. "As long as you are alive then that is all that matters to me."

"It will be a new beginning, whatever happens."

"Perhaps but I want my new beginning to be with you rather than without you." They had stopped walking and now she stepped into the circle of his embrace, shielded by the wall which ran to the river. "I want happy ever after."

"So do I." He leaned down and kissed her, the pulse in his throat jumping erratically. "I want that more than anything." He kissed her lips and then her eyes. "Forever," he whispered after each kiss, "I want forever."

***

In the dim light of early dawn Edmund Beaufort, Duke of Somerset, stood before Kate in his armour, polished to a glowing sheen and decorated with a blue and white surcoat badged with the gold Beaufort lions on their red background, his triangular shield painted with the Somerset insignia, strapped across his shoulders and his helm and gauntlets held by the newly knighted Gethin Rhys. Behind her, their escort waited to take the ladies to the priory, some of whom were taking leave of their men-folk as she was, and others who stood patiently.

"Madame." He bowed over her hand, bringing her knuckle formally to his lips.

"My Lord." She curtseyed deeply, her eyes never leaving his, trying to convey her pride and love in this very public farewell.

"You will be safe at the priory." He did not let go of her hand. "With the Queen."

"Yes." She squeezed his fingers.

"Don't leave until I get there or you have news of me from Gethin."

"Yes, my Lord."

"I will return for you this evening."

"Yes, my Lord."

"Katherine…" His voice was very low, his eyes burning with intensity as he let go of her hand and kissed his fingertips, placing them over his heart. "Forever," he moued. Her heart swooped and own eyes filled with tears but she found a dazzling smile for him.

"Forever," she whispered.

"Go with God, my Lady." He bowed once more.

"God keep you safe, my Lord." She curtseyed as he turned away, flicking his hand at Gethin to follow.

***

"So the time has finally come." Beau looked across at the army ranged before them, the tall figure of Edward of York prominent in the centre astride a showy white stallion, messengers galloping backwards and forwards along the lines to the commanders of the right and the vanguard. His heart picked up pace in anticipation, and John Langstrother beside him seemed to sense his excitement.

"Aye, lad." The older man said softly. "And let us hope that it is our time."

"If all do what is expected of them then I am sure it will be." Beau flashed a quicksilver grin, teeth very white in the gloom of the early morning. Last night they had assessed the battle area and Beau had come up with a plan of surprise attack from the place where Edward would least expect it. He would take a party of two hundred men and hide them in the trees at the top of the hillock adjacent to the battlefield. If all went according to plan then he would be attacking Gloucester's left flank at a point where he would be at his most vulnerable fending off an attack from the Lancastrian right, then Wenlock would join the fray with his Prince and hopefully they would prevail.

"Where is our Prince?" Langstrother looked around him, up the lines and back.

"With Wenlock," Beau said shortly. "Madame wanted him safe and so we thought it would be best if he kept with Wenlock."

"I am not surprised she is wary of his safety. He is but young yet to be so blooded." Langstrother was indulgent.

"Gloucester is the same age and is commanding York's van." Beau looked at the other man, his own feeling of exasperation mirrored on his face.

"Aye, well..." Langstrother shook his head and then smiled briefly. "Well I cannot tarry here so go with God, my friend, and God willing I will see you at the end."

"Aye, God willing." Beau returned his smile and the other man wheeled his mount about and cantered away.

***

'Whosoever could think war glamorous must be off their heads,' was the first thought which went through Edward Prince of Wales' mind as the battle commenced. As the lines clashed with bruising force and the noise of steel crashed onto steel, men grunting or crying out as they were wounded filled the air, he felt the bile rise in his throat and for one awful moment thought that he might disgrace himself by being sick in front of all of Wenlock's men. He swallowed fiercely as saliva filled his mouth again and again, not daring to unclench his jaw until he was certain that the danger had receded.

"It gets us all like that first time, my Lord," a soft voice said at his side, and turning he looked into the sympathetic blue eyes of one of Wenlock's knights. He smiled tightly, hating to be caught out in his weakness.

"Does it?"

"Yes, my Lord." The Knight warmed to his theme and to the unfamiliar young man that they were fighting for. "I puked by my stallion my first time."

"And me." The man next to him grinned. "'tis the right of passage for all soldiers."

"I am Sir John Lascells of Sturton. I was Warwick's man and now with my Lord Wenlock." The first man inclined his head deferentially. "And this is Sir William Carey."

"My Lords." Edward smiled as best he could, thinking how incongruous it was that they should be meeting now, for the first time, on the battlefield. "Is it always like this?" He gestured to the melee below them. "How can you be sure you are fighting the right men?"

"You stay close to your most known companions, my Lord, and hope for the best, but sometimes accidents do happen, even to those with the best of intentions as happened to my Lord Warwick at Barnet." Lascells shook his head sadly. "It was a terrible thing and a terrible end to a great man." As if sensing the flicker of fear which shot through Edward's stomach, Lascells added quickly, "You are to stick close to us, my Lord, and we will see you safely through."

"I am not a child to be coddled," Edward said stiffly and Carey grinned.

"We never thought you were, my Lord. But it would be foolish for us all to fight for you only to find that it was for nothing because no one watched your back."

"I cannot see anyone watching York's back or Gloucester's." Edward was still feeling his courage was in question and it showed in his tone. Neither Lascells nor Carey took offence.

"You would be surprised, my Lord," was all that Lascells said.

"So what happens n...?" Edward's words were cut off by Carey's shout.

"Here comes my Lord Somerset!" He gestured towards the hill at the side of the field and Edward saw movement as men emerged from the trees heading straight for the Yorkist vanguard. His heart surged into his throat and his hands tightened on the reins, causing his stallion to shake his head and flick out a hind hoof irritably, but Edward did not notice. He tensed his muscles and waited for Wenlock's order to charge.

***

"What the hell is happening?" Edward of York shouted at the bloodied messenger who had just arrived at his side. "Why is my brother giving ground?" The young squire looked warily at the King's snapping chestnut stallion, evading hooves and teeth as he came to Richard's stirrup.

"Lancaster has launched an attack on his flank. They came out of the trees and took him by surprise. His flank has given under the attack and the Duke needs you to press ahead hard and drive them back while he sends men to aid the left."

"What is he going to do?"

"He asks for some of your men to counter." The messenger grinned suddenly, a macabre sight in his bloodied face. "We think Wenlock was meant to join the fight at that point but he has not, has stayed his ground. If that is the case then the Duke says if you hold hard and push on, we will win the day."

"So the old bastard has turned his coat again." Edward was cramming his helm on as he spat the words.

"Aye, but this time to our advantage." The messenger's smile did not falter. "What shall I tell the Duke?"

"Tell him, I hear his men are on the way." Edward smiled grimly. "And we will win the day."

***

"You whoreson!" Beau appeared at full tilt through the throng in front of John Wenlock like a menacing spectre. "You misbegotten son of a fucking treacherous whore!" He reined Hercules to a sliding halt, coming to a stop at the old man's stirrup.

"Treacherous?" Wenlock said, his lip curling, his hand going to his sword hilt. "Who are you calling treacherous?"

"Why did you not come?" Beau's voice cracked on the words, emotion overwhelming him. "I had York where I needed him and you did not come."

"I am not a fool, Somerset. I could see with my own eyes you had no chance. I will not risk my men on your whim!"

"Why?" Beau sneered, his eyes a vulpine yellow. "Because it was not your plan?"

"No, because it was foolhardy." The old man smiled bitterly. "I have fought with the greatest of warriors and none of them would have followed such a foolhardy plan."

"Would they not?" Beau's expression took on a dangerous light but Wenlock was not cowed.

"No they would not," he said quietly. "My Lord Warwick and Edward of York would never have countenanced such a plan."

"Then you should have stayed with York, shouldn't you?"

"Maybe I should and then I would be sure of victory, wouldn't I?"

"Would you?"

"I think so, don't you?"

"Well, you will not get the chance to ever find out." Beau's arm came up in a sweeping motion and Wenlock saw the battle axe in his hand, his face registering, first shock and then disbelief, as the younger man swung first up and then hard down, burying the axe deep into the white haired skull, almost rending it in two with the force of his anger. Their eyes met for a second before the old man's glazed over and his life was gone.

As Wenlock toppled to the ground, Beau wiped blood and brains from his armour, his haunted eyes taking in the frightened men in front of him.

"Where is my Prince?" he shouted hoarsely. "Where is he?"

"Gone, my Lord." John Lascells squinted up at him, his own face smeared with his master's brains. "When my Lord would not join you, he went. Took men into the fray. We have not seen him since."

"You let him go?" Beau stared at the man, his expression feral.

"I could not stop him. He would not listen." Tears seeped under the man's lashes as he looked down at the corpse at his feet. "He would not listen."

"Fucking hell!" Beau wheeled his stallion around.

"What shall we do, my Lord?" Lascells called.

"Run for your lives or stay here and die." Beau stuck his spurs in Hercules' side. "I care not which."

***

"Where is he?" Edward jerked off his helm and ran his hand through his sweat-soaked hair, showering all those close by with droplets. His stallion caviled to the left and bumped Will Hastings' roan destrier who snapped at the bigger animal testily. Will grabbed his reins and cursed for a moment before flipping up his visor and regarding Edward with weary grey eyes.

"There are unconfirmed reports that some of Lancaster's men are in Tewkesbury Abbey, seeking sanctuary."

"Is Beaufort one of them?"

"I don't know." Will shrugged. "I've sent one of my men down there."

"Tewkesbury Abbey is not a recognised sanctuary." Edward's voice was hard. "If he is in there then we will take him out, even if I have to go and tell the Abbot myself. I want him and Langstrother. All the rest are accounted for."

"And the women?" Will unfastened his chin strap and pulled off his helm, throwing it to his squire, shaking sweat out of his own hair with what felt like the last of his strength. At thirty-nine he was starting to feel his age.

"The women are close by. I've sent Stanley to find them and bring them to Coventry."

"Even the French bitch?" Will was surprised that Edward would want her near him.

"Especially the French bitch." White teeth flashed in a begrimed face. "I have told him to tell her nothing. I want to be the one to deliver the sad tidings."

"The boy is definitely dead then?" Will was surprised they had such clear news so close to the end of the battle.

"Yes. We got one of Wenlock's men to identify him."

"Apparently, Edmund Beaufort split Wenlock's head in two with a battle axe because he didn't bring his men into the fight." Richard of Gloucester joined them, climbing down from his stallion and handing the reins to Will Hastings' squire.

"Really?" Edward laughed suddenly. "That was a bit of a comeuppance for the old bastard!"

"When Beaufort came with his men down the hillock, it had been agreed that Wenlock would enter the battle and he didn't. Beaufort appeared like a wild animal and killed him in front of the men before telling them to fight or flight, and galloping off!"

"Who told you all this?" Will stared at the young man.

"The same man who identified Edward of Lancaster."

"True, do you think?" Edward was sceptical.

"I don't know." Richard shrugged. "Perhaps if we capture him I'll ask him." He smiled and Edward laughed.

"I think you sh..."

"My liege!" His words were cut off by a shout from a man in Hastings' colours galloping towards them at full tilt. "My liege, Edmund Beaufort is in the abbey. I tried to gain entry but the Abbot turned me away."

"Good man." Edward smiled grimly at his companions. "Come on, let's go and inform my Lord Abbot where his priorities lie!"

"You are not going to ride into a house of God, are you?" Richard looked appalled. Will looked from one to the other, as always struck by the differences between the two brothers; Edward with practically no scruples and Richard with his high moral character, and wondered how they could have been bred from the same parents. It almost gave credence to the old story that Edward was not the son of the Duke of York but the son of Rouen archer.

"I will if the Abbot will not hand him over."

"Jesus, Ned!"

"Don't 'Jesus, Ned' me." Edward shook his head in exasperation. "I told you at the beginning that if I had the chance I would end this once and for all and this is my chance! Are you with me?" The boy hesitated for only a fraction.

"Yes," he said. "I am with you."

***

"They will come back." Beau leaned his head back against the wall and closed his eyes. "For you and I."

"I know." John Langstrother could barely speak, so broken was his voice from rallying his men.

"I find myself questioning God's will." The younger man looked at the ribbon, no longer green, around his wrist. "Why give so much, only to take it away?"

"Ah, lad." The old man did not know what to say.

"A year ago, I would not have cared that I am sat here now waiting for someone to come and take me to my death." Beau rubbed his face wearily. "The loss of my brother and my Prince would have been enough to make me long for my life to end. Then God gives me a reason to live but takes my life anyway. Makes no sense to me."

"You cannot apply logic to the will of God, my friend." Langstrother touched the other man's forearm briefly.

"No, but that does not mean I have to accept it." At that moment, the younger man was too emotionally spent to feel anything, but Langstrother guessed the onslaught would come when he regained his strength and the realisation that he would never see his child born or grow old with his family.

"It is best to die accepting God than to deny him." The old man croaked, coughed and then swallowed hard on a raw throat. "That path will bring you no solace."

"I'm not sure God can console me at this point, John." Beau gave a mirthless snort and then stopped, cocking an ear. "They are back," he said very softly, getting to his feet as other men stirred and stood up.

"Jesus, the horses are in the church!" a man whispered. Beau's hand went to his sword hilt as the chapel door swung open and Edward of York stood, framed by the arch, his amour filthy with mud and blood.

"I have come for Edmund Beaufort," he said conversationally into the quiet. "And the Prior of Jerusalem. Declare them to me and the rest of you can go free." None of the men moved, just stared at Edward's powerful frame and the Rose en Soleil on his dirty blue surcoat. "Or you can all die." He shrugged and began to turn away.

"I am here." Beau's husky voice cut through the silence and the men parted as he walked toward his arch enemy.

"Hello Beau; long time no see." Edward smiled, stepping aside so two of his men could take Beau and tie his hands behind his back.

"Langstrother is not here." Beau looked the slightly taller man in the eye, his expression impassive.

"Where is he?" Edward's bright blue eyes narrowed.

"I don't know." Beau shrugged. "I'm not his keeper."

"Take them all." Edward flung over his shoulder at the men behind him and turned away.

"I am here." Langstrother came forward, his hand touching Beau's shoulder as he passed. "Take me, but spare them." Edward stopped and thought for a moment and then turned back.

"You are not hiding anyone else in there?"

"No, the rest are dead. Jack Beaufort, Courtenay, Wenlock, my Prince; all dead." Langstrother's voice caught and he took a deep, shaky breath. "Somerset and I are all that's left. These men are but knights and common soldiers."

"Let them go." Edward turned away and began walking back to the main door of the abbey. "I am a man of my word." He stopped at the door where his groom stood with his horse and the Abbot was anxiously twisting his hands. "My Lord Abbot, you will find a place for my Lords Beaufort and Langstrother to wait until my brother of Gloucester deals with them. Meanwhile I am off to Coventry." He turned back to Beau and smiled triumphantly. "Where, hopefully, if Will Stanley has done his job properly, I can close some unfinished business with my lovely red haired cousin." And laughing at Beau's outraged expression, he mounted his stallion and clattered showily away.

Tewkesbury Abbey
May 1471

"Father John, I need to ask of you a very great favour." Beau fervently clasped the hand of the priest in greeting, not wasting time on pleasantries. "I need you to deliver this to the Duke of Gloucester." He held out the sealed package, thanking heaven and earth for the devoted Gethin who had appeared this morning at his prison with clean clothes, writing implements and fresh water. He had also brought the one thing that could get Beau anything he needed in his abbey cell, and that was money, a bag of coins that must have been the lad's life savings. He had even managed to get some garments for his prison companion, Langstrother. Gratefully Beau had washed the battle grime from his body and changed into his fresh shirt and chausses, his feet in his familiar long boots. Then he had sat down close to the small window and written his letter to Richard of Gloucester, his bold black hand a little shaky to his own eyes, the words tumbling out over the page as he tried to get his message across. Since his eviction from sanctuary the day before, he had slowly reconciled himself to the certain death that awaited him, but he could not reconcile himself to the loss of his wife and the grief that she would have to suffer when she heard of his death. He had to know that she was going to be cared for, hence the letter to Gloucester, the only one of the brothers of York who had any integrity; the only one that he felt he could turn to.

"My Lord I...I don't know how to get access to him." The priest looked more than a little terrified of the mission that was being given to him. "He has been shut away since yesterday, dealing with business for the King."

"Where is York?" Beau could not bring himself to use the title.

"He has gone to Coventry, my Lord. The Duke of Gloucester is his deputy here as Constable of England."

"All that responsibility and only eighteen!"

"And surrounded by soldiers and courtiers and impossible to get near." The priest shook his head.

"You'll think of something, my friend." Beau gave the man a brief smile and then squeezed his hand hard. "I just need him to get the letter, Father. I need to know that he will take care of my wife." Father John's eyes filled with sudden sympathy and he nodded.

"Of course, my Lord," he said softly. "I understand." He took the parchment and scuttled out of the room.

"I think you are wasting your time." Langstrother's cracked and broken voice cut into his thoughts. "I cannot see Gloucester caring about the fate of Warwick's daughter."

"They grew up together." Beau chewed the inside of his lip and then paced to the small window and looked out. "I have to hope that that is enough."

"You have not told him she is your wife, have you?"

"God, no!" Beau looked back, his eyes darting round the room restlessly. "Though it seems so unfair that I must brand her a whore."

"It is for the child's sake."

"I know." Beau sighed and rubbed his face hard; he seemed to be constantly on the cusp of breaking down these last hours.

"Sit down, lad. Fretting will serve for naught." Langstrother patted his pallet and when Beau hesitated, patted it again. "With any luck we will be beyond earthly cares by this time tomorrow." It was offered as a comfort but Beau's mouth twisted and his eyes glittered suddenly.

"But Katherine won't be." He heeled his eyes and shook his head. "When I think about what she must go through, I cannot bear it."

"Ah lad." Langstrother laid his hand on the younger man's shoulder and squeezed it. There was nothing that the older man could say to that; nothing that could comfort a man so unfortunate that he loved his wife to distraction. Most men would be worried about the family they left behind but for Edmund Beaufort, his wife's suffering was a physical hurt, and that, coupled with the fact that he would never see the child he had longed for, made it so very difficult for him. Beau knew that Langstrother had in recent times changed his opinion of him; that he had once thought him to be nothing more than a brash, womanising popinjay with no substance behind the pride and arrogance. But in the last weeks he knew the older man had come to appreciate his fierce and determined desire to get Lancaster back into power coupled with his sound command of strategy and war. He had turned Marguerite away from returning to France and had driven the men hard to get them into Wales, winning much respect, failing only because of the super-human efforts of his opponent, and if now he was on the verge of despair, it was for those he loved, not for himself, for he had made his peace with God and reconciled himself to death. They sat in silence, the older man's arm around the younger one, drawing comfort from each other as the light began to dim and afternoon drew into evening. The turning of the key in the door made them start and they looked at each other, a momentary flash of fear in both their eyes. They waited for the door to open and were not reassured by the sight of the soldier who stood there.

"My Lord Somerset?" The young man gave him the courtesy of his attainted title. Beau stood up.

"Yes."

"Could you accompany me please, Sir."

"May I ask where to?" Beau reached for his tunic and dragged it over his head, swiftly lacing the front and adjusting his shirt. He fastened the points to his chausses and smoothed the front, determined that he should still look like the Duke who carried royal plantagenet blood in his veins, even when he was a prisoner.

"To the prior's chamber, my Lord." The young man led the way and immediately he was surrounded by armed men. He said nothing but walked along the corridors until he was ushered into a large chamber which seemed to be full of people. The throng parted, with a few curious glances thrown his way and then, to his surprise, Richard of Gloucester appeared from behind a screen and beckoned them over.

"Somerset," he said in his low, pleasant voice, indicating politely to a bench.

"Gloucester." Beau sat down and waited quietly whilst Gloucester spoke to a waiting squire and then joined him at the trestle, out of sight of prying eyes. For a few seconds, they sat in silence and then Gloucester said,

"I am told that you split Wenlock's head clean in half when you realised he had betrayed you?"

"Yes and I would do the same again if I had to." Beau's face was hard but the boy grinned delightedly.

"God, I wish I had seen that!" He laughed suddenly. "I would like to have seen the look on his proud face when he realised." He laughed again and Beau grinned in spite of himself.

"His last expression was one of surprise, to say the least," he said.

"Well, any man who can surprise a smug old bastard like Wenlock cannot be all bad in my book." Gloucester's expression was surprisingly friendly. "I never liked him. I could never see what my cousin Warwick saw in him."

"Loyalty I suppose, and he was loyal." Beau shrugged. "But the loyalty was to Richard Neville, not to me or to Lancaster."

"He seemed to take men that way, my cousin." Gloucester's gaze was inward.

"Yes." They sat for a moment, Beau's heart apprehensively picking up pace, and then Gloucester roused himself.

"Obviously I got your message." He smiled briefly. "Your messenger was quite inventive to get himself in front of me. "Beau tried to return the smile but could not, and then to his horror his eyes filled with tears. He turned his face away but not quick enough to avoid the look of pity which flickered in Gloucester's dark eyes. "You were concerned for the welfare of my cousin Katherine Neville," the young man continued quietly. "I am aware of your... relationship with her."

"It is...was...an honourable liaison." Beau blinked rapidly and turned back, black lashes matted with moisture but his gaze level. "I care very much for her."

"I wanted you to know that I intend to take her home." Gloucester ignored the other man's statement.

"Home?" Beau echoed.

"The King has given me Middleham and I plan to take Kate and her sister Anne back there if that is what they want."

"It was a place Katherine often talked about." Beau's voice caught and he bit his lip. He had had plans to ask Harry for Middleham so that Kate could go home, and now this slight young man was going to be the one to take her there, not as a duchess as he had hoped but, once more, as the outsider. His chest contracted and he fought hard for control.

"The child will also be welcome in my household," Gloucester continued, ignoring the tension in the other man. "Hopefully he or she will be the first of many to grace the nursery at Middleham. I am the father of a small son myself and I have another child on the way so I hope that my wife, whoever she may be, will welcome all three when the time comes." The boy looked at him and Beau realised it was not pity he had seen in the depths of those deep blue eyes but sympathy.

"Warwick told me that he once had you earmarked for my Princess?" he said huskily, pushing away the crowding images of his dead. Richard coloured and something flickered in his eyes which Beau could not read.

"Yes, I expect he did," Gloucester muttered. Then he took a deep breath and asked the question that was real the reason why he had been brought to the prior's chamber. "Do you think Anne Neville could be with child?" His eyes flickered again and Beau realised there was more to the question than an enquiry into the possibility of an heir to Lancaster.

"She could be." He smiled to soften the words and then, because he liked the boy, softened them still further. "It was not a love match, not on her part anyway, but I believe they shared a bed at least until they came to England. There was not much opportunity after." He thought of his nights under trees and the stars and his stomach lurched nausea through his body. He gripped the trestle edge until his knuckles went white and the sick feeling passed. "I would suggest your brother keeps her close for a couple of months, just to make sure."

"Thank you, we will bear that in mind." The young man rose, the meeting obviously at an end. Gloucester held out his hand and, after a brief hesitation, Beau took it and shook it firmly.

"Thank you," he said hoarsely, emotion threatening him once more. "For taking the time..." He gestured at the people waiting beyond the screen. Gloucester regarded him thoughtfully for a few moments longer and then he said,

"I remember when I was seven being plucked off the streets of Ludlow by a man on a big black destrier who gave me some good advice."

"That was a long time ago." Beau snorted a mirthless laugh. "Things have changed since then."

"Maybe, but the advice remains true." Gloucester leaned across the table earnestly. "I cannot offer you your life, Somerset, but I can take away your burdens. I will take care of Kate so all you have to do is to take care of your conscience."

Tewkesbury Square
May 1471

Beau stood in the square in just his chausses and boots, his hands tied behind his back, his face impassive, gold eyes flicking across the crowd until they came to rest on a familiar face. He twitched a crooked smile and saw Gethin nod and smile tightly in acknowledgement. With a pang, he saw that the young Knight was still wearing his colours, still had on his chest the Beaufort lions, and every now and then, as he watched him, his hand went to the badge and touched it briefly.

John Langstrother stood ahead of him, broad shoulders straight, his carriage proud, knowing that he would be next to the block. He wanted to reach out and lay his hand on the man's shoulder to give him some comfort but, bound as he was, he could not, so instead he leaned forward and murmured,

"Go with God, my friend."

"And you, lad." The old man glanced back with a bleak smile. "Shall I wait for you on the other side?" Beau snorted a laugh.

"Aye, but if I'm not there in five minutes you will know I am sent elsewhere for my sins."

"You are assuming I am a man of virtue."

"Don't tell me. You had a secret life!" Beau laughed again and Langstrother grinned.

"I'll tell you later." A young soldier, wearing the Blanc Sanglier of Richard of Gloucester, came to his side and took Langstrother's arm. "I am not such an old fool that I cannot walk by myself," he growled, snatching his arm away and heading for the block set up by the cross in the centre of the square. Beau watched, his throat aching, as the proud man, stripped to just his chausses, all the trappings of his office taken from him, waited for the soldier to untie his hands and then knelt by the block. Beau forced himself to watch the axe fall and the head roll away, mouth still moving in prayer. Bile rose into his throat and he swallowed it away, fighting the desire to retch. There would be none here who could say that Edmund Beaufort, Duke of Somerset, had not died with pride and dignity. Puking was not part of his plan. He closed his eyes for a second and took a deep breath, setting his expression to blankness. Then slowly he walked forward as Langstrother had done, his eyes once more searching until they found their target. As his hands were untied he met the midnight blue eyes of Richard of Gloucester, held his gaze for a moment and then nodded. The young man looked at him squarely and then gave a sad flick of a smile and returned the acknowledgement. There was nothing left to do now but kneel, hands on either side of the block, and wait for oblivion.

"Forgive me, Katherine," he whispered. "Forgive me, my love."

Epilogue

Tewkesbury Abbey, April 1472

"We laid him to rest here, my Lady." The monk had opened the door to the chapel and gestured to the altar of St John and the newly engraved stone before it. "My Lord Duke and his brother, side-by-side in the place where he was happiest. I attended them myself." He felt the girl's distress and saw that her face was blanched of colour but her eyes remained dry.

"Then I am in your debt, Father John." She found a smile for him and he was struck afresh by the fragility of her beauty.

"He looked very fine, my Lady, and we made sure that the ring and the ribbon were wrapped in a kerchief and placed over his heart as he wished." He looked at the altar for a moment and then back at the girl. "He was a brave man, my Lady and died with great courage and dignity."

"I would not have expected anything less." Her voice was almost a whisper. "And I try to take strength from his fortitude." She smiled her unbearably sad smile again and then turned to the young Knight at her side. "Will you help Alice with Jack, Geth?" she said softly. "I expect she would be grateful."

"Yes of course, my Lady, but I thought you would want him with you. My Lord Duke...."

He already knows his son, Geth." Her smile did not waver, but her voice was firm. "His spirit is with us always but today I have come to see my Lord's earthly resting place and Jack does not need to be with me." The monk was impressed by the certainty of her belief.

"Sir Thomas and I will leave you with your prayers," he said, guiding the reluctant young man towards the exit. "I have laid the items the Duke left for you on a prayer cushion over there, my Lady." He pointed past the altar and then, still ushering Gethin out of the door, closed it behind them.

***

She stood for a moment, listening as their footsteps receded and then smiled.

"Hey," she said very softly, sitting herself down next to the prayer cushion beside the dark slab in the floor and arranging her skirts around her. "I thought they would never go." She picked up the sealed package and looked at it, her mouth twisting at the sight of his bold black handwriting. "Oh dear, this is going to be harder than I thought," she whispered. She broke the seal and opened the square. Inside were two documents, one very obviously a letter and the other…she was not sure. Underneath those, wrapped in a note which said 'for our child' were his rings and his Somerset lozenge on the leather strap. Blinking back tears she tucked the letter into her bodice and picked up the other document, and realised as she began to read that it was a marriage contract, drawn up by Abbot Strensham, the Tewkesbury prior, to validate their marriage. "Oh Beau!" she said, letting the tears fall at last, "You knew." And she cried afresh for all the thought he had given her in his last hours before death, for the fact that he had given her something real to hold onto, a contract of marriage which stopped their life from receding into the realm of fairy tale. Not that she would ever show it to anyone but at least she could take it out and see that she had not dreamed her life with Edmund Beaufort; that it was real and that Jack really was his legitimate son. Gradually the sense of loss receded and her tears began to ease, as she wiped her eyes with the wet and crumpled kerchief in her hand. "I don't need to tell you how hard it has been for little Jack and me," she said after a long while, as she laid her other hand on the warm stone. "I know you have been with us often; I saw you looking in his cradle when he was born. I know you wanted to take him but thank you for letting me keep him and I am sorry it has taken nearly a year for me to come here. Ned would not let me visit my father or come to you until he thought I was well enough, and I know that you know how sick I was. So, what with that and all the trouble between George and Richard over the betrothal, and poor Anne almost Richard's wife but not yet, it has been so hard to get away." She stroked the stone. "I so wanted to come to you, my love, and it was only you telling me I had to stay with Jack because he needed me so much that made me try and get well." She smiled tremulously. "Gethin has been a godsend and I am sure I would not be here without him and Alice. They nursed me for so long and Alice got Jack a wet nurse and made sure he was cared for as he should be when I could not be a mother to him. Jack loves Gethin and he loves little Jack as if he were his father but I will make sure my boy knows all about his real father and how much I loved him when the time comes, and that he knows how much he was loved and wanted in return." She traced her finger around the stark engraving in the stone, showing just the names of its occupants. "I miss you, Beau, so much and every time Jack does something new I wish you were with me and you could see how clever he is. But I have come here today to tell you that I know and so do you, that it is time for me to move on with my life. If I cannot be with you then I have to let go and try and be happy." Tears streaked her cheeks again. "I know you will always be with me and my heart will always belong first and foremost to you but I also know that until it is my time and I can be with you, I must live my life." She hiccupped against a fresh sob. "I will never forget you, my love. I will think of you every day, I promise, but this has to be a new beginning. I wanted that new beginning to be with you, but if it cannot be then I must begin anew on my own." She leaned down and laid her lips to the stone. "I will love you forever, Beau," she whispered. "Forever, I promise."

Author's Note

As a staunch Yorkist and Ricardian my original intention was to pen a novel about the times of Edward IV and Richard III seen from the point of someone who was present at all the major events in their lives; hence the creation of the fictional Katherine Neville as Warwick's illegitimate daughter. But as I began writing, Edmund Beaufort came to the fore and flowed from my keyboard as if he was desperate to be heard. Driven by a desire to find out more about him, I started to research the man that was the staunchest of supporters of the House of Lancaster and found that very little is known or written about him. I found it interesting that he has only ever warranted mention in books which deal with the creation of the House of Beaufort for the children of John of Gaunt and his mistress of more than twenty year, Katherine Swynford (who subsequently became his third and final wife). Yet Edmund has never been brought to the fore as a key figure in the wars between Lancaster and York, later known as the 'Wars of the Roses'. The only personal description I could find about him was in a book by Geoffrey Richardson called *A Pride of Bastards* which described him as handsome, vain, arrogant and brash, and dealt very briefly with his role in the life of Marguerite of Anjou and then the Battle of Tewkesbury. So with a novelists' license, using those four words of description, I allowed him to create himself, and before I knew it he had become the central character of the novel. I found myself deviating entirely from my 'Yorkist sympathies' to write what I hope is a believable and empathetic character who was a product of his times and who lived a difficult and turbulent life trying to support his Queen and provide for his brother.

Nothing is known about his relationship with Richard Neville, Earl of Warwick, as no letters or communications survive that may

411

have shed light on it so I have taken the liberty of creating my own interpretation of their truce and the events which followed.

I would like also to add that there is some evidence that both John of Gaunt and his brother the Black Prince suffered from depression; in fact, the Black Prince may even have been bi-polar, and that this could have continued through the generations, creating the intensity of character that Edmund Beaufort displays.

There is no evidence that the Beaufort brothers were ever introduced to Margaret of York at her wedding to the Duke of Burgundy or that Edmund Beaufort encountered Richard of Gloucester on the streets of Ludlow or in the centre of Bruges.

I have written this novel very much from the human perspective about the larger than life characters of the period and how they dealt with the turbulence of their lives and relationships that may have existed at the time.